COUNT ROBERT OF PARIS

Walter Scott

CHAPTER THE FIRST

Leontius.—— That power that kindly spreads
The clouds, a signal of impending showers, To warn
the wandering linnet to the shade, Beheld without
concern expiring Greece, And not one prodigy
foretold our fate.

Demetrius. A thousand horrid prodigies foretold it: A feeble
government, eluded laws,
A factious populace, luxurious nobles, And all the
maladies of sinking states. When public villany, too
strong for justice, Shows his bold front, the
harbinger of ruin, Can brave Leontius call for airy
wonders,
Which cheats interpret, and which fools regard? IRENE,
Act I.

The close observers of vegetable nature have remarked, that when a new graft
is taken from an aged tree, it possesses indeed in exterior form the appearance
of a youthful shoot, but has in fact attained to
the same state of maturity, or even decay, which has been reached by the
parent stem. Hence, it is said, arises the general decline and death that about
the same season is often observed to spread itself through individual trees of
some particular species, all of which, deriving
their vital powers from the parent stock, are therefore incapable of
protracting their existence longer than it does.

In the same manner, efforts have been made by the mighty of the earth to
transplant large cities, states, and communities, by one great and sudden
exertion, expecting to secure to the new capital the wealth, the dignity, the
magnificent decorations and unlimited extent of the ancient city, which they
desire to renovate; while, at the same time, they hope to begin a new
succession of ages from the date of

the new structure, to last, they imagine, as long, and with as much fame, as its predecessor, which the founder hopes his new metropolis may replace in all its youthful glories. But nature has her laws, which seem to apply to the social, as well as the vegetable system. It appears to be a general rule, that what is to last long should be slowly matured and gradually improved, while every

sudden effort, however gigantic, to bring about the speedy execution of a plan calculated to endure for ages, is doomed to exhibit symptoms of premature decay from its very commencement. Thus,

in a beautiful Oriental tale, a dervise explains to the sultan how he had reared the magnificent trees among which they walked, by nursing their shoots from the seed; and the prince's pride is damped when he reflects, that those plantations, so simply raised, were gathering new vigour from each returning sun, while his own exhausted cedars, which had been transplanted by one violent effort, were drooping their majestic heads in the Valley of Orez. [Footnote: Tale of Mirglip the Persian, in the Tales of the Genii.]

It has been allowed, I believe, by all men of taste, many of whom have been late visitants of Constantinople, that if it were possible to survey the whole globe with a view to fixing a seat of universal empire, all who are capable of making such a choice, would give their preference to the city of Constantine, as including the great recommendations of beauty, wealth, security, and eminence. Yet with all these advantages of situation and climate, and with all the architectural splendour of its churches and halls, its quarries of marble, and its treasure–houses of gold, the imperial founder must himself have learned, that although he could employ all these rich materials in obedience to his own wish, it was the mind of man itself, those intellectual faculties refined by the ancients to the

highest degree, which had produced the specimens of talent at which men paused and wondered, whether as subjects of art or of moral labour. The power of the Emperor might indeed strip other cities of their statues and their shrines, in order to decorate that which he had fixed upon as his new capital; but the men who had performed great actions, and those, almost equally esteemed, by whom such deeds were celebrated, in poetry, in painting, and in music, had ceased to exist. The nation, though still the most civilised in the world, had passed beyond that period of society, when the desire of fair fame is

of itself the sole or chief motive for the labour of the historian or the poet, the painter or the statuary. The slavish and despotic constitution introduced into the empire, had long since entirely
destroyed that public spirit which animated the free history of Rome, leaving nothing but feeble recollections, which produced no emulation.

To speak as of an animated substance, if Constantine could have regenerated his new metropolis, by transfusing into it the vital and vivifying principles of old Rome,—that brilliant spark no longer remained for Constantinople to borrow, or for Rome to lend.

In one most important circumstance, the state of the capital of Constantine had been totally changed, and unspeakably to its advantage. The world was now Christian, and, with the Pagan code, had got rid of its load of disgraceful superstition. Nor is there the least doubt, that the better faith produced its natural and desirable fruits in society, in gradually ameliorating the hearts, and taming the passions, of the people. But while many of the converts were turning meekly towards their new creed, some, in the arrogance of their understanding, were limiting the Scriptures by their own devices, and others failed not to make religious character or spiritual rank the means of rising to temporal power. Thus it happened at this critical period, that the effects of this great change in the religion of the country, although producing an immediate harvest, as well as sowing much good seed which was to grow hereafter, did not, in the fourth century, flourish so as to shed at once that predominating influence which its principles might have taught men to expect.

Even the borrowed splendour, in which Constantine decked his city, bore in it something which seemed to mark premature decay. The imperial founder, in seizing upon the ancient statues, pictures, obelisks, and works of art, acknowledged his own incapacity to supply their place with the productions of later genius; and when the world, and particularly Rome, was plundered to adorn Constantinople, the Emperor, under whom the work was carried on, might be compared to a prodigal youth, who strips an aged parent of her youthful ornaments, in order to decorate a flaunting paramour, on whose brow all must consider them as misplaced.

Constantinople, therefore, when in 324 it first arose in imperial majesty out of the humble Byzantium, showed, even in its birth, and amid its adventitious splendour, as we have already said, some intimations of that speedy decay to which the whole civilised world, then limited within the Roman empire, was internally and imperceptibly tending. Nor was it many ages ere these prognostications of declension were fully verified.

In the year 1080, Alexius Comnenus [Footnote: See Gibbon, Chap. xlviii, for the origin and early history of the house of the Comneni.] ascended the throne of the Empire; that is, he was declared sovereign of Constantinople, its precincts and dependencies; nor, if he was disposed to lead a life of relaxation, would the savage incursions of the Scythians or the Hungarians frequently disturb the imperial slumbers, if limited to his own capital. It may be supposed that this safety did not extend much farther; for it is said that the Empress Pulcheria had built a church to the Virgin Mary, as remote as possible from the gate of the city, to save her devotions from the risk of being interrupted by the hostile yell of the barbarians, and the reigning Emperor had constructed a palace near the same spot, and for the same reason.

Alexius Comnenus was in the condition of a monarch who rather derives consequence from the wealth and importance of his predecessors, and the great extent of their original dominions, than from what remnants of fortune had descended to the present generation. This Emperor, except nominally, no more ruled over his dismembered provinces, than a half– dead horse can exercise power over those limbs, on which the hooded crow and the vulture have already begun to settle and select their prey.

In different parts of his territory, different enemies arose, who waged successful or dubious war against the Emperor; and, of the numerous nations with whom he was engaged in hostilities, whether the Franks from the west, the Turks advancing from the east, the Cumans and Scythians pouring their barbarous numbers and unceasing storm of arrows from the north, and the Saracens, or the tribes into which they were divided, pressing from the south, there was not one for whom the Grecian empire did not spread a tempting repast. Each of

these various enemies had their own particular habits of war, and a way of manoeuvring in battle peculiar to themselves. But the Roman, as the unfortunate subject of the Greek empire was still called, was by far the weakest, the most ignorant, and most timid, who could be dragged into the field; and the Emperor was happy in
his own good luck, when he found it possible to conduct a defensive war on a counterbalancing principle, making use of the Scythian to repel the Turk, or of both these savage people to drive back the fiery–footed Frank, whom Peter the Hermit had, in the time of Alexius, waked to double fury, by the powerful influence of the crusades.

If, therefore, Alexius Comnenus was, during his anxious seat upon the throne of the East, reduced to use a base and truckling course of policy—if he was sometimes reluctant to fight when he had a conscious doubt of the valour of his troops—if he commonly employed cunning and dissimulation instead of wisdom, and perfidy instead of courage—his expedients were the disgrace of the age, rather than his own.

Again, the Emperor Alexius may be blamed for affecting a degree of state which was closely allied to imbecility. He was proud of assuming in his own person, and of bestowing upon others, the painted show of various orders of nobility, even now, when the rank within the prince's gift was become an additional reason for the free barbarian despising the imperial noble. That the Greek court was encumbered with unmeaning ceremonies, in order to make amends for the want of that veneration which ought to have been called forth by real worth, and the presence of actual power, was not the particular fault of that prince, but belonged to the system of the government of Constantinople for ages. Indeed, in its trumpery etiquette, which provided rules for the most trivial points of a man's behaviour during the day, the Greek empire resembled no existing power in its minute follies, except that of Pekin; both, doubtless, being influenced by the same vain wish, to add seriousness and an appearance of importance to objects, which, from their trivial nature, could admit no such distinction.

Yet thus far we must justify Alexius, that humble as were the expedients he had recourse to, they were more useful to his empire than the measures of a more proud and high–spirited prince might have proved in the same circumstances. He was no champion to break a lance against the breast–plate of his Frankish rival, the famous Bohemond of Antioch,[Footnote: Bohemond, son of Robert Guiscard, the Norman conqueror of Apulia, Calabria, and Sicily, was, at the time when the first crusade began, Count of Tarentum. Though far advanced in life, he eagerly joined the expedition of the Latins, and became Prince of Antioch. For details of his adventures, death, and extraordinary character, see Gibbon, chap. lix, and Mills' History of the Crusades, vol. i.] but there were many occasions on which he hazarded his life freely; and, so far as we can see, from a minute perusal of his achievements, the Emperor of Greece was never so dangerous "under shield," as when any foeman desired to stop him while retreating from a conflict in which he had been worsted.

But, besides that he did not hesitate, according to the custom of the time, at least occasionally, to commit his person to the perils of close combat, Alexius also possessed such knowledge of a general's profession, as is required in our modern days. He knew how to occupy military positions to the best advantage, and often covered defeats, or improved dubious conflicts, in a manner highly to the disappointment of those who deemed that the work of war was done only on the field of battle.

If Alexius Comnenus thus understood the evolutions of war, he was still better skilled in those of politics, where, soaring far above the express purpose of his immediate negotiation, the Emperor was sure to gain some important and permanent advantage; though very often he was ultimately defeated by the unblushing fickleness, or avowed treachery of the barbarians, as the Greeks generally termed all other nations, and particularly those tribes, (they can hardly be termed states,) by which their own empire was surrounded.

We may conclude our brief character of Comnenus, by saying, that, had he not been called on to fill the station of a monarch who was under the necessity of making himself dreaded, as one who was exposed to all manner of conspiracies, both in and out of his own family, he might, in all probability, have been regarded as an honest and humane prince. Certainly he showed himself a good–natured man, and dealt less in cutting off heads and extinguishing eyes, than had been the practice of his predecessors, who generally took this method of shortening the ambitious views of competitors.

It remains to be mentioned, that Alexius had his full share of the superstition of the age, which he covered with a species of hypocrisy. It is even said, that his wife, Irene, who of course was best acquainted with the real character of the Emperor, taxed her dying husband with practising, in his last moments, the dissimulation which had been his companion during life. [Footnote: See Gibbon, chap. lvi.] He took also a deep interest in all matters respecting the Church, where heresy, which the Emperor held, or affected to hold, in great horror, appeared to him to lurk. Nor do we discover in his treatment of the Manichaeans, or Paulicians, that pity for their speculative errors, which modern times might think had been well purchased by the extent of the temporal services of these unfortunate sectaries. Alexius knew no indulgence for those who misinterpreted the mysteries of the Church, or of its doctrines; and the duty of defending religion against schismatics was, in his opinion, as peremptorily demanded from him, as that of protecting the empire against the numberless tribes of barbarians who were encroaching on its boundaries on every side.

Such a mixture of sense and weakness, of meanness and dignity, of prudent discretion and poverty of spirit, which last, in the European mode of viewing things, approached to cowardice, formed the leading traits of the character of Alexius Comnenus, at a period when the fate of Greece, and all that was left in that country of art and civilization, was trembling in the balance, and likely to be saved or lost, according to the abilities of the Emperor for playing the very difficult game which was put into his hands.

These few leading circumstances will recall, to any one who is tolerably well read in history, the peculiarities of the period at which we have found a resting–place for the foundation of our story.

Chapter the Second

Othus. —––– This superb successor
Of the earth's mistress, as thou vainly speakest, Stands
midst these ages as, on the wide ocean, The last spared
fragment, of a spacious land, That in some grand and
awful ministration
Of mighty nature has engulfed been, Doth lift
aloft its dark and rocky cliffs
O'er the wild waste around, and sadly frowns
In lonely majesty.
CONSTANTINE PALEOLOGUS, *Scene I.*

Our scene in the capital of the Eastern Empire opens at what is termed the
Golden Gate of Constantinople; and it may be said in passing, that this
splendid epithet is not so lightly bestowed as may be expected from the
inflated language of the Greeks, which throws such an appearance of
exaggeration about them, their buildings, and monuments.

The massive, and seemingly impregnable walls with which Constantine
surrounded the city, were greatly improved and added to by Theodosius,
called the Great. A triumphal arch, decorated with
the architecture of a better, though already a degenerate age, and serving, at
the same time, as a useful entrance, introduced the stranger into the city. On
the top, a statue of bronze represented Victory, the goddess who had
inclined the scales of battle in favour
of Theodosius; and, as the artist determined to be wealthy if he could not be
tasteful, the gilded ornaments with which the inscriptions
were set off, readily led to the popular name of the gate. Figures carved in a
distant and happier period of the art, glanced from the walls, without assorting
happily with the taste in which these were built. The more modern ornaments
of the Golden Gate bore, at the period of our story, an aspect very different
from those indicating the

"conquest brought back to the city," and the "eternal peace" which the flattering inscriptions recorded as having been extorted by the sword of Theodosius. Four or five military engines, for throwing darts of the largest size, were placed upon the summit of the arch; and what had been originally designed as a specimen of architectural embellishment, was now applied to the purposes of defence.

It was the hour of evening, and the cool and refreshing breeze from the sea inclined each passenger, whose business was not of a very urgent description, to loiter on his way, and cast a glance at the romantic gateway, and the various interesting objects of nature and art, which the city of Constantinople presented, as well to the inhabitants as to strangers. [Footnote: The impression which the imperial city was calculated to make on such visitors as the Crusaders of the West, is given by the ancient French chronicler Villehardouin, who was present at the capture of A. D. 1203. "When we had come," he says, "within three leagues, to a certain Abbey, then we could plainly survey Constantinople. There the ships and the galleys came to anchor; and much did they who had never been in that quarter before, gaze upon the city. That such a city could be in the world they had never conceived, and they were never weary of staring at the high walls and towers with which it was entirely encompassed, the rich palaces and lofty churches, of which there were so many that no one could have believed it, if he had not seen with his own eyes that city, the Queen of all cities. And know that there was not so bold a heart there, that it did not feel some terror at the strength of Constantinople."—Chap. 66.

Again,—"And now many of those of the host went to see Constantinople within, and the rich palaces and stately churches, of which it possesses so many, and the riches of the place, which are such as no other city ever equalled. I need not speak of the sanctuaries, which are as many as are in all the world beside."— Chap. 100.]

One individual, however, seemed to indulge more wonder and curiosity than could have been expected from a native of the city, and looked upon the rarities around with a quick and startled eye, that marked an imagination awakened by sights that were new and strange. The appearance of this person bespoke a foreigner of military habits, who seemed, from his complexion, to have his birthplace far from the Grecian metropolis, whatever chance had at present brought him to the Golden Gate, or whatever place he filled in the Emperor's service.

This young man was about two–and–twenty years old, remarkably finely–formed and athletic—qualities well understood by the citizens of Constantinople, whose habits of frequenting the public games had taught them at least an acquaintance with the human person, and where, in the select of their own countrymen, they saw the handsomest specimens of the human race.

These were, however, not generally so tall as the stranger at the Golden Gate, while his piercing blue eyes, and the fair hair which descended from under a light helmet gaily ornamented with silver, bearing on its summit a crest resembling a dragon in the act of expanding his terrible jaws, intimated a northern descent, to which the extreme purity of his complexion also bore witness. His beauty, however, though he was eminently distinguished both in features and in person, was not liable to the charge of effeminacy. From this
it was rescued, both by his strength, and by the air of confidence and self–possession with which the youth seemed to regard the wonders around him, not indicating the stupid and helpless gaze of a mind equally inexperienced, and incapable of receiving instruction, but expressing the bold intellect which at once understands the greater part of the information which it receives, and commands the spirit to toil in search of the meaning of that which it has not comprehended, or may fear it has misinterpreted. This look of awakened attention and intelligence gave interest to the young barbarian; and while the bystanders were amazed that a savage from some unknown or
remote corner of the universe should possess a noble countenance bespeaking a mind so elevated, they respected him for the
composure with which he witnessed so many things, the fashion, the splendour, nay, the very use of which, must have been recently new to him.

The young man's personal equipments exhibited a singular mixture
of splendour and effeminacy, and enabled the experienced spectators

to ascertain his nation, and the capacity in which he served. We have already mentioned the fanciful and crested helmet, which was a distinction of the foreigner, to which the reader must add in his imagination a small cuirass, or breastplate of silver, so sparingly fashioned as obviously to afford little security to the broad chest, on which it rather hung like an ornament than covered as a buckler; nor, if a well–thrown dart, or strongly–shod arrow, should alight full on this rich piece of armour, was there much hope that it could protect the bosom which it partially shielded.

From betwixt the shoulders hung down over the back what had the appearance of a bearskin; but, when more closely examined, it was only a very skilful imitation, of the spoils of the chase, being in reality a surcoat composed of strong shaggy silk, so woven as to exhibit, at a little distance, no inaccurate representation of a bear's hide. A light crooked sword, or scimitar, sheathed in a scabbard of gold and ivory, hung by the left side of the stranger, the ornamented hilt of which appeared much too small for the large–jointed hand of the young Hercules who was thus gaily attired. A dress, purple in colour, and setting close to the limbs, covered the body of the soldier to a little above the knee; from thence the knees and legs were bare
to the calf, to which the reticulated strings of the sandals rose from the instep, the ligatures being there fixed by a golden coin of the reigning Emperor, converted into a species of clasp for the purpose.

But a weapon which seemed more particularly adapted to the young barbarian's size, and incapable of being used by a man of less formidable limbs and sinews, was a battle–axe, the firm iron– guarded staff of which was formed of tough elm, strongly inlaid and defended with brass, while many a plate and ring were indented in the handle, to hold the wood and the steel parts together. The axe itself was composed of two blades, turning different ways, with a sharp steel spike projecting from between them. The steel part, both spike and blade, was burnished as bright as a mirror; and though its ponderous size must have been burdensome to one weaker than himself, yet the young soldier carried it as carelessly along, as if it were but a feather's weight. It was, indeed, a skilfully constructed weapon, so well balanced, that it was much lighter in striking and in recovery, than he who saw it in the hands of another could easily have believed.

The carrying arms of itself showed that the military man was a stranger. The native Greeks had that mark of a civilized people, that they never bore weapons during the time of peace, unless the wearer chanced to be numbered among those whose military profession and employment required them to be always in arms. Such soldiers by profession were easily distinguished from the peaceful citizens; and it was with some evident show of fear as well as dislike, that the passengers observed to each other, that the stranger was a Varangian, an expression which intimated a barbarian of the imperial body–guard.

To supply the deficiency of valour among his own subjects, and to procure soldiers who should be personally dependent on the Emperor, the Greek sovereigns had been, for a great many years, in the custom of maintaining in their pay, as near their person as they could, the steady services of a select number of mercenaries in the capacity of body–guards, which were numerous enough, when their steady discipline and inflexible loyalty were taken in conjunction with their personal strength and indomitable courage, to defeat, not only any traitorous attempt on the imperial person, but to quell open rebellions, unless such were supported by a great proportion of the military force. Their pay was therefore liberal; their rank and established character for prowess gave them a degree of consideration among the people, whose reputation for valour had not
for some ages stood high; and if, as foreigners, and the members of a privileged body, the Varangians were sometimes employed in arbitrary and unpopular services, the natives were so apt to fear, while they disliked them, that the hardy strangers disturbed themselves but little about the light in which they were regarded by the inhabitants of Constantinople. Their dress and accoutrements, while within the city, partook of the rich, or rather gaudy costume, which we have described, bearing only a sort of affected resemblance to that which the Varangians wore in their native forests. But the individuals of this select corps were, when their services were required beyond the city, furnished with armour and weapons more resembling those which they were accustomed to wield in their own country, possessing much less of the splendour of

war, and a far greater portion of its effective terrors; and thus they were summoned to take the field.

This body of Varangians (which term is, according to one interpretation merely a general expression for barbarians) was, in an early age of the empire, formed of the roving and piratical inhabitants of the north, whom a love of adventure, the greatest perhaps that ever was indulged, and a contempt of danger, which never had a parallel in the history of human nature, drove forth upon the pathless ocean. "Piracy," says Gibbon, with his usual spirit, "was the exercise, the trade, the glory, and the virtue of the Scandinavian youth. Impatient of a bleak climate and narrow limits, they started from the banquet, grasped their arms, sounded their horn, ascended their ships, and explored every coast that promised either spoil or settlement." [Footnote: Decline and Fall of the Roman Empire.
Chap. lv. vol. x. p. 221, 8vo edition.]

The conquests made in France and Britain by these wild sea–kings, as they were called, have obscured the remembrance of other northern champions, who, long before the time of Comnenus, made excursions as far as Constantinople, and witnessed with their own eyes the wealth and the weakness of the Grecian empire itself. Numbers found their way thither through the pathless wastes of Russia; others navigated the Mediterranean in their sea–serpents, as they termed their piratical vessels. The Emperors, terrified at the appearance of these daring inhabitants of the frozen zone, had recourse to the usual policy of a rich and unwarlike people, bought with gold the service of their swords, and thus formed a corps of satellites more distinguished for valour than the famed Praetorian Bands of Rome, and, perhaps because fewer in number, unalterably loyal to their new princes.

But, at a later period of the empire, it began to be more difficult for the Emperors to obtain recruits for their favourite and selected corps, the northern nations having now in a great measure laid aside the piratical and roving habits, which had driven their ancestors from the straits of Elsinore to those of Sestos and Abydos. The corps of the Varangians must therefore have died out, or have been filled up with less worthy materials, had not the conquests made by the Normans in the far distant west, sent to the aid of Comnenus a large body of the dispossessed inhabitants of the islands of Britain, and particularly of England, who furnished recruits to his chosen body– guard. These were, in fact, Anglo–Saxons; but, in the confused idea of geography received at the court of Constantinople, they were naturally enough called Anglo–Danes, as their native country was confounded with the Thule of the ancients, by which expression the archipelago of Zetland and Orkney is properly to be understood, though, according to the notions of the Greeks, it comprised either Denmark or Britain. The emigrants, however, spoke a language not very dissimilar to the original Varangians, and adopted the name more readily, that it seemed to remind them of their unhappy fate, the appellation being in one sense capable of being interpreted as exiles. Excepting one or two chief commanders, whom the Emperor judged worthy of such high trust, the Varangians were officered by men of their own nation; and with so many privileges, being joined by many of their countrymen from time to time, as the crusades, pilgrimages, or discontent at home, drove fresh supplies of the Anglo– Saxons, or Anglo–Danes, to the east, the Varangians subsisted in strength to the last days of the Greek empire, retaining their native language, along with the unblemished loyalty, and unabated martial spirit, which characterised their fathers.

This account of the Varangian Guard is strictly historical, and might be proved by reference to the Byzantine historians; most of whom, and also Villehardouin's account of the taking of the city of Constantinople by the Franks and Venetians, make repeated mention of this celebrated and singular body of Englishmen, forming a mercenary guard attendant on the person of the Greek Emperors. [Footnote: Ducange has poured forth a tide of learning on this curious subject, which will be found in his Notes on Villehardouin's Constantinople under the French Emperors.—Paris, 1637, folio, p. 196. Gibbon's History may also be consulted, vol. x. p. 231.

Villehardouin, in describing the siege of Constantinople, A. D. 1203, says, "'Li murs fu mult garnis d'Anglois et de Danois,"—hence the dissertation of Ducange here quoted, and several articles besides in his Glossarium, as *Varangi*, Warengangi, etc. The etymology of the name is left uncertain, though the German *fort–ganger*, *i. e.* forth–

goer, wanderer, *exile*, seems the most probable. The term occurs in various Italian and Sicilian documents, anterior to the establishment of the Varangian Guards at Constantinople, and collected by Muratori: as, for instance, in an edict of one of the Lombard kings, "Omnes Warengrangi, qui de extens finibus in regni nostri finibus advenerint seque sub scuto potestatis nostrae subdiderint, legibus nostris Longobardorum vivere debeant,"—and in another, "De Warengangis, nobilibus, mediocribus, et rusticis hominibus, qui usque nune in terra vestra fugiti sunt, habeatis eos."—*Muratori*, vol. ii. p. 261.

With regard to the origin of the Varangian Guard, the most distinct testimony is that of Ordericus Vittalis, who says, "When therefore the English had lost their liberty, they turned themselves with zeal to discover the means of throwing off the unaccustomed yoke. Some fled to Sueno, King of the Danes, to excite him to the recovery of the inheritance of his grandfather, Canute. Not a few fled into exile in other regions, either from the mere desire of escaping from under the Norman rule, or in the hope of acquiring wealth, and so being one day in a condition to renew the struggle at home. Some of these, in the bloom of youth, penetrated into a far distant land, and offered themselves to the military service of the Constantinopolitan Emperor — that wise prince, against whom Robert Guiscard, Duke of Apulia, had then raised all his forces. The English exiles were favourably received, and opposed in battle to the Normans, for whose encounter the Greeks themselves were too weak. Alexius began to build a town for the English, a little above Constantinople, at a place called *Chevelot*, but the trouble of the Normans from Sicily still increasing, he soon recalled them to the capital, and intrusted the princial palace with all its treasures to their keeping. This was the method in which the Saxon English found their way to Ionia, where they still remain, highly valued by the Emperor and the people."—Book iv. p. 508.]

Having said enough to explain why an individual Varangian should be strolling about the Golden Gate, we may proceed in the story which we have commenced.

Let it not be thought extraordinary, that this soldier of the life– guard should be looked upon with some degree of curiosity by the passing citizens. It must be supposed, that, from their peculiar duties, they were not encouraged to hold frequent intercourse or communication with the inhabitants; and, besides that they had duties of police occasionally to exercise amongst them, which made them generally more dreaded than beloved, they were at the same time conscious, that their high pay, splendid appointments, and immediate dependence on the Emperor, were subjects of envy to the other forces. They, therefore, kept much in the neighbourhood of their own barracks, and were seldom seen straggling remote from them, unless they had a commission of government intrusted to their charge.

This being the case, it was natural that a people so curious as the Greeks should busy themselves in eyeing the stranger as he loitered in one spot, or wandered to and fro, like a man who either could not find some place which he was seeking, or had failed to meet some person with whom he had an appointment, for which the ingenuity of the passengers found a thousand different and inconsistent reasons. "A Varangian," said one citizen to another, "and upon duty
—ahem! Then I presume to say in your ear"—

"What do you imagine is his object?" enquired the party to whom this information was addressed.

"Gods and goddesses! do you think I can tell you? but suppose that he is lurking here to hear what folk say of the Emperor," answered the *quid–nunc* of Constantinople.

"That is not likely,"' said the querist; "these Varangians do not speak our language, and are not extremely well fitted for spies, since few of them pretend to any intelligible notion of the Grecian tongue. It is not likely, I think, that the Emperor would employ as a spy a man who did not understand the language of the country."

"But if there are, as all men fancy," answered the politician, "persons among these barbarian soldiers who can speak almost all languages, you will admit that such are excellently qualified for seeing clearly around them, since they possess the talent of beholding and
reporting, while no one has the slightest idea of suspecting them."

"It may well be," replied his companion; "but since we see so clearly the fox's foot and paws protruding from beneath the seeming sheep's fleece, or rather, by your leave, the *bear's* hide yonder, had we not better be jogging homeward, ere it be pretended we have insulted a Varangian Guard?"

This surmise of danger insinuated by the last speaker, who was a much older and more experienced politician than his friend, determined both on a hasty retreat. They adjusted their cloaks, caught hold of each other's arm, and, speaking fast and thick as they started new subjects of suspicion, they sped, close coupled together, towards their habitations, in a different and distant quarter of the town.

In the meantime, the sunset was nigh over; and the long shadows of the walls, bulwarks, and arches, were projecting from the westward in deeper and blacker shade. The Varangian seemed tired of the short and lingering circle in which he had now trodden for more than an hour, and in which he still loitered like an unliberated spirit, which cannot leave the haunted spot till licensed by the spell which has brought it hither. Even so the barbarian, casting an impatient glance to the sun, which was setting in a blaze of light behind a rich grove of cypress– trees, looked for some accommodation on the benches of stone which were placed under shadow of the triumphal arch of Theodosius, drew the axe, which was his principal weapon, close to his side, wrapped his cloak about him, and, though his dress was not in other respects a fit attire for slumber, any more than the place well selected for repose, yet in less than three minutes he was fast asleep. The irresistible impulse which induced him to seek for repose in a place very indifferently fitted for the purpose, might be weariness consequent upon the military vigils, which had proved a part of his duty on the preceding evening. At the same time, his spirit was so alive within him, even while he gave way to this transient fit of oblivion, that he remained almost awake even with shut eyes, and no hound ever seemed to sleep more lightly than our Anglo–Saxon at the Golden Gate of Constantinople.

And now the slumberer, as the loiterer had been before, was the subject of observation to the accidental passengers. Two men entered the porch in company. One was a somewhat slight made, but alert–looking man, by name Lysimachus, and by profession a designer. A roll of paper in his hand, with a little satchel containing a few chalks, or pencils, completed his stock in trade; and his acquaintance with the remains of ancient art gave him a power of talking on the subject, which unfortunately bore more than due proportion to his talents of execution. His companion, a magnificent–looking man in form, and so far resembling the young barbarian, but more clownish and peasant–like in the expression of his features, was Stephanos the wrestler, well known in the Palestra.

"Stop here, my friend," said the artist, producing his pencils, "till I make a sketch for my youthful Hercules."

"I thought Hercules had been a Greek," said the wrestler. "This sleeping animal is a barbarian."

The tone intimated some offence, and the designer hastened to soothe the displeasure which he had thoughtlessly excited. Stephanos, known by the surname of Castor, who was highly distinguished for gymnastic exercises, was a sort of patron to the little artist, and not unlikely by his own reputation to bring the talents of his friend into notice.

"Beauty and strength," said the adroit artist, "are of no particular nation; and may our Muse never deign me her prize, but it is my greatest pleasure to compare them, as existing in the uncultivated savage of the north, and when they are found in the darling of an enlightened people, who has added the height of gymnastic skill to the most distinguished natural qualities, such as we can now only see in the works of Phidias and Praxiteles—or in our living model of the gymnastic champions of antiquity."

"Nay, I acknowledge that the Varangian is a proper man," said the athletic hero, softening his tone; "but the poor savage hath not, perhaps, in his lifetime, had a single drop of oil on his bosom! Hercules instituted the Isthmian Games"—

"But hold! what sleeps he with, wrapt so close in his bear–skin?" said the artist. "Is it a club?"

"Away, away, my friend!" cried Stephanos, as they looked closer on the sleeper. "Do you not know that is the instrument of their barbarous office? They do not war with swords or lances, as if destined to attack men of flesh and blood; but with maces and axes, as if they were to hack limbs formed of stone, and sinews of oak. I will wager my crown [of withered parsley] that he lies here to arrest some distinguished commander who has offended the government! He would not have been thus formidably armed otherwise— Away, away, good Lysimachus; let us respect the slumbers of the bear."

So saying, the champion of the Palestra made off with less apparent confidence than his size and strength might have inspired.

Others, now thinly straggling, passed onward as the evening closed, and the shadows of the cypress–trees fell darker around. Two females of the lower rank cast their eyes on the sleeper. "Holy Maria!" said one, "if he does not put me in mind of the Eastern tale, how the Genie brought a gallant young prince from his nuptial chamber in Egypt, and left him sleeping at the gate of Damascus. I will awake the poor lamb, lest he catch harm from the night dew."

"Harm?" answered the older and crosser looking woman. "Ay, such harm as the cold water of the Cydnus does to the wild–swan. A lamb?—ay, forsooth! Why he's a wolf or a bear, at least a Varangian, and no modest matron would exchange a word with such an unmannered barbarian. I'll tell you what one of, these English Danes did to me"—

So saying, she drew on her companion, who followed with some reluctance, seeming to listen to her gabble, while she looked back upon the sleeper.

The total disappearance of the sun, and nearly at the same time the departure of the twilight, which lasts so short time in that tropical region—one of the few advantages which a more temperate climate possesses over it, being the longer continuance of that sweet and placid light—gave signal to the warders of the city to shut the
folding leaves of the Golden Gate, leaving a wicket lightly bolted for the passage of those whom business might have detained too late

without the walls, and indeed for all who chose to pay a small coin. The position and apparent insensibility of the Varangian did not escape those who had charge of the gate, of whom there was a strong guard, which belonged to the ordinary Greek forces.

"By Castor and by Pollux," said the centurion—for the Greeks swore by the ancient deities, although they no longer worshipped them, and preserved those military distinctions with which "the steady Romans shook the world," although they were altogether degenerated from their original manners—"By Castor and Pollux, comrades, we
cannot gather gold in this gate, according as its legend tells us: yet it will be our fault if we cannot glean a goodly crop of silver; and though the golden age be the most ancient and honourable, yet in
this degenerate time it is much if we see a glimpse of the inferior metal."

"Unworthy are we to follow the noble centurion Harpax," answered one of the soldiers of the watch, who showed the shaven head and the single tuft [Footnote: One tuft is left on the shaven head of the Moslem, for the angel to grasp by when conveying him to Paradise.] of a Mussulman, "if we do not hold silver a sufficient cause to bestir
ourselves, when there has been no gold to be had—as, by the faith of an honest man, I think we can hardly tell its colour—whether out of the imperial treasury, or obtained at the expense of individuals, for many long moons !"

"But this silver," said the centurion, "thou shalt see with thine own eye, and hear it ring a knell in the purse which holds our common stock." "Which *did* hold it, as thou wouldst say, most valiant commander," replied the inferior warder; "but what that purse holds now, save a few miserable oboli for purchasing certain pickled potherbs and salt fish, to relish our allowance of stummed wine, I cannot tell, but willingly give my share of the contents to the devil, if either purse or platter exhibits symptom of any age richer than the age of copper."

"I will replenish our treasury," said the centurion, "were our stock yet lower than it is. Stand up close by the wicket, my masters. Bethink you we are the Imperial Guards, or the guards of the

Imperial City, it is all one, and let us have no man rush past us on a sudden;—and now that we are on our guard, I will unfold to you— But stop," said the valiant centurion, "are we all here true brothers? Do all well understand the ancient and laudable customs of our watch—keeping all things secret which concern the profit and advantage of this our vigil, and aiding and abetting the common cause, without information or treachery?"

"You are strangely suspicious to–night," answered the sentinel. "Methinks we have stood by you without tale–telling in matters which were more weighty. Have you forgot the passage of the jeweller—which was neither the gold nor silver age; but if there were a diamond one"—

"Peace, good Ismail the Infidel," said the centurion,—"for, I thank Heaven, we are of all religions, so it is to be hoped we must have the true one amongst us,—Peace, I say; it is unnecessary to prove thou canst keep new secrets, by ripping up old ones. Come hither—look through the wicket to the stone bench, on the shady side of the grand porch—tell me, old lad, what dost thou see there?"

"A man asleep," said Ismail. "By Heaven, I think from what I can see by the moonlight, that it is one of those barbarians, one of those island dogs, whom the Emperor sets such store by!"

"And can thy fertile brain," said the centurion, "spin nothing out of his present situation, tending towards our advantage?"

"Why, ay," said Ismail; "they have large pay, though they are not only barbarians, but pagan dogs, in comparison with us Moslems and Nazarenes. That fellow hath besotted himself with liquor, and hath not found his way home to his barracks in good time. He will be severely punished, unless we consent to admit him; and to prevail on us to do so, he must empty the contents of his girdle."

"That, at least—that, at least," answered the soldiers of the city watch, but carefully suppressing their voices, though they spoke in an eager tone. "And is that all that you would make of such an opportunity?" said Harpax, scornfully. "No, no, comrades. If this outlandish animal indeed escape us, he must at least leave his fleece behind. See you not the gleams from his headpiece and his cuirass? I presume these betoken substantial silver, though it may be of the thinnest. There lies the silver mine I spoke of, ready to enrich the dexterous hands who shall labour it."

"But," said timidly a young Greek, a companion of their watch lately enlisted in the corps, and unacquainted with their habits, "still this barbarian, as you call him, is a soldier of the Emperor; and if we are convicted of depriving him of his arms, we shall be justly punished for a military crime."

"Hear to a new Lycurgus come to teach us our duty!" said the centurion. "Learn first, young man, that the metropolitan cohort never can commit a crime; and next, of course, that they can never be convicted of one. Suppose we found a straggling barbarian, a Varangian, like this slumberer, perhaps a Frank, or some other of these foreigners bearing unpronounceable names, while they dishonour us by putting on the arms and apparel of the real Roman soldier, are we, placed to defend an important post, to admit a man so suspicious within our postern, when the event may probably be to betray both the Golden Gate and the hearts of gold who guard it,—to have the one seized, and the throats of the others handsomely cut?"

"Keep him without side of the gate, then," replied the novice, "if you think him so dangerous. For my part, I should not fear him, were he deprived of that huge double–edged axe, which gleams from under his cloak, having a more deadly glare than the comet which astrologers prophesy such strange things of."

"Nay, then, we agree together," answered Harpax, "and you speak like a youth of modesty and sense; and I promise you the state will lose nothing in the despoiling of this same barbarian. Each of these savages hath a double set of accoutrements, the one wrought with gold, silver, inlaid work, and ivory, as becomes their duties in the prince's household; the other fashioned of triple steel, strong, weighty, and irresistible. Now, in taking from this suspicious character his silver helmet and cuirass, you reduce him to his proper weapons, and you will see him start up in arms fit for duty."

"Yes," said the novice; "but I do not see that this reasoning will do more than warrant our stripping the Varangian of his armour, to be afterwards heedfully returned to him on the morrow, if he prove a true man. How, I know not, but I had adopted some idea that it was to be confiscated for our joint behoof."

"Unquestionably," said Harpax; "for such has been the rule of our watch ever since the days of the excellent centurion Sisyphus, in whose time it first was determined, that all contraband commodities or suspicious weapons, or the like, which were brought into the city during the nightwatch, should be uniformly forfeited to the use of the soldiery of the guard; and where the Emperor finds the goods or arms unjustly seized, I hope he is rich enough to make it up to the sufferer."

"But still—but still," said Sebastes of Mitylene, the young Greek aforesaid, "were the Emperor to discover"—

"Ass!" replied Harpax, "he cannot discover, if he had all the eyes of Argus's tail.—Here are twelve of us sworn according to the rules of the watch, to abide in the same story. Here is a barbarian, who, if he remembers any thing of the matter—which I greatly doubt—his choice of a lodging arguing his familiarity with the wine–pot—tells but a wild tale of losing his armour, which we, my masters," (looking round to his companions,) "deny stoutly—I hope we have courage enough for that—and which party will be believed? The companions of the watch, surely!"

"Quite the contrary," said Sebastes. "I was born at a distance from hence; yet even in the island of Mitylene, the rumour had reached me that the cavaliers of the city–guard of Constantinople were so accomplished in falsehood, that the oath of a single barbarian would
outweigh the Christian oath of the whole body, if Christians some of them are—for example, this dark man with a single tuft on his head."

"And if it were even so," said the centurion, with a gloomy and sinister look, "there is another way of making the transaction a safe one."

Sebastes, fixing his eye on his commander, moved his hand to the hilt of an Eastern poniard which he wore, as if to penetrate his exact meaning. The centurion nodded in acquiescence.

"Young as I am," said Sebastes, "I have been already a pirate five years at sea, and a robber three years now in the hills, and it is the first time I have seen or heard a man hesitate, in such a case, to take the only part which is worth a brave man's while to resort to in a pressing affair."

Harpax struck his hand into that of the soldier, as sharing his uncompromising sentiments; but when he spoke, it was in a tremulous voice.

"How shall we deal with him?" said he to Sebastes, who, from the most raw recruit in the corps, had now risen to the highest place in his estimation.

"Any how," returned the islander; "I see bows here and shafts, and if no other person can use them"—

"They are not," said the centurion, "the regular arms of our corps." "The

fitter you to guard the gates of a city," said the young soldier,
with a horse–laugh, which had something insulting in it. "Well—be it so. I can shoot like a Scythian," he proceeded; "nod but with your head, one shaft shall crash among the splinters of his skull and his brains; the second shall quiver in his heart."

"Bravo, my noble comrade!" said Harpax, in a tone of affected rapture, always lowering his voice, however, as respecting the slumbers of the Varangian. "Such were the robbers of ancient days, the Diomedes, Corvnetes, Synnes, Scyrons, Procrustes, whom it required demigods to bring to what was miscalled justice, and whose compeers and fellows will remain masters of the continent and isles of Greece, until Hercules and Theseus shall again appear upon earth. Nevertheless, shoot not, my valiant Sebastes—draw not the bow, my invaluable Mitylenian; you may wound and not kill." "I am little wont to do so," said Sebastes, again repeating the hoarse, chuckling, discordant laugh, which grated upon the ears of the centurion,
though he could hardly tell the reason why it was so uncommonly

unpleasant. "If I look not about me," was his internal reflection, "we shall have two centurions of the watch, instead of one. This Mitylenian, or be he who the devil will, is a bow's length beyond me. I must keep my eye on him." He then spoke aloud, in a tone of authority. "But, come, young man, it is hard to discourage a young beginner. If you have been such a rover of wood and river as you tell us of, you know how to play the Sicarius: there lies your object, drunk or asleep, we know not which;—you will deal with him in either case."

"Will you give me no odds to stab a stupefied or drunken man, most noble centurion?" answered the Greek. "You would perhaps love the commission yourself?" he continued, somewhat ironically.

"Do as you are directed, friend," said Harpax, pointing to the turret staircase which led down from the battlement to the arched entrance underneath the porch.

"He has the true cat–like stealthy pace," half muttered the centurion, as his sentinel descended to do such a crime as he was posted there to prevent. "This cockerel's comb must be cut, or he will become king of the roost. But let us see if his hand be as resolute as his tongue; then we will consider what turn to give to the conclusion."

As Harpax spoke between his teeth, and rather to himself than any of his companions, the Mitylenian emerged from under the archway, treading on tiptoe, yet swiftly, with an admirable mixture of silence and celerity. His poniard, drawn as he descended, gleamed in his hand, which was held a little behind the rest of his person, so as to conceal it. The assassin hovered less than an instant over the sleeper, as if to mark the interval between the ill–fated silver corslet, and the body which it was designed to protect, when, at the instant the blow was rushing to its descent, the Varangian started up at once, arrested the armed hand of the assassin, by striking it upwards with the head of his battle–axe; and while he thus parried the intended stab, struck the Greek a blow heavier than Sebastes had ever learned at the Pancration, which left him scarce the power to cry help to his comrades on the battlements. They saw what had happened,
however, and beheld the barbarian set his foot on their companion,

and brandish high his formidable weapon, the whistling sound of which made the old arch ring ominously, while he paused an instant, with his weapon upheaved, ere he gave the finishing blow to his enemy. The warders made a bustle, as if some of them would descend to the assistance of Sebastes, without, however, appearing very eager to do so, when Harpax, in a rapid whisper, commanded them to stand fast.

"Each man to his place," he said, "happen what may. Yonder comes a captain of the guard—the secret is our own, if the savage has killed the Mitylenian, as I well trust, for he stirs neither hand nor foot. But if he lives, my comrades, make hard your faces as flints—he is but one man, we are twelve. We know nothing of his purpose, save that he went to see wherefore the barbarian slept so near the post."

While the centurion thus bruited his purpose in busy insinuation to the companions of his watch, the stately figure of a tall soldier, richly armed, and presenting a lofty crest, which glistened as he stept from the open moonlight into the shade of the vault, became visible beneath. A whisper passed among the warders on the top of the gate.

"Draw bolt, shut gate, come of the Mitylenian what will," said the centurion; "we are lost men if we own him.—Here comes the chief of the Varangian axes, the Follower himself."

"Well, Hereward," said the officer who came last upon the scene, in a sort of *lingua Franca*, generally used by the barbarians of the guard, "hast thou caught a night–hawk?"

"Ay, by Saint George!" answered the soldier; "and yet, in my country, we would call him but a kite."

"What is he?" said the leader.

"He will tell you that himself," replied the Varangian, "when I take my grasp from his windpipe."

"Let him go, then," said the officer.

The Englishman did as he was commanded; but, escaping as soon as

he felt himself at liberty, with an alertness which could scarce have been anticipated, the Mitylenian rushed out at the arch, and, availing himself of the complicated ornaments which had originally graced the exterior of the gateway, he fled around buttress and projection, closely pursued by the Varangian, who, encumbered with his
armour, was hardly a match in the course for the light–footed Grecian, as he dodged his pursuer from one skulking place to another. The officer laughed heartily, as the two figures, like shadows appearing and disappearing as suddenly, held rapid flight and chase around the arch of Theodosius.

"By Hercules! it is Hector pursued round the walls of Ilion by Achilles," said the officer; "but my Pelides will scarce overtake the son of Priam. What, ho! goddess–born—son of the white–footed Thetis!— But the allusion is lost on the poor savage—Hollo, Hereward! I say, stop—know thine own most barbarous name." These last words were muttered; then raising his voice, "Do not out– run thy wind, good Hereward. Thou mayst have more occasion for breath to–night."

"If it had been my leader's will," answered the Varangian, coming back in sulky mood, and breathing like one who had been at the top of his speed, "I would have had him as fast as ever grey–hound held hare, ere I left off the chase. Were it not for this foolish armour, which encumbers without defending one, I would not have made two bounds without taking him by the throat."

"As well as it is," said the officer, who was, in fact, the Acoulonthos, or *Follower*, so called because it was the duty of this highly– trusted officer of the Varangian Guards constantly to attend on the person of the Emperor. "But let us now see by what means we are to regain our entrance through the gate; for if, as I suspect, it was one of those warders who was willing to have played thee a trick, his companions may not let us enter willingly." "And is it not," said the Varangian, "your Valour's duty to probe this want of discipline to the bottom?"

"Hush thee here, my simple–minded savage! I have often told you, most ignorant Hereward, that the skulls of those who come from your cold and muddy Boentia of the North, are fitter to bear out twenty blows with a sledge–hammer, than turn off one witty or ingenious idea. But follow me, Hereward, and although I am aware that showing the fine meshes of Grecian policy to the coarse eye of an unpractised barbarian like thee, is much like casting pearls before swine, a thing forbidden in the Blessed Gospel, yet, as thou hast so good a heart, and so trusty, as is scarce to be met with among my Varangians themselves, I care not if, while thou art in attendance on my person, I endeavour to indoctrinate thee in some of that policy by which I myself—the Follower—the chief of the Varangians, and therefore erected by their axes into the most valiant of the valiant, am content to guide myself, although every way qualified to bear me through the cross currents of the court by main pull of oar and press of sail—a condescension in me, to do that by policy, which no man in this imperial court, the chosen sphere of superior wits, could so well accomplish by open force as myself. What think'st thou, good savage?"

"I know," answered the Varangian, who walked about a step and a half behind his leader, like an orderly of the present day behind his officer's shoulder, "I should be sorry to trouble my head with what I could do by my hands at once."

"Did I not say so?" replied the Follower, who had now for some minutes led the way from the Golden Gate, and was seen gliding along the outside of the moonlight walls, as if seeking an entrance elsewhere. "Lo, such is the stuff of what you call your head is made! Your hands and arms are perfect Ahitophels, compared to it.
Hearken to me, thou most ignorant of all animals,—but, for that very reason, thou stoutest of confidants, and bravest of soldiers,—I will tell thee the very riddle of this night–work, and yet, even then I doubt if thou canst understand me."

"It is my present duty to try to comprehend your Valour," said the Varangian—"I would say your policy, since you condescend to expound it to me. As for your valour," he added, "I should be unlucky if I did not think I understand its length and breadth already."

The Greek General coloured a little, but replied, with unaltered voice, "True, good Hereward. We have seen each other in battle."

Hereward here could not suppress a short cough, which to those grammarians of the day who were skilful in applying the use of accents, would have implied no peculiar eulogium on his officer's military bravery. Indeed, during their whole intercourse, the conversation of the General, in spite of his tone of affected importance and superiority, displayed an obvious respect for his companion, as one who, in many points of action, might, if brought to the test, prove a more effective soldier than himself. On the other hand, when the powerful Northern warrior replied, although it was with all observance of discipline and duty, yet the discussion might sometimes resemble that between an ignorant macaroni officer, before the Duke of York's reformation of the British army, and a steady sergeant of the regiment in which they both served. There was a consciousness of superiority, disguised by external respect, and half admitted by the leader.

"You will grant me, my simple friend," continued the chief, in the same tone as before, "in order to lead thee by a short passage into the deepest principle of policy which pervades this same court of Constantinople, that the favour of the Emperor"—(here the officer raised his casque, and the soldier made a semblance of doing so also)
— "who (be the place where he puts his foot sacred!) is the vivifying principle of the sphere in which we live, as the sun itself is that of humanity"—

"I have heard something like this said by our tribunes," said the Varangian.

"It is their duty so to instruct you," answered the leader; "and I trust that the priests also, in their sphere, forget not to teach my Varangians their constant service to their Emperor."

"They do not omit it," replied the soldier, "though we of the exiles know our duty."

"God forbid I should doubt it," said the commander of the battle–axes. "All I mean is to make thee understand, my dear Hereward, that as there are, though perhaps such do not exist in thy dark and

gloomy climate, a race of insects which are born in the first rays of the morning, and expire with those of sunset, (thence called by us ephemeras, as enduring one day only,) such is the case of a favourite at court, while enjoying the smiles of the most sacred Emperor. And happy is he whose favour, rising as the person of the sovereign emerges from the level space which extends around the throne, displays itself in the first imperial blaze of glory, and who, keeping his post during the meridian splendour of the crown, has only the
fate to disappear and die with the last beam of imperial brightness."

"Your Valour," said the islander, "speaks higher language than my Northern wits are able to comprehend. Only, methinks, rather than part with life at the sunset, I would, since insect I must needs be, become a moth for two or three dark hours."

"Such is the sordid desire of the vulgar, Hereward," answered the Follower, with assumed superiority, "who are contented to enjoy life, lacking distinction; whereas we, on the other hand, we of choicer quality, who form the nearest and innermost circle around the Imperial Alexius, in which he himself forms the central point, are watchful, to woman's jealousy, of the distribution of his favours, and omit no opportunity, whether by leaguing with or against each other, to recommend ourselves individually to the peliar light of his countenance."

"I think I comprehend what you mean," said the guardsman; "although as for living such a life of intrigue—but that matters not."

"It does indeed matter not, my good Hereward," said his officer, "and thou art lucky in having no appetite for the life I have described. Yet have I seen barbarians rise high in the empire, and if they have not altogether the flexibility, the malleability, as it is called—that happy ductility which can give way to circumstances, I
have yet known those of barbaric tribes, especially if bred up at court from their youth, who joined to a limited portion of this flexile
quality enough of a certain tough durability of temper, which, if it does not excel in availing itself of opportunity, has no contemptible talent at creating it. But letting comparisons pass, it follows, from this emulation of glory, that is, of royal favour, amongst the servants

of the imperial and most sacred court, that each is desirous of distinguishing himself by showing to the Emperor, not only that he fully understands the duties of his own employments, but that he is capable, in case of necessity, of discharging those of others."

"I understand," said the Saxon; "and thence it happens that the under ministers, soldiers, and assistants of the great crown–officers, are perpetually engaged, not in aiding each other, but in acting as spies on their neighbours' actions?"

"Even so," answered the commander; "it is but few days since I had a disagreeable instance of it. Every one, however dull in the intellect, hath understood thus much, that the great Protospathaire, [Footnote: Literally, the First Swordsman.] which title thou knowest signifies the General–in–chief of the forces of the empire, hath me at hatred, because I am the leader of those redoubtable Varangians, who enjoy and well deserve, privileges exempting them from the absolute command which he possesses over all other corps of the army—an authority which becomes Nicanor, notwithstanding the victorious sound of his name, nearly as well as a war– saddle would become a bullock."

"How!" said the Varangian, "does the Protospathaire pretend to any authority over the noble exiles?—By the red dragon, under which we will live and die, we will obey no man alive but Alexius Comnenus himself, and our own officers!"

"Rightly and bravely resolved," said the leader; "but, my good Hereward, let not your just indignation hurry you so far as to name the most sacred Emperor, without raising your hand to your casque, and adding the epithets of his lofty rank."

"I will raise my hand often enough and high enough," said the Norseman, "when the Emperor's service requires it."

"I dare be sworn thou wilt," said Achilles Tatius, the commander of the Varangian Imperial Body Guard, who thought the time was unfavourable for distinguishing himself by insisting on that exact observance of etiquette, which was one of his great pretensions to the name of a soldier. "Yet were it not for the constant vigilance of your leader, my child, the noble Varangians would be trode down, in the common mass of the army, with the heathen cohorts of Huns, Scythians, or those turban'd infidels the renegade Turks; and even for this is your commander here in peril, because he vindicates his axe–men as worthy of being prized above the paltry shafts of the Eastern tribes and the javelins of the Moors, which are only fit to be playthings for children."

"You are exposed to no danger," said the soldier, closing up to Achilles in a confidential manner, "from which these axes can protect you."

"Do I not know it?" said Achilles. "But it is to your arms alone that the Follower of his most sacred Majesty now intrusts his safety."

"In aught that a soldier may do," answered Hereward; "make your own computation, and then reckon this single arm worth two against any man the Emperor has, not being of our own corps."

"Listen, my brave friend," continued Achilles. "This Nicanor was daring enough to throw a reproach on our noble corps, accusing them—gods and goddesses!—of plundering in the field, and, yet more sacrilegious, of drinking the precious wine which was prepared for his most sacred Majesty's own blessed consumption. I, the sacred person of the Emperor being present, proceeded, as thou may'st well believe"—

"To give him the lie in his audacious throat!" burst in the Varangian — "named a place of meeting somewhere in the vicinity, and called the attendance of your poor follower, Hereward of Hampton, who is your bond–slave for life long, for such an honour! I wish only you had told me to get my work–day arms; but, however, I have my battle–axe, and"— Here his companion seized a moment to break in, for he was somewhat abashed at the lively tone of the young soldier.

"Hush thee, my son," said Achilles Tatius; "speak low, my excellent Hereward. Thou mistakest this thing. With thee by my side, I would not, indeed, hesitate to meet five such as Nicanor; but such is not the law of this most hallowed empire, nor the sentiments of the three times illustrious Prince who now rules it. Thou art debauched, my soldier, with the swaggering stories of the Franks, of whom we hear more and more every day."

"I would not willingly borrow any thing from those whom you call Franks, and we Normans," answered the Varangian, in a disappointed, dogged tone.

"Why, listen, then," said the officer as they proceeded on their walk, "listen to the reason of the thing, and consider whether such a custom can obtain, as that which they term the duello, in any country of civilization and common sense, to say nothing of one which is blessed with the domination of the most rare Alexius Comnenus.
Two great lords, or high officers, quarrel in the court, and before the reverend person of the Emperor. They dispute about a point of fact. Now, instead of each maintaining his own opinion by argument or evidence, suppose they had adopted the custom of these barbarous Franks,—'Why, thou liest in thy throat,' says the one; 'and thou liest in thy very lungs,' says another; and they measure forth the lists of battle in the next meadow. Each swears to the truth of his quarrel, though probably neither well knows precisely how the fact stands. One, perhaps the hardier, truer, and better man of the two, the Follower of the Emperor, and father of the Varangians, (for death, my faithful follower, spares no man,) lies dead on the ground, and the other comes back to predominate in the court, where, had the matter been enquired into by the rules of common sense and reason,
the victor, as he is termed, would have been sent to the gallows. And yet this is the law of arms, as your fancy pleases to call it, friend Hereward!"

"May it please your Valour," answered the barbarian, "there is a show of sense in what you say; but you will sooner convince me that this blessed moonlight is the blackness of a wolf's mouth, than that I ought to hear myself called liar, without cramming the epithet down the speaker's throat with the spike of my battle–axe. The lie is to a man the same as a blow, and a blow degrades him into a slave and a beast of burden, if endured without retaliation."

"Ay, there it is!" said Achilles; "could I but get you to lay aside that inborn barbarism, which leads you, otherwise the most disciplined soldiers who serve the sacred Emperor, into such deadly quarrels and feuds"—

"Sir Captain," said the Varangian, in a sullen tone, "take my advice, and take the Varangians as you have them; for, believe my word, that if you could teach them to endure reproaches, bear the lie, or tolerate stripes, you would hardly find them, when their discipline is completed, worth the single day's salt which they cost to his holiness, if that be his title. I must tell you, moreover, valorous sir, that the Varangians will little thank their leader, who heard them called marauders, drunkards, and what not, and repelled not the charge on the spot."

"Now, if I knew not the humours of my barbarians," thought Tatius, in his own mind, "I should bring on myself a quarrel with these untamed islanders, who the Emperor thinks can be so easily kept in discipline. But I will settle this sport presently." Accordingly, he addressed the Saxon in a soothing tone.

"My faithful soldier," he proceeded aloud, "we Romans, according to the custom of our ancestors, set as much glory on actually telling the truth, as you do in resenting the imputation of falsehood; and I could not with honour return a charge of falsehood upon Nicanor, since what he said was substantially true."

"What! that we Varangians were plunderers, drunkards, and the like?" said Hereward, more impatient than before.

"No, surely, not in that broad sense," said Achilles; "but there was too much foundation for the legend."

"When and where?" asked the Anglo–Saxon.

"You remember," replied his leader, "the long march near Laodicea, where the Varangians beat off a cloud of Turks, and retook a train of the imperial baggage? You know what was done that day—how you quenched your thirst, I mean?"

"I have some reason to remember it," said Hereward of Hampton; "for we were half choked with dust, fatigue, and, which was worst of all, constantly fighting with our faces to the rear, when we found some firkins of wine in certain carriages which were broken down— down our throats it went, as if it had been the best ale in Southampton."

"Ah, unhappy!" said the Follower; "saw you not that the firkins were stamped with the thrice excellent Grand Butler's own inviolable seal, and set apart for the private use of his Imperial Majesty's most
sacred lips?"

"By good Saint George of merry England, worth a dozen of your Saint George of Cappadocia, I neither thought nor cared about the matter," answered Hereward. "And I know your Valour drank a mighty draught yourself out of my head–piece; not this silver bauble, but my steel–cap, which is twice as ample. By the same token, that whereas before you were giving orders to fall back, you were a changed man when you had cleared your throat of the dust, and
cried, 'Bide the other brunt, my brave and stout boys of Britain!'"

"Ay," said Achilles, "I know I am but too apt to be venturous in action. But you mistake, good Hereward; the wine I tasted in the extremity of martial fatigue, was not that set apart for his sacred Majesty's own peculiar mouth, but a secondary sort, preserved for
the Grand Butler himself, of which, as one of the great officers of the household, I might right lawfully partake—the chance was nevertheless sinfully unhappy."

"On my life," replied Hereward, "I cannot see the infelicity of drinking when we are dying of thirst."

"But cheer up, my noble comrade," said Achilles, after he had hurried over his own exculpation, and without noticing the Varangian's light estimation of the crime, "his Imperial Majesty, in his ineffable graciousness, imputes these ill–advised draughts as a crime to no one who partook of them. He rebuked the Protospathaire for fishing up this accusation, and said, when he had recalled the bustle and confusion of that toilsome day, 'I thought myself well off amid that seven times heated furnace, when we obtained a draught of the barley–wine drank by my poor Varangians; and I drank their health, as well I might, since, had it not been for their services, I had drunk my last; and well fare their hearts, though they quaffed my wine in return!' And with that he turned off, as one who said, 'I have too much of this, being a finding of matter and ripping up of stories against Achilles Tatius and his gallant Varangians.'"

"Now, may God bless his honest heart for it!" said Hereward, with more downright heartiness than formal respect. "I'll drink to his health in what I put next to my lips that quenches thirst, whether it may be ale, wine, or ditch–water."

"Why, well said, but speak not above thy breath! and remember to put thy hand to thy forehead, when naming, or even thinking of the Emperor!—Well, thou knowest, Hereward, that having thus obtained the advantage, I knew that the moment of a repulsed attack is always that of a successful charge; and so I brought against the Protospathaire, Nicanor, the robberies which have been committed at the Golden Gate, and other entrances of the city, where a merchant was but of late kidnapped and murdered, having on him certain jewels, the property of the Patriarch."

"Ay! indeed?" said the Varangian; "and what said Alex—I mean the most sacred Emperor, when he heard such things said of the city warders?— though he had himself given, as we say in our land, the fox the geese to keep."

"It may be he did," replied Achilles; "but he is a sovereign of deep policy, and was resolved not to proceed against these treacherous warders, or their general, the Protospathaire, without decisive proof. His Sacred Majesty, therefore, charged me to obtain specific circumstantial proof by thy means."

"And that I would have managed in two minutes, had you not called me off the chase of yon cut–throat vagabond. But his grace knows the word of a Varangian, and I can assure him that either lucre of my silver gaberdine, which they nickname a cuirass, or the hatred of my corps, would be sufficient to incite any of these knaves to cut the throat of a Varangian, who appeared to be asleep.—So we go, I suppose, captain, to bear evidence before the Emperor to this night's work?"

"No, my active soldier, hadst thou taken the runaway villain, my first act must have been to set him free again; and my present charge to you is, to forget that such an adventure has ever taken place."

"Ha!" said the Varangian; "this is a change of policy indeed!" "Why,

yes, brave Hereward; ere I left the palace this night, the Patriarch made overtures of reconciliation betwixt me and the Protospathaire, which, as our agreement is of much consequence to the state, I could not very well reject, either as a good soldier or a good Christian. All offences to my honour are to be in the fullest degree repaid, for which the Patriarch interposes his warrant. The Emperor, who will rather wink hard than see disagreements, loves better the matter should be slurred over thus."

"And the reproaches upon the Varangians." said Hereward—

"Shall be fully retracted and atoned for," answered Achilles; "and a weighty donative in gold dealt among the corps of the Anglo–Danish axemen. Thou, my Hereward, mayst be distributor; and thus, if well– managed, mayst plate thy battle–axe with gold."

"I love my axe better as it is," said the Varangian. "My father bore it against the robber Normans at Hastings. Steel instead of gold for my money."

"Thou mayst make thy choice, Hereward," answered his officer; "only, if thou art poor, say the fault was thine own."

But here, in the course of their circuit round Constantinople, the officer and his soldier came to a very small wicket or sallyport, opening on the interior of a large and massive advanced work, which terminated an entrance to the city itself. Here the officer halted, and made his obedience, as a devotee who is about to enter a chapel of peculiar sanctity.

CHAPTER THE THIRD

Here, youth, thy foot unbrace, Here,
youth, thy brow unbraid; Each tribute
that may grace
The threshold here be paid. Walk with
the stealthy pace Which Nature
teaches deer, When, echoing in the
chase, The hunter's horn they hear.
THE COURT.

Before entering, Achilles Tatius made various gesticulations, which were
imitated roughly and awkwardly by the unpractised Varangian, whose service
with his corps had been almost entirely in the field,
his routine of duty not having, till very lately, called him to serve as one of the
garrison of Constantinople. He was not, therefore, acquainted with the minute
observances which the Greeks, who were the most formal and ceremonious
soldiers and courtiers in the world, rendered not merely to the Greek Emperor
in person, but throughout the sphere which peculiarly partook of his influence.

Achilles, having gesticulated after his own fashion, at length touched the door
with a rap, distinct at once and modest. This was thrice repeated, when the
captain whispered to his attendant, "The interior!
— for thy life, do as thou seest me do." At the same moment he started back,
and, stooping his head on his breast, with his hands over his eyes, as if to
save them from being dazzled by an expected
burst of light, awaited the answer to his summons. The Anglo–Dane, desirous
to obey his leader, imitating him as near as he could, stood side by side in the
posture of Oriental humiliation. The little portal opened inwards, when no
burst of light was seen, but four of the Varangians were made visible in the
entrance, holding each his battle–axe, as if about to strike down the intruders
who had disturbed

the silence of their watch.

"Acoulouthos," said the leader, by way of password.

"Tatius and Acoulouthos," murmured the warders, as a countersign. Each

sentinel sunk his weapon.

Achilles then reared his stately crest, with a conscious dignity at making this display of court influence in the eyes of his soldiers. Hereward observed an undisturbed gravity, to the surprise of his officer, who marvelled in his own mind how he could be such a barbarian as to regard with apathy a scene, which had in his eyes the most impressive and peculiar awe. This indifference he imputed to the stupid insensibility of his companion.

They passed on between the sentinels, who wheeled backward in file, on each side of the portal, and gave the strangers entrance to a long narrow plank, stretched across the city–moat, which was here drawn within the enclosure of an external rampart, projecting beyond the principal wall of the city.

"This," he whispered to Hereward, "is called the Bridge of Peril, and it is said that it has been occasionally smeared with oil, or strewed with dried peas, and that the bodies of men, known to have been in company with the Emperor's most sacred person, have been taken out of the Golden Horn, [Footnote: The harbour of Constantinople.] into which the moat empties itself."

"I would not have thought," said the islander, raising his voice to its usual rough tone, "that Alexius Comnenus"—

"Hush, rash and regardless of your life!" said Achilles Tatius; "to awaken the daughter of the imperial arch, [Footnote: The daughter of the arch was a courtly expression for the echo, as we find explained by the courtly commander himself.] is to incur deep penalty at all times; but when a rash delinquent has disturbed her with reflections on his most sacred Highness the Emperor, death is a punishment far too light for the effrontery which has interrupted her blessed slumber!—Ill hath been my fate, to have positive commands laid on

me, enjoining me to bring into the sacred precincts a creature who hath no more of the salt of civilization in him than to keep his mortal frame from corruption, since of all mental culture he is totally incapable. Consider thyself, Hereward, and bethink thee what thou art. By nature a poor barbarian— thy best boast that thou hast slain certain Mussulmans in thy sacred master's quarrel; and here art thou admitted into the inviolable enclosure of the Blaquernal, and in the hearing not only of the royal daughter of the imperial arch, which means," said the eloquent leader, "the echo of the sublime vaults; but
—Heaven be our guide,—for what I know, within the natural hearing of the Sacred Ear itself!"

"Well, my captain," replied the Varangian, "I cannot presume to speak my mind after the fashion of this place; but I can easily suppose I am but ill qualified to converse in the presence of the court, nor do I mean therefore to say a word till I am spoken to, unless when I shall see no better company than ourselves. To be
plain, I find difficulty in modelling my voice to a smoother tone than nature has given it. So, henceforth, my brave captain, I will be mute, unless when you give me a sign to speak."

"You will act wisely," said the captain. "Here be certain persons of high rank, nay, some that have been born in the purple itself, that will, Hereward, (alas, for thee!) prepare to sound with the line of their courtly understanding the depths of thy barbarous and shallow conceit. Do not, therefore, then, join their graceful smiles with thy inhuman bursts of cachinnation, with which thou art wont to thunder forth when opening in chorus with thy messmates."

"I tell thee I will be silent," said the Varangian, moved somewhat beyond his mood. "If you trust my word, so; if you think I am a jackdaw that must be speaking, whether in or out of place and purpose, I am contented to go back again, and therein we can end the matter."

Achilles, conscious perhaps that it was his best policy not to drive his subaltern to extremity, lowered his tone somewhat in reply to the uncourtly note of the soldier, as if allowing something for the rude manners of one whom he considered as not easily matched among the Varangians themselves, for strength and valour; qualities which, in despite of Hereward's discourtesy, Achilles suspected in his heart were fully more valuable than all those nameless graces which a more courtly and accomplished soldier might possess.

The expert navigator of the intricacies of the imperial residence, carried the Varangian through two or three small complicated courts, forming a part of the extensive Palace of the Blaquernal, [Footnote: This palace derived its name from the neighbouring Blachernian
Gate and Bridge.] and entered the building itself by a side door— watched in like manner by a sentinel of the Varangian Guard, whom they passed on being recognized. In the next apartment was stationed the Court of Guard, where were certain soldiers of the same corps amusing themselves at games somewhat resembling the modern draughts and dice, while they seasoned their pastime with frequent applications to deep flagons of ale, which were furnished to them while passing away their hours of duty. Some glances passed
between Hereward and his comrades, and he would have joined them, or at least spoke to them; for, since the adventure of the Mitylenian, Hereward had rather thought himself annoyed than distinguished by his moonlight ramble in the company of his commander, excepting always the short and interesting period during which he conceived they were on the way to fight a duel. Still, however negligent in the strict observance of the ceremonies of the sacred palace, the Varangians had, in their own way, rigid notions of calculating their military duty; in consequence of which Hereward, without speaking to his companions, followed his leader through the guard–room, and one or two antechambers adjacent, the splendid
and luxurious furniture of which convinced him that he could be nowhere else save in the sacred residence of his master the Emperor.

At length, having traversed passages and apartments with which the captain seemed familiar, and which he threaded with a stealthy, silent, and apparently reverential pace, as if, in his own inflated phrase, afraid to awaken the sounding echoes of those lofty and monumental halls, another species of inhabitants began to be visible. In different entrances, and in different apartments, the northern soldier beheld those unfortunate slaves, chiefly of African descent,
raised occasionally under the Emperors of Greece to great power and

honours, who, in that respect, imitated one of the most barbarous points of Oriental despotism. These slaves were differently occupied; some standing, as if on guard, at gates or in passages, with their drawn sabres in their hands; some were sitting in the Oriental fashion, on carpets, reposing themselves, or playing at various games, all of a character profoundly silent. Not a word passed between the guide of Hereward, and the withered and deformed beings whom they thus encountered. The exchange of a glance with the principal soldier seemed all that was necessary to ensure both an uninterrupted passage.

After making their way through several apartments, empty or thus occupied, they, at length entered one of black marble, or some other dark–coloured stone, much loftier and longer than the rest. Side passages opened into it, so far as the islander could discern, descending from several portals in the wall; but as the oils and gums with which the lamps in these passages were fed diffused a dim vapour around, it was difficult to ascertain, from the imperfect light, either the shape of the hall, or the style of its architecture. At the upper and lower ends of the chamber, there was a stronger and clearer light. It was when they were in the middle of this huge and long apartment, that Achilles said to the soldier, in the sort of cautionary whisper which he appeared to have substituted in place of his natural voice since he had crossed the Bridge of Peril—

"Remain here till I return, and stir from this hall on no account." "To hear is to obey," answered the Varangian, an expression of obedience, which, like many other phrases and fashions, the empire, which still affected the name of Roman, had borrowed from the barbarians of the East. Achilles Tatius then hastened up the steps which led to one of the side–doors of the hall, which being slightly pressed, its noiseless hinge gave way and admitted him.

Left alone to amuse himself as he best could, within the limits permitted to him, the Varangian visited in succession both ends of the hall, where the objects were more visible than elsewhere. The lower end had in its centre a small low–browed door of iron. Over it was displayed the Greek crucifix in bronze, and around and on every side, the representation of shackles, fetter bolts, and the like, were also executed in bronze, and disposed as appropriate ornaments over the entrance. The door of the dark archway was half open, and Hereward naturally looked in, the orders of his chief not prohibiting his satisfying his curiosity thus far. A dense red light, more like a distant spark than a lamp, affixed to the wall of what seemed a very narrow and winding stair, resembling in shape and size a draw–well, the verge of which opened on the threshold of the iron door, showed a descent which seemed to conduct to the infernal regions. The Varangian, however obtuse he might be considered by the quick– witted Greeks, had no difficulty in comprehending that a staircase having such a gloomy appearance, and the access to which was by a portal decorated in such a melancholy style of architecture, could only lead to the dungeons of the imperial palace, the size and complicated number of which were neither the least remarkable, nor the least awe–imposing portion of the sacred edifice. Listening profoundly, he even thought he caught such accents as befit those graves of living men, the faint echoing of groans and sighs, sounding as it were from the deep abyss beneath. But in this respect his fancy probably filled up the sketch which his conjectures bodied out.

"I have done nothing," he thought, "to merit being immured in one of these subterranean dens. Surely though my captain, Achilles Tatius, is, under favour, little better than an ass, he cannot be so false of word as to train me to prison under false pretexts? I trow he shall first see for the last time how the English axe plays, if such is to be the sport of the evening. But let us see the upper end of this
enormous vault; it may bear a better omen."

Thus thinking, and not quite ruling the tramp of his armed footstep according to the ceremonies of the place, the large–limbed Saxon strode to the upper end of the black marble hall. The ornament of the portal here was a small altar, like those in the temples of the heathen deities, which projected above the centre of the arch. On this altar smoked incense of some sort, the fumes of which rose curling in a thin cloud to the roof, and thence extending through the hall, enveloped in its column of smoke a singular emblem, of which the Varangian could make nothing. It was the representation of two human arms and hands, seeming to issue from the wall, having the

palms extended and open, as about to confer some boon on those who approached the altar. These arms were formed of bronze, and being placed farther back than the altar with its incense, were seen through the curling smoke by lamps so disposed as to illuminate the whole archway. "The meaning of this," thought the simple barbarian, "I should well know how to explain, were these fists clenched, and were the hall dedicated to the *pancration*, which we call boxing; but as even these helpless Greeks use not their hands without their
fingers being closed, by St. George I can make out nothing of their meaning."

At this instant Achilles entered the black marble hall at the same door by which he had left it, and came up to his neophyte, as the Varangian might be termed.

"Come with me now, Hereward, for here approaches the thick of the onset. Now, display the utmost courage that thou canst summon up, for believe me thy credit and name also depend on it."

"Fear nothing for either," said Hereward, "if the heart or hand of one man can bear him through the adventure by the help of a toy like this."

"Keep thy voice low and submissive, I have told thee a score of times," said the leader, "and lower thine axe, which, as I bethink me, thou hadst better leave in the outer apartment."

"With your leave, noble captain," replied Hereward, "I am unwilling to lay aside my bread–winner. I am one of those awkward clowns who cannot behave seemly unless I have something to occupy my hands, and my faithful battle–axe comes most natural to me."

"Keep it then; but remember thou dash it not about according to thy custom, nor bellow, nor shout, nor cry as in a battle–field; think of the sacred character of the place, which exaggerates riot into blasphemy, and remember the persons whom thou mayst chance to see, an offence to some of whom, it may be, ranks in the same sense with blasphemy against Heaven itself."

This lecture carried the tutor and the pupil so far as to the side–door, and thence inducted them into a species of anteroom, from which Achilles led his Varangian forward, until a pair of folding–doors, opening into what proved to be a principal apartment of the palace, exhibited to the rough–hewn native of the north a sight equally new and surprising.

It was an apartment of the palace of the Blaquernal, dedicated to the special service of the beloved daughter of the Emperor Alexius, the Princess Anna Comnena, known to our times by her literary talents, which record the history of her father's reign. She was seated, the queen and sovereign of a literary circle, such as an imperial Princess, porphyrogenita, or born in the sacred purple chamber itself, could assemble in those days, and a glance around will enable us to form
an idea of her guests or companions.

The literary Princess herself had the bright eyes, straight features, and comely and pleasing manners, which all would have allowed to the Emperor's daughter, even if she could not have been, with severe truth, said to have possessed them. She was placed upon a small bench, or sofa, the fair sex here not being permitted to recline, as
was the fashion of the Roman ladies. A table before her was loaded with books, plants, herbs, and drawings. She sat on a slight elevation, and those who enjoyed the intimacy of the Princess, or to whom she wished to speak in particular, were allowed, during such sublime colloquy, to rest their knees on the little dais, or elevated place where her chair found its station, in a posture half standing, half kneeling. Three other seats, of different heights, were placed on the dais, and under the same canopy of state which overshadowed that of the Princess Anna.

The first, which strictly resembled her own chair in size and convenience, was one designed for her husband, Nicephorus Briennius. He was said to entertain or affect the greatest respect for his wife's erudition, though the courtiers were of opinion he would have liked to absent himself from her evening parties more frequently than was particularly agreeable to the Princess Anna and her imperial parents. This was partly explained by the private tattle of the court, which averred, that the Princess Anna Comnena had
been more beautiful when she was less learned; and that, though still

a fine woman, she had somewhat lost the charms of her person as she became enriched in her mind.

To atone for the lowly fashion of the seat of Nicephorus Briennius, it was placed as near to his princess as it could possibly be edged by the ushers, so that she might not lose one look of her handsome spouse, nor he the least particle of wisdom which might drop from the lips of his erudite consort.

Two other seats of honour, or rather thrones,—for they had footstools placed for the support of the feet, rests for the arms, and embroidered pillows for the comfort of the back, not to mention the glories of the outspreading canopy, were destined for the imperial couple, who frequently attended their daughter's studies, which she prosecuted in public in the way we have intimated. On such occasions, the Empress Irene enjoyed the triumph peculiar to the mother of an accomplished daughter, while Alexius, as it might happen, sometimes listened with complacence to the rehearsal of his own exploits in the inflated language of the Princess, and sometimes mildly nodded over her dialogues upon the mysteries of philosophy, with the Patriarch Zosimus, and other sages.

All these four distinguished seats for the persons of the Imperial family, were occupied at the moment which we have described, excepting that which ought to have been filled by Nicephorus Briennius, the husband of the fair Anna Comnena. To his negligence and absence was perhaps owing the angry spot on the brow of his fair bride. Beside her on the platform were two white–robed nymphs of her household; female slaves, in a word, who reposed themselves on their knees on cushions, when their assistance was not wanted as a species of living book–desks, to support and extend the parchment rolls, in which the Princess recorded her own wisdom, or from which she quoted that of others. One of these young maidens, called Astarte, was so distinguished as a calligrapher, or beautiful writer of various alphabets and languages, that she narrowly escaped being sent as a present to the Caliph, (who could neither read nor write,) at a time when it was necessary to bribe him into peace. Violante, usually called the Muse, the other attendant of the Princess, a mistress of the vocal and instrumental art of music, was actually sent in a compliment to soothe the temper of Robert Guiscard, the Archduke of Apulia, who being aged and stone–deaf, and the girl under ten years old at the time, returned the valued present to the imperial donor, and, with the selfishness which was one of that wily Norman's characteristics, desired to have some one sent him who could contribute to his pleasure, instead of a twangling squalling infant.

Beneath these elevated seats there sat, or reposed on the floor of the hall, such favourites as were admitted. The Patriarch Zosimus, and one or two old men, were permitted the use of certain lowly stools, which were the only seats prepared for the learned members of the Princess's evening parties, as they would have been called in our days. As for the younger magnates, the honour of being permitted to join the imperial conversation was expected to render them far superior to the paltry accommodation of a joint–stool. Five or six courtiers, of different dress and ages, might compose the party, who either stood, or relieved their posture by kneeling, along the verge of an adorned fountain, which shed a mist of such very small rain as to dispel almost insensibly, cooling the fragrant breeze which breathed from the flowers and shrubs, that were so disposed as to send a
waste of sweets around. One goodly old man, named Michael Agelastes, big, burly, and dressed like an ancient Cynic philosopher, was distinguished by assuming, in a great measure, the ragged garb and mad bearing of that sect, and by his inflexible practice of the strictest ceremonies exigible by the Imperial family. He was known by an affectation of cynical principle and language, and of
republican philosophy, strangely contradicted by his practical deference to the great. It was wonderful how long this man, now sixty years old and upwards, disdained to avail himself of the accustomed privilege of leaning, or supporting his limbs, and with what regularity he maintained either the standing posture or that of absolute kneeling; but the first was so much his usual attitude, that he acquired among his court friends the name of Elephas, or the Elephant, because the ancients had an idea that the half–reasoning animal, as it is called, has joints incapable of kneeling down.

"Yet I have seen them kneel when I was in the country of the Gymnosophists," said a person present on the evening of Hereward's introduction.

"To take up their master on their shoulders? so will ours," said the Patriarch Zosimus, with the slight sneer which was the nearest advance to a sarcasm that the etiquette of the Greek court permitted; for on all ordinary occasions, it would not have offended the Presence more surely, literally, to have drawn a poniard, than to exchange a repartee in the imperial circle. Even the sarcasm, such as it was, would have been thought censurable by that ceremonious court in any but the Patriarch, to whose high rank some license was allowed.

Just as he had thus far offended decorum, Achilles Tatius, and his soldier Hereward, entered the apartment. The former bore him with even more than his usual degree of courtliness, as if to set his own good– breeding off by a comparison with the inexpert bearing of his follower; while, nevertheless, he had a secret pride in exhibiting, as one under his own immediate and distinct command, a man whom he was accustomed to consider as one of the finest soldiers of the army of Alexius, whether appearance or reality were to be considered.

Some astonishment followed the abrupt entrance of the new comers. Achilles indeed glided into the presence with the easy and quiet extremity of respect which intimated his habitude in these regions. But Hereward started on his entrance, and perceiving himself in company of the court, hastily strove to remedy his disorder. His commander, throwing round a scarce visible shrug of apology, made then a confidential and monitory sign to Hereward to mind his conduct. What he meant was, that he should doff his helmet and fall prostrate on the ground. But the Anglo–Saxon, unaccustomed to interpret obscure inferences, naturally thought of his military duties, and advanced in front of the Emperor, as when he rendered his military homage. He made reverence with his knee, half touched his cap, and then recovering and shouldering his axe, stood in advance
of the imperial chair, as if on duty as a sentinel.

A gentle smile of surprise went round the circle as they gazed on the manly appearance, and somewhat unceremonious but martial deportment of the northern soldier. The various spectators around consulted the Emperor's face, not knowing whether they were to take the intrusive manner of the Varangian's entrance as matter of ill– breeding, and manifest their horror, or whether they ought rather to consider the bearing of the life–guardsman as indicating blunt and manly zeal, and therefore to be received with applause.

It was some little time ere the Emperor recovered himself sufficiently to strike a key–note, as was usual upon such occasions. Alexius Comnenus had been wrapt for a moment into some species of slumber, or at least absence of mind. Out of this he had been startled by the sudden appearance of the Varangian; for though he was accustomed to commit the outer guards of the palace to this trusty corps, yet the deformed blacks whom we have mentioned, and who sometimes rose to be ministers of state and commanders of armies, were, on all ordinary occasions, intrusted with the guard of the interior of the palace. Alexius, therefore, awakened from his slumber, and the military phrase of his daughter still ringing in his ears as she was reading a description of the great historical work, in which she had detailed the conflicts of his reign, felt somewhat unprepared for the entrance and military deportment of one of the Saxon guard, with whom he was accustomed to associate, in general, scenes of blows, danger, and death.

After a troubled glance around, his look rested on Achilles Tatius. "Why here," he said, "trusty Follower? why this soldier here at this time of night?" Here, of course, was the moment for modelling the visages *regis ad exemplum;* but, ere the Patriarch could frame his countenance into devout apprehension of danger, Achilles Tatius had spoken a word or two, which reminded Alexius' memory that the soldier had been brought there by his own special orders. "Oh, ay! true, good fellow," said he, smoothing his troubled brow; "we had forgot that passage among the cares of state." He then spoke to the Varangian with a countenance more frank, and a heartier accent than he used to his courtiers; for, to a despotic monarch, a faithful life– guardsman is a person of confidence, while an officer of high rank is always in some degree a subject of distrust. "Ha!" said he, "our worthy Anglo–Dane, how fares he?"— This unceremonious
salutation surprised all but him to whom it was addressed. Hereward

answered, accompanying his words with a military obeisance which partook of heartiness rather than reverence, with a loud unsubdued voice, which startled the presence still more that the language was Saxon, which these foreigners occasionally used, "*Waes hael Kaisar mirrig und machtigh!*"—that is, Be of good health, stout and mighty Emperor. The Emperor, with a smile of intelligence, to show he could speak to his guards in their own foreign language, replied, by the well–known counter–signal—"*Drink hael!*"

Immediately a page brought a silver goblet of wine. The Emperor put his lips to it, though he scarce tasted the liquor, then commanded it to be handed to Hereward, and bade the soldier drink. The Saxon did not wait till he was desired a second time, but took off the contents without hesitation. A gentle smile, decorous as the presence required, passed over the assembly, at a feat which, though by no means wonderful in a hyperborean, seemed prodigious in the estimation of the moderate Greeks. Alexius himself laughed more loudly than his courtiers thought might be becoming on their part, and mustering what few words of Varangian he possessed, which he eked out with Greek, demanded of his life– guardsman—"Well, my bold Briton, or Edward, as men call thee, dost thou know the flavour of that wine?"

"Yes," answered the Varangian, without change of countenance, "I tasted it once before at Laodicea"—

Here his officer, Achilles Tatius, became sensible that his soldier approached delicate ground, and in vain endeavoured to gain his attention, in order that he might furtively convey to him a hint to be silent, or at least take heed what he said in such a presence. But the soldier, who, with proper military observance, continued to have his eye and attention fixed on the Emperor, as the prince whom he was bound to answer or to serve, saw none of the hints, which Achilles at length suffered to become so broad, that Zosimus and the Protospathaire exchanged expressive glances, as calling on each other to notice the by–play of the leader of the Varangians. In the meanwhile, the dialogue between the Emperor and his soldier continued:—"How," said Alexius, "did this draught relish compared with the former?"

"There is fairer company here, my liege, than that of the Arabian archers," answered Hereward, with a look and bow of instinctive good– breeding; "Nevertheless, there lacks the flavour which the heat of the sun, the dust of the combat, with the fatigue of wielding
such a weapon as this" (advancing his axe) "for eight hours together, give to a cup of rare wine."

"Another deficiency there might be," said Agelastes the Elephant, "provided I am pardoned hinting at it," he added, with a look to the throne,—"it might be the smaller size of the cup compared with that at Laodicea." "By Taranis, you say true," answered the life– guardsman; "at Laodicea I used my helmet."

"Let us see the cups compared together, good friend," said
Agelastes, continuing his raillery, "that we may be sure thou hast not swallowed the present goblet; for I thought, from the manner of the draught, there was a chance of its going down with its contents."

"There are some things which I do not easily swallow," answered the Varangian, in a calm and indifferent tone; "but they must come from a younger and more active man than you."

The company again smiled to each other, as if to hint that the philosopher, though also parcel wit by profession, had the worst of the encounter. The Emperor at the same time interfered—"Nor did I send for thee hither, good fellow, to be baited by idle taunts."

Here Agelastes shrunk back in the circle, as a hound that has been rebuked by the huntsman for babbling—and the Princess Anna Comnena, who had indicated by her fair features a certain degree of impatience, at length spoke— "Will it then please you, my imperial and much–beloved father, to inform those blessed with admission to the Muses' temple, for what it is that you have ordered this soldier to be this night admitted to a place so far above his rank in life? Permit me to say, we ought not to waste, in frivolous and silly jests, the time which is sacred to the welfare of the empire, as every moment of your leisure must be."

"Our daughter speaks wisely," said the Empress Irene, who, like most mothers who do not possess much talent themselves, and are not very capable of estimating it in others, was, nevertheless, a great admirer of her favourite daughter's accomplishments, and ready to draw them out on all occasions. "Permit me to remark, that in this divine and selected palace of the Muses, dedicated to the studies of our well– beloved and highly–gifted daughter, whose pen will preserve your reputation, our most imperial husband, till the desolation of the universe, and which enlivens and delights this society, the very flower of the wits of our sublime court;—permit me to say, that we have, merely by admitting a single life–guardsman, given our conversation the character of that which distinguishes a barrack."

Now the Emperor Alexius Comnenus had the same feeling with many an honest man in ordinary life when his wife begins a long oration, especially as the Empress Irene did not always retain the observance consistent with his awful rule and right supremacy, although especially severe in exacting it from all others, in reference to her lord. Therefore, though, he had felt some pleasure in gaining a short release from the monotonous recitation of the Princess's
history, he now saw the necessity of resuming it, or of listening to the matrimonial eloquence of the Empress. He sighed, therefore, as he said, "I crave your pardon, good our imperial spouse, and our daughter born in the purple chamber. I remember me, our most amiable and accomplished daughter, that last night you wished to know the particulars of the battle of Laodicea, with the heathenish Arabs, whom Heaven confound. And for certain considerations which moved ourselves to add other enquiries to our own recollection, Achilles Tatius, our most trusty Follower, was commissioned to introduce into this place one of those soldiers under his command, being such a one whose courage and presence
of mind could best enable him to remark what passed around him on that remarkable and bloody day. And this I suppose to be the man brought to us for that purpose."

"If I am permitted to speak, and live," answered the Follower, "your Imperial Highness, with those divine Princesses, whose name is to us as those of blessed saints, have in your presence the flower of my Anglo–Danes, or whatsoever unbaptized name is given to my soldiers. He is, as I may say, a barbarian of barbarians; for, although in birth and breeding unfit to soil with his feet the carpet of this precinct of accomplishment and eloquence, he is so brave—so trusty —so devotedly attached—and so unhesitatingly zealous, that"—

"Enough, good Follower," said the Emperor; "let us only know that he is cool and observant, not confused and fluttered during close battle, as we have sometimes observed in you and other great commanders—and, to speak truth, have even felt in our imperial self on extraordinary occasions. Which difference in man's constitution is not owing to any inferiority of courage, but, in us, to a certain consciousness of the importance of our own safety to the welfare of the whole, and to a feeling of the number of duties which at once devolve on us. Speak then, and speak quickly, Tatius; for I discern that our dearest consort, and our thrice fortunate daughter born in the imperial chamber of purple, seem to wax somewhat impatient."

"Hereward," answered Tatius, "is as composed and observant in battle, as another in a festive dance. The dust of war is the breath of his nostrils; and he will prove his worth in combat against any four others, (Varangians excepted,) who shall term themselves your Imperial Highness's bravest servants."

"Follower," said the Emperor, with a displeased look and tone, "instead of instructing these poor, ignorant barbarians in the rules and civilization of our enlightened empire, you foster, by such boastful words, the idle pride and fury of their temper, which hurries them into brawls with the legions of other foreign countries, and even breeds quarrels among themselves."

"If my mouth may be opened in the way of most humble excuse," said the Follower, "I would presume to reply, that I but an hour hence talked with this poor ignorant Anglo–Dane, on the paternal care with which the Imperial Majesty of Greece regards the preservation of that concord which unites the followers of his standard, and how desirous he is to promote that harmony, more especially amongst the various nations who have the happiness to serve you, in spite of the bloodthirsty quarrels of the Franks, and other northern men, who are never free from civil broil. I think the poor youth's understanding can bear witness to this much in my

behalf." He then looked towards Hereward, who gravely inclined his head in token of assent to what his captain said. His excuse thus ratified, Achilles proceeded in his apology more firmly. "What I
have said even now was spoken without consideration; for, instead of pretending that this Hereward would face four of your Imperial Highness's servants, I ought to have said, that he was willing to defy six of your Imperial Majesty's most deadly *enemies*, and permit them to choose every circumstance of time, arms, and place of combat."

"That hath a better sound," said the Emperor; "and in truth, for the information of my dearest daughter, who piously has undertaken to record the things which I have been the blessed means of doing for the Empire, I earnestly wish that she should remember, that though the sword of Alexius hath not slept in its sheath, yet he hath never sought his own aggrandizement of fame at the price of bloodshed among his subjects."

"I trust," said Anna Comnena, "that in my humble sketch of the life of the princely sire from whom I derive my existence, I have not forgot to notice his love of peace, and care for the lives of his soldiery, and abhorrence of the bloody manners of the heretic Franks, as one of his most distinguishing characteristics."

Assuming then an attitude more commanding, as one who was about to claim the attention of the company, the Princess inclined her head gently around to the audience, and taking a roll of parchment from the fair amanuensis, which she had, in a most beautiful handwriting, engrossed to her mistress's dictation, Anna Comnena prepared to
read its contents.

At this moment, the eyes of the Princess rested for an instant on the barbarian Hereward, to whom she deigned this greeting—"Valiant barbarian, of whom my fancy recalls some memory, as if in a dream, thou art now to hear a work, which, if the author be put into comparison with the subject, might be likened to a portrait of Alexander, in executing which, some inferior dauber has usurped the pencil of Apelles; but which essay, however it may appear unworthy of the subject in the eyes of many, must yet command some envy in those who candidly consider its contents, and the difficulty of portraying the great personage concerning whom it is written. Still, I pray thee, give thine attention to what I have now to read, since this account of the battle of Laodicea, the details thereof being

principally derived from his Imperial Highness, my excellent father, from the altogether valiant Protospathaire, his invincible general, together with Achilles Tatius, the faithful Follower of our victorious Emperor, may nevertheless be in some circumstances inaccurate. For it is to be thought, that the high offices of those great commanders retained them at a distance from some particularly active parts of the fray, in order that they might have more cool and accurate opportunity to form a judgment upon the whole, and transmit their orders, without being disturbed by any thoughts of personal safety. Even so, brave barbarian, in the art of embroidery, (marvel not that we are a proficient in that mechanical process, since it is patronized by Minerva, whose studies we affect to follow,) we reserve to ourselves the superintendence of the entire web, and commit to our maidens and others the execution of particular parts. Thus, in the same manner, thou, valiant Varangian, being engaged in the very thickest of the affray before Laodicea, mayst point out to us, the unworthy historian of so renowned a war, those chances which befell where men fought hand to hand, and where the fate of war was decided by the edge of the sword. Therefore, dread not, thou bravest of the axe– men to whom we owe that victory, and so many others,

to correct any mistake or misapprehension which we may have been led into concerning the details of that glorious event."

"Madam," said the Varangian, "I shall attend with diligence to what your Highness may be pleased to read to me; although, as to presuming to blame the history of a Princess born in the purple, far be such a presumption from me; still less would it become a barbaric Varangian to pass a judgment on the military conduct of the Emperor, by whom he is liberally paid, or of the commander, by whom he is well treated. Before an action, if our advice is required,

it is ever faithfully tendered; but according to my rough wit, our censure after the field is fought would be more invidious than useful. Touching the Protospathaire, if it be the duty of a general to absent himself from close action, I can safely say, or swear, were it necessary, that the invincible commander was never seen by me within a javelin's cast of aught that looked like danger."

This speech, boldly and bluntly delivered, had a general effect on the company present. The Emperor himself, and Achilles Tatius, looked like men who had got off from a danger better than they expected. The Protospathaire laboured to conceal a movement of resentment. Agelastes whispered to the Patriarch, near whom he was placed,

"The northern battle–axe lacks neither point nor edge."

"Hush!" said Zosimus, "let us hear how this is to end; the Princess is about to speak."

CHAPTER THE FOURTH

We heard the Tecbir, so these Arabs call
Their shout of onset, when with loud acclaim
They challenged Heaven, as if demanding conquest. The
battle join'd, and through the barb'rous herd, Fight, fight! and
Paradise was all their cry.
THE SIEGE OF DAMASCUS.

The voice of the northern soldier, although modified by feelings of respect to the Emperor, and even attachment to his captain, had more of a tone of blunt sincerity, nevertheless, than was usually heard by the sacred echoes of the imperial palace; and though the Princess Anna Comnena began to think that she had invoked the opinion of a severe judge, she was sensible, at the same time, by the deference of his manner, that his respect was of a character more real, and his applause, should she gain it, would prove more truly flattering, than the gilded assent of the whole court of her father. She gazed with some surprise and attention on Hereward, already described as a very handsome young man, and felt the natural desire to please, which is easily created in the mind towards a fine person of the other sex. His attitude was easy and bold, but neither clownish nor uncourtly. His title of a barbarian, placed him at once free from the forms of civilized life, and the rules of artificial politeness. But his character for valour, and the noble self-confidence of his bearing, gave him a deeper interest than would have been acquired by a more studied and anxious address, or an excess of reverential awe.

In short, the Princess Anna Comnena, high in rank as she was, and born in the imperial purple, which she herself deemed the first of all attributes, felt herself, nevertheless, in preparing to resume the recitation of her history, more anxious to obtain the approbation of this rude soldier, than that of all the rest of the courteous audience. She knew them well, it is true, and felt nowise solicitous about the applause which the daughter of the Emperor was sure to receive with full hands from those of the Grecian court to whom she might choose to communicate the productions of her father's daughter. But she had now a judge of a new character, whose applause, if bestowed, must have something in it intrinsically real, since it could only be obtained by affecting his head or his heart.

It was perhaps under the influence of these feelings, that the Princess was somewhat longer than usual in finding out the passage in the roll of history at which she purposed to commence. It was also noticed, that she began her recitation with a diffidence and embarrassment surprising to the noble hearers, who had often seen her in full possession of her presence of mind before what they conceived a more distinguished, and even more critical audience.

Neither were the circumstances of the Varangian such as rendered the scene indifferent to him. Anna Comnena had indeed attained her fifth lustre, and that is a period after which Grecian beauty is understood to commence its decline. How long she had passed that critical period, was a secret to all but the trusted ward–women of the purple chamber. Enough, that it was affirmed by the popular tongue, and seemed to be attested by that bent towards philosophy and literature, which is not supposed to be congenial to beauty in its earlier buds, to amount to one or two years more. She might be seven–and–twenty.

Still Anna Comnena was, or had very lately been, a beauty of the very first rank, and must be supposed to have still retained charms to captivate a barbarian of the north; if, indeed, he himself was not careful to maintain an heedful recollection of the immeasurable distance between them. Indeed, even this recollection might hardly have saved Hereward from the charms of this enchantress, bold, free–born, and fearless as he was; for, during that time of strange revolutions, there were many instances of successful generals sharing the couch of imperial princesses, whom perhaps they had themselves rendered widows, in order to make way for their own pretensions. But, besides the influence of other recollections, which the reader may learn hereafter, Hereward, though flattered by the unusual degree of attention which the Princess bestowed upon him, saw in her only the daughter of his Emperor and adopted liege lord, and the wife of a noble prince, whom reason and duty alike forbade him to think of in any other light.

It was after one or two preliminary efforts that the Princess Anna began her reading, with an uncertain voice, which gained strength and fortitude as she proceeded with the following passage from a well–known part of her history of Alexius Comnenus, but which unfortunately has not been republished in the Byzantine historians. The narrative cannot, therefore, be otherwise than acceptable to the antiquarian reader; and the author hopes to receive the thanks of the learned world for the recovery of a curious fragment, which, without
his exertions, must probably have passed to the gulf of total oblivion. THE

RETREAT OF LAODICEA.

NOW FIRST PUBLISHED FROM THE GREEK OF THE
PRINCESS COMNENA'S HISTORY OF HER FATHER.

"The sun had betaken himself to his bed in the ocean, ashamed, it would seem, to see the immortal army of our most sacred Emperor Alexius surrounded by those barbarous hordes of unbelieving barbarians, who, as described in our last chapter, had occupied the various passes both in front and rear of the Romans, [Footnote: More properly termed the Greeks; but we follow the phraseology of the
fair authoress.] secured during the preceding night by the wily barbarians. Although, therefore, a triumphant course of advance had brought us to this point, it now became a serious and doubtful question whether our victorious eagles might be able to penetrate any farther into the country of the enemy, or even to retreat with safety into their own.

"The extensive acquaintance of the Emperor with military affairs, in which he exceeds most living princes, had induced him, on the preceding evening, to ascertain, with marvellous exactitude and foresight, the precise position of the enemy. In this most necessary service he employed certain light–armed barbarians, whose habits and discipline had been originally derived from the wilds of Syria; and, if I am required to speak according to the dictation of Truth, seeing she ought always to sit upon the pen of a historian, I must needs say they were infidels like their enemies; faithfully attached, however, to the Roman service, and, as I believe, true slaves of the Emperor, to whom they communicated the information required by him respecting the position of his dreaded opponent Jezdegerd. These men did not bring in their information till long after the hour when the Emperor usually betook himself to rest.

"Notwithstanding this derangement of his most sacred time, our imperial father, who had postponed the ceremony of disrobing, so important were the necessities of the moment, continued, until deep in the night, to hold a council of his wisest chiefs, men whose depth of judgment might have saved a sinking world, and who now consulted what was to be done under the pressure of the circumstances in which they were now placed. And so great was the urgency, that all ordinary observances of the household were set aside, since I have heard from those who witnessed the fact, that the royal bed was displayed in the very room where the council assembled, and that the sacred lamp, called the Light of the Council, and which always burns when the Emperor presides in person over the deliberations of his servants, was for that night—a thing unknown in our annals—fed with unperfumed oil!!"

The fair speaker here threw her fine form into an attitude which expressed holy horror, and the hearers intimated their sympathy in the exciting cause by corresponding signs of interest; as to which we need only say, that the sigh of Achilles Tatius was the most pathetic; while the groan of Agelastes the Elephant was deepest and most tremendously bestial in its sound. Hereward seemed little moved, except by a slight motion of surprise at the wonder expressed by the others. The Princess, having allowed due time for the sympathy of her hearers to exhibit itself, proceeded as follows:—

"In this melancholy situation, when even the best–established and most sacred rites of the imperial household gave way to the necessity of a hasty provision for the morrow, the opinions of the counsellors were different, according to their tempers and habits; a thing, by the way, which may be remarked as likely to happen among the best and wisest on such occasions of doubt and danger.

"I do not in this place put down the names and opinions of those whose counsels were proposed and rejected, herein paying respect to the secrecy and freedom of debate justly attached to the imperial cabinet. Enough it is to say, that some there were who advised a speedy attack upon the enemy, in the direction of our original advance. Others thought it was safer, and might be easier, to force our way to the rear, and retreat by the same course which had brought us hither; nor must it be concealed, that there were persons of unsuspected fidelity, who proposed a third course, safer indeed than the others, but totally alien to the mind of our most magnanimous father. They recommended that a confidential slave, in company with a minister of the interior of our imperial palace, should be sent to the tent of Jezdegerd, in order to ascertain upon what terms the barbarian would permit our triumphant father to retreat in safety at the head of his victorious army. On learning such opinion, our imperial father was heard to exclaim, 'Sancta Sophia!' being the nearest approach to an adjuration which he has been known to permit himself, and was apparently about to say something violent both concerning the dishonour of the advice, and the cowardice of those by whom, it was preferred, when, recollecting the mutability of human things, and the misfortune of several of his Majesty's gracious predecessors, some of whom had been compelled to surrender their sacred persons to the infidels in the same region,
his Imperial Majesty repressed his generous feelings, and only suffered his army counsellors to understand his sentiments by a speech, in which he declared so desperate and so dishonourable a course would be the last which he would adopt, even in the last extremity of danger. Thus did the judgment of this mighty Prince at once reject counsel that seemed shameful to his arms, and thereby encourage the zeal of his troops, while privately he kept this postern in reserve, which in utmost need might serve for a safe, though not altogether, in less urgent circumstances, an honourable retreat.

"When the discussion had reached this melancholy crisis, the renowned Achilles Tatius arrived with the hopeful intelligence, that he himself and some soldiers of his corps had discovered an opening on the left flank of our present encampment, by which, making indeed a considerable circuit, but reaching, if we marched with vigour, the town of Laodicea, we might, by falling back on our resources, be in some measure in surety from the enemy.

"So soon as this ray of hope darted on the troubled mind of our gracious father, he proceeded to make such arrangements as might secure the full benefit of the advantage. His Imperial Highness would not permit the brave Varangians, whose battle–axes he accounted the flower of his imperial army, to take the advanced posts of assailants on the present occasion. He repressed the love of battle by which these generous foreigners have been at all times distinguished, and directed that the Syrian forces in the army, who have been before mentioned, should be assembled with as little noise as possible in the vicinity of the deserted pass, with instructions to occupy it. The good genius of the empire suggested that, as their speech, arms, and appearance, resembled those of the enemy, they might be permitted unopposed to take post in the defile with their light–armed forces, and thus secure it for the passage of the rest of
the army, of which he proposed that the Varangians, as immediately attached to his own sacred person, should form the vanguard. The well–known battalions, termed the Immortals, came next, comprising the gross of the army, and forming the centre and rear. Achilles Tatius, the faithful Follower of his Royal Master, although mortified that he was not permitted to assume the charge of the rear,
which he had proposed for himself and his valiant troops, as the post of danger at the time, cheerfully acquiesced, nevertheless, in the arrangement proposed by the Emperor, as most fit to effect the imperial safety, and that of the army.

"The imperial orders, as they were sent instantly abroad, were in like manner executed with the readiest punctuality, the rather that they indicated a course of safety which had been almost despaired of even by the oldest soldiers. During the dead period of time, when, as the divine Homer tells us, gods and men are alike asleep, it was found that the vigilance and prudence of a single individual had provided safety for the whole Roman army. The pinnacles of the mountain passes were scarcely touched by the earliest beams of the dawn, when these beams were also reflected from the steel caps and spears of the Syrians, under the command of a captain named Monastras, who, with his tribe, had attached himself to the empire. The Emperor, at the head of his faithful Varangians, defiled through the passes in order to gain that degree of advance on the road to the city of Laodicea which was desired, so as to avoid coming into collision with the barbarians.

"It was a goodly sight to see the dark mass of northern warriors, who now led the van of the army, moving slowly and steadily through the defiles of the mountains, around the insulated rocks and precipices, and surmounting the gentler acclivities, like the course of a strong and mighty river; while the loose bands of archers and javelin–men, armed after the Eastern manner, were dispersed on the steep sides of the defiles, and might be compared to light foam upon the edge of
the torrent. In the midst of the squadrons of the life–guard might be seen the proud war–horse of his Imperial Majesty, which pawed the earth indignantly, as if impatient at the delay which separated, him from his august burden. The Emperor Alexius himself travelled in a litter, borne by eight strong African slaves, that he might rise perfectly refreshed if the army should be overtaken by the enemy. The valiant Achilles Tatius rode near the couch of his master, that none of those luminous ideas, by which our august sire so often decided the fate of battle, might be lost for want of instant communication to those whose duty it was to execute them. I may also say, that there were close to the litter of the Emperor, three or four carriages of the same kind; one prepared for the Moon, as she may be termed, of the universe, the gracious Empress Irene. Among the others which might be mentioned, was that which contained the authoress of this history, unworthy as she may be of distinction, save as the daughter of the eminent and sacred persons whom the
narration chiefly concerns. In this manner the imperial army pressed on through the dangerous defiles, where their march was exposed to insults from the barbarians. They were happily cleared without any opposition. When we came to the descent of the pass which looks down on the city of Laodicea, the sagacity of the Emperor commanded the van—which, though the soldiers composing the same were heavily armed, had hitherto marched extremely fast—to halt, as well that they themselves might take some repose and refreshment, as to give the rearward forces time to come up, and close various gaps which the rapid movement of those in front had occasioned in, the line of march.

"The place chosen for this purpose was eminently beautiful, from the small and comparatively insignificant ridge of hills which melt irregularly down into the plains stretching between the pass which
we occupied and Laodicea. The town was about one hundred stadia distant, and some of our more sanguine warriors pretended that they could already discern its towers and pinnacles, glittering in the early beams of the sun, which had not as yet risen high into the horizon. A mountain torrent, which found its source at the foot of a huge rock, that yawned to give it birth, as if struck by the rod of the prophet Moses, poured its liquid treasure down to the more level country, nourishing herbage and even large trees, in its descent, until, at the distance of some four or five miles, the stream, at least in dry seasons, was lost amid heaps of sand and stones, which in the rainy season marked the strength and fury of its current.

"It was pleasant to see the attention of the Emperor to the comforts of the companions and guardians of his march. The trumpets from time to time gave license to various parties of the Varangians to lay down their arms, to eat the food which was distributed to them, and quench their thirst at the pure stream, which poured its bounties down the hill, or they might be seen to extend their bulky forms upon the turf around them. The Emperor, his most serene spouse,
arid the princesses and ladies, were also served with breakfast, at the fountain formed by the small brook in its very birth, and which the reverent feelings of the soldiers had left unpolluted by vulgar touch, for the use of that family, emphatically said to be born in the purple. Our beloved husband was also present on this occasion, and was among the first to detect one of the disasters of the day. For,
although all the rest of the repast had been, by the dexterity of the officers of the imperial mouth, so arranged, even on so awful an occasion, as to exhibit little difference from the ordinary provisions of the household, yet, when his Imperial Highness called for wine, behold, not only was the sacred liquor, dedicated to his own peculiar imperial use, wholly exhausted or left behind, but, to use the language of Horace, not the vilest Sabine vintage could be procured; so that his Imperial Highness was glad to accept the offer of a rude Varangian, who proffered his modicum of decocted barley, which these barbarians prefer to the juice of the grape. The Emperor, nevertheless, accepted of this coarse tribute."

"Insert," said the Emperor, who had been hitherto either plunged in deep contemplation or in an incipient slumber, "insert, I say, these very words: 'And with the heat of the morning, and anxiety of so rapid a march, with a numerous enemy in his rear, the Emperor was so thirsty, as never in his life to think beverage more delicious.'"

In obedience to her imperial father's orders, the Princess resigned the manuscript to the beautiful slave by whom it was written, repeating to the fair scribe the commanded addition, requiring her to note it, as made by the express sacred command of the Emperor, and then proceeded thus:— "More had I said here respecting the favourite liquor of your Imperial Highnesses faithful Varangians; but your Highness having once graced it with a word of commendation, this *ail*, as they call it, doubtless because removing all disorders, which they term 'ailments,' becomes a theme too lofty for the discussion of any inferior person. Suffice it to say, that thus were we all pleasantly engaged, the ladies and slaves trying to find some amusement for the imperial ears; the soldiers, in a long line down the ravine, seen in different postures, some straggling to the watercourse, some keeping guard over the arms of their comrades, in which duty they relieved each other, while body after body of the remaining troops, under command of the Protospathaire, and particularly those called Immortals, [Footnote: The [Greek: Athanatoi], or Immortals, of the army of Constantinople, were a select body, so named, in imitation of the ancient Persians. They were first embodied, according to Ducange, by Michael Ducas] joined the main army as they came up. Those soldiers who were already exhausted, were allowed to take a short repose, after which they were sent forward, with directions to advance steadily on the road to Laodicea; while their leader was instructed, so soon as he should open a free communication with that city, to send thither a command for reinforcements and refreshments, not forgetting fitting provision of the sacred wine for the imperial mouth. Accordingly, the Roman bands of Immortals and others had resumed their march, and held some way on their journey, it being the imperial pleasure that the Varangians, lately the vanguard, should now form the rear of the whole army, so as to bring off in safety the Syrian light troops, by whom the hilly pass was still occupied, when we heard upon the other side of this defile, which he had traversed with so much safety, the awful sound of the *Lelies*, as the Arabs name their shout of onset, though in what language it is expressed, it would be hard to say. Perchance some in this audience may enlighten my ignorance."

"May I speak and live," said the Acoulouthos Achilles, proud of his literary knowledge, "the words are, *Alla illa alla, Mohamed resoul alla*.[Footnote: i. e. "God is god—Mahomet is the prophet of God."] These, or something like them, contain the Arabs' profession of faith, which they always call out when they join battle; I have heard them many times."

"And so have I," said the Emperor; "and as thou didst, I warrant me, I have sometimes wished myself anywhere else than within hearing."

All the circle were alive to hear the answer of Achilles Tatius. He was too good a courtier, however, to make any imprudent reply. "It was my duty," he replied, "to desire to be as near your Imperial Highness as your faithful Follower ought, wherever you might wish yourself for the time."

Agelastes and Zosimus exchanged looks, and the Princess Anna Comnena proceeded in her recitation.

"The cause of these ominous sounds, which came in wild confusion up the rocky pass, was soon explained to us by a dozen cavaliers, to whom the task of bringing intelligence had been assigned.

"These informed us, that the barbarians, whose host had been dispersed around the position in which they had encamped the preceding day, had not been enabled to get their forces together until our light troops were evacuating the post they had occupied for securing the retreat of our army. They were then drawing off from the tops of the hills into the pass itself, when, in despite of the rocky ground, they were charged furiously by Jezdegerd, at the head of a large body of his followers, which, after repeated exertions, he had at length brought to operate on the rear of the Syrians. Notwithstanding that the pass was unfavourable for cavalry, the personal exertions of the infidel chief made his followers advance with a degree of resolution unknown to the Syrians of the Roman army, who, finding themselves at a distance from their companions,

formed the injurious idea that they were left thereto be sacrificed, and thought of flight in various directions, rather than of a combined and resolute resistance. The state of affairs, therefore, at the further end of the pass, was less favourable than we could wish, and those whose curiosity desired to see something which might be termed the rout of the rear of an army, beheld the Syrians pursued from the hill tops, overwhelmed, and individually cut down and made prisoners
by the bands of caitiff Mussulmans.

"His Imperial Highness looked upon the scene of battle for a few minutes, and, much commoved at what he saw, was somewhat hasty in his directions to the Varangians to resume their arms, and precipitate their march towards Laodicea; whereupon one of those northern soldiers said boldly, though in opposition to the imperial command, 'If we attempt to go hastily down this hill, our rear–guard will be confused, not only by our own hurry, but by these runaway scoundrels of Syrians, who in their headlong flight will not fail to mix themselves among our ranks. Let two hundred Varangians, who will live and die for the honour of England, abide in the very throat of this pass with me, while the rest escort the Emperor to this
Laodicea, or whatever it is called. We may perish in our defence, but we shall die in our duty; and I have little doubt but we shall furnish such a meal as will stay the stomach of these yelping hounds from seeking any farther banquet this day.'

"My imperial father at once discovered the importance of this advice, though it made him wellnigh weep to see with what unshrinking fidelity these poor barbarians pressed to fill up the number of those who were to undertake this desperate duty—with what kindness they took leave of their comrades, and with what jovial shouts they followed their sovereign with their eyes as he proceeded on his march down the hill, leaving them behind to resist and perish. The Imperial eyes were filled with tears; and I am not ashamed to confess, that amid the terror of the moment, the Empress, and I myself, forgot our rank in paying a similar tribute to these bold and self–devoted men.

"We left their leader carefully arraying his handful of comrades in defence of the pass, where the middle path was occupied by their centre, while their wings on either side were so disposed as to act upon the flanks of the enemy, should he rashly press upon such as appeared opposed to him in the road. We had not proceeded half way towards the plain, when a dreadful shout arose, in which the yells of the Arabs were mingled with the deep and more regular shouts which these strangers usually repeat thrice, as well when bidding hail to their commanders and princes, as when in the act of engaging in battle. Many a look was turned back by their comrades, and many a form was seen in the ranks which might have claimed the chisel of a sculptor, while the soldier hesitated whether to follow the line of his duty, which called him to march forward with his Emperor, or the impulse of courage, which prompted him to rush back to join his companions. Discipline, however, prevailed, and the main body marched on.

"An hour had elapsed, during which we heard, from time to time, the noise of battle, when a mounted Varangian presented himself at the side of the Emperor's litter. The horse was covered with foam, and had obviously, from his trappings, the fineness of his limbs, and the smallness of his joints, been the charger of some chief of the desert, which had fallen by the chance of battle into the possession of the northern warrior. The broad axe which the Varangian bore was also stained with blood, and the paleness of death itself was upon his countenance. These marks of recent battle were held sufficient to excuse the irregularity of his salutation, while he exclaimed, —'Noble Prince, the Arabs are defeated, and you may pursue your march at more leisure.'

"'Where is Jezdegerd?' said the Emperor, who had many reasons for dreading this celebrated chief.

"'Jezdegerd,' continued the Varangian, 'is where brave men are who fall in their duty.'

"'And that is'—said the Emperor, impatient to know distinctly the fate of so formidable an adversary—

"'Where I am now going,' answered the faithful soldier, who dropped from his horse as he spoke, and expired at the feet of the litter–

bearers. The Emperor called to his attendants to see that the body of this faithful retainer, to whom he destined an honourable sepulchre, was not left to the jackal or vulture; and some of his brethren, the Anglo–Saxons, among whom he was a man of no mean repute,
raised the body on their shoulders, and resumed their march with this additional encumbrance, prepared to fight for their precious burden, like the valiant Menelaus for the body of Patroclus."

The Princess Anna Comnena here naturally paused; for, having attained what she probably considered as the rounding of a period, she was willing to gather an idea of the feelings of her audience. Indeed, but that she had been intent upon her own manuscript, the emotions of the foreign soldier must have more early attracted her attention. In the beginning of her recitation, he had retained the same attitude which he had at first assumed, stiff and rigid as a sentinel upon duty, and apparently remembering nothing save that he was performing that duty in presence of the imperial court. As the narrative advanced, however, he appeared to take more interest in what was read. The anxious fears expressed by the various leaders in the midnight council, he listened to with a smile of suppressed contempt, and he almost laughed at the praises bestowed upon the leader of his own corps, Achilles Tatius. Nor did, even the name of the Emperor, though listened to respectfully, gain that applause for which his daughter fought so hard, and used so much exaggeration.

Hitherto the Varangian's countenance indicated very slightly any internal emotions; but they appeared to take a deeper hold on his mind as she came to the description of the halt after the main army had cleared the pass; the unexpected advance of the Arabs; the retreat of the column which escorted the Emperor; and the account of the distant engagement. He lost, on hearing the narration of these events, the rigid and constrained look of a soldier, who listened to the history of his Emperor with the same feelings with which he would have mounted guard at his palace. His colour began to come and go; his eyes to fill and to sparkle; his limbs to become more agitated than their owner seemed to assent to; and his whole appearance was changed into that of a listener, highly interested by the recitation which he hears, and insensible, or forgetful, of
whatever else is passing before him, as well as of the quality of those

who are present.

As the historian proceeded, Hereward became less able to conceal his agitation; and at the moment the Princess looked round, his feelings became so acute, that, forgetting where he was, he dropped his ponderous axe upon the floor, and, clasping his hands together, exclaimed,—"My unfortunate brother!"

All were startled by the clang of the falling weapon, and several persons at once attempted to interfere, as called upon to explain a circumstance so unusual. Achilles Tatius made some small progress in a speech designed to apologize for the rough mode of venting his sorrows to which Hereward had given way, by assuring the eminent persons present, that the poor uncultivated barbarian was actually younger brother to him who had commanded and fallen at the memorable defile. The Princess said nothing, but was evidently struck, and affected, and not ill–pleased, perhaps, at having given rise to feelings of interest so flattering to her as an authoress. The others, each in their character, uttered incoherent words of what was meant to be consolation; for distress which flows from a natural cause, generally attracts sympathy even from the most artificial characters. The voice of Alexius silenced all these imperfect speakers: "Hah, my brave soldier, Edward!" said the Emperor, "I must have been blind that I did not sooner recognise thee, as I think there is a memorandum entered, respecting five hundred pieces of gold due from us to Edward the Varangian; we have it in our secret scroll of such liberalities for which we stand indebted to our servitors, nor shall the payment be longer deferred." "Not to me, if it may please you, my liege," said the Anglo–Dane, hastily composing his countenance into its rough gravity of lineament, "lest it should be to one who can claim no interest in your imperial munificence. My name is Hereward; that of Edward is borne by three of my companions, all of them as likely as I to have deserved your Highness's reward for the faithful performance of their duty."

Many a sign was made by Tatius in order to guard his soldier against the folly of declining the liberality of the Emperor. Agelastes spoke more plainly: "Young man," he said, "rejoice in an honour so unexpected, and answer henceforth to no other name save that of

Edward, by which it hath pleased the light of the world, as it poured a ray upon thee, to distinguish thee from other barbarians. What is to thee the font–stone, or the priest officiating thereat, shouldst thou have derived from either any epithet different from that by which it hath now pleased the Emperor to distinguish thee from the common mass of humanity, and by which proud distinction thou hast now a right to be known ever afterwards?"

"Hereward was the name of my father," said the soldier, who had now altogether recovered his composure. "I cannot abandon it while I honour his memory in death. Edward is the title of my comrade—I must not run the risk of usurping his interest."

"Peace all!" interrupted the Emperor. "If we have made a mistake, we are rich enough to right it; nor shall Hereward be the poorer, if an Edward shall be found to merit this gratuity."

"Your Highness may trust that to your affectionate consort," answered the Empress Irene.

"His most sacred Highness," said the Princess Anna Comnena, "is so avariciously desirous to do whatever is good and gracious, that he leaves no room even for his nearest connexions to display generosity or munificence. Nevertheless, I, in my degree, will testify my gratitude to this brave man; for where his exploits are mentioned in this history, I will cause to be recorded,— 'This feat was done by Hereward the Anglo–Dane, whom it hath pleased his Imperial Majesty to call Edward.' Keep this, good youth," she continued, bestowing at the same time a ring of price, "in token that we will not forget our engagement."

Hereward accepted the token with a profound obeisance, and a discomposure which his station rendered not unbecoming. It was obvious to most persons present, that the gratitude of the beautiful Princess was expressed in a manner more acceptable to the youthful life– guardsman, than that of Alexius Comnenus. He took the ring with great demonstration of thankfulness:— "Precious relic!" he said, as he saluted this pledge of esteem by pressing it to his lips; "we may not remain long together, but be assured," bending reverently to the

Princess, "that death alone shall part us."

"Proceed, our princely daughter," said the Empress Irene; "you have done enough to show that valour is precious to her who can confer fame, whether it be found in a Roman or a barbarian."

The Princess resumed her narrative with some slight appearance of embarrassment.

"Our movement upon Laodicea was now resumed, and continued with good hopes on the part of those engaged in the march. Yet instinctively we could not help casting our eyes to the rear, which had been so long the direction in which we feared attack. At length, to our surprise, a thick cloud of dust was visible on the descent of the hill, half way betwixt us and the place at which we had halted. Some of the troops who composed our retreating body, particularly those in the rear, began to exclaim 'The Arabs! the Arabs!' and their march assumed a more precipitate character when they believed themselves pursed by the enemy. But the Varangian guards affirmed with one voice, that the dust was raised by the remains of their own comrades, who, left in the defence of the pass, had marched off after having so valiantly maintained the station intrusted to them. They fortified their opinion by professional remarks that the cloud of dust was more concentrated than if raised by the Arab horse, and they even pretended to assert, from their knowledge of such cases, that the number of their comrades had been much diminished in the action. Some Syrian horsemen, despatched to reconnoitre the approaching body, brought intelligence corresponding with the opinion of the Varangians in every particular. The portion of the body–guard had beaten back the Arabs, and their gallant leader had slain their chief Jezdegerd, in which service he was mortally wounded, as this history hath already mentioned. The survivors of the detachment, diminished by one half, were now on their march to join the Emperor, as fast as the encumbrance of bearing their wounded to a place of safety would permit.

"The Emperor Alexius, with one of those brilliant and benevolent ideas which mark his paternal character towards his soldiers, ordered all the litters, even that for his own most sacred use, to be instantly sent back to relieve the bold Varangians of the task of bearing the wounded. The shouts of the Varangians' gratitude may be more easily conceived than described, when they beheld the Emperor himself descend from his litter, like an ordinary cavalier, and assume his war-horse, at the same time that the most sacred Empress, as well as the authoress of this history, with other princesses born in the purple, mounted upon mules in order to proceed upon the march, while their litters were unhesitatingly assigned for the accommodation of the wounded men. This was indeed a mark, as well of military sagacity as of humanity; for the relief afforded to the bearers of the wounded, enabled the survivors of those who had defended the defile at the fountain, to join us sooner than would otherwise have been possible.

"It was an awful thing to see those men who had left us in the full splendour which military equipment gives to youth and strength, again appearing in diminished numbers—their armour shattered— their shields full of arrows—their offensive weapons marked with blood, and they themselves exhibiting all the signs of desperate and recent battle. Nor was it less interesting to remark the meeting of the soldiers who had been engaged, with the comrades whom they had rejoined. The Emperor, at the suggestion of the trusty Acoulouthos, permitted them a few moments to leave their ranks, and learn from each other the fate of the battle.

"As the two bands mingled, it seemed a meeting where grief and joy had a contest together. The most rugged of these barbarians,—and I who saw it can bear witness to the fact,—as he welcomed with a grasp of his strong hand some comrade whom he had given up for lost, had his large blue eyes filled with tears at hearing of the loss of some one whom he had hoped might have survived. Other veterans reviewed the standards which had been in the conflict, satisfied themselves that they had all been brought back in honour and safety, and counted the fresh arrow- shots with which they had been pierced, in addition to similar marks of former battles. All were loud in the praises of the brave young leader they had lost, nor were the acclamations less general in laud of him who had succeeded to the command, who brought up the party of his deceased brother—and whom," said the Princess, in a few words which seemed apparently interpolated for the occasion, "I now assure of the high honour and estimation in which he is held by the author of this history—that is, I would say, by every member of the imperial family— for his gallant services in such an important crisis."

Having hurried over her tribute to her friend the Varangian, in which emotions mingled that are not willingly expressed before so many hearers, Anna Comnena proceeded with composure in the part of her history which was less personal.

"We had not much time to make more observations on what passed among those brave soldiers; for a few minutes having been allowed to their feelings, the trumpet sounded the advance towards Laodicea, and we soon beheld the town, now about four miles from us, in
fields which were chiefly covered with trees. Apparently the garrison had already some notice of our approach, for carts and wains were seen advancing from the gates with refreshments, which the heat of the day, the length of the march, and columns of dust, as well as the want of water, had rendered of the last necessity to us. The soldiers joyfully mended their pace in order to meet the sooner with the supplies of which they stood so much in need. But as the cup doth not carry in all cases the liquid treasure to the lips for which it was intended, however much it may be longed for, what was our mortification to behold a cloud of Arabs issue at full gallop from the wooded plain betwixt the Roman army and the city, and
throw themselves upon the waggons, slaying the drivers, and making havoc and spoil of the contents! This, we afterwards learned, was a body of the enemy, headed by Varanes, equal in military fame, among those infidels, to Jezdegerd, his slain brother. When this chieftain saw that it was probable that the Varangians would succeed in their desperate defence of the pass, he put himself at the head of a large body of the cavalry; and as these infidels are mounted on
horses unmatched either in speed or wind, performed a long circuit, traversed the stony ridge of hills at a more northerly defile, and placed himself in ambuscade in the wooded plain I have mentioned, with the hope of making an unexpected assault upon the Emperor and his army, at the very time when they might be supposed to reckon upon an undisputed retreat. This surprise would certainly have taken place, and it is not easy to say what might have been the

consequence, had not the unexpected appearance of the train of waggons awakened the unbridled rapacity of the Arabs, in spite of their commander's prudence, and attempts to restrain them. In this manner the proposed ambuscade was discovered.

"But Varanes, willing still to gain some advantage from the rapidity of his movements, assembled as many of his horsemen as could be collected from the spoil, and pushed forward towards the Romans, who had stopped short on their march at so unlooked for an apparition. There was an uncertainty and wavering in our first ranks which made their hesitation known even to so poor a judge of military demeanour as myself. On the contrary, the Varangians joined in a unanimous cry of 'Bills' [Footnote: Villehardouin says, "Les Anglois et Danois mult bien rombattoint avec leurs *haches*."] (that is, in their language, battle–axes,) 'to the front!' and the Emperor's most gracious will acceding to their valorous desire, they
pressed forward from the rear to the head of the column. I can hardly say how this manoeuvre was executed, but it was doubtless by the wise directions of my most serene father, distinguished for his presence of mind upon such difficult occasions. It was, no doubt, much facilitated by the good will of the troops themselves; the Roman bands, called the Immortals, showing, as it seemed to me, no less desire to fall into the rear, than did the Varangians to occupy the places which the Immortals left vacant in front. The manoeuvre was so happily executed, that before Varanes and his Arabs had arrived at the van of our troops, they found it occupied by the inflexible guard of northern soldiers. I might have seen with my own eyes, and called upon them as sure evidences of that which chanced upon the occasion. But, to confess the truth, my eyes were little used to look upon such sights; for of Varanes's charge I only beheld, as it were, a thick cloud of dust rapidly driven forward, through which were seen the glittering points of lances, and the waving plumes of turban'd cavaliers imperfectly visible. The tecbir was so loudly uttered, that I was scarcely aware that kettle–drums and brazen cymbals were sounding in concert with it. But this wild and outrageous storm was met as effectually as if encountered by a rock.

"The Varangians, unshaken by the furious charge of the Arabs, received horse and rider with a shower of blows from their massive battle–axes, which the bravest of the enemy could not face, nor the strongest endure. The guards strengthened their ranks also, by the hindmost pressing so close upon those that went before, after the manner of the ancient Macedonians, that the fine–limbed, though slight steeds of those Idumeans could not make the least inroad upon the northern phalanx. The bravest men, the most gallant horses, fell in the first rank. The weighty, though short, horse javelins, flung from the rear ranks of the brave Varangians, with good aim and sturdy arm, completed the confusion of the assailants, who turned their back in affright, and fled from the field in total confusion.

"The enemy thus repulsed, we proceeded on our march, and only halted when we recovered our half–plundered waggons. Here, also, some invidious remarks were made by certain officers of the interior of the household, who had been on duty over the stores, and having fled from their posts on the assault of the infidels, had only returned upon their being repulsed. These men, quick in malice, though slow in perilous service, reported that, on this occasion, the Varangians so far forgot their duty as to consume a part of the sacred wine reserved for the imperial lips alone. It would be criminal to deny that this was a great and culpable oversight; nevertheless, our imperial hero passed it over as a pardonable offence; remarking, in a jesting manner, that since he had drunk the *ail*, as they termed it, of his trusty guard, the Varangians had acquired a right to quench the thirst, and to relieve the fatigue, which they had undergone that day in his defence, though they used for these purposes the sacred contents of the imperial cellar.

"In the meantime, the cavalry of the army were despatched in pursuit of the fugitive Arabs; and having succeeded in driving them behind the chain of hills which had so recently divided them from the Romans, the imperial arms might justly be considered as having obtained a complete and glorious victory.

"We are now to mention the rejoicings of the citizens of Laodicea, who, having witnessed from their ramparts, with alternate fear and hope, the fluctuations of the battle, now descended to congratulate the imperial conqueror."

Here the fair narrator was interrupted. The principal entrance of the apartment flew open, noiselessly indeed, but with both folding leaves at once, not as if to accommodate the entrance of an ordinary courtier, studying to create as little disturbance as possible, but as if there was entering a person, who ranked so high as to make it indifferent how much attention was drawn to his motions. It could only be one born in the purple, or nearly allied to it, to whom such freedom was lawful; and most of the guests, knowing who were likely to appear in that Temple of the Muses, anticipated, from the degree of bustle, the arrival of Nicephorus Briennius, the son–in–law of Alexius Comnenus, the husband to the fair historian, and in the rank of Caesar, which, however, did not at that period imply, as in early ages, the dignity of second person in the empire. The policy of Alexius had interposed more than one person of condition between the Caesar and his original rights and rank, which had once been second to those only of the Emperor himself.

CHAPTER THE FIFTH

The storm increases—'tis no sunny shower, Foster'd in
the moist breast of March or April, Or such as parched
Summer cools his lip with:
Heaven's windows are flung wide; the inmost deeps
Call in hoarse greeting one upon another;
On comes the flood in all its foaming horrors, And
where's the dike shall stop it!
THE DELUGE, *a Poem.*

The distinguished individual who entered was a noble Grecian, of stately
presence, whose habit was adorned with every mark of dignity, saving those
which Alexius had declared sacred to the Emperor's own person and that of
the Sebastocrator, whom he had established as next in rank to the head of the
empire. Nicephorus Briennius, who was in the bloom of youth, retained all
the marks of that manly beauty which had made the match acceptable to
Anna Comnena; while political considerations, and the desire of attaching a
powerful house as friendly adherents of the throne, recommended the union
to the Emperor.

We have already hinted that the royal bride had, though in no great degree,
the very doubtful advantage of years. Of her literary talents we have seen
tokens. Yet it was not believed by those who best knew, that, with the aid of
those claims to respect, Anna Comnena was successful in possessing the
unlimited attachment of her handsome husband. To treat her with apparent
neglect, her connexion with the crown rendered impossible; while, on the
other hand, the power of Nicephorus's family was too great to permit his
being dictated to even by the Emperor himself. He was possessed of talents,
as it was believed, calculated both for war and peace. His
advice was, therefore, listened to, and his assistance required, so that he
claimed complete liberty with respect to his own time, which he

sometimes used with less regular attendance upon the Temple of the Muses, than the goddess of the place thought herself entitled to, or than the Empress Irene was disposed to exact on the part of her daughter. The good–humoured Alexius observed a sort of neutrality in this matter, and kept it as much as possible from becoming visible to the public, conscious that it required the whole united strength of his family to maintain his place in so agitated an empire.

He pressed his son–in–law's hand, as Nicephorus, passing his father– in– law's seat, bent his knee in token of homage. The constrained manner of the Empress indicated a more cold reception of her son– in–law, while the fair muse herself scarcely deigned to signify her attention to his arrival, when her handsome mate assumed the vacant seat by her side, which we have already made mention of.

There was an awkward pause, during which the imperial son–in– law, coldly received when he expected to be welcomed, attempted to enter into some light conversation with the fair slave Astarte, who knelt behind her mistress. This was interrupted by the Princess commanding her attendant to enclose the manuscript within its appropriate casket, and convey it with her own hands to the cabinet of Apollo, the usual scene of the Princess's studies, as the Temple of the Muses was that commonly dedicated to her recitations.

The Emperor himself was the first to break an unpleasant silence. "Fair son–in–law," he said, "though it now wears something late in the night, you will do yourself wrong if you permit our Anna to send away that volume, with which this company have been so delectably entertained that they may well say, that the desert hath produced roses, and the barren rocks have poured forth milk and honey, so agreeable is the narrative of a toilsome and dangerous campaign, in the language of our daughter."

"The Caesar," said the Empress, "seems to have little taste for such dainties as this family can produce. He hath of late repeatedly absented himself from this Temple of the Muses, and found doubtless more agreeable conversation and amusement elsewhere."

"I trust, madam," said Nicephorus, "that my taste may vindicate me

from the charge implied. But it is natural that our sacred father
should be most delighted with the milk and honey which is produced for his
own special use."

The Princess spoke in the tone of a handsome woman offended by her
lover, and feeling the offence, yet not indisposed to a reconciliation.

"If," she said, "the deeds of Nicephorus Briennius are less frequently
celebrated in that poor roll of parchment than those of my illustrious father,
he must do me the justice to remember that such was his own special request;
either proceeding from that modesty which is justly ascribed to him as serving
to soften and adorn his other attributes, or because he with justice distrusts his
wife's power to compose their eulogium."

"We will then summon back Astarte," said the Empress, "who cannot
yet have carried her offering to the cabinet of Apollo."

"With your imperial pleasure," said Nicephorus, "it might incense the Pythian
god were a deposit to be recalled of which he alone can fitly estimate the
value. I came hither to speak with the Emperor upon pressing affairs of state,
and not to hold a literary conversation with a company which I must needs
say is something of a miscellaneous description, since I behold an ordinary
life– guardsman in the imperial circle."

"By the rood, son–in–law," said Alexius, "you do this gallant man wrong. He
is the brother of that brave Anglo–Dane who secured the victory at Laodicea
by his valiant conduct and death; he himself is that Edmund— or
Edward—or Hereward—to whom we are ever bound for securing the
success of that victorious day. He was called into our presence, son– in–law,
since it imports that you should know so much, to refresh the memory of any
Follower, Achilles
Tatius, as well as mine own, concerning some transactions of the day of which
we had become in some degree oblivious."

"Truly, imperial sir," answered Briennius, "I grieve that, by having intruded
on some such important researches, I may have, in some degree, intercepted
a portion of that light which is to illuminate

future ages. Methinks that in a battle–field, fought under your imperial guidance, and that of your great captains, your evidence might well supersede the testimony of such a man as this.—Let me know," he added, turning haughtily to the Varangian, "what particular thou canst add, that is unnoticed in the Princess's narrative?"

The Varangian replied instantly, "Only that when we made a halt at the fountain, the music that was there made by the ladies of the Emperor's household, and particularly by those two whom I now behold, was the most exquisite that ever reached my ears."

"Hah! darest thou to speak so audacious an opinion?" exclaimed Nicephorus; "is it for such as thou to suppose for a moment that the music which the wife and daughter of the Emperor might condescend to make, was intended to afford either matter of pleasure or of criticism to every plebeian barbarian who might hear them? Begone from this place! nor dare, on any pretext, again to appear before mine eyes— under allowance always of our imperial father's pleasure."

The Varangian bent his looks upon Achilles Tatius, as the person from whom he was to take his orders to stay or withdraw. But the Emperor himself took up the subject with considerable dignity.

"Son," he said, "we cannot permit this. On account of some love quarrel, as it would seem, betwixt you and our daughter, you allow yourself strangely to forget our imperial rank, and to order from our presence those whom we have pleased to call to attend us. This is neither right nor seemly, nor is it our pleasure that this same Hereward—or Edward— or whatever be his name— either leave us at this present moment, or do at any time hereafter regulate himself by any commands save our own, or those of our Follower, Achilles Tatius. And now, allowing this foolish affair, which I think was blown among us by the wind, to pass as it came, without farther notice, we crave to know the grave matters of state which brought you to our presence at so late an hour.—You look again at this Varangian.—Withhold not your words, I pray you, on account of his presence; for he stands as high in our trust, and we are convinced with as good reason, as any counsellor who has been sworn our domestic servant."

"To hear is to obey," returned the Emperor's son–in–law, who saw that Alexius was somewhat moved, and knew that in such cases it was neither safe nor expedient to drive him to extremity. "What I have to say," continued he, "must so soon be public news, that it little matters who hears it; and yet the West, so full of strange changes, never sent to the Eastern half of the globe tidings so alarming as those I now come to tell your Imperial Highness. Europe, to borrow an expression from this lady, who honours me by calling me husband, seems loosened from its foundations and about to precipitate itself upon Asia"—

"So I did express myself," said the Princess Anna Comnena, "and, as I trust, not altogether unforcibly, when we first heard that the wild impulse of those restless barbarians of Europe had driven a tempest as of a thousand nations upon our western frontier, with the extravagant purpose, as they pretended, of possessing themselves of Syria, and the holy places there marked as the sepulchres of
prophets, the martyrdom of saints, and the great events detailed in the blessed gospel. But that storm, by all accounts, hath burst and passed away, and we well hoped that the danger had gone with it. Devoutly shall we sorrow to find it otherwise."

"And otherwise we must expect to find it," said her husband. "It is very true, as reported to us, that a huge body of men, of low rank and little understanding, assumed arms at the instigation of a mad hermit, and took the road from Germany to Hungary, expecting miracles to be wrought in their favour, as when Israel was guided through the wilderness by a pillar of flame and a cloud. But no showers of
manna or of quails relieved their necessities, or proclaimed them the chosen people of God. No waters gushed from the rock for their refreshment. They were enraged at their sufferings, and endeavoured to obtain supplies by pillaging the country. The Hungarians, and other nations on our western frontiers, Christians, like themselves,
did not hesitate to fall upon this disorderly rabble; and immense piles of bones, in wild passes and unfrequented deserts, attest the calamitous defeats which extirpated these unholy pilgrims."

"All this," said the Emperor, "we knew before;—but what new evil now threatens, since we have already escaped so important a one?"

"Knew before?" said the Prince Nicephorus. "We knew nothing of our real danger before, save that a wild herd of animals, as brutal and as furious as wild bulls, threatened to bend their way to a pasture for which they had formed a fancy, and deluged the Grecian empire, and its vicinity, in their passage, expecting that Palestine, with its streams of milk and honey, once more awaited them, as God's predestined people. But so wild and disorderly an invasion had no terrors for a civilized nation like the Romans. The brute herd was terrified by our Greek fire; it was snared and shot down by the wild nations who, while they pretend to independence, cover our frontier as with a protecting fortification. The vile multitude has been consumed even by the very quality of the provisions thrown in their way,—those wise means of resistance which were at once suggested by the paternal care of the Emperor, and by his unfailing policy. Thus wisdom has played its part, and the bark over which the tempest had poured its thunder, has escaped, notwithstanding all its violence. But the second storm, by which the former is so closely followed, is of a new descent of these Western nations, more formidable than any which we or our fathers have yet seen. This consists not of the ignorant or of the fanatical—not of the base, the needy, and the improvident. Now,—all that wide Europe possesses of what is wise and worthy, brave and noble, are united by the most religious vows, in the same purpose."

"And what is that purpose? Speak plainly," said Alexius. "The destruction of our whole Roman empire, and the blotting out the very name of its chief from among the princes of the earth, among which it has long been predominant, can alone be an adequate motive for a confederacy such as thy speech infers."

"No such design is avowed," said Nicephorus; "and so many princes, wise men, and statesmen of eminence, aim, it is pretended, at nothing else than the same extravagant purpose announced by the brute multitude who first appeared in these regions. Here, most gracious Emperor, is a scroll, in which you will find marked down a list of the various armies which, by different routes, are approaching the vicinity of the empire. Behold, Hugh of Vermandois, called from his dignity Hugh the Great, has set sail from the shores of Italy. Twenty knights have already announced their coming, sheathed in armour of steel, inlaid with gold, bearing this proud greeting:—'Let the Emperor of Greece, and his lieutenants, understand that Hugo, Earl of Vermandois, is approaching his territories. He is brother to the king of kings—The King of France,[Footnote: Ducange pours

out a whole ocean of authorities to show that the King of France was in those days styled *Rex*, by way of eminence. See his notes on the Alexiad. Anna Comnena in her history makes Hugh, of Vermandois assume to himself the titles which could only, in the most enthusiastic Frenchman's opinion, have been claimed by his older brother, the reigning monarch.] namely—and is attended by the flower of the French nobility. He bears the blessed banner of St. Peter, intrusted to his victorious care by the holy successor of the apostle, and warns thee of all this, that thou mayst provide a reception suitable to his rank.'"

"Here are sounding words," said the Emperor; "but the wind which whistles loudest is not always most dangerous to the vessel. We

know something of this nation of France, and have heard more. They are as petulant at least as they are valiant; we will flatter their vanity till we get time and opportunity for more effectual defence. Tush! if words can pay debt, there is no fear of our exchequer becoming insolvent.—What follows here, Nicephorus? A list, I suppose, of the followers of this great count?"

"My liege, no!" answered Nicephorus Briennius; "so many independent chiefs, as your Imperial Highness sees in that memorial, so many independent European armies are advancing by different routes towards the East, and announce the conquest of Palestine

from the infidels as their common object."

"A dreadful enumeration," said the Emperor, as he perused the list; "yet so far happy, that its very length assures us of the impossibility that so many princes can be seriously and consistently united in so wild a project. Thus already my eyes catch the well–known name of an old friend, our enemy— for such are the alternate chances of peace and war—Bohemond of Antioch. Is not he the son of the celebrated Robert of Apulia, so renowned among his countrymen, who raised himself to the rank of grand duke from a simple cavalier, and became sovereign of those of his warlike nation, both in Sicily and Italy? Did not the standards of the German Emperor, of the Roman Pontiff, nay, our own imperial banners, give way before him; until, equally a wily statesman and a brave warrior, he became the terror of Europe, from being a knight whose Norman castle would have been easily garrisoned by six cross–bows, and as many lances? It is a dreadful family, a race of craft as well as power. But Bohemond, the son of old Robert, will follow his father's politics. He may talk of Palestine and of the interests of Christendom, but if I can make his interests the same with mine, he is not likely to be guided

by any other object. So then, with the knowledge I already possess of his wishes and projects, it may chance that Heaven sends us an ally in the guise of an enemy.—Whom have we next? Godfrey [Footnote: Godfrey of Bouillon, Duke of Lower Lorraine—the great Captain of the first Crusade, afterwards King of Jerusalem. See Gibbon,—or Mills, *passim*.] Duke of Bouillon— leading, I see, a most formidable band from the banks of a huge river called the Rhine. What is this person's character?"

"As we hear," replied Nicephorus, "this Godfrey is one of the wisest, noblest, and bravest of the leaders who have thus strangely put themselves in motion; and among a list of independent princes, as many in number as those who assembled for the siege of Troy, and followed, most of them, by subjects ten times more numerous, this Godfrey may be regarded as the Agamemnon. The princes and

counts esteem him, because he is the foremost in the ranks of those whom they fantastically call Knights, and also on account of the good faith and generosity which he practises in all his transactions. The clergy give him credit for the highest zeal for the doctrines of religion, and a corresponding respect for the Church and its dignitaries. Justice, liberality, and frankness, have equally attached

to this Godfrey the lower class of the people. His general attention to moral obligations is a pledge to them that his religion is real; and, gifted with so much that is excellent, he is already, although inferior in rank, birth, and power to many chiefs of the crusade, justly regarded as one of its principal leaders."

"Pity," said the Emperor, "that a character such as you describe this Prince to be, should be under the dominion of a fanaticism scarce worthy of Peter the Hermit, or the clownish multitude which he led, or of the very ass which he rode upon! which I am apt to think the wisest of the first multitude whom we beheld, seeing that it ran away towards Europe as soon as water and barley became scarce."

"Might I be permitted here to speak, and yet live," said Agelastes, "I would remark that the Patriarch himself made a similar retreat so soon as blows became plenty and food scarce."

"Thou hast hit it, Agelastes," said the Emperor; "but the question now is, whether an honorable and important principality could not be formed out of part of the provinces of the Lesser Asia, now laid waste by the Turks. Such a principality, methinks, with its various advantages of soil, climate, industrious inhabitants, and a healthy atmosphere, were well worth the morasses of Bouillon. It might be held as a dependence upon the sacred Roman empire, and garrisoned, as it were, by Godfrey and his victorious Franks, would be a bulwark on that point to our just and sacred person. Ha! most holy patriarch, would not such a prospect shake the most devout Crusader's attachment to the burning sands of Palestine?"

"Especially," answered the Patriarch, "if the prince for whom such a rich *theme* [Footnote: These provinces were called *Themes*.] was changed into a feudal appanage, should be previously converted to the only true faith, as your Imperial Highness undoubtedly means."

"Certainly—most unquestionably," answered the Emperor, with a due affectation of gravity, notwithstanding he was internally conscious how often he had been compelled, by state necessities, to admit, not only Latin Christians, but Manicheans, and other heretics, nay, Mahomedan barbarians, into the number of his subjects, and that without experiencing opposition from the scruples of the Patriarch. "Here I find," continued the Emperor, "such a numerous list of princes and principalities in the act of approaching our boundaries, as might well rival the armies of old, who were said to have drunk up rivers, exhausted realms, and trode down forests, in their wasteful advance." As he pronounced these words, a shade of paleness came over the Imperial brow, similar to that which had already clothed in sadness most of his counsellors.

"This war of nations," said Nicephorus, "has also circumstances distinguishing it from every other, save that which his Imperial Highness hath waged in former times against those whom we are accustomed to call Franks. We must go forth against a people to whom the strife of combat is as the breath of their nostrils; who, rather than not be engaged in war, will do battle with their nearest neighbours, and challenge each other to mortal fight, as much in sport as we would defy a comrade to a chariot–race. They are covered with an impenetrable armour of steel, defending them from blows of the lance and sword, and which the uncommon strength of their horses renders them able to support, though one of ours could
as well bear Mount Olympus upon his loins. Their foot–ranks carry a missile weapon unknown to us, termed an arblast, or cross–bow. It is not drawn with the right hand, like the bow of other nations, but by placing the feet upon the weapon itself, and pulling with the whole force of the body; and it despatches arrows called bolts, of hard
wood pointed with iron, which the strength of the bow can send through the strongest breastplates, and even through stone walls, where not of uncommon thickness."

"Enough," said the Emperor; "we have seen with our own eyes the lances of Frankish knights, and the cross–bows of their infantry. If Heaven has allotted them a degree of bravery, which to other nations seems wellnigh preternatural, the Divine will has given to the Greek councils that wisdom which it hath refused to barbarians; the art of achieving conquest by wisdom rather than brute force—obtaining by our skill in treaty advantages which victory itself could not have procured. If we have not the use of that dreadful weapon, which our son–in–law terms the cross–bow, Heaven, in its favour, has concealed from these western barbarians the composition and use of the Greek fire—well so called, since by Grecian hands alone it is prepared, and by such only can its lightnings be darted upon the astonished foe." The Emperor paused, and looked around him; and although the faces of his counsellors still looked blank, he boldly proceeded:—"But to return yet again to this black scroll, containing the names of those nations who approach our frontier, here occur

more than one with which, methinks, old memory should make us familiar, though our recollections are distant and confused. It becomes us to know who these men are, that we may avail ourselves of those feuds and quarrels among them, which, being blown into life, may happily divert them from the prosecution of this extraordinary attempt in which they are now united. Here is, for example, one Robert, styled Duke of Normandy, who commands a goodly band of counts, with which title we are but too well acquainted; of *earls*, a word totally strange to us, but apparently some barbaric title of honour; and of knights whose names are
compounded, as we think, chiefly of the French language, but also of another jargon, which we are not ourselves competent to understand. To you, most reverend and most learned Patriarch, we may fittest apply for information on this subject."

"The duties of my station," replied the patriarch Zosimus, "have withheld my riper years from studying the history of distant realms; but the wise Agelastes, who hath read as many volumes as would fill the shelves of the famous Alexandrian library, can no doubt satisfy your Imperial Majesty's enquiries."

Agelastes erected himself on those enduring legs which had procured him the surname of Elephant, and began a reply to the enquiries of the Emperor, rather remarkable for readiness than accuracy. "I have read," said he, "in that brilliant mirror which reflects the time of our fathers, the volumes of the learned Procopius, that the people separately called Normans and Angles are in truth the same race, and that Normandy, sometimes so called, is in fact a part of a district of Gaul. Beyond, and nearly opposite to it, but separated by an arm of the sea, lies a ghastly region, on which clouds and tempests for ever rest, and which is well known to its continental neighbours as the abode to which departed spirits are sent after this life. On one side of the strait dwell a few fishermen, men possessed
of a strange charter, and enjoying singular privileges, in consideration of their being the living ferrymen who, performing the office of the heathen Charon, carry the spirits of the departed to the island which is their residence after death. At the dead of night, these fishermen are, in rotation, summoned to perform the duty by which they seem to hold the permission to reside on this strange coast. A

knock is heard at the door of his cottage who holds the turn of this singular service, sounded by no mortal hand. A whispering, as of a decaying breeze, summons the ferryman to his duty. He hastens to his bark on the sea–shore, and has no sooner launched it than he perceives its hull sink sensibly in the water, so as to express the weight of the dead with whom it is filled. No form is seen, and though voices are heard, yet the accents are undistinguishable, as of one who speaks in his sleep. Thus he traverses the strait between the continent and the island, impressed with the mysterious awe which affects the living when they are conscious of the presence of the dead. They arrive upon the opposite coast, where the cliffs of white chalk form a strange contrast with the eternal darkness of the atmosphere. They stop at a landing–place appointed, but disembark not, for the land is never trodden by earthly feet. Here the passage– boat is gradually lightened of its unearthly inmates, who wander forth in the way appointed to them, while the mariners slowly return to their own side of the strait, having performed for the time this singular service, by which they hold their fishing–huts and their possessions on that strange coast." Here he ceased, and the Emperor replied,—

"If this legend be actually told us by Procopius, most learned Agelastes, it shows that that celebrated historian came more near the heathen than the Christian belief respecting the future state. In truth, this is little more than the old fable of the infernal Styx. Procopius, we believe, lived before the decay of heathenism, and, as we would gladly disbelieve much which he hath told us respecting our ancestor and predecessor Justinian, so we will not pay him much credit in future in point of geographical knowledge.—Meanwhile, what ails thee, Achilles Tatius, and why dost thou whisper with that soldier?"

"My head," answered Achilles Tatius, "is at your imperial command, prompt to pay for the unbecoming trespass of my tongue. I did but ask of this Hereward here what he knew of this matter; for I have heard my Varangians repeatedly call themselves Anglo–Danes, Normans, Britons, or some other barbaric epithet, and I am sure that one or other, or it may be all, of these barbarous sounds, at different times serve to designate the birth–place of these exiles, too happy in being banished from the darkness of barbarism, to the luminous vicinity of your imperial presence."

"Speak, then, Varangian, in the name of Heaven," said the Emperor, "and let us know whether we are to look for friends or enemies in those men of Normandy who are now approaching our frontier. Speak with courage, man; and if thou apprehendest danger, remember thou servest a prince well qualified to protect thee."

"Since I am at liberty to speak," answered the life–guardian, "although my knowledge of the Greek language, which you term the Roman, is but slight, I trust it is enough to demand of his Imperial Highness, in place of all pay, donative, or gift whatsoever, since he has been pleased to talk of designing such for me, that he would place me in the first line of battle which shall be formed against
these same Normans, and their Duke Robert; and if he pleases to allow me the aid of such Varangians as, for love of me, or hatred of their ancient tyrants, may be disposed to join their arms to mine, I have little doubt so to settle our long accounts with these men, that the Grecian eagles and wolves shall do them the last office, by tearing the flesh from their bones."

"What dreadful feud is this, my soldier," said the Emperor, "that after so many years still drives thee to such extremities when the very name of Normandy is mentioned?"

"Your Imperial Highness shall be judge!" said the Varangian. "My fathers, and those of most, though not all of the corps to whom I belong, are descended from a valiant race who dwelt in the North of Germany, called Anglo–Saxons. Nobody, save a priest possessed of the art of consulting ancient chronicles, can even guess how long it is since they came to the island of Britain, then distracted with civil war. They came, however, on the petition of the natives of the island, for the aid of the Angles was requested by the southern inhabitants. Provinces were granted in recompense of the aid thus liberally afforded, and the greater proportion of the island became, by degrees, the property of the Anglo–Saxons, who occupied it at first as several principalities, and latterly as one kingdom, speaking the language, and observing the laws, of most of those who now form your imperial body–guard of Varangians, or exiles. In process of time, the Northmen became known to the people of the more southern climates. They were so called from their coming from the distant regions of the Baltic Sea—an immense ocean, sometimes frozen with ice as hard as the cliffs of Mount Caucasus. They came seeking milder regions than nature had assigned them at home; and the climate of France being delightful, and its people slow in battle, they extorted from them the grant of a large province which was, from the name of the new settlers, called Normandy, though I have heard my father say that was not its proper appellation. They settled there under a Duke, who acknowledged the superior authority of the King of France, that is to say, obeying him when it suited his convenience so to do.

"Now, it chanced many years since, while these two nations of Normans and Anglo–Saxons were quietly residing upon different sides of the salt–water channel which divides France from England, that William, Duke of Normandy, suddenly levied a large army, came over to Kent, which is on the opposite side of the channel, and there defeated in a great battle, Harold, who was at that time King of the Anglo–Saxons. It is but grief to tell what followed. Battles have been fought in old time, that have had dreadful results, which years, nevertheless, could wash away; but at Hastings—O woe's me!— the banner of my country fell, never again to be raised up. Oppression has driven her wheel over us. All that was valiant amongst us have left the land; and of Englishmen— for such is our proper designation —no one remains in England save as the thrall of the invaders. Many men of Danish descent, who had found their way on different occasions to England, were blended in the common calamity. All was laid desolate by the command of the victors. My father's home lies now an undistinguished ruin, amid an extensive forest, composed out of what were formerly fair fields and domestic pastures, where a manly race derived nourishment by cultivating a friendly soil. The fire has destroyed the church where sleep the fathers of my race; and I, the last of their line, am a wanderer in other climates—a fighter of the battles of others—the servant of a foreign, though a kind master; in a word, one of the banished—a Varangian."

"Happier in that station" said Achilles Tatius, "than in all the barbaric simplicity which your forefathers prized so highly, since you are now under the cheering influence of that smile which is the life of the world."

"It avails not talking of this," said the Varangian, with a cold gesture. "These

Normans" said the Emperor, "are then the people by whom the celebrated island of Britain is now conquered and governed?" "It is but

too true" answered the Varangian.

"They are, then, a brave and warlike people?"—said Alexius.

"It would be base and false to say otherwise of an enemy" said Hereward. "Wrong have they done me, and a wrong never to be atoned; but to speak falsehood of them were but a woman's vengeance. Mortal enemies as they are to me, and mingling with all my recollections as that which is hateful and odious, yet were the troops of Europe mustered, as it seems they are likely to be, no nation or tribe dared in gallantry claim the advance of the haughty Norman."

"And this Duke Robert, who is he?"

"That," answered the Varangian, "I cannot so well explain. He is the son—the eldest son, as men say, of the tyrant William, who subdued England when I hardly existed, or was a child in the cradle. That William, the victor of Hastings, is now dead, we are assured by concurring testimony; but while it seems his eldest son Duke Robert has become his heir to the Duchy of Normandy, some other of his children have been so fortunate as to acquire the throne of England,
—unless, indeed, like the petty farm of some obscure yeoman, the fair kingdom has been divided among the tyrant's issue."

"Concerning this," said the Emperor, "we have heard something, which we shall try to reconcile with the soldier's narrative at leisure, holding the words of this honest Varangian as positive proof, in whatsoever he avers from his own knowledge.—And now, my grave and worthy counsellors, we must close this evening's service in the Temple of the Muses, this distressing news, brought us by our dearest son–in–law the Caesar, having induced us to prolong our worship of these learned goddesses, deeper into the night than is consistent with the health of our beloved wife and daughter; while to ourselves, this intelligence brings subject for grave deliberation."

The courtiers exhausted their ingenuity in forming the most ingenious prayers, that all evil consequences should be averted which could attend this excessive vigilance.

Nicephorus and his fair bride spoke together as a pair equally desirous to close an accidental breach between them. "Some things thou hast said, my Caesar," observed the lady, "in detailing this dreadful intelligence, as elegantly turned as if the nine goddesses, to whom this temple is dedicated, had lent each her aid to the sense and expression."

"I need none of their assistance," answered Nicephorus, "since I possess a muse of my own, in whose genius are included all those attributes which the heathens vainly ascribed to the nine deities of Parnassus!"

"It is well," said the fair historian, retiring by the assistance of her husband's arm; "but if you will load your wife with praises far beyond her merits, you must lend her your arm to support her under the weighty burden you have been pleased to impose." The council parted when the imperial persons had retired, and most of them sought to indemnify themselves in more free though less dignified circles, for the constraint which they had practised in the Temple of the Muses.

CHAPTER THE SIXTH

Vain man! thou mayst, esteem thy love as fair
As fond hyperboles suffice to raise.
She may be all that's matchless in her person, And all–
divine in soul to match her body;
But take this from me—thou shalt never call her
Superior to her sex, while *one* survives, And I
am her true votary.
OLD PLAY.

Achilles Tatius, with his faithful Varangian close by his shoulder, melted from
the dispersing assembly silently and almost invisibly, as snow is dissolved
from its Alpine abodes as the days become more genial. No lordly step, nor
clash of armour, betokened the retreat of the military persons. The very idea
of the necessity of guards was
not ostentatiously brought forward, because, so near the presence of the
Emperor, the emanation supposed to flit around that divinity of earthly
sovereigns, had credit for rendering it impassive and unassailable. Thus the
oldest and most skilful courtiers, among whom our friend Agelastes was not
to be forgotten, were of opinion, that, although the Emperor employed the
ministry of the Varangians and other guards, it was rather for form's sake,
than from any danger of the commission of a crime of a kind so heinous, that
it was the
fashion to account it almost impossible. And this doctrine, of the rare
occurrence of such a crime, was repeated from month to month in those very
chambers, where it had oftener than once been
perpetrated, and sometimes by the very persons who monthly laid schemes
for carrying some dark conspiracy against the reigning Emperor into
positive execution.

At length the captain of the life–guardsmen, and his faithful attendant, found
themselves on the outside of the Blacquernal Palace. The passage which
Achilles found for their exit, was closed

by a postern which a single Varangian shut behind, them, drawing, at the same time, bolt and bar with an ill–omened and jarring sound. Looking back at the mass of turrets, battlements, and spires, out of which they had at length emerged, Hereward could not but feel his heart lighten to find "himself once more under the deep blue of a Grecian heaven, where the planets were burning with unusual lustre. He sighed and rubbed his hands with pleasure, like a man newly restored to liberty. He even spoke to his leader, contrary to his custom unless addressed:—"Methinks the air of yonder halls, valorous Captain, carries with it a perfume, which, though it may be well termed sweet, is so suffocating, as to be more suitable to sepulchrous chambers, than to the dwellings of men. Happy I am
that I am free, as I trust, from its influences."

"Be happy, then," said Achilles Tatius, "since thy vile, cloddish spirit feels suffocation rather than refreshment in gales, which, instead of causing death, might recall the dead themselves to life. Yet this I will say for thee, Hereward, that, born a barbarian, within the narrow circle of a savage's desires and pleasures, and having no idea of life, save what thou derivest from such vile and base connexions, thou art, nevertheless, designed by nature for better things, and hast this day sustained a trial, in which, I fear me, not even one of mine own noble corps, frozen as they are into lumps of unfashioned barbarity, could have equalled thy bearing. And speak now in true faith, hast not thou been rewarded?"

"That will I never deny," said the Varangian. "The pleasure of knowing, twenty–four hours perhaps before my comrades, that the Normans are coming hither to afford us a full revenge of the bloody day of Hastings, is a lordly recompense, for the task of spending some hours in hearing the lengthened chat of a lady, who has written about she knows not what, and the flattering commentaries of the bystanders, who pretended to give her an account of what they did not themselves stop to witness."

"Hereward, my good youth," said Achilles Tatius, "thou ravest, and I think I should do well to place thee under the custody of some person of skill. Too much hardihood, my valiant soldier, is in soberness allied to over–daring. It was only natural that thou shouldst feel a becoming pride in thy late position; yet, let it but taint thee with vanity, and the effect will be little short of madness. Why, thou hast looked boldly in the face of a Princess born in the purple, before whom my own eyes, though well used to such spectacles, are never raised beyond the foldings of her veil."

"So be it in the name of Heaven!" replied Hereward. "Nevertheless, handsome faces were made to look upon, and the eyes of young men to see withal."

"If such be their final end," said Achilles, "never did thine, I will freely suppose, find a richer apology for the somewhat overbold license which thou tookest in thy gaze upon the Princess this evening."

"Good leader, or Follower, whichever is your favourite title," said the Anglo–Briton, "drive not to extremity a plain man, who desires to hold his duty in all honour to the imperial family. The Princess, wife of the Caesar, and born, you tell me, of a purple colour, has now inherited, notwithstanding, the features of a most lovely woman. She hath composed a history, of which I presume not to form a judgment, since I cannot understand it; she sings like an angel; and to conclude, after the fashion of the knights of this day—though I deal not ordinarily with their language—I would say cheerfully, that I am ready to place myself in lists against any one whomsoever, who dares detract from the beauty of the imperial Anna Comnena's person, or from the virtues of her mind. Having said this, my noble captain, we have said all that it is competent for you to inquire into, or for me to answer. That there are hansomer women than the Princess, is unquestionable; and I question it the less, that I have myself seen a person whom I think far her superior; and with that let us close the dialogue."

"Thy beauty, thou unparalleled fool," said Achilles, "must, I ween, be the daughter of the large–bodied northern boor, living next door to him upon whose farm was brought up the person of an ass, curst with such intolerable want of judgment."

"You may say your pleasure, captain," replied Hereward: "because it is the safer for us both that thou canst not on such a topic either offend me, who hold thy judgment as light as thou canst esteem mine, or speak any derogation of a person whom you never saw, but whom, if you had seen, perchance I might not so patiently have brooked any reflections upon, even at the hands of a military superior."

Achilles Tatius had a good deal of the penetration necessary for one in his situation. He never provoked to extremity the daring spirits whom he commanded, and never used any freedom with them beyond the extent that he knew their patience could bear. Hereward was a favourite soldier, and had, in that respect at least, a sincere liking and regard for his commander: when, therefore, the Follower, instead of resenting his petulance, good–humouredly apologized for having hurt his feelings, the momentary displeasure between them was at an end; the officer at once reassumed his superiority, and the soldier sunk back with a deep sigh, given to some period which was long past, into his wonted silence and reserve. Indeed the Follower had another and further design upon Hereward, of which he was as yet unwilling to do more than give a distant hint.

After a long pause, during which they approached the barracks, a gloomy fortified building constructed for the residence of their corps, the captain motioned his soldier to draw close up to his side, and proceeded to ask him, in a confidential tone—"Hereward, my
friend, although it is scarce to be supposed that in the presence of the imperial family thou shouldst mark any one who did not partake of their blood, or rather, as Homer has it, who did not participate of the divine *ichor*, which, in their sacred persons, supplies the place of
that vulgar fluid; yet, during so long an audience, thou mightst possibly, from his uncourtly person and attire, have distinguished Agelastes, whom we courtiers call the Elephant, from his strict observation of the rule which forbids any one to sit down or rest in the Imperial presence?"

"I think," replied the soldier, "I marked the man you mean; his age was some seventy and upwards,—a big burly person;—and the baldness which reached to the top of his head was well atoned for by a white beard of prodigious size, which descended in waving curls over his breast, and reached to the towel with which his loins were girded, instead of the silken sash used by other persons of rank."

"Most accurately marked, my Varangian," said the officer. "What else didst thou note about this person?"

"His cloak was in its texture as coarse as that of the meanest of the people, but it was strictly clean, as if it had been the intention of the wearer to exhibit poverty, or carelessness and contempt of dress, avoiding, at the same time, every particular which implied anything negligent, sordid, or disgusting."

"By St. Sophia!" said the officer, "thou astonishest me! The Prophet Baalam was not more surprised when his ass turned round her head and spoke to him!—And what else didst thou note concerning this man? I see those who meet thee must beware of thy observation, as well as of thy battle–axe."

"If it please your Valour" answered the soldier, "we English have eyes as well as hands; but it is only when discharging our duty that we permit our tongues to dwell on what we have observed. I noted but little of this man's conversation, but from what I heard, it seemed he was not unwilling to play what we call the jester, or jack– pudding, in the conversation, a character which, considering the man's age and physiognomy, is not, I should be tempted to say, natural, but assumed for some purpose of deeper import."

"Hereward," answered his officer, "thou hast spoken like an angel sent down to examine men's bosoms: that man, Agelastes, is a contradiction, such as earth has seldom witnessed. Possessing all that wisdom which in former times united the sages of this nation with
the gods themselves, Agelastes has the same cunning as the elder Brutus, who disguised his talents under the semblance of an idle jester. He appears to seek no office—he desires no consideration— he pays suit at court only when positively required to do so; yet what shall I say, my soldier, concerning the cause of an influence gained without apparent effort, and extending almost into the very thoughts of men, who appear to act as he would desire, without his soliciting them to that purpose? Men say strange things concerning the extent

of his communications with other beings, whom our fathers worshipped with prayer and sacrifice. I am determined, however, to know the road by which he climbs so high and so easily towards the point to which all men aspire at court, and it will go hard but he shall either share his ladder with me, or I will strike its support from under him. Thee, Hereward, I have chosen to assist me in this matter, as

the knights among these Frankish infidels select, when going upon an adventure, a sturdy squire, or inferior attendant, to share the dangers and the recompense; and this I am moved to, as much by the shrewdness thou hast this night manifested, as by the courage which thou mayst boast, in common with, or rather beyond, thy companions."

"I am obliged, and I thank your Valour," replied the Varangian, more coldly perhaps than his officer expected; "I am ready, as is my duty, to serve you in anything consistent with God and the Emperor's claims upon my service. I would only say, that, as a sworn inferior soldier, I will do nothing contrary to the laws of the empire, and, as a sincere though ignorant Christian, I will have nothing to do with the gods of the heathens, save to defy them in the name and strength of the holy saints."

"Idiot!" said Achilles Tatius, "dost thou think that I, already possessed of one of the first dignities of the empire, could meditate anything contrary to the interests of Alexius Comnenus? or, what would be scarce more atrocious, that I, the chosen friend and ally of the reverend Patriarch Zosimus, should meddle with anything bearing a relation, however remote, to heresy or idolatry?"

"Truly," answered the Varangian, "no one would be more surprised or grieved than I should; but when we walk in a labyrinth, we must assume and announce that we have a steady and forward purpose, which is one mode at least of keeping a straight path. The people of this country have so many ways of saying the same thing, that one can hardly know at last what is their real meaning. We English, on the other hand, can only express ourselves in one set of words, but it is one out of which all the ingenuity of the world could not extract a double meaning."

"'Tis well," said his officer, "to–morrow we will talk more of this, for which purpose thou wilt come to my quarters a little after sunset. And, hark thee, to–morrow, while the sun is in heaven, shall be thine own, either to sport thyself or to repose. Employ thy time in the latter, by my advice, since to–morrow night, like the present, may find us both watchers."

So saying, they entered the barracks, where they parted company— the commander of the life–guards taking his way to a splendid set of apartments which belonged to him in that capacity, and the Anglo– Saxon seeking his humble accommodations as a subaltern officer of the same corps.

Chapter the Seventh

Such forces met not, nor so vast a camp, When
Agrican, with all his northern powers, Besieged
Albraeca, as romances tell.
The city of Gallaphron, from thence to win
The fairest of her sex, Angelica,
His daughter, sought by many prowess'd knights, Both
Paynim, and the Peers of Charlemagne. PARADISE
REGAINED.

Early on the morning of the day following that which we have
commemorated, the Imperial Council was assembled, where the number of
general officers with sounding titles, disguised under a thin veil the real
weakness of the Grecian empire. The commanders were numerous and the
distinctions of their rank minute, but the soldiers were very few in
comparison. The offices formerly filled by prefects, praetors, and questors,
were now held by persons who had gradually risen into the authority of those
officers, and who, though designated from their domestic duties about the
Emperor, yet, from that very circumstance, possessed what, in that despotic
court, was the most effectual source of power. A long train of officers entered
the great hall of the Castle of Blacquernal, and proceeded so far together as
their different grades admitted, while in each chamber through which they
passed in succession, a certain number of the train whose rank permitted them
to advance no farther, remained behind the others. Thus, when the interior
cabinet of audience was gained, which was not until their passage through ten
anterooms,
five persons only found themselves in the presence of the Emperor in this
innermost and most sacred recess of royalty, decorated by all the splendour
of the period.

The Emperor Alexius sat upon a stately throne, rich with barbaric gems and
gold, and flanked on either hand, in imitation probably of

Solomon's magnificence, with the form of a couchant lion in the same precious metal. Not to dwell upon other marks of splendour, a tree whose trunk seemed also of gold, shot up behind the throne, which it over–canopied with its branches. Amid the boughs were birds of various kinds curiously wrought and enamelled, and fruit composed of precious stones seemed to glisten among the leaves. Five officers alone, the highest in the state, had the privilege of entering this sacred recess when the Emperor held council. These were—the Grand Domestic, who might be termed of rank with a modern prime minister—the Logothete, or chancellor—the Protospathaire, or commander of the guards, already mentioned—the Acolyte, or Follower, and leader of the Varangians—and the Patriarch.

The doors of this secret apartment, and the adjacent antechamber, were guarded by six deformed Nubian slaves, whose writhen and withered countenances formed a hideous contrast with their snow– white dresses and splendid equipment. They were mutes, a species of wretches borrowed from the despotism of the East, that they might be unable to proclaim the deeds of tyranny of which they were the unscrupulous agents. They were generally held in a kind of horror, rather than compassion, for men considered that slaves of this sort had a malignant pleasure in avenging upon others the irreparable wrongs which had severed themselves from humanity. It was a general custom, though, like many other usages of the Greeks, it would be held childish in modern times, that by means of machinery easily conceived, the lions, at the entrance of a stranger, were made, as it were, to rouse themselves and roar, after which a wind seemed to rustle the foliage of the tree, the birds hopped from branch to branch, pecked the fruit, and appeared to fill the chamber with their carolling. This display had alarmed many an ignorant foreign ambassador, and even the Grecian counsellors themselves were expected to display the same sensations of fear, succeeded by surprise, when they heard the roar of the lions, followed by the concert of the birds, although perhaps it was for the fiftieth time. On this occasion, as a proof of the urgency of the present meeting of the council, these ceremonies were entirely omitted.

The speech of the Emperor himself seemed to supply by its

commencement the bellowing of the lions, while it ended in a strain more resembling the warbling of the birds.

In his first sentences, he treated of the audacity and unheard–of boldness of the millions of Franks, who, under the pretence of wresting Palestine from the infidels, had ventured to invade the sacred territories of the empire. He threatened them with such chastisement as his innumerable forces and officers would, he affirmed, find it easy to inflict. To all this the audience, and especially the military officers, gave symptoms of ready assent. Alexius, however, did not long persist in the warlike intentions which he at first avowed. The Franks, he at length seemed to reflect, were, in profession, Christians. They might possibly be serious in their pretext of the crusade, in which case their motives claimed a degree of indulgence, and, although erring, a certain portion of
respect. Their numbers also were great, and their valour could not be despised by those who had seen them fight at Durazzo, [Footnote: For the battle of Durazzo, Oct. 1081, in which Alexius was defeated with great slaughter by Robert Guiscard, and escaped only by the swiftness of his horse, see Gibbon, ch. 56.] and elsewhere. They
might also, by the permission of Supreme Providence, be, in the long run, the instruments of advantage to the most sacred empire, though they approached it with so little ceremony. He had, therefore, mingling the virtues of prudence, humanity, and generosity, with
that valour which must always burn in the heart of an Emperor, formed a plan, which he was about to submit to their consideration, for present execution; and, in the first place, he requested of the Grand Domestic, to let him know what forces he might count upon on the western side of the Bosphorus.

"Innumerable are the forces of the empire as the stars in heaven, or the sand on the sea–shore," answered the Grand Domestic.

"That is a goodly answer," said the Emperor, "provided there were strangers present at this conference; but since we hold consultation in private, it is necessary that I know precisely to what number that
army amounts which I have to rely upon. Reserve your eloquence till some fitter time, and let me know what you, at this present moment, mean by the word *innumerable?*"

The Grand Domestic paused, and hesitated for a short space; but as he became aware that the moment was one in which the Emperor could not be trifled with, (for Alexius Comnenus was at times dangerous,) he answered thus, but not without hesitation. "Imperial master and lord, none better knows that such an answer cannot be hastily made, if it is at the same time to be correct in its results. The number of the imperial host betwixt this city and the western frontier of the empire, deducting those absent on furlough, cannot be counted upon as amounting to more than twenty–five thousand men, or thirty thousand at most."

Alexius struck his forehead with his hand; and the counsellors, seeing him give way to such violent expressions of grief and surprise, began to enter into discussions, which they would otherwise have reserved for a fitter place and time.

"By the trust your Highness reposes in me," said the Logothete, "there has been drawn from your Highness's coffers during the last year, gold enough to pay double the number of the armed warriors whom the Grand Domestic now mentions."

"Your Imperial Highness," retorted the impeached minister, with no small animation, "will at once remember the stationary garrisons, in addition to the movable troops, for which this figure–caster makes no allowance."

"Peace, both of you!" said Alexius, composing himself hastily; "our actual numbers are in truth less than we counted on, but let us not by wrangling augment the difficulties of the time. Let those troops be dispersed in valleys, in passes, behind ridges of hills, and in difficult ground, where a little art being used in the position, can make few men supply the appearance of numbers, between this city and the western frontier of the empire. While this disposal is made, we will continue to adjust with these crusaders, as they call themselves, the terms on which we will consent to let them pass through our dominions; nor are we without hope of negotiating with them, so as to gain great advantage to our kingdom. We will insist that they pass through our country only by armies of perhaps fifty thousand at once, whom we will successively transport into Asia, so that no

greater number shall, by assembling beneath our walls, ever
endanger the safety of the metropolis of the world.

"On their way towards the banks of the Bosphorus, we will supply them
with provisions, if they march peaceably, and in order; and if any straggle
from their standards, or insult the country by marauding, we suppose our
valiant peasants will not hesitate to repress their excesses, and that without
our giving positive orders,
since we would not willingly be charged with any thing like a breach of
engagement. We suppose, also, that the Scythians, Arabs, Syrians, and other
mercenaries in our service, will not suffer our subjects to
be overpowered in their own just defence; as, besides that there is no justice
in stripping our own country of provisions, in order to feed strangers, we will
not be surprised nor unpardonably displeased to learn, that of the ostensible
quantity of flour, some sacks should be found filled with chalk, or lime, or
some such substance. It is,
indeed, truly wonderful, what the stomach of a Frank will digest comfortably.
Their guides, also, whom you shall choose with reference to such duty, will
take care to conduct the crusaders by difficult and circuitous routes; which
will be doing them a real service, by inuring them to the hardships of the
country and climate, which they would otherwise have to face without
seasoning.

"In the meantime, in your intercourse with their chiefs, whom they call
counts, each of whom thinks himself as great as an Emperor, you will take
care to give no offence to their natural presumption,
and omit no opportunity of informing them of the wealth and bounty of our
government. Sums of money may be even given to persons of note, and
largesses of less avail to those under them. You, our Logothete, will take good
order for this, and you, our Grand Domestic, will take care that such soldiers
as may cut off detached parties of the Franks shall be presented, if possible, in
savage dress, and under the show of infidels. In commending these injunctions
to your care, I purpose that, the crusaders having found the value of our
friendship, and also in some sort the danger of our enmity, those whom we
shall safely transport to Asia, shall be, however unwieldy, still a smaller and
more compact body, whom we may deal with in
all Christian prudence. Thus, by using fair words to one, threats to another,
gold to the avaricious, power to the ambitious, and reasons

to those that are capable of listening to them, we doubt not but to prevail upon those Franks, met as they are from a thousand points, and enemies of each other, to acknowledge us as their common superior, rather than choose a leader among themselves, when they are made aware of the great fact, that every village in Palestine, from Dan to Beersheba, is the original property of the sacred Roman empire, and that whatever Christian goes to war for their recovery, must go as our subject, and hold any conquest which he may make, as our vassal. Vice and virtue, sense and folly, ambition and disinterested devotion, will alike recommend to the survivors of these singular–minded men, to become the feudatories of the empire, not its foe, and the shield, not the enemy, of your paternal Emperor."

There was a general inclination of the head among the courtiers, with the Eastern acclamation of,—"Long live the Emperor!"

When the murmur of this applausive exclamation had subsided, Alexius proceeded:—"Once more, I say, that my faithful Grand Domestic, and those who act under him, will take care to commit the execution of such part of these orders as may seem aggressive, to troops of foreign appearance and language, which, I grieve to say, are more numerous in our imperial army than our natural–born and orthodox subjects."

The Patriarch here interposed his opinion.—"There is a consolation," he said,"in the thought, that the genuine Romans in the imperial army are but few, since a trade so bloody as war, is most fitly prosecuted by those whose doctrines, as well as their doings, on earth, merit eternal condemnation in the next world."

"Reverend Patriarch," said the Emperor, "we would not willingly hold with the wild infidels, that Paradise is to be gained by the sabre; nevertheless, we would hope that a Roman dying in battle for his religion and his Emperor, may find as good hope of acceptation, after the mortal pang is over, as a man who dies in peace, and with unblooded hand."

"It is enough for me to say," resumed the Patriarch, "that the Church's doctrine is not so indulgent: she is herself peaceful, and her

promises of favour are for those who have been men of peace. Yet think not I bar the gates of Heaven against a soldier, as such, if believing all the doctrines of our Church, and complying with all our observances; far less would I condemn your Imperial Majesty's wise precautions, both for diminishing the power and thinning the ranks
of those Latin heretics, who come hither to despoil us, and plunder perhaps both church and temple, under the vain pretext that Heaven would permit them, stained with so many heresies, to reconquer that Holy Land, which true orthodox Christians, your Majesty's sacred predecessors, have not been enabled to retain from the infidel. And well I trust that no settlement made under the Latins will be permitted by your Majesty to establish itself, in which the Cross shall not be elevated with limbs of the same length, instead of that irregular and most damnable error which prolongs, in western churches, the nether limb of that most holy emblem."

"Reverend Patriarch," answered the Emperor, "do not deem that we think lightly of your weighty scruples; but the question is now, not in what manner we may convert these Latin heretics to the true faith,
but how we may avoid being overrun by their myriads, which resemble those of the locusts by which their approach was preceded and intimated."

"Your Majesty," said the Patriarch, "will act with your usual wisdom; for my part, I have only stated my doubts, that I may save my own soul alive."

"Our construction," said the Emperor, "does your sentiments no wrong, most reverend Patriarch; and you," addressing himself to the other counsellors, "will attend to these separate charges given out for directing the execution of the commands which have been generally intimated to you. They are written out in the sacred ink, and our sacred subscription is duly marked with the fitting tinge of green and purple. Let them, therefore, be strictly obeyed. Ourselves will
assume the command of such of the Immortal Bands as remain in the city, and join to them the cohorts of our faithful Varangians. At the head of these troops, we will await the arrival of these strangers
under the walls of the city, and, avoiding combat while our policy can postpone it, we will be ready, in case of the worst, to take

whatsoever chance it shall please the Almighty to send us."

Here the council broke up, and the different chiefs began to exert themselves in the execution of their various instructions, civil and military, secret or public, favourable or hostile to the crusaders. The peculiar genius of the Grecian people was seen upon this occasion. Their loud and boastful talking corresponded with the ideas which the Emperor wished to enforce upon the crusaders concerning the extent of his power and resources. Nor is it to be disguised, that the wily selfishness of most of those in the service of Alexius, endeavoured to find some indirect way of applying the imperial instruction, so as might best suit their own private ends.

Meantime, the news had gone abroad in Constantinople of the arrival of the huge miscellaneous army of the west upon the limits of the Grecian empire, arid of their purpose to pass to Palestine. A
thousand reports magnified, if that was possible, an event so wonderful. Some said, that their ultimate view was the conquest of Arabia, the destruction of the Prophet's tomb, and the conversion of his green banner into a horse– cloth for the King of France's brother. Others supposed that the ruin and sack of Constantinople was the
real object of the war. A third class thought it was in order to compel the Patriarch to submit himself to the Pope, adopt the Latin form of the cross, and put an end to the schism.

The Varangians enjoyed an addition to this wonderful news, seasoned as it everywhere was with something peculiarly suited to the prejudices of the hearers. It was gathered originally from what our friend Hereward, who was one of their inferior officers, called sergeants or constables, had suffered to transpire of what he had heard the preceding evening. Considering that the fact must be soon matter of notoriety, he had no hesitation to give his comrades to understand that a Norman army was coming hither under Duke Robert, the son of the far–famed William the Conqueror, and with hostile intentions, he concluded, against them in particular. Like all other men in peculiar circumstances, the Varangians adopted an explanation applicable to their own condition. These Normans, who hated the Saxon nation, and had done so much to dishonour and oppress them, were now following them, they supposed, to the

foreign capital where they had found refuge, with the purpose of making war on the bountiful prince who protected their sad remnant. Under this belief, many a deep oath was sworn in Norse and Anglo– Saxon, that their keen battle–axes should avenge the slaughter of Hastings, and many a pledge, both in wine and ale, was quaffed who should most deeply resent, and most effectually revenge, the wrongs which the Anglo–Saxons of England had received at the hand of
their oppressors.

Hereward, the author of this intelligence, began soon to be sorry that he had ever suffered it to escape him, so closely was he cross– examined concerning its precise import, by the enquiries of his comrades, from whom he thought himself obliged to keep concealed the adventures of the preceding evening, and the place in which he had gained his information.

About noon, when he was effectually tired with returning the same answer to the same questions, and evading similar others which were repeatedly put to him, the sound of trumpets announced the presence of the Acolyte, Achilles Tatius, who came immediately, it was industriously whispered, from the sacred Interior, with news of the immediate approach of war.

The Varangians, and the Roman bands called Immortal, it was said, were to form a camp under the city, in order to be prompt to defend
it at the shortest notice. This put the whole barracks into commotion, each man making the necessary provision for the approaching campaign. The noise was chiefly that of joyful bustle and acclamation; and it was so general, that Hereward, whose rank permitted him to commit to a page or esquire the task of preparing his equipments, took the opportunity to leave the barracks, in order
to seek some distant place apart from his comrades, and enjoy his solitary reflections upon the singular connexion into which he had been drawn, and his direct communication with the Imperial family.

Passing through the narrow streets, then deserted, on account of the heat of the sun, he reached at length one of those broad terraces, which, descending as it were by steps, upon the margin of the Bosphorus, formed one of the most splendid walks in the universe, and still, it is believed, preserved as a public promenade for the pleasure of the Turks, as formerly for that of the Christians. These graduated terraces were planted with many trees, among which the cypress, as usual, was most generally cultivated. Here bands of the inhabitants were to be seen: some passing to and fro, with business and anxiety in their faces; some standing still in groups, as if discussing the strange and weighty tidings of the day, and some, with the indolent carelessness of an eastern climate, eating their noontide refreshment in the shade, and spending their time as if their sole object was to make much of the day as it passed, and let the cares of to–morrow answer for themselves.

While the Varangian, afraid of meeting some acquaintance in this concourse, which would have been inconsistent with the desire of seclusion which had brought him thither, descended or passed from one terrace to another, all marked him with looks of curiosity and enquiry, considering him to be one, who, from his arms and connexion with the court, must necessarily know more than others concerning the singular invasion by numerous enemies, and from various quarters, which was the news of the day.

None, however, had the hardihood to address the soldier of the guard, though all looked at him with uncommon interest. He walked from the lighter to the darker alleys, from the more closed to the more open terraces, without interruption from any one, yet not without a feeling that he must not consider himself as alone.

The desire that he felt to be solitary rendered him at last somewhat watchful, so that he became sensible that he was dogged by a black slave, a personage not so unfrequent in the streets of Constantinople as to excite any particular notice. His attention, however, being at length fixed on this individual, he began to be desirous to escape his observation; and the change of place which he had at first adopted to avoid society in general, he had now recourse to, in order to rid himself of this distant, though apparently watchful attendant. Still, however, though he by change of place had lost sight of the negro for a few minutes, it was not long ere he again discovered him at a distance too far for a companion, but near enough to serve all the purposes of a spy. Displeased at this, the Varangian turned short in his walk, and choosing a spot where none was in sight but the object of his resentment, walked suddenly up to him, and demanded wherefore, and by whose orders, he presumed to dog his footsteps. The negro answered in a jargon as bad as that in which he was addressed though of a different kind, "that he had orders to remark whither he went."

"Orders from whom?" said the Varangian.

"From my master and yours," answered the negro, boldly.

"Thou infidel villain!" exclaimed the angry soldier, "when was it that we became fellow–servants, and who is it that thou darest to call my master?"

"One who is master of the world," said the slave, "since he commands his own passions."

"I shall scarce command mine," said the Varangian, "if thou repliest to my earnest questions with thine affected quirks of philosophy. Once more, what dost thou want with me? and why hast thou the boldness to watch me?"

"I have told thee already," said the slave, "that I do my master's commands."

"But I must know who thy master is," said Hereward.

"He must tell thee that himself," replied the negro; "he trusts not a poor slave like me with the purpose of the errands on which he sends me."

"He has left thee a tongue, however," said the Varangian, "which some of thy countrymen would. I think, be glad to possess. Do not provoke me to abridge it by refusing me the information which I have a right to demand."

The black meditated, as it seemed from the grin on his face, further evasions, when Hereward cut them short by raising the staff of his battle–axe. "Put me not" he said, "to dishonour myself by striking thee with this weapon, calculated for a use so much more noble."

"I may not do so, valiant sir," said the negro, laying aside an impudent, half–gibing tone which he had hitherto made use of, and betraying personal fear in his manner. "If you beat the poor slave to death, you cannot learn what his master hath forbid him to tell. A short walk will save your honour the stain, and yourself the trouble, of beating what cannot resist, and me the pain of enduring what I can neither retaliate nor avoid."

"Lead on then," said the Varangian. "Be assured thou shalt not fool me by thy fair words, and I will know the person who is impudent enough to assume the right of watching my motions."

The black walked on with a species of leer peculiar to his physiognomy, which might be construed as expressive either of malice or of mere humour. The Varangian followed him with some suspicion, for it happened that he had had little intercourse with the unhappy race of Africa, and had not totally overcome the feeling of surprise with which he had at first regarded them, when he arrived a stranger from the north. So often did this man look back upon him during their walk, and with so penetrating and observing a cast of countenance, that Hereward felt irresistibly renewed in his mind the English prejudices, which assigned to the demons the sable colour and distorted cast of visage of his conductor. The scene into which he was guided, strengthened an association which was not of itself unlikely to occur to the ignorant and martial islander.

The negro led the way from the splendid terraced walks which we have described, to a path descending to the sea–shore, when a place appeared, which, far from being trimmed, like other parts of the coast, into walks of embankments, seemed, on the contrary, abandoned to neglect, and was covered with the mouldering ruins of antiquity, where these had not been overgrown by the luxuriant vegetation of the climate. These fragments of building, occupying a sort of recess of the bay, were hidden by steep banks on each side, and although in fact they formed part of the city, yet they were not seen from any part of it, and, embosomed in the manner we have described, did not in turn command any view of the churches, palaces, towers, and fortifications, amongst which they lay. The sight of this solitary, and apparently deserted spot, encumbered with ruins, and overgrown with cypress and other trees, situated as it was in the midst of a populous city, had something in it impressive and awful to the imagination. The ruins were of an ancient date, and in the style of a foreign people. The gigantic remains of a portico, the mutilated fragments of statues of great size, but executed in a taste and attitude so narrow and barbaric as to seem perfectly the reverse of the Grecian, and the half–defaced hieroglyphics which could be traced on some part of the decayed sculpture, corroborated the popular account of their origin, which we shall briefly detail.

According to tradition, this had been a temple dedicated to the Egyptian goddess Cybele, built while the Roman Empire was yet heathen, and while Constantinople was still called by the name of Byzantium. It is well known that the superstition of the Egyptians— vulgarly gross in its literal meaning as well as in its mystical interpretation, and peculiarly the foundation of many wild doctrines,
—was disowned by the principles of general toleration, and the system of polytheism received by Rome, and was excluded by repeated laws from the respect paid by the empire to almost every other religion, however extravagant or absurd. Nevertheless, these Egyptian rites had charms for the curious and the superstitious, and had, after long opposition, obtained a footing in the empire.

Still, although tolerated, the Egyptian priests were rather considered as sorcerers than as pontiffs, and their whole ritual had a nearer relation, to magic in popular estimation, than to any regular system of devotion.

Stained with these accusations, even among the heathen themselves, the worship of Egypt was held in more mortal abhorrence by the Christians, than the other and more rational kinds of heathen devotion; that is, if any at all had a right to be termed so. The brutal worship of Apis and Cybele was regarded, not only as a pretext for obscene and profligate pleasures, but as having a direct tendency to open and encourage a dangerous commerce with evil spirits, who were supposed to take upon themselves, at these unhallowed altars, the names and characters of these foul deities. Not only, therefore, the temple of Cybele, with its gigantic portico, its huge and inelegant statues, and its fantastic hieroglyphics, was thrown down and defaced when the empire was converted to the Christian faith, but the very ground on which it stood was considered as polluted and unhallowed; and no Emperor having yet occupied the site with a Christian church, the place still remained neglected and deserted as we have described it.

The Varangian Hereward was perfectly acquainted with the evil reputation of the place; and when the negro seemed disposed to advance into the interior of the ruins, he hesitated, and addressed his guide thus:—"Hark thee, my black friend, these huge fantastic images, some having dogs' heads, some cows' heads, and some no heads at all, are not held reverently in popular estimation. Your own colour, also, my comrade, is greatly too like that of Satan himself, to render you an unsuspicious companion amid ruins, in which the false spirit, it is said, daily walks his rounds. Midnight and Noon are the times, it is rumoured, of his appearance. I will go no farther with you, unless you assign me a fit reason for so doing."

"In making so childish a proposal" said the negro, "you take from me, in effect, all desire to guide you to my master. I thought I spoke to a man of invincible courage, and of that good sense upon which courage is best founded. But your valour only emboldens you to beat a black slave, who has neither strength nor title to resist you; and your courage is not enough to enable you to look without trembling on the dark side of a wall, even when the sun is in the heavens."

"Thou art insolent," said Hereward, raising his axe.

"And thou art foolish," said the negro, "to attempt to prove thy manhood and thy wisdom by the very mode which gives reason for calling them both in question. I have already said there can be little valour in beating a wretch like me; and no man, surely, who wishes to discover his way, would begin by chasing away his guide."

"I follow thee" said Hereward, stung with the insinuation of cowardice; "but if thou leadest me into a snare, thy free talk shall not save thy bones, if a thousand of thy complexion, from earth or hell, were standing ready to back thee."

"Thou objectest sorely to my complexion," said the negro; "how knowest thou that it is, in fact, a thing to be counted and acted upon as matter of reality? Thine own eyes daily apprize thee, that the colour of the sky nightly changes from bright to black, yet thou knowest that this is by no means owing to any habitual colour of the heavens themselves. The same change that takes place in the hue of the heavens, has existence in the tinge of the deep sea—How canst thou tell, but what the difference of my colour from thine own may be owing to some deceptions change of a similar nature—not real in itself, but only creating an apparent reality?"

"Thou mayst have painted thyself, no doubt," answered the Varangian, upon reflection, "and thy blackness, therefore, may be only apparent; but I think thy old friend himself could hardly have presented these grinning lips, with the white teeth and flattened nose, so much to the life, unless that peculiarity of Nubian physiognomy,
as they call it, had accurately and really an existence; and to save thee some trouble, my dark friend, I will tell thee, that though thou speakest to an uneducated Varangian, I am not entirely unskilled in the Grecian art of making subtle words pass upon the hearers instead of reason."

"Ay?" said the negro, doubtfully, and somewhat surprised; "and may the slave Diogenes—for so my master has christened me—enquire into the means by which you reached knowledge so unusual?"

"It is soon told," replied Hereward. "My countryman, Witikind, being a constable of our bands, retired from active service, and spent the end of a long life in this city of Constantinople. Being past all toils of battle, either those of reality, as you word it, or the pomp and fatigue of the exercising ground, the poor old man, in despair of something to pass his time, attended the lectures of the philosophers."

"And what did he learn there?" said the negro; "for a barbarian, grown grey under the helmet, was not, as I think, a very hopeful student in our schools."

"As much though, I should think, as a menial slave, which I understand to be thy condition," replied the soldier. "But I have understood from him, that the masters of this idle science make it their business to substitute, in their argumentations, mere words instead of ideas; and as they never agree upon the precise meaning of the former, their disputes can never arrive at a fair or settled conclusion, since they do not agree in the language in which they express them. Their theories, as they call them, are built on the sand, and the wind and tide shall prevail against them."

"Say so to my master," answered the black, in a serious tone.

"I will," said the Varangian; "and he shall know me as an ignorant soldier, having but few ideas, and those only concerning my religion and my military duty. But out of these opinions I will neither be beaten by a battery of sophisms, nor cheated by the arts or the terrors of the friends of heathenism, either in this world or the next."

"You may speak your mind to him then yourself," said Diogenes. He stepped aside as if to make way for the Varangian, to whom he motioned to go forward.

Hereward advanced accordingly, by a half–worn and almost imperceptible path leading through the long rough grass, and, turning round a half–demolished shrine, which exhibited the remains of Apis, the bovine deity, he came immediately in front of
the philosopher, Agelastes, who, sitting among the ruins, reposed his limbs on the grass.

CHAPTER THE EIGHTH

Through the vain webs which puzzle sophists' skill, Plain
sense and honest meaning work their way;
So sink the varying clouds upon the hill, When the
clear dawning—brightens into day. DR. WATTS.

The old man rose from the ground with alacrity, as Hereward approached.
"My bold Varangian" he said, "thou who valuest men and things not
according to the false estimate ascribed to them in this world, but to their real
importance and actual value, thou art welcome, whatever has brought thee
hither—thou art welcome to a place, where it is held the best business of
philosophy to strip man of his borrowed ornaments, and reduce him to the just
value of his own attributes of body and mind, singly considered."

"You are a courtier, sir," said the Saxon, "and as a permitted companion of the
Emperor's Highness, you must be aware, that there are twenty times more
ceremonies than such a man as I can be acquainted with, for regulating the
different ranks in society; while a plain man like myself may be well excused
from pushing himself
into the company of those above him, where he does not exactly know
how he should comport himself."

"True," said the philosopher; "but a man like yourself, noble Hereward,
merits more consideration in the eyes of a real philosopher, than a thousand
of those mere insects, whom the smiles of a court call into life, and whom its
frowns reduce to annihilation."

"You are yourself, grave sir, a follower of the court," said Hereward. "And a

most punctilious one," said Agelastes. "There is not, I trust, a
subject in the empire who knows better the ten thousand punctilios exigible
from those of different ranks, and clue to different

authorities. The man is yet to be born who has seen me take advantage of any more commodious posture than that of standing in presence of the royal family. But though I use those false scales in society, and so far conform to its errors, my real judgment is of a more grave character, and more worthy of man, as said to be formed in the image of his Creator."

"There can be small occasion," said the Varangian, "to exercise your judgment in any respect upon me, nor am I desirous that any one should think of me otherwise than I am; a poor exile, namely, who endeavours to fix his faith upon Heaven, and to perform his duty to the world he lives in, and to the prince in whose service he is engaged. And now, grave sir, permit me to ask, whether this meeting is by your desire, and for what is its purpose? An African slave, whom I met in the public walks, and who calls himself Diogenes, tells me that you desired to speak with me; he hath somewhat the humour of the old scoffer, and so he may have lied. If so, I will even forgive him the beating which I owe his assurance, and make my excuse at the same time for having broken in upon your retirement, which I am totally unfit to share."

"Diogenes has not played you false," answered Agelastes; "he has his humours, as you remarked even now, and with these some qualities also that put him upon a level with those of fairer complexion and better features."

"And for what," said the Varangian, "have you so employed him? Can your wisdom possibly entertain a wish to converse with me?"

"I am an observer of nature and of humanity," answered the philosopher; "is it not natural that I should tire of those beings who are formed entirely upon artifice, and long to see something more fresh from the hand of nature?"

"You see not that in me," said the Varangian; "the rigour of military discipline, the camp—the centurion—the armour—frame a man's sentiments and limbs to them, as the sea–crab is framed to its shell. See one of us, and you see us all."

"Permit me to doubt that," said Agelastes; "and to suppose that in

Hereward, the son of Waltheoff, I see an extraordinary man, although he himself may be ignorant, owing to his modesty, of the rarity of his own good qualities."

"The son of Waltheoff!" answered the Varangian, somewhat startled. —"Do you know my father's name?"

"Be not surprised," answered the philosopher, "at my possessing so simple a piece of information. It has cost me but little trouble to attain it, yet I would gladly hope that the labour I have taken in that matter may convince you of my real desire to call you friend."

"It was indeed an unusual compliment," said Hereward, "that a man of your knowledge and station should be at the trouble to enquire, among the Varangian cohorts, concerning the descent of one of their constables. I scarcely think that my commander, the Acolyte himself, would think such knowledge worthy of being collected or preserved."

"Greater men than he," said Agelastes, "certainly would not——You know one in high office, who thinks the names of his most faithful soldiers of less moment than those of his hunting dogs or his hawks, and would willingly save himself the trouble of calling them otherwise than by a whistle."

"I may not hear this," answered the Varangian.

"I would not offend you," said the philosopher, "I would not even shake your good opinion of the person I allude to; yet it surprises me that such should be entertained by one of your great qualities."

"A truce with this, grave sir, which is in fact trifling in a person of your character and appearance," answered the Anglo–Saxon. "I am like the rocks of my country; the fierce winds cannot shake me, the soft rains cannot melt me; flattery and loud words are alike lost upon me."

"And it is even for that inflexibility of mind," replied Agelastes, "that steady contempt of every thing that approaches thee, save in the light of a duty, that I demand, almost like a beggar, that personal acquaintance, which thou refusest like a churl."

"Pardon me," said Hereward, "if I doubt this. Whatever stories you may have picked up concerning me, not unexaggerated probably— since the Greeks do not keep the privilege of boasting so entirely to themselves but the Varangians have learned a little of it—you can have heard nothing of me which can authorise your using your present language, excepting in jest."

"You mistake, my son," said Agelastes; "believe me not a person to mix in the idle talk respecting you, with your comrades at the ale- cup. Such as I am, I can strike on this broken image of Anubis"— (here he touched a gigantic fragment of a statue by his side)—"and bid the spirit who long prompted the oracle, descend, and once more reanimate the trembling mass. We that are initiated enjoy high privileges—we stamp upon those ruined vaults, and the echo which dwells there answers to our demand. Do not think, that although I crave thy friendship, I Heed therefore supplicate thee for information either respecting thyself or others."

"Your words are wonderful," said the Anglo–Saxon; "but by such promising words I have heard that many souls have been seduced from the path of heaven. My grandsire, Kenelm, was wont to say, that the fair words of the heathen philosophy were more hurtful to the Christian faith than the menaces of the heathen tyrants."

"I know him," said Agelastes. "What avails it whether it was in the body or in the spirit?—He was converted from the faith of Woden by a noble monk, and died a priest at the shrine of saint Augustin." [Footnote: At Canterbury.]

"True"—said Hereward; "all this is certain—and I am the rather bound to remember his words now that he is dead and gone. When I hardly knew his meaning, he bid me beware of the doctrine which causeth to err, which is taught by false prophets, who attest their doctrine by unreal miracles."

"This," said Agelastes, "is mere superstition. Thy grandsire was a good and excellent man, but narrow–minded, like other priests; and, deceived by their example, he wished but to open a small wicket in the gate of truth, and admit the world only on that limited scale. Seest thou, Hereward, thy grandsire and most men of religion would fain narrow our intellect to the consideration of such parts of the Immaterial world as are essential to our moral guidance here, and our final salvation hereafter; but it is not the less true, that man has liberty, provided he has wisdom and courage, to form intimacies with beings more powerful than himself, who can defy the bounds of space by which he is circumscribed, and overcome, by their metaphysical powers, difficulties which, to the timid and unlearned, may appear wild and impossible."

"You talk of a folly," answered Hereward, "at which childhood gapes and manhood smiles."

"On the contrary," said the sage, "I talk of a longing wish which every man feels at the bottom of his heart, to hold communication with beings more powerful than himself, and who are not naturally accessible to our organs. Believe me, Hereward, so ardent and universal an aspiration had not existed in our bosoms, had there not also been means, if steadily and wisely sought, of attaining its accomplishment. I will appeal to thine own heart, and prove to thee even by a single word, that what I say is truth. Thy thoughts are even now upon a being long absent or dead, and with the name of BERTHA, a thousand emotions rush to thy heart, which in thy ignorance thou hadst esteemed furled up for ever, like spoils of the dead hung above a tombstone!—Thou startest and changest thy colour—I joy to see by these signs, that the firmness and indomitable courage which men ascribe to thee, have left the avenues of the heart as free as ever to kindly and to generous affections, while they have barred them against those of fear, uncertainty, and all the caitiff tribe of meatier sensations. I have proffered to esteem thee, and I have no hesitation in proving it. I will tell thee, If thou desirest to know it, the fate of that very Bertha, whose memory thou hast cherished in thy breast in spite of thee, amidst the toil of the day and the repose of the night, in the battle and in the truce, when sporting with thy companions in fields of exercise, or attempting to prosecute the study of Greek learning, in which if thou wouldst advance, I can teach it by a short road."

While Agelastes thus spoke, the Varangian in some degree recovered his composure, and made answer, though his voice was somewhat tremulous,— "Who thou art, I know not—what thou wouldst with me, I cannot tell—by what means thou hast gathered intelligence of such consequence to me, and of so little to another, I have no conception—But this I know, that by intention or accident, thou hast pronounced a name which agitates my heart to its deepest recesses; yet am I a Christian and Varangian, and neither to my God nor to my adopted prince will I willingly stagger in my faith. What is to be wrought by idols or by false deities, must be a treason to the real divinity. Nor is it less certain that thou hast let glance some arrows, though the rules of thy allegiance strictly forbid it, at the Emperor himself. Henceforward, therefore, I refuse to communicate with thee, be it for weal or woe. I am the Emperor's waged soldier, and although I affect not the nice precisions of respect and obedience, which are exacted in so many various cases, and by so many various rules, yet I am his defence, and my battle–axe is his body–guard."

"No one doubts it," said the philosopher. "But art not thou also bound to a nearer dependence upon' the great Acolyte, Achilles Tatius?"

"No. He is my general, according to the rules of our service," answered the Varangian; "to me he has always shown himself a kind and good– natured man, and, his dues of rank apart, I may say has deported himself as a friend rather than a commander. He is, however, my master's servant as well as I am; nor do I hold the difference of great amount, which the word of a man can give or take away at pleasure."

"It is nobly spoken," said Agelastes; "and you yourself are surely entitled to stand erect before one whom you supersede in courage and in the art of war."

"Pardon me," returned the Briton, "if I decline the attributed compliment, as what in no respect belongs to me. The Emperor chooses his own officers, in respect of their power of serving him as he desires to be served. In this it is likely I might fail; I have said already, I owe my Emperor my obedience, my duty, and my service, nor does it seem to me necessary to carry our explanation farther."

"Singular man!" said Agelastes; "is there nothing than can move thee but things that are foreign to thyself? The name of thy Emperor and thy commander are no spell upon thee, and even that of the object thou has loved"—

Here the Varangian interrupted him.

"I have thought," he said, "upon the words thou hast spoken—thou hast found the means to shake my heart–strings, but not to unsettle my principles. I will hold no converse with thee on a matter in which thou canst not have interest.—Necromancers, it is said, perform their spells by means of the epithets of the Holiest; no marvel, then,
should they use the names of the purest of his creation to serve their unhallowed purposes. I will none of such truckling, disgraceful to the dead perhaps as to the living. Whatever has been thy purpose,
old man— for, think not thy strange words have passed unnoticed— be thou assured I bear that in my heart which defies alike the seduction of men and of fiends."

With this the soldier turned, and left the ruined temple, after a slight inclination of his head to the philosopher.

Agelastes, after the departure of the soldier, remained alone, apparently absorbed in meditation, until he was suddenly disturbed by the entrance, into the ruins, of Achilles Tatius. The leader of the Varangians spoke not until he had time to form some result from the philosopher's features. He then said, "Thou remainest, sage Agelastes, confident in the purpose of which we have lately spoke together?"

"I do," said Agelastes, with gravity and firmness.

"But," replied Achilles Tatius, "thou hast not gained to our side that proselyte, whose coolness and courage would serve us better in our hour of need than the service of a thousand cold–hearted slaves?"

"I have not succeeded," answered the philosopher.

"And thou dost not blush to own it?" said the imperial officer in reply.

"Thou, the wisest of those who yet pretend to Grecian wisdom, the most powerful of those who still assert the skill by words, signs, names, periapts, and spells, to exceed the sphere to which thy faculties belong, hast been foiled in thy trade of persuasion, like an infant worsted in debate with its domestic tutor? Out upon thee, that thou canst not sustain in argument the character which thou wouldst so fain, assume to thyself!"

"Peace!" said the Grecian. "I have as yet gained nothing, it is true, over this obstinate and inflexible man; but, Achilles Tatius, neither have I lost. We both stand where yesterday we did, with this advantage on my side, that I have suggested to him such an object of interest as he shall never be able to expel from his mind, until he hath had recourse to me to obtain farther knowledge concerning it.— And now let this singular person remain for a time unmentioned; yet, trust me, though flattery, avarice, and ambition may fail to gain him, a bait nevertheless remains, that shall make him as completely our own as any that is bound within our mystic and inviolable contract. Tell me then, how go on the affairs of the empire? Does this tide of Xiatin warriors, so strangely set aflowing, still rush on to the banks of the Bosphorus? and does Alexius still entertain hopes to diminish and divide the strength of numbers, which he could in vain hope to defy?"

"Something further of intelligence has been gained, even within a very few hours," answered Achilles Tatius. "Bohemond came to the city with some six or eight light horse, and in a species of disguise. Considering how often he had been the Emperor's enemy, his project was a perilous one. But when is it that these Franks draw back on account of danger? The Emperor perceived at once that the Count was come to see what he might obtain, by presenting himself as the very first object of his liberality, and by offering his assistance as mediator with Godfrey of Bouillon and the other princes of the crusade."

"It is a species of policy," answered the sage, "for which he would receive full credit from the Emperor."

Achilles Tatius proceeded:—"Count Bohemond was discovered to the imperial court as if it were by mere accident, and he was welcomed with marks of favour and splendour which had never been even mentioned as being fit for any one of the Frankish race. There was no word of ancient enmity or of former wars, no mention of Bohemond as the ancient usurper of Antioch, and the encroacher upon the empire. But thanks to Heaven were returned on all sides, which had sent a faithful ally to the imperial assistance at a moment of such imminent peril."

"And what said Bohemond?" enquired the philosopher.

"Little or nothing," said the captain of the Varangians, "until, as I learned from the domestic slave Narses, a large sum of gold had been abandoned to him. Considerable districts were afterwards agreed to be ceded to him, and other advantages granted, on condition he should stand on this occasion the steady friend of the empire and its master. Such was the Emperor's munificence towards
the greedy barbarian, that a chamber in the palace was, by chance, as it were, left exposed to his view, containing large quantities of manufactured silks, of jewellers' work, of gold and silver, and other articles of great value. When the rapacious Frank could not forbear some expressions of admiration, he was assured, that the contents of the treasure–chamber were his own, provided he valued them as showing forth the warmth and sincerity of his imperial ally towards his friends; and these precious articles were accordingly conveyed to the tent of the Norman leader. By such measures, the Emperor must make himself master of Bohemond, both body and soul, for the Franks themselves say it is strange to see a man of undaunted bravery, and towering ambition, so infected, nevertheless, with avarice, which they term a mean and unnatural vice."

"Bohemond," said Agelastes, "is then the Emperor's for life and death—always, that is, till the recollection of the royal munificence be effaced by a greater gratuity. Alexius, proud as he naturally is of his management with this important chieftain, will no doubt expect to prevail by his counsels, on most of the other crusaders, and even on Godfrey of Bouillon himself, to take an oath of submission and fidelity to the Emperor, which, were it not for the sacred nature of their warfare, the meanest gentleman among them would not submit to, were it to be lord of a province. There, then, we rest. A few days must determine what we have to do. An earlier discovery would be destruction."

"We meet not then to–night?" said the Acolyte.

"No," replied the sage; "unless we are summoned to that foolish stage– play or recitation; and then we meet as playthings in the hand of a silly woman, the spoiled child of a weak–minded parent."

Tatius then took his leave of the philosopher, and, as if fearful of being seen in each other's company, they left their solitary place of meeting by different routes. The Varangian, Hereward, received, shortly after, a summons from his superior, who acquainted him, that he should not, as formerly intimated, require his attendance that evening.

Achilles then paused, and added,—"Thou hast something on thy lips thou wouldst say to me, which, nevertheless hesitates to break forth."

"It is only this," answered the soldier: "I have had an interview with the man called Agelastes, and he seems something so different from what he appeared when we last spoke of him, that I cannot forbear mentioning to you what I have seen. He is not an insignificant trifler, whose object it is to raise a laugh at his own expense, or that of any other. He is a deep–thinking and far–reaching man, who, for some reason or other, is desirous of forming friends, and drawing a party
to himself. Your own wisdom will teach you to beware of him."

"Thou art an honest fellow, my poor Hereward," said Achilles Tatius, with an affectation of good–natured contempt. "Such men as Agelastes do often frame their severest jests in the shape of formal gravity—they will pretend to possess the most unbounded power over elements and elemental spirits—they will make themselves masters of the names and anecdotes best known to those whom they make their sport; and any one who shall listen to them, shall, in the words of the Divine Homer, only expose himself to a flood of

inextinguishable laughter. I have often known him select one of the rawest and most ignorant persons in presence, and to him for the amusement of the rest, he has pretended to cause the absent to appear, the distant to draw near, and the dead themselves to burst the
cerements of the grave. Take care, Hereward, that his arts make not a stain on the credit of one of my bravest Varangians."

"There is no danger," answered Hereward. "I shall not be fond of being often with this man. If he jests upon one subject which he hath mentioned to me, I shall be but too likely to teach him seriousness after a rough manner. And if he is serious in his pretensions in such mystical matters, we should, according to the faith of my
grandfather, Kenelm, do insult to the deceased, whose name is taken in the mouth of a soothsayer, or impious enchanter. I will not, therefore, again go near this Agelastes, be he wizard, or be he impostor."

"You apprehend me not," said the Acolyte, hastily; "you mistake my meaning. He is a man from whom, if he pleases to converse with such as you, you may derive much knowledge; keeping out of the reach of those pretended secret arts, which he will only use to turn thee into ridicule." With these words, which he himself would perhaps have felt it difficult to reconcile, the leader and his follower parted.

CHAPTER THE NINTH

Between the foaming jaws of the white torrent, The
skilful artist draws a sudden mound;
By level long he subdivides their strength, Stealing
the waters from their rocky bed, First to diminish
what he means to conquer; Then, for the residue he
forms a road,
Easy to keep, and painful to desert,
And guiding to the end the planner aim'd at. THE
ENGINEER

It would have been easy for Alexius, by a course of avowed suspicion, or
any false step in the manner of receiving this tumultuary invasion of the
European nations, to have blown into a flame the numerous but smothered
grievances under which they
laboured; and a similar catastrophe would not have been less certain, had he at
once abandoned all thoughts of resistance, and placed his hope of safety in
surrendering to the multitudes of the west whatsoever they accounted worth
taking. The Emperor chose a middle course; and, unquestionably, in the
weakness of the Greek empire, it was the only one which would have given
him at once safety, and a great degree of consequence in the eyes of the Frank
invaders and those of his own subjects. The means with, which he acted were
of various kinds, and, rather from policy than inclination, were often stained
with falsehood or meanness; therefore it follows that the measures of the
Emperor resembled those of the snake, who twines himself through the grass,
with the purpose of stinging insidiously those whom he fears to approach with
the step of the
bold and generous lion. We are not, however, writing the History of the
Crusades, and what we have already said of the Emperor's precautions on the
first appearance of Godfrey of Bouillon, and his associates, may suffice for
the elucidation of our story.

About four weeks had now passed over, marked by quarrels and reconcilements between the crusaders and the Grecians of the empire. The former were, as Alexius's policy dictated, occasionally and individually, received with extreme honour, and their leaders loaded with respect and favour; while, from time to time, such bodies of them as sought distant or circuitous routes to the capital,
were intercepted and cut to pieces by light–armed troops, who easily passed upon their ignorant opponents for Turks, Scythians, or other infidels, and sometimes were actually such, but in the service of the Grecian monarch. Often, too, it happened, that while the more powerful chiefs of the crusade were feasted by the Emperor and his ministers with the richest delicacies, and their thirst slaked with iced wines, their followers were left at a distance, where, intentionally supplied with adulterated flour, tainted provisions, and bad water, they contracted diseases, and died in great numbers, without having once seen a foot of the Holy Land, for the recovery of which they had abandoned their peace, their competence, and their native country. These aggressions did not pass without complaint. Many of
the crusading chiefs impugned the fidelity of their allies, exposed the losses sustained by their armies as evils voluntarily inflicted on them by the Greeks, and on more than one occasion, the two nations stood opposed to each other on such terms that a general war seemed to be inevitable.

Alexius, however, though obliged to have recourse to every finesse, still kept his ground, and made peace with the most powerful chiefs, under one pretence or other. The actual losses of the crusaders by the sword he imputed to their own aggressions—their misguidance, to accident and to wilfulness—the effects produced on them by the adulterated provisions, to the vehemence of their own appetite for raw fruits and unripened wines. In short, there was no disaster of any kind whatsoever which could possibly befall the unhappy pilgrims, but the Emperor stood prepared to prove that it was the natural consequence of their own violence, wilfulness of conduct, or hostile precipitancy.

The chiefs, who were not ignorant of their strength, would not, it was likely, have tamely suffered injuries from a power so inferior to their own, were it not that they had formed extravagant ideas of the wealth of the Eastern empire, which Alexius seemed willing to share with them with an excess of bounty as new to the leaders as the rich productions of the East were tempting to their followers.

The French nobles would perhaps have been the most difficult to be brought into order when differences arose; but an accident, which the Emperor might have termed providential, reduced the high– spirited Count of Vermandois to the situation, of a suppliant, when he expected to hold that of a dictator. A fierce tempest surprised his fleet after he set sail from Italy, and he was finally driven on the coast of Greece. Many ships were destroyed, and those troops who got ashore were so much distressed, that they were obliged to surrender themselves to the lieutenants of Alexius. So that the Count of Vermandois, so haughty in his bearing when he first embarked, was sent to the court of Constantinople, not as a prince, but as a prisoner. In this case, the Emperor instantly set the soldiers at
liberty, and loaded them with presents. [Footnote: See Mills' History of the Crusades, vol. i, p. 96]

Grateful, therefore, for attentions in which Alexius was unremitting, Count Hugh was by gratitude as well as interest, inclined to join the opinion of those who, for other reasons, desired the subsistence of peace betwixt the crusaders and the empire of Greece. A better principle determined the celebrated Godfrey, Raymond of
Thoulouse, and some others, in whom devotion was something more than a mere burst of fanaticism. These princes considered with what scandal their whole journey must be stained, if the first of their exploits should be a war upon the Grecian empire, which might
justly be called the barrier of Christendom. If it was weak, and at the same time rich—if at the same time it invited rapine, and was unable to protect itself against it—it was the more their interest and duty, as Christian soldiers, to protect a Christian state, whose existence was
of so much consequence to the common cause, even when it could not defend itself. It was the wish of these frank–hearted men to receive the Emperor's professions of friendship with such sincere returns of amity—to return his kindness with so much usury, as to convince him that their purpose towards him was in every respect fair and honourable, and that it would be his interest to abstain from every injurious treatment which might induce or compel them to

alter their measures towards him.

It was with this accommodating spirit towards Alexius, which, for many different and complicated reasons, had now animated most of the crusaders, that the chiefs consented to a measure which, in other circumstances, they would probably have refused, as undue to the Greeks, and dishonourable to themselves. This was the famous resolution, that, before crossing the Bosphorus to go in quest of that Palestine which they had vowed to regain, each chief of crusaders would acknowledge individually the Grecian Emperor, originally lord paramount of all these regions, as their liege lord and suzerain.

The Emperor Alexius, with trembling joy, beheld the crusaders approach a conclusion to which he had hoped to bribe them rather by interested means than by reasoning, although much might be said why provinces reconquered from the Turks or Saracens should, if recovered from the infidel, become again a part of the Grecian empire, from which they had been rent without any pretence, save that of violence.

Though fearful, and almost despairing of being able to manage the rude and discordant army of haughty chiefs, who were wholly independent of each other, Alexius failed not, with eagerness and dexterity, to seize upon the admission of Godfrey and his compeers, that the Emperor was entitled to the allegiance of all who should war on Palestine, and natural lord paramount of all the conquests which should be made in the course of the expedition. He was resolved to make this ceremony so public, and to interest men's minds in it by such a display of the imperial pomp and munificence, that it should not either pass unknown, or be readily forgotten.

An extensive terrace, one of the numerous spaces which extend along the coast of the Propontis, was chosen for the site of the magnificent ceremony. Here was placed an elevated and august throne, calculated for the use of the Emperor alone. On this occasion, by suffering no other seats within view of the pageant, the
Greeks endeavoured to secure a point of ceremony peculiarly dear to their vanity, namely, that none of that presence, save the Emperor himself, should be seated. Around the throne of Alexius Comnenus

were placed in order, but standing, the various dignitaries of his splendid court, in their different ranks, from the Protosebastos and the Caesar, to the Patriarch, splendid in his ecclesiastical robes, and to Agelastes, who, in his simple habit, gave also the necessary attendance. Behind and around the splendid display of the Emperor's court, were drawn many dark circles of the exiled Anglo–Saxons. These, by their own desire, were not, on that memorable day, accoutred in the silver corslets which were the fashion of an idle court, but sheathed in mail and plate. They desired, they said, to be known as warriors to warriors. This was the more readily granted, as there was no knowing what trifle might infringe a truce between parties so inflammable as were now assembled.

Beyond the Varangians, in much greater numbers, were drawn up the bands of Grecians, or Romans, then known by the title of Immortals, which had been borrowed by the Romans originally from the empire of Persia. The stately forms, lofty crests, and splendid apparel of these guards, would have given the foreign princes
present a higher idea of their military prowess, had there not occurred in their ranks a frequent indication of loquacity and of motion, forming a strong contrast to the steady composure and death–like silence with which the well–trained Varangians stood in the parade, like statues made of iron.

The reader must then conceive this throne in all the pomp of Oriental greatness, surrounded by the foreign and Roman troops of the empire, and closed on the rear by clouds of light–horse, who shifted their places repeatedly, so as to convey an idea of their multitude, without affording the exact means of estimating it. Through the dust which they raised by these evolutions, might be seen banners and standards, among which could be discovered by glances, the celebrated LABARUM, [Footnote: Ducange fills half a column of his huge page with the mere names of the authors who have written at length on the *Labarum*, or principal standard of the empire for the time of Constantine. It consisted of a spear of silver, or plated with that metal, having suspended from, a cross beam below the spoke a small square silken banner, adorned with portraits of the reigning family, and over these the famous Monogram which expresses at once the figure of the cross and the initial letters of the name of

Christ. The bearer of the *Labarum* was an officer of high rank down to the last days of the Byzantine government.—See Gibbon, chap. 20.

Ducange seems to have proved, from the evidence of coins and triumphial monuments, that a standard of the form of the *Labarum* was used by various barbarous nations long before it was adopted by their Roman conquerors, and he is of opinion that its name also was borrowed from either Teutonic Germany, or Celtic Gaul, or Sclavonic Illyria. It is certain that either the German language or the Welsh may afford at this day a perfectly satisfactory etymon: *Lap– heer* in the former and *Lab–hair* in the latter, having precisely the same meaning— *the cloth of the host.*

The form of the *Labarum* may still be recognised in the banners carried in ecclesiastical processions in all Roman Catholic countries.] the pledge of conquest to the imperial banners, but whose sacred efficacy had somewhat failed of late days. The rude soldiers of the West, who viewed the Grecian army, maintained that the standards which were exhibited in front of their line, were at least sufficient for the array of ten times the number of soldiers.

Far on the right, the appearance of a very large body of European cavalry drawn up on the sea–shore, intimated the presence of the crusaders. So great was the desire to follow the example of the chief Princes, Dukes, and Counts, in making the proposed fealty, that the number of independent knights and nobles who were to perform this service, seemed very great when collected together for that purpose; for every crusader who possessed a tower, and led six lances, would have thought himself abridged of his dignity if he had not been called to acknowledge the Grecian Emperor, and hold the lands he should conquer of his throne, as well as Godfrey of Bouillon, or Hugh the Great, Count of Vermandois. And yet, with strange inconsistency, though they pressed to fulfil the homage, as that which was paid by greater persons than themselves, they seemed, at the very same time, desirous to find some mode of intimating that the homage which they rendered they felt as an idle degradation, and in fact held the whole show as a mere piece of mockery.

The order of the procession had been thus settled:—The Crusaders, or, as the Grecians called them, the *Counts*,—that being the most common title among them,—were to advance from the left of their body, and passing the Emperor one by one, were apprized, that, in passing, each was to render to him, in as few words as possible, the homage which had been previously agreed on. Godfrey of Bouillon, his brother Baldwin, Bohemond of Antioch, and several other crusaders of eminence, were the first to perform the ceremony, alighting when their own part was performed, and remaining in attendance by the Emperor's chair, to prevent, by the awe of their presence, any of their numerous associates from being guilty of petulance or presumption during the solemnity. Other crusaders of less degree retained their station near the Emperor, when they had once gained it, out of mere curiosity, or to show that they were as much at liberty to do so as the greater commanders who assumed that privilege.

Thus two great bodies of troops, Grecian and European, paused at some distance from each other on the banks of the Bosphorus canal, differing in language, arms, and appearance. The small troops of horse which from time to time issued forth from these bodies, resembled the flashes of lightning passing from one thunder–cloud to another, which communicate to each other by such emissaries their overcharged contents. After some halt on the margin of the Bosphorus, the Franks who had performed homage, straggled irregularly forward to a quay on the shore, where innumerable galleys and smaller vessels, provided for the purpose, lay with sails and oars prepared to waft the warlike pilgrims across the passage, and place them on that Asia which they longed so passionately to visit, and from which but few of them were likely to return. The gay appearance of the vessels which were to receive them, the readiness
with which they were supplied with refreshments, the narrowness of the strait they had to cross, the near approach of that active service which they had vowed and longed to discharge, put the warriors into gay spirits, and songs and music bore chorus to the departing oars.

While such was the temper of the crusaders, the Grecian Emperor did his best through the whole ceremonial to impress on the armed multitude the highest ideas of his own grandeur, and the importance of the occasion which had brought them together. This was readily admitted by the higher chiefs; some because their vanity had been propitiated,—some because their avarice had been gratified,—some because their ambition had been inflamed,—and a few, a very few, because to remain friends with Alexius was the most probable means of advancing the purposes of their expedition. Accordingly the great lords, from these various motives, practised a humility which

perhaps they were far from feeling, and carefully abstained from all which might seem like irreverence at the solemn festival of the Grecians. But there were very many of a different temper.

Of the great number of counts, lords, and knights, under whose variety of banners the crusaders were led to the walls of Constantinople, many were too insignificant to be bribed to this distasteful measure of homage; and these, though they felt it dangerous to oppose resistance, yet mixed their submission with taunts, ridicule, and such contraventions of decorum, as plainly intimated that they entertained resentment and scorn at the step they were about to take, and esteemed it as proclaiming themselves vassals to a prince, heretic in his faith, limited in the exercise of his boasted power, their enemy when he dared to show himself such, and the friend of those only among their number, who were able to compel him to be so; and who, though to them an obsequious ally, was to the others, when occasion offered, an insidious and murderous enemy.

The nobles of Frankish origin and descent were chiefly remarkable for their presumptuous contempt of every other nation engaged in the crusade, as well as for their dauntless bravery, and for the scorn with which they regarded the power and authority of the Greek empire. It was a common saying among them, that if the skies should fall, the French crusaders alone were able to hold them up with their lances. The same bold and arrogant disposition showed itself in occasional quarrels with their unwilling hosts, in which the Greeks, notwithstanding all their art, were often worsted; so that Alexius was determined, at all events, to get rid of these intractable and fiery allies, by ferrying them over the Bosphorus with all

manner of diligence. To do this with safety, he availed himself of the presence of the Count of Vermandois, Godfrey of Bouillon, and other chiefs of great influence, to keep in order the lesser Frankish knights, who were so numerous and unruly. [Footnote: See Mills, vol. i. chap. 3.]

Struggling with his feelings of offended pride, tempered by a prudent degree of apprehension, the Emperor endeavoured to receive with complacence a homage tendered in mockery. An incident shortly took place of a character highly descriptive of the nations brought together in so extraordinary a manner, and with such different feelings and sentiments. Several bands of French had passed, in a sort of procession, the throne of the Emperor, and rendered, with some appearance of gravity, the usual homage. On this occasion they bent their knees to Alexius, placed their hands within his, and in that posture paid the ceremonies of feudal fealty. But when it came to the turn of Bohemond of Antioch, already mentioned, to render this fealty, the Emperor, desirous to show every species of honour to this wily person, his former enemy, and now apparently his ally, advanced two or three paces towards the sea– side, where the boats lay as if in readiness for his use.

The distance to which the Emperor moved was very small, and it was assumed as a piece of deference to Bohemond; but it became the means of exposing Alexius himself to a cutting affront, which his guards and subjects felt deeply, as an intentional humiliation. A half score of horsemen, attendants of the Frankish Count who was next to perform the homage, with their lord at their head, set off at full gallop from the right flank of the French squadrons, and arriving before the throne, which was yet empty, they at once halted. The rider at the head of the band was a strong herculean figure, with a decided and stern countenance, though extremely handsome, looking out from thick black curls. His head was surmounted with a barret cap, while his hands, limbs, and feet were covered with garments of chamois leather, over which he in general wore the ponderous and complete armour of his country. This, however, he had laid aside for personal convenience, though in doing so he evinced a total neglect of the ceremonial which marked so important a meeting. He waited not a moment for the Emperor's return, nor regarded the impropriety of obliging Alexius to hurry his steps back to his throne, but sprung from his gigantic horse, and threw the reins loose, which were instantly seized by one of the attendant pages. Without a moment's hesitation the Frank seated himself in the vacant throne of the Emperor, and extending his half–armed and robust figure on the golden cushions which were destined for Alexius, he indolently began to caress a large wolf–hound which had followed him, and which, feeling itself as much at ease as its master, reposed its grim form on the carpets of silk and gold damask, which tapestried the imperial foot–stool. The very hound stretched itself with a bold, ferocious insolence, and seemed to regard no one with respect, save the stern knight whom it called master.

The Emperor, turning back from the short space which, as a special mark of favour, he had accompanied Bohemond, beheld with astonishment his seat occupied by this insolent Frank. The bands of the half–savage Varangians who were stationed around, would not have hesitated an instant in avenging the insult, by prostrating the violator of their master's throne even in this act of his contempt, had they not been restrained by Achilles Tatius and other officers, who were uncertain what the Emperor would do, and somewhat timorous of taking a resolution for themselves.

Meanwhile, the unceremonious knight spoke aloud, in a speech which, though provincial, might be understood by all to whom the French language was known, while even those who understood it not, gathered its interpretation from his tone and manner. "What churl is this," he said, "who has remained sitting stationary like a block of wood, or the fragment of a rock, when so many noble knights, the flower of chivalry and muster of gallantry, stand uncovered around, among the thrice conquered Varangians?"

A deep, clear accent replied, as if from the bottom of the earth, so like it was to the accents of some being from the other world,—"If the Normans desire battle of the Varangians, they will meet them in the lists man to man, without the poor boast of insulting the Emperor of Greece, who is well known to fight only by the battle–axes of his guard."

The astonishment was so great when this answer was heard, as to affect even the knight, whose insult upon the Emperor had occasioned it; and amid the efforts of Achilles to retain his soldiers within the bounds of subordination and silence, a loud murmur seemed to intimate that they would not long remain so. Bohemond returned through the press with a celerity which did not so well suit the dignity of Alexius, and catching the crusader by the arm, he, something between fair means and a gentle degree of force, obliged him to leave the chair of the Emperor, in which he had placed himself so boldly.

"How is it," said Bohemond, "noble Count of Paris? Is there one of this great assembly who can see with patience, that your name, so widely renowned for valour, is now to be quoted in an idle brawl with hirelings, whose utmost boast it is to bear a mercenary battle– axe in the ranks of the Emperor's guards? For shame—for shame— do not, for the discredit of Norman chivalry, let it be so!"

"I know not," said the crusader, rising reluctantly—"I am not nice in choosing the degree of my adversary, when he bears himself like one who is willing and forward in battle. I am good–natured, I tell thee, Count Bohemond; and Turk or Tartar, or wandering Anglo–Saxon, who only escapes from the chain of the Normans to become the
slave of the Greek, is equally welcome to whet his blade clean against my armour, if he desires to achieve such an honourable office."

The Emperor had heard what passed—had heard it with indignation, mixed with fear; for he imagined the whole scheme of his policy was about to be overturned at once by a premeditated plan of personal affront, and probably an assault upon his person. He was about to
call to arms, when, casting his eyes on the right flank of the crusaders, he saw that all remained quiet after the Frank Baron had transferred himself from thence. He therefore instantly resolved to let the insult pass, as one of the rough pleasantries of the Franks, since the advance of more troops did not give any symptom of an actual onset.

Resolving on his line of conduct with the quickness of thought, he glided back to his canopy, and stood beside his throne, of which, however, he chose not instantly to take possession, lest he should give the insolent stranger some ground for renewing and persisting in a competition for it.

"What bold Vavasour is this," said he to Count Baldwin, "whom, as is apparent from his dignity, I ought to have received seated upon my throne, and who thinks proper thus to vindicate his rank?"

"He is reckoned one of the bravest men in our host," answered Baldwin, "though the brave are as numerous there as the sands of the sea. He will himself tell you his name and rank."

Alexius looked at the Vavasour. He saw nothing in his large, well– formed features, lighted by a wild touch of enthusiasm which spoke in his quick eye, that intimated premeditated insult, and was induced to suppose that what had occurred, so contrary to the form and ceremonial of the Grecian court, was neither an intentional affront, nor designed as the means of introducing a quarrel. He therefore spoke with comparative ease, when he addressed the stranger thus:
—"We know not by what dignified name to salute you: but we are aware, from Count Baldwin's information, that we are honoured in having in our presence one of the bravest knights whom a sense of the wrongs done to the Holy Land has brought thus far on his way to Palestine, to free it from its bondage."

"If you mean to ask my name," answered the European knight, "any one of these pilgrims can readily satisfy you, and more gracefully than I can myself; since we use to say in our country, that many a fierce quarrel is prevented from being fought out by an untimely disclosure of names, when men, who might have fought with the fear of God before their eyes, must, when their names are manifested, recognise each other as spiritual allies, by baptism, gossipred, or some such irresistible bond of friendship; whereas, had they fought first and told their names afterwards, they could have had some assurance of each other's valour, and have been able to view their relationship as an honour to both."

"Still," said the Emperor, "methinks I would know if you, who, in this extraordinary press of knights, seem to assert a precedence to yourself, claim the dignity due to a king or prince?"

"How speak you that?" said the Frank, with a brow somewhat over– clouded; "do you feel that I have not left you unjostled by my advance to these squadrons of yours?"

Alexius hastened to answer, that he felt no particular desire to connect the Count with an affront or offence; observing, that in the extreme necessity of the Empire, it was no time for him, who was at the helm, to engage in idle or unnecessary quarrels.

The Frankish knight heard him, and answered drily—"Since such are your sentiments, I wonder that you have ever resided long enough within the hearing of the French language to learn to speak it as you do. I would have thought some of the sentiments of the chivalry of the nation, since you are neither a monk nor a woman, would, at the same time with the words of the dialect, have found their way into your heart." "Hush, Sir Count," said Bohemond, who remained by
the Emperor to avert the threatening quarrel. "It is surely requisite to answer the Emperor with civility; and those who are impatient for warfare, will have infidels enough to wage it with. He only
demanded your name and lineage, which you of all men can have the least objection to disclose."

"I know not if it will interest this prince, or Emperor as you term him," answered the Frank Count; "but all the account I can give of myself is this:— In the midst of one of the vast forests which, occupy the centre of France, my native country, there stands a chapel, sunk so low into the ground, that it seems as if it were become decrepid
by its own great age. The image of the Holy Virgin who presides over its altar, is called by all men our Lady of the Broken Lances, and is accounted through the whole kingdom the most celebrated for military adventures. Four beaten roads, each leading from an opposite point in the compass, meet before the principal door of the chapel; and ever and anon, as a good knight arrives at this place, he passes in to the performance of his devotions in the chapel, having first sounded his horn three times, till ash and oak–tree quiver and ring. Having then kneeled down to his devotions, he seldom arises from the mass of Her of the Broken Lances, but there is attending on his leisure some adventurous knight ready to satisfy the new comer's desire of battle. This station have I held for a month and more

against all comers, and all gave me fair thanks for the knightly manner of quitting myself towards them, except one, who had the evil hap to fall from his horse, and did break his neck; and another, who was struck through the body, so that the lance came out behind his back about a cloth–yard, all dripping with blood. Allowing for such accidents, which cannot easily be avoided, my opponents parted with me with fair acknowledgment of the grace I had done them."

"I conceive, Sir Knight," said the Emperor, "that a form like yours, animated by the courage you display, is likely to find few equals even among your adventurous countrymen; far less among men who are taught that to cast away their lives in a senseless quarrel among themselves, is to throw away, like a boy, the gift of Providence."

"You are welcome to your opinion," said the Frank, somewhat contemptuously; "yet I assure you, if you doubt that our gallant strife was unmixed with sullenness and anger, and that we hunt not the hart or the boar with merrier hearts in the evening, than we discharge our task of chivalry by the morn had arisen, before the portal of the old chapel, you do us foul injustice."

"With the Turks you will not enjoy this amiable exchange of courtesies," answered Alexius. "Wherefore I would advise you neither to stray far into the van nor into the rear, but to abide by the standard where the best infidels make their efforts, and the best knights are required to repel them."

"By our Lady of the Broken Lances," said the Crusader, "I would not that the Turks were more courteous than they are Christian, and am well pleased that unbeliever and heathen hound are a proper description for the best of them, as being traitor alike to their God and to the laws of chivalry; and devoutly do I trust that I shall meet with them in the front rank of our army, beside our standard, or elsewhere, and have an open field to my devoir against them, both as the enemies of our Lady and the holy saints, and as, by their evil customs, more expressly my own. Meanwhile you have time to seat yourself and receive my homage, and I will be bound to you for despatching this foolish ceremony with as little waste and delay of time as the occasion will permit."

The Emperor hastily seated himself, and received into his the sinewy hands of the Crusader, who made the acknowledgment of his homage, and was then guided off by Count Baldwin, who walked with the stranger to the ships, and then, apparently well pleased at seeing him in the course of going on board, returned back to the side of the Emperor.

"What is the name," said the Emperor, "of that singular and assuming man?"

"It is Robert, Count of Paris," answered Baldwin, "accounted one of the bravest peers who stand around the throne of France."

After a moment's recollection, Alexius Comnenus issued orders, that the ceremonial of the day should be discontinued, afraid, perhaps, lest the rough and careless humour of the strangers should produce some new quarrel. The crusaders were led, nothing loth, back to palaces in which they had been hospitably received, and readily resumed the interrupted feast, from which they had been called to pay their homage. The trumpets of the various leaders blew the
recall of the few troops of an ordinary character who were attendant, together with the host of knights and leaders, who, pleased with the indulgences provided for them, and obscurely foreseeing that the passage of the Bosphorus would be the commencement of their actual suffering, rejoiced in being called to the hither side.

It was not probably intended; but the hero, as he might be styled, of the tumultuous day, Count Robert of Paris, who was already on his road to embarkation on the strait, was disturbed in his purpose by the sound of recall which was echoed around; nor could Bohemond, Godfrey, or any one who took upon him to explain the signal, alter his resolution of returning to Constantinople. He laughed to scorn
the threatened displeasure of the Emperor, and seemed to think there would be a peculiar pleasure in braving Alexius at his own board, or, at least, that nothing could be more indifferent than whether he gave offence or not.

To Godfrey of Bouillon, to whom he showed some respect, he was still far from paying deference; and that sagacious prince, having used every argument which might shake his purpose of returning to the imperial city, to the very point of making it a quarrel with him in person, at length abandoned him to his own discretion, and pointed him out to the Count of Thoulouse, as he passed, as a wild knight– errant, incapable of being influenced by any thing save his own wayward fancy. "He brings not five hundred men to the crusade," said Godfrey; "and I dare be sworn, that even in this, the very outset of the undertaking, he knows not where these five hundred men are, and how their wants are provided for. There is an eternal trumpet in his ear sounding to assault, nor has he room or time to hear a milder or more rational signal. See how he strolls along yonder, the very emblem of an idle schoolboy, broke out of the school–bounds upon a holyday, half animated by curiosity and half by love of mischief."

"And," said Raymond, Count of Thoulouse, "with resolution sufficient to support the desperate purpose of the whole army of devoted crusaders. And yet so passionate a Rodomont is Count Robert, that he would rather risk the success of the whole expedition, that omit an opportunity of meeting a worthy antagonist *en champ– clos*, or lose, as he terms it, a chance of worshipping our Lady of the Broken Lances. Who are yon with whom he has now met, and who are apparently walking, or rather strolling in the same way with him, back to Constantinople?"

"An armed knight, brilliantly equipped—yet of something less than knightly stature," answered Godfrey. "It is, I suppose, the celebrated lady who won Robert's heart in the lists of battle, by bravery and valour equal to his own; and the pilgrim form in the long vestments may be their daughter or niece."

"A singular spectacle, worthy Knight," said the Count of Thoulouse, "do our days present to us, to which we have had nothing similar, since Gaita, [Footnote: This Amazon makes a conspicuous figure in Anna Comnena's account of her father's campaigns against Robert Guiscard. On one occasion (Alexiad, lib. iv. p. 93) she represents her as thus recalling the fugitive soldiery of her husband to their duty,— [Greek: Hae de ge Taita Aeallas allae, kan mae Athaenae kat auton megisaen apheisa phonaen, monon ou to Homaerikon epos tae idia dialektio legein eokei. Mechri posou pheuxesthou; ataete aneres ese. Hos de eti pheugontas toutous eora, dory makron enagkalisamenae, holous rhytaeras endousa kata ton pheugonton ietai].—That is, exhorting them, in all but Homeric language, at the top of her voice; and when this failed, brandishing a long spear, and rushing upon the fugitives at the utmost speed of her horse.

This heroic lady, according to the *Chronigue Scandaleuse*, of those days, was afterwards deluded by some cunning overtures of the Greek Emperor, and poisoned her husband in expectation of gaining a place on the throne of Constantinople. Ducange, however, rejects the story, and so does Gibbon.] wife of Robert Guiscard, first took upon her to distinguish herself by manly deeds of emprise, and rival her husband, as well in the front of battle as at the dancing–room or banquet."

"Such is the custom of this pair, most noble knight," answered another Crusader, who had joined them, "and Heaven pity the poor man who has no power to keep domestic peace by an appeal to the stronger hand!"

"Well!" replied Raymond, "if it be rather a mortifying reflection, that the lady of our love is far past the bloom of youth, it is a consolation that she is too old–fashioned to beat us, when we return back with no more of youth or manhood than a long crusade has left. But come, follow on the road to Constantinople, and in the rear of this most doughty knight."

CHAPTER THE TENTH

Those were wild times—the antipodes of ours: Ladies
were there, who oftener saw themselves In the broad
lustre of a foeman's shield
Than in a mirror, and who rather sought
To match themselves in battle, than in dalliance To meet
a lover's onset.—But though Nature Was outraged thus,
she was not overcome. FEUDAL TIMES.

Brenhilda, Countess of Paris, was one of those stalwart dames who willingly hazarded themselves in the front of battle, which, during the first crusade, was as common as it was possible for a very unnatural custom to be, and, in fact, gave the real instances of the
Marphisas and Bradamantes, whom the writers of romance delighted to paint, assigning them sometimes the advantage of invulnerable armour, or a spear whose thrust did not admit of being resisted, in order to soften the improbability of the weaker sex being frequently victorious over the male part of the creation.

But the spell of Brenhilda was of a more simple nature, and rested chiefly in her great beauty.

From a girl she despised the pursuits of her sex; and they who ventured to become suitors for the hand of the young Lady of Aspramonte, to which warlike fief she had succeeded, and which perhaps encouraged her in her fancy, received for answer, that they must first merit it by their good behaviour in the lists. The father of Brenhilda was dead; her mother was of a gentle temper, and easily kept under management by the young lady herself.

Brenhilda's numerous suitors readily agreed to terms which were too much according to the manners of the age to be disputed. A tournament was held at the Castle of Aspramonte, in which one half of the gallant assembly rolled headlong before their successful rivals, and withdrew from the lists mortified and disappointed. The successful party among the suitors were expected to be summoned to joust among themselves. But they were surprised at being made acquainted with the lady's further will. She aspired to wear armour herself, to wield a lance, and back a steed, and prayed the knights

that they would permit a lady, whom they professed to honour so highly, to mingle in their games of chivalry. The young knights courteously received their young mistress in the lists, and smiled at the idea of her holding them triumphantly against so many gallant champions of the other sex. But the vassals and old servants of the Count, her father, smiled to each other, and intimated a different result than the gallants anticipated. The knights who encountered the fair Brenhilda were one by one stretched on the sand; nor was it to

be denied, that the situation of tilting with one of the handsomest women of the time was an extremely embarrassing one. Each youth was bent to withhold his charge in full volley, to cause his steed to swerve at the full shock, or in some other way to flinch from doing the utmost which was necessary to gain the victory, lest, in so gaining it, he might cause irreparable injury to the beautiful opponent he tilted with. But the Lady of Aspramonte was not one who could be conquered by less than the exertion of the whole strength and talents of the victor. The defeated suitors departed from the lists the more mortified at their discomfiture, because Robert of Paris arrived at sunset, and, understanding what was going forward, sent his name to the barriers, as that of a knight who would willingly forego the reward of the tournament, in case he had the fortune to gain it, declaring, that neither lauds nor ladies' charms were what he came thither to seek. Brenhilda, piqued and mortified, chose a new lance, mounted her best steed, and advanced into the lists as one determined to avenge upon the new assailant's brow the slight of her charms which he seemed to express. But whether her displeasure had somewhat interfered with her usual skill, or whether she had, like others of her sex, felt a partiality towards one whose heart was not particularly set upon gaining hers—or whether, as is often said on such occasions, her fated hour was come, so it was that Count

Robert tilted with his usual address and good fortune. Brenhilda of Aspramonte was unhorsed and unhelmed, and stretched on the earth, and the beautiful face, which faded from very red to deadly pale

before the eyes of the victor, produced its natural effect in raising the value of his conquest. He would, in conformity with his resolution, have left the castle after having mortified the vanity of the lady; but her mother opportunely interposed; and when she had satisfied herself that no serious injury had been sustained by the young
heiress, she returned her thanks to the stranger knight who had
taught her daughter a lesson, which, she trusted, she would not easily forget. Thus tempted to do what he secretly wished, Count Robert gave ear to those sentiments, which naturally whispered to him to be in no hurry to withdraw.

He was of the blood of Charlemagne, and, what was still of more consequence in the young lady's eyes, one of the most renowned of Norman knights in that jousting day. After a residence of ten days in the castle of Aspramonte, the bride and bridegroom set out, for such was Count Robert's will, with a competent train, to our Lady of the Broken Lances, where it pleased him to be wedded. Two knights who were waiting to do battle, as was the custom of the place, were rather disappointed at the nature of the cavalcade, which seemed to interrupt their purpose. But greatly were they surprised when they received a cartel from the betrothed couple, offering to substitute their own persons in the room of other antagonists, and congratulating themselves in commencing their married life in a manner so consistent with that which they had hitherto led. They
were victorious as usual; and the only persons having occasion to rue the complaisance of the Count and his bride, were the two strangers, one of whom broke an arm in the rencontre, and the other dislocated
a collar–bone.

Count Robert's course of knight–errantry did not seem to be in the least intermitted by his marriage; on the contrary, when he was called upon to support his renown, his wife was often known also in military exploits, nor was she inferior to him in thirst after fame. They both assumed the cross at the same time, that being then the predominating folly in Europe.

The Countess Brenhilda was now above six–and–twenty years old, with as much beauty as can well fall to the share of an Amazon. A figure, of the largest feminine size, was surmounted by a noble countenance, to which even repeated warlike toils had not given more than a sunny hue, relieved by the dazzling whiteness of such parts of her face as were not usually displayed.

As Alexius gave orders that his retinue should return to Constantinople, he spoke in private to the Follower, Achilles Tatius. The Satrap answered with a submissive bend of the head, and separated with a few attendants from the main body of the Emperor's train. The principal road to the city was, of course, filled with the troops, and with the numerous crowds of spectators, all of whom were inconvenienced in some degree by the dust and heat of the weather.

Count Robert of Paris had embarked his horses on board of ship, and all his retinue, except an old squire or valet of his own, and an attendant of his wife. He felt himself more incommoded in this
crowd than he desired, especially as his wife shared it with him, and began to look among the scattered trees which fringed the shores, down almost to the tide–mark, to see if he could discern any by–path which might carry them more circuitously, but more pleasantly, to
the city, and afford them at the same time, what was their principal object in the East, strange sights, or adventures of chivalry. A broad and beaten path seemed to promise them all the enjoyment which shade could give in a warm climate. The ground through which it wound its way was beautifully broken by the appearance of temples, churches, and kiosks, and here and there a fountain distributed its silver produce, like a benevolent individual, who, self–denying to himself, is liberal to all others who are in necessity. The distant sound of the martial music still regaled their way; and, at the same time, as it detained the populace on the high–road, prevented the strangers from becoming incommoded with fellow–travellers.

Rejoicing in the abated heat of the day–wondering, at the same time, at the various kinds of architecture, the strange features of the landscape, or accidental touches of manners, exhibited by those who met or passed them upon their journey, they strolled easily onwards. One figure particularly caught the attention of the Countess Brenhilda. This was an old man of great stature, engaged,
apparently, so deeply with the roll of parchment which he held in his

hand, that he paid no attention to the objects which were passing around him. Deep thought appeared to reign on his brow, and his eye was of that piercing kind which seems designed to search and winnow the frivolous from the edifying part of human discussion,

and limit its inquiry to the last. Raising his eyes slowly from the parchment on which he had been gazing, the look of Agelastes—for it was the sage himself—encountered those of Count Robert and his lady, and addressing them, with the kindly epithet of "my children," he asked if they had missed their road, or whether there was any thing in which he could do them any pleasure.

"We are strangers, father," was the answer, "from a distant country, and belonging to the army which has passed hither upon pilgrimage; one object brings us here in common, we hope, with all that host.

We desire to pay our devotions where the great ransom was paid for us, and to free, by our good swords, enslaved Palestine, from the usurpation and tyranny of the infidel. When we have said this, we have announced our highest human motive. Yet Robert of Paris and his Countess would not willingly set their foot on a land, save what should resound its echo. They have not been accustomed to move in silence upon the face of the earth, and they would purchase an eternal life of fame, though it were at the price of mortal existence."

"You seek, then, to barter safety for fame," said Agelastes, "though you may, perchance, throw death into the scale by which you hope to gain it?"

"Assuredly," said Count Robert; "nor is there one wearing such a belt as this, to whom such a thought is stranger."

"And as I understand," said Agelastes, "your lady shares with your honourable self in these valorous resolutions?—Can this be?"

"You may undervalue my female courage, father, if such is your will," said the Countess; "but I speak in presence of a witness who can attest the truth, when I say that a man of half your years had not doubted the truth with impunity."

"Nay, Heaven protect me from the lightning of your eyes," said Agelastes, "whether in anger or in scorn. I bear an aegis about myself against what I should else have feared. But age, with its incapacities, brings also its apologies. Perhaps, indeed, it is one like me whom you seek to find, and in that case I should be happy to render to you such services as it is my duty to offer to all worthy knights."

"I have already said," replied Count Robert, "that after the accomplishment of my vow,"—he looked upwards and crossed himself,— "there is nothing on earth to which I am more bound than to celebrate my name in arms as becomes a valiant cavalier. When men die obscurely, they die for ever. Had my ancestor Charles never left the paltry banks of the Saale, he had not now been much better known than any vine– dresser who wielded his pruning–hook in the same territories. But he bore him like a brave man, and his name is deathless in the memory of the worthy."

"Young man," said the old Grecian, "although it is but seldom that such as you, whom I was made to serve and to value, visit this country, it is not the less true that I am well qualified to serve you in the matter which you have so much at heart. My acquaintance with nature has been so perfect and so long, that, during its continuance, she has disappeared, and another world has been spread before me,
in which she has but little to do. Thus the curious stores which I have assembled are beyond the researches of other men, and not to be laid before those whose deeds of valour are to be bounded by the
ordinary probabilities of everyday nature. No romancer of your romantic country ever devised such extraordinary adventures out of his own imagination, and to feed the idle wonder of those who sat listening around, as those which I know, not of idle invention, but of real positive existence, with the means of achieving and accomplishing the conditions of each adventure."

"If such be your real profession," said the French Count, "you have met one of those whom you chiefly search for; nor will my Countess and I stir farther upon our road until you have pointed out to us some one of those adventures which, it is the business of errant–knights to be industrious in seeking out."

So saying, he sat down by the side of the old man; and his lady, with a degree of reverence which had something in it almost diverting, followed his example.

"We have fallen right, Brenhilda," said Count Robert; "our guardian. angel has watched his charge carefully. Here have we come among an, ignorant set of pedants, chattering their absurd language, and holding more important the least look that a cowardly Emperor can give, than the best blow that a good knight can deal. Believe me, I was wellnigh thinking that we had done ill to take the cross—God forgive such an impious doubt! Yet here, when we were even despairing to find the road to fame, we have met with one of those excellent men whom the knights of yore were wont to find sitting by springs, by crosses, and by altars, ready to direct the wandering knight where fame was to be found. Disturb him not, my Brenhilda," said the Count, "but let him recall to himself his stories of the
ancient time, and thou shalt see he will enrich us with the treasures of his information."

"If," replied Agelastes, after some pause, "I have waited for a longer term than human life is granted to most men, I shall still be overpaid by dedicating what remains of existence to the service of a pair so devoted to chivalry. What first occurs to me is a story of our Greek country, so famous in adventures, and which I shall briefly detail to you:—

"Afar hence, in our renowned Grecian Archipelago, amid storms and whirlpools, rocks which, changing their character, appear to precipitate themselves against each other, and billows that are never in a pacific state, lies the rich island of Zulichium, inhabited, notwithstanding its wealth, by a very few natives, who live only
upon the sea–coast. The inland part of the island is one immense mountain, or pile of mountains, amongst which, those who dare approach near enough, may, we are assured, discern the moss–grown and antiquated towers and pinnacles of a stately, but ruinous castle, the habitation of the sovereign of the island, in which she has been, enchanted for a great many years.

"A bold knight, who came upon, a pilgrimage to Jerusalem, made a vow to deliver this unhappy victim of pain and sorcery; feeling, with

justice, vehemently offended, that the fiends of darkness should exercise any authority near the Holy Land, which might be termed the very fountain of light. Two of the oldest inhabitants of the island undertook to guide him as near to the main gate as they durst, nor
did they approach it more closely than the length of a bow–shot. Here, then, abandoned to himself, the brave Frank set forth upon his enterprise, with a stout heart, and Heaven alone to friend. The fabric which he approached showed, by its gigantic size, and splendour of outline, the power and wealth of the potentate who had erected it. The brazen gates unfolded themselves as if with hope and pleasure; and aerial voices swept around the spires and turrets, congratulating the genius of the place, it might be, upon the expected approach of its deliverer.

"The knight passed on, not unmoved with wonder, though untainted by fear; and the Gothic splendours which he saw were of a kind highly to exalt his idea of the beauty of the mistress for whom a prison–house had been so richly decorated. Guards there were in Eastern dress and arms, upon bulwark and buttress, in readiness, it appeared, to bend their bows; but the warriors were motionless and silent, and took no more notice of the armed step of the knight than if a monk or hermit had approached their guarded post. They were living, and yet, as to all power and sense, they might be considered among the dead. If there was truth in the old tradition, the sun had shone and the rain had fallen upon them for more than four hundred changing seasons, without their being sensible of the genial warmth of the one or the coldness of the other. Like the Israelites in the desert, their shoes had not decayed, nor their vestments waxed old. As Time left them, so and without alteration was he again to find
them." The philosopher began now to recall what he had heard of the cause of their enchantment.

"The sage to whom this potent charm is imputed, was one of the
Magi who followed the tenets of Zoroaster. He had come to the court of this youthful Princess, who received him with every attention which gratified vanity could dictate, so that in a short time her awe
of this grave personage was lost in the sense of ascendency which her beauty gave her over him. It was no difficult matter—in fact it happens every day—for the beautiful woman to lull the wise man

into what is not inaptly called a fool's paradise. The sage was induced to attempt feats of youth which his years rendered ridiculous; he could command the elements, but the common course of nature was beyond his power. When, therefore, he exerted his magic strength, the mountains bent and the seas receded; but when the philosopher attempted to lead forth the Princess of Zulichium in the youthful dance, youths and maidens turned their heads aside lest they should make too manifest the ludicrous ideas with which they were impressed.

"Unhappily, as the aged, even the wisest of them, will forget themselves, so the young naturally enter into an alliance to spy out, ridicule, and enjoy their foibles. Many were the glances which the Princess sent among her retinue, intimating the nature of the amusement which she received from the attentions of her formidable lover. In process of time she lost her caution, and a glance was detected, expressing to the old man the ridicule and contempt in which he had been all along held by the object of his affections.
Earth has no passion so bitter as love converted to hatred; and while the sage bitterly regretted what he had done, he did not the less resent the light–hearted folly of the Princess by whom he had been duped.

"If, however, he was angry, he possessed the art to conceal it. Not a word, not a look expressed the bitter disappointment which he had received. A shade of melancholy, or rather gloom, upon his brow, alone intimated the coming storm. The Princess became somewhat alarmed; she was besides extremely good–natured, nor had her intentions of leading the old man into what would render him ridiculous, been so accurately planned with malice prepense, as they were the effect of accident and chance. She saw the pain which he suffered, and thought to end it by going up to him, when about to retire, and kindly wishing him good– night.

"'You say well, daughter,' said the sage, 'good–night—but who, of the numbers who hear me, shall say good–morning?'

"The speech drew little attention, although two or three persons to whom the character of the sage was known, fled from the island that very night, and by their report made known the circumstances attending the first infliction of this extraordinary spell on those who remained within the Castle. A sleep like that of death fell upon them, and was not removed. Most of the inhabitants left the island; the few who remained were cautious how they approached the Castle, and watched until some bold adventurer should bring that happy awakening which the speech of the sorcerer seemed in some degree to intimate.

"Never seemed there a fairer opportunity for that awakening to take place than when the proud step of Artavan de Hautlieu was placed upon those enchanted courts. On the left, lay the palace and donjon– keep; but the right, more attractive, seemed to invite to the apartment of the women. At a side door, reclined on a couch, two guards of the haram, with their naked swords grasped in their hands, and features fiendishly contorted between sleep and dissolution, seemed to menace death to any who should venture to approach. This threat deterred not Artavan de Hautlieu. He approached the entrance, when the doors, like those of the great entrance to the Castle, made themselves instantly accessible to him. A guard–room of the same effeminate soldiers received him, nor could the strictest examination have discovered to him whether it was sleep or death which arrested the eyes that seemed to look upon and prohibit his advance. Unheeding the presence of these ghastly sentinels, Artavan pressed forward into an inner apartment, where female slaves of the most distinguished beauty were visible in the attitude of those who had already assumed their dress for the night. There was much in this scene which might have arrested so young a pilgrim as Artavan of Hautlieu; but his heart was fixed on achieving the freedom of the beautiful Princess, nor did he suffer himself to be withdrawn from that object by any inferior consideration. He passed on, therefore, to
a little ivory door, which, after a moment's pause, as if in maidenly hesitation, gave way like the rest, and yielded access to the sleeping apartment of the Princess herself. A soft light, resembling that of evening, penetrated into a chamber where every thing seemed contrived to exalt the luxury of slumber. The heaps of cushions, which formed a stately bed, seemed rather to be touched than impressed by the form of a nymph of fifteen, the renowned Princess of Zulichium."

"Without interrupting you, good father," said the Countess Brenhilda, "it seems to me that we can comprehend the picture of a woman asleep without much dilating upon it, and that such a subject is little recommended either by our age or by yours."

"Pardon me, noble lady," answered Agelastes, "the most approved part of my story has ever been this passage, and while I now suppress it in obedience to your command, bear notice, I pray you, that I sacrifice the most beautiful part of the tale."

"Brenhilda," added the Count, "I am surprised you think of interrupting a story which has hitherto proceeded with so much fire; the telling of a few words more or less will surely have a much greater influence upon, the sense of the narrative, than such an addition can possibly possess over our sentiments of action."

"As you will," said his lady, throwing herself carelessly back upon the seat; "but methinks the worthy father protracts this discourse, till it becomes of a nature more trifling than interesting."

"Brenhilda," said the Count, "this is the first time I have remarked in you a woman's weakness."

"I may as well say, Count Robert, that it is the first time," answered Brenhilda, "that you have shown to me the inconstancy of your sex."

"Gods and goddesses," said the philosopher, "was ever known a quarrel more absurdly founded! The Countess is jealous of one whom her husband probably never will see, nor is there any prospect that the Princess of Zulichium will be hereafter better known, to the modern world, than if the curtain hung before her tomb."

"Proceed," said Count Robert of Paris; "if Sir Artavan of Hautlieu has not accomplished the enfranchisement of the Princess of Zulichium, I make a vow to our Lady of the Broken Lances,"—

"Remember," said his lady interfering, "that you are already under a vow to free the Sepulchre of God; and to that, methinks, all lighter engagements might give place."

"Well, lady—well," said Count Robert, but half satisfied with this interference, "I will not engage myself, you may be assured, on any adventure which may claim precedence of the enterprise of the Holy Sepulchre, to which we are all bound."

"Alas!" said Agelastes, "the distance of Zulichium from the speediest route to the sepulchre is so small that"—

"Worthy father," said the Countess, "we will, if it pleases you, hear your tale to an end, and then determine what we will do. We Norman ladies, descendants of the old Germans, claim a voice with our lords in the council which precedes the battle; nor has our assistance in the conflict been deemed altogether useless."

The tone in which this was spoken conveyed an awkward innuendo to the philosopher, who began to foresee that the guidance of the Norman knight would be more difficult than he had foreseen, while his consort remained by his side. He took up, therefore, his oratory on somewhat a lower key than before, and avoided those warm descriptions which had given such offence to the Countess Brenhilda.

"Sir Artavan de Hautlieu, says the story, considered in what way he should accost the sleeping damsel, when it occurred to him in what manner the charm would be most likely to be reversed. I am in your judgment, fair lady, if he judged wrong in resolving that the method of his address should be a kiss upon the lips." The colour of Brenhilda was somewhat heightened, but she did not deem the observation worthy of notice.

"Never had so innocent an action," continued the philosopher, "an effect more horrible. The delightful light of a summer evening was instantly changed into a strange lurid hue, which, infected with sulphur, seemed to breathe suffocation through the apartment. The rich hangings, and splendid furniture of the chamber, the very walls themselves, were changed into huge stones tossed together at
random, like the inside of a wild beast's den, nor was the den without an inhabitant. The beautiful and innocent lips to which Artavan de Hautlieu had approached his own, were now changed into the

hideous and bizarre form, and bestial aspect of a fiery dragon. A moment she hovered upon the wing, and it is said, had Sir Artavan found courage to repeat his salute three times, he would then have remained master of all the wealth, and of the disenchanted princess. But the opportunity was lost, and the dragon, or the creature who seemed such, sailed out at a side window upon its broad pennons, uttering loud wails of disappointment."

Here ended the story of Agelastes. "The Princess," he said, "is still supposed to abide her doom in the Island of Zulichium, and several knights have undertaken the adventure; but I know not whether it was the fear of saluting the sleeping maiden, or that of approaching the dragon into which she was transformed, but so it is, the spell remains unachieved. I know the way, and if you say the word, you may be to– morrow on the road to the castle of enchantment."

The Countess heard this proposal with the deepest anxiety, for she knew that she might, by opposition, determine her husband irrevocably upon following out the enterprise. She stood therefore with a timid and bashful look, strange in a person whose bearing was generally so dauntless, and prudently left it to the uninfluenced mind of Count Robert to form the resolution which should best please
him.

"Brenhilda," he said, taking her hand, "fame and honour are dear to thy husband as ever they were to knight who buckled a brand upon his side. Thou hast done, perhaps, I may say, for me, what I might in vain have looked for from ladies of thy condition; and therefore thou mayst well expect a casting voice in such points of deliberation.— Why dost thou wander by the side of a foreign and unhealthy shore, instead of the banks of the lovely Seine?—Why dost thou wear a dress unusual to thy sex?—Why dost thou seek death, and think it little in comparison of shame?—Why? but that the Count of Paris may have a bride worthy of him.—Dost thou think that this affection is thrown away? No, by the saints! Thy knight repays it as he best ought, and sacrifices to thee every thought which thy affection may less than entirely approve."

Poor Brenhilda, confused as she was by the various emotions with which she was agitated, now in vain endeavoured to maintain the heroic deportment which her character as an Amazon required from her. She attempted to assume the proud and lofty look which was properly her own, but failing in the effort, she threw herself into the Count's arms, hung round his neck, and wept like a, village maiden, whose true love is pressed for the wars. Her husband, a little ashamed, while he was much moved by this burst of affection in one to whose character it seemed an unusual attribute, was, at the same time, pleased and proud that he could have awakened an affection so genuine and so gentle in a soul so high–spirited and so unbending.

"Not thus," he said, "my Brenhilda! I would not have it thus, either for thine own sake or for mine. Do not let this wise old man suppose that thy heart is made of the malleable stuff which forms that of
other maidens; and apologize to him, as may well become thee, for having prevented my undertaking the adventure of Zulichium, which he recommends."

It was not easy for Brenhilda to recover herself, after having afforded so notable an instance how nature can vindicate her rights, with whatever rigour she may have been disciplined and tyrannized over. With a look of ineffable affection, she disjoined herself from her husband, still keeping hold of his hand, and turning to the old man with a countenance in which the half–effaced tears were succeeded by smiles of pleasure and of modesty, she spoke to
Agelastes as she would to a person whom she respected, and towards whom she had some offence to atone. "Father," she said,
respectfully, "be not angry with me that I should have been an obstacle to one of the best knights that ever spurred steed, undertaking the enterprise of thine enchanted Princess; but the truth is, that in our land, where knighthood and religion agree in permitting only one lady love, and one lady wife, we do not quite so willingly see our husbands run into danger—especially of that kind where lonely ladies are the parties relieved—and—and kisses are the ransom paid. I have as much confidence in my Robert's fidelity, as a lady can have in a loving knight, but still"—

"Lovely lady," said Agelastes, who, notwithstanding his highly artificial character, could not help being moved by the simple and sincere affection of the handsome young pair, "you have done no evil. The state of the Princess is no worse than it was, and there cannot be a doubt that the knight fated to relieve her, will appear at the destined period." The Countess smiled sadly, and shook her head. "You do not know," she said, "how powerful is the aid of

which I have unhappily deprived this unfortunate lady, by a jealousy which I now feel to have been alike paltry and unworthy; and, such

is my regret, that I could find in my heart to retract my opposition to Count Robert's undertaking this adventure." She looked at her husband with some anxiety, as one that had made an offer she would not willingly see accepted, and did not recover her courage until he said, decidedly, "Brenhilda, that may not be."

"And why, then, may not Brenhilda herself take the adventure," continued the Countess, "since she can neither fear the charms of the Princess nor the terrors of the dragon?"

"Lady," said Agelastes, "the Princess must be awakened by the kiss of love, and not by that of friendship."

"A sufficient reason," said the Countess, smiling, "why a lady may not wish her lord to go forth upon an adventure of which the conditions are so regulated."

"Noble minstrel, or herald, or by whatever name this country calls you," said Count Robert, "accept a small remuneration for an hour pleasantly spent, though spent, unhappily, in vain. I should make some apology for the meanness of my offering, but French knights, you may have occasion to know, are more full of fame than of wealth."

"Not for that, noble sir," replied Agelastes, "would I refuse your munificence; a besant from your worthy hand, or that of your noble– minded lady, were centupled in its value, by the eminence of the persons from whom it came. I would hang it round my neck by a string of pearls, and when I came into the presence of knights and of ladies, I would proclaim that this addition to my achievement of armorial distinction, was bestowed by the renowned Count Robert of Paris, and his unequalled lady." The Knight and the Countess looked on each other, and the lady, taking from her finger a ring of pure gold, prayed the old man to accept of it, as a mark of her esteem and her husband's. "With one other condition," said the philosopher, "which I trust you will not find altogether unsatisfactory. I have, on the way to the city by the most pleasant road, a small kiosk, or hermitage, where I sometimes receive my friends, who, I venture to say, are among the most respectable personages of this empire. Two or three of these will probably honour my residence today, and partake of the provision it affords. Could I add to these the company of the noble Count and Countess of Paris, I should deem my poor habitation honoured for ever."

"How say you, my noble wife?" said the Count. "The company of a minstrel befits the highest birth, honours the highest rank, and adds to the greatest achievements; and the invitation does us too much credit to be rejected."

"It grows somewhat late," said the Countess: "but we came not here to shun a sinking sun or a darkening sky, and I feel it my duty, as well as my satisfaction, to place at the command of the good father every pleasure which it is in my power to offer to him, for having been the means of your neglecting his advice."

"The path is so short," said Agelastes, "that we had better keep our present mode of travelling, if the lady should not want the assistance of horses."

"No horses on my account," said the Lady Brenhilda. "My waiting– woman, Agatha, has what necessaries I may require; and, for the rest, no knight ever travelled so little embarrassed with baggage as my husband."

Agelastes, therefore, led the way through the deepening wood, which was freshened by the cooler breath of evening, and his guests accompanied him.

CHAPTER THE ELEVENTH

Without, a ruin, broken, tangled, cumbrous, Within,
it was a little paradise,
Where Taste had made her dwelling. Statuary, First—
born of human art, moulded her images, And bade men.
mark and worship. ANONYMOUS.

The Count of Paris and his lady attended the old man, whose advanced age,
his excellence in the use of the French language, which he spoke to
admiration,—above all, his skill in applying it to poetical and romantic
subjects, which was essential to what was then termed history and belles
lettres,—drew from the noble hearers a degree of applause, which, as
Agelastes had seldom been vain enough to consider as his due, so, on the part
of the Knight of Paris and his lady, had it been but rarely conferred. They had
walked for some time by a path which sometimes seemed to hide itself among
the woods that came down to the shore of the Propontis, sometimes
emerged from concealment, and skirted the open margin of the strait, while, at
every turn, it seemed guided by the desire to select a choice and contrast of
beauty. Variety of scenes and manners enlivened, from their novelty, the
landscape to the pilgrims. By the sea–shore, nymphs were seen dancing, and
shepherds piping, or beating the tambourine to their steps, as represented in
some groups of ancient statuary. The very faces had a singular resemblance to
the antique. If old, their long robes, their attitudes, and magnificent heads,
presented the ideas which distinguish prophets and saints; while, on the other
hand, the features of the young recalled the expressive countenances of the
heroes of antiquity, and the charms of those lovely females by whom their
deeds were inspired. But the race of the Greeks was no longer to be seen,
even in its native country, unmixed, or in absolute purity; on the contrary,
they saw groups of persons with features which argued a different descent.

In a retiring bosom of the shore, which was traversed by the path, the rocks, receding from the beach, rounded off a spacious portion of level sand, and, in some degree, enclosed it. A party of heathen Scythians whom they beheld, presented the deformed features of the demons they were said to worship— flat noses with expanded nostrils, which seemed to admit the sight to their very brain; faces which extended rather in breadth than length, with strange unintellectual eyes placed in the extremity; figures short and dwarfish, yet garnished with legs and arms of astonishing sinewy strength, disproportioned to their bodies. As the travellers passed, the savages held a species of tournament, as the Count termed it. In this they exercised themselves by darting at each other long reeds, or canes, balanced for the purpose, which, in this rude sport, they threw with such force, as not unfrequently to strike each other from their steeds, and otherwise to cause serious damage. Some of the combatants being, for the time, out of the play, devoured with greedy looks the beauty of the Countess, and eyed her in such a manner, that she said to Count Robert,—"I have never known fear, my husband, nor is it for me to acknowledge it now; but if disgust be an ingredient of it, these misformed brutes are qualified to inspire it." "What, ho, Sir Knight!" exclaimed one of the infidels, "your wife, or your lady love, has committed a fault against the privileges of the Imperial Scythians, and not small will be the penalty she has incurred. You may go your way as fast as you will out of this place, which is, for the present; our hippodrome, or atmeidan, call it which you will, as you prize the Roman or the Saracen language; but for your wife, if the sacrament has united you, believe my word, that she parts not so soon or so easy."

"Scoundrel heathen," said the Christian Knight, "dost thou hold that language to a Peer of France?"

Agelastes here interposed, and using the sounding language of a Grecian courtier, reminded the Scythians, (mercenary soldiers, as they seemed, of the empire,) that all violence against the European pilgrims was, by the Imperial orders, strictly prohibited under pain of death.

"I know better," said the exulting savage, shaking one or two javelins with broad steel heads, and wings of the eagle's feather, which last were dabbled in blood. "Ask the wings of my javelin," he said, "in whose heart's blood these feathers have been dyed. They shall reply to you, that if Alexius Comnenus be the friend of the European pilgrims, it is only while he looks upon them; and we are too exemplary soldiers to serve our Emperor otherwise than he wishes to be served."

"Peace, Toxartis," said the philosopher, "thou beliest thine Emperor."

"Peace thou!" said Toxartis, "or I will do a deed that misbecomes a soldier, and rid the world of a prating old man."

So saying, he put forth his hand to take hold of the Countess's veil. With the readiness which frequent use had given to the warlike lady, she withdrew herself from the heathen's grasp, and with her trenchant sword dealt him so sufficient a blow, that Toxartis lay lifeless on the plain. The Count leapt on the fallen leader's steed, and crying his war–cry, "Son of Charlemagne, to the rescue!" he rode amid the rout of heathen cavaliers with a battle–axe, which he found at the saddlebow of the deceased chieftain, and wielding it with remorseless dexterity, he soon slew or wounded, or compelled to flight, the objects of his resentment; nor was there any of them who abode an instant to support the boast which they had made. "The despicable churls!" said the Countess to Agelastes; "it irks me that a drop of such coward blood should stain the hands of a noble knight. They call their exercise a tournament, although in their whole exertions every blow is aimed behind the back, and not one has the courage to throw his windlestraw while he perceives that of another pointed against himself."

"Such is their custom," said Agelastes; "not perhaps so much from cowardice as from habit, in exercising before his Imperial Majesty. I have seen that Toxartis literally turn his back upon the mark when he bent his bow in full career, and when in the act of galloping the farthest from his object, he pierced it through the very centre with a broad arrow."

"A force of such soldiers," said Count Robert, who had now rejoined his friends, "could not, methinks, be very formidable, where there was but an ounce of genuine courage in the assailants."

"Mean time, let us pass on to my kiosk," said Agelastes, "lest the fugitives find friends to encourage them in thoughts of revenge."

"Such friends," said Count Robert, "methinks the insolent heathens ought not to find in any land which calls itself Christian; and if I survive the conquest of the Holy Sepulchre, I shall make it my first business to enquire by what right your Emperor retains in his service a band of Paynim and unmannerly cut-throats, who dare offer injury upon the highway, which ought to be sacred to the peace of God and the king, and to noble ladies and inoffensive pilgrims. It is one of a list of many questions which, my vow accomplished, I will not fail to put to him; ay, and expecting an answer, as they say, prompt and categorical."

"You shall gain no answer from me though," said Agelastes to himself. "Your demands, Sir Knight, are over–peremptory, and imposed under too rigid conditions, to be replied to by those who can evade them." He changed the conversation, accordingly, with easy dexterity; and they had not proceeded much farther, before they reached a spot, the natural beauties of which called forth the admiration of his foreign companions. A copious brook, gushing out of the woodland, descended to the sea with no small noise and tumult; and, as if disdaining a quieter course, which it might have gained by a little circuit to the right, it took the readiest road to the ocean, plunging over the face of a lofty and barren precipice which overhung the sea–shore, and from thence led its little tribute, with as much noise as if it had the stream of a full river to boast of, to the waters of the Hellespont.

The rock, we have said, was bare, unless in so far as it was clothed with the foaming waters of the cataract; but the banks on each side were covered with plane–trees, walnut–trees, cypresses, and other kinds of large timber proper to the East. The fall of water, always agreeable in a warm climate, and generally produced by artificial means, was here natural, and had been chosen, something like the

Sibyl's temple at Tivoli, for the seat of a goddess to whom the invention of Polytheism had assigned a sovereignty over the department around. The shrine was small and circular, like many of the lesser temples of the rustic deities, and enclosed by the wall of an outer court. After its desecration, it had probably been converted into a luxurious summer retreat by Agelastes, or some Epicurean philosopher. As the building, itself of a light, airy, and fantastic character, was dimly seen through the branches and foliage on the edge of the rock, so the mode by which it was accessible was not at first apparent amongst the mist of the cascade. A pathway, a good deal hidden, by vegetation, ascended by a gentle acclivity, and prolonged by the architect by means of a few broad and easy marble steps, making part of the original approach, conducted the passenger to a small, but exquisitely lovely velvet lawn, in front of the turret or temple we have described, the back part of which building overhung the cataract.

CHAPTER THE TWELFTH

The parties met. The wily, wordy Greek,
Weighing each word, and canvassing each syllable; Evading,
arguing, equivocating.
And the stern Frank came with his two–hand sword,
Watching to see which way the balance sways,
That he may throw it in, and turn the scales.
PALESTINE.

At a signal made by Agelastes, the door of this romantic retreat was opened by Diogenes, the negro slave, to whom our readers have been already introduced; nor did it escape the wily old man, that the Count and his lady testified some wonder at his form and
lineaments, being the first African perhaps whom they had ever seen so closely. The philosopher lost not the opportunity of making an impression on their minds, by a display of the superiority of his knowledge.

"This poor being," he observed, "is of the race of Ham, the undutiful son of Noah; for his transgressions against his parent, he was banished to the sands of Africa, and was condemned to be the father of a race doomed to be the slaves of the issue of his more dutiful brethren."

The knight and his lady gazed on the wonderful appearance before them, and did not, it may be believed, think of doubting the information which was so much of a piece with their prejudices, while their opinion of their host was greatly augmented by the supposed extent of his knowledge.

"It gives pleasure to a man of humanity," continued Agelastes, "when, in old age, or sickness, we must employ the services of others, which is at other times scarce lawful, to choose his assistants out of a race of beings, hewers of wood and drawers of water—from their birth upwards destined to slavery; and to whom, therefore, by employing them as slaves, we render no injury, but carry into effect, in a slight degree, the intentions of the Great Being who made us all."

"Are there many of a race," said the Countess, "so singularly unhappy in their destination? I have hitherto thought the stories of black men as idle as those which minstrels tell of fairies and ghosts."

"Do not believe so," said the philosopher; "the race is numerous as the sands of the sea, neither are they altogether unhappy in discharging the duties which their fate has allotted them. Those who are of worse character suffer even in this life the penance due to their guilt; they become the slaves of the cruel and tyrannical, are beaten, starved, and mutilated. To those whose moral characters are better, better masters are provided, who share with their slaves, as with their children, food and raiment, and the other good things which they themselves enjoy. To some, Heaven allots the favour of kings and of conquerors, and to a few, but those the chief favourites of the species, hath been assigned a place in the mansions of philosophy, where, by availing themselves of the lights which their masters can afford, they gain a prospect into that world which is the residence of true happiness."

"Methinks I understand you," replied the Countess, "and if so, I ought rather to envy our sable friend here than to pity him, for having been allotted in the partition of his kind to the possession of his present master, from whom, doubtless, he has acquired the desirable knowledge which you mention."

"He learns, at least," said Agelastes, modestly, "what I can teach, and, above all, to be contented with his situation.—Diogenes, my good child," said he, changing his address to the slave, "thou seest I have company—What does the poor hermit's larder afford, with which he may regale his honoured guests?"

Hitherto they had advanced no farther than a sort of outer room, or hall of entrance, fitted up with no more expense than might have suited one who desired at some outlay, and more taste, to avail himself of the ancient building for a sequestered and private retirement. The chairs and couches were covered with Eastern wove mats, and were of the simplest and most primitive form. But on touching a spring, an interior apartment was displayed, which had considerable pretension to splendour and magnificence. The furniture and hangings of this apartment were of straw–coloured silk, wrought on the looms of Persia, and crossed with embroidery, which produced a rich, yet simple effect. The ceiling was carved in Arabesque, and the four corners of the apartment were formed into recesses for statuary, which had been produced in a better age of the art than that which existed at the period of our story. In one nook, a shepherd seemed to withdraw himself, as if ashamed to produce his scantily–covered person, while he was willing to afford the audience the music of the reed which he held in his hand. Three damsels, resembling the Graces in the beautiful proportions of their limbs, and the slender clothing which they wore, lurked in different attitudes, each in her own niche, and seemed but to await the first sound of the music, to bound forth from thence and join in the frolic dance. The subject was beautiful, yet somewhat light, to ornament the study of such a sage as Agelastes represented himself to be.

He seemed to be sensible that this might attract observation.
—"These figures," he said, "executed at the period of the highest excellence of Grecian art, were considered of old as the choral nymphs assembled to adore the goddess of the place, waiting but the music to join in the worship of the temple. And, in truth, the wisest may be interested in seeing how near to animation the genius of
these wonderful men could bring the inflexible marble. Allow but for the absence of the divine afflatus, or breath of animation, and an unenlightened heathen might suppose the miracle of Prometheus was about to be realized. But we," said he, looking upwards, "are taught
to form a better judgment between what man can do and the
productions of the Deity."

Some subjects of natural history were painted on the walls, and the philosopher fixed the attention of his guests upon the half–reasoning elephant, of which he mentioned several anecdotes, which they listened to with great eagerness.

A distant strain was here heard, as if of music in the woods, penetrating by fits through the hoarse roar of the cascade, which, as it sunk immediately below the windows, filled the apartment with its deep voice.

"Apparently," said Agelastes, "the friends whom I expected are approaching, and bring with them the means of enchanting another sense. It is well they do so, since wisdom tells us that we best honour the Deity by enjoying the gifts he has provided us."

These words called the attention of the philosopher's Frankish guests to the preparations exhibited in this tasteful saloon. These were made for an entertainment in the manner of the ancient Romans, and couches, which were laid beside a table ready decked, announced that the male guests, at least, were to assist at the banquet in the usual recumbent posture of the ancients; while seats, placed among the couches, seemed to say that females were expected, who would observe the Grecian customs, in eating seated. The preparations for good cheer were such as, though limited in extent, could scarce be excelled in quality, either by the splendid dishes which decked Trimalchio's banquet of former days, or the lighter delicacies of Grecian cookery, or the succulent and highly–spiced messes indulged in by the nations of the East, to whichever they happened to give the preference; and it was with an air of some vanity that Agelastes asked his guests to share a poor pilgrim's meal.

"We care little for dainties," said the Count; "nor does our present course of life as pilgrims, bound by a vow, allow us much choice on such subjects. Whatever is food for soldiers, suffices the Countess and myself; for, with our will, we would at every hour be ready for battle, and the less time we use in preparing for the field, it is even so much the better. Sit then, Brenhilda, since the good man will have it so, and let us lose no time in refreshment, lest we waste that which should be otherwise employed." "A moment's forgiveness," said Agelastes, "until the arrival of my other friends, whose music you may now hear is close at hand, and who will not long, I may safely promise, divide you from your meal."

"For that," said the Count, "there is no haste; and since you seem to account it a part of civil manners, Brenhilda and I can with ease postpone our repast, unless you will permit us, what I own would be more pleasing, to take a morsel of bread and a cup of water presently; and, thus refreshed, to leave the space clear for your more curious and more familiar guests."

"The saints above forbid!" said Agelastes; "guests so honoured never before pressed these cushions, nor could do so, if the sacred family of the imperial Alexius himself even now stood at the gate."

He had hardly uttered these words, when the full–blown peal of a trumpet, louder in a tenfold degree than the strains of music they had before heard, was now sounded in the front of the temple, piercing through the murmur of the waterfall, as a Damascus blade penetrates the armour, and assailing the ears of the hearers, as the sword pierces the flesh of him who wears the harness.

"You seem surprised or alarmed, father," said Count Robert. "Is there danger near, and do you distrust our protection?"

"No," said Agelastes, "that would give me confidence in any extremity; but these sounds excite awe, not fear. They tell me that some of the Imperial family are about to be my guests. Yet fear nothing, my noble friends—they, whose look is life, are ready to shower their favours with profusion upon strangers so worthy of honour as they will see here. Meantime, my brow must touch my threshold, in order duly to welcome them." So saying, he hurried to the outer door of the building.

"Each land has its customs," said the Count, as he followed his host, with his wife hanging on his arm; "but, Brenhilda, as they are so various, it is little wonder that they appear unseemly to each other. Here, however, in deference to my entertainer, I stoop my crest, in the manner which seems to be required." So saying, he followed Agelastes into the anteroom, where a new scene awaited them.

CHAPTER THE THIRTEENTH

Agelastes gained his threshold before Count Robert of Paris and his lady. He had, therefore, time to make his prostrations before a huge animal, then unknown to the western world, but now universally distinguished as the elephant. On its back was a pavilion or palanquin, within which were enclosed the august persons of the Empress Irene, and her daughter Anna Comnena. Nicephorus Briennius attended the Princesses in the command of a gallant body of light horse, whose splendid armour would have given more pleasure to the crusader, if it had possessed less an air of useless wealth and effeminate magnificence. But the effect which it produced in its appearance was as brilliant as could well be conceived. The officers alone of this *corps de garde* followed

Nicephorus to the platform, prostrated themselves while the ladies of the Imperial house descended, and rose up again under a cloud of waving plumes and flashing lances, when they stood secure upon the platform in front of the building. Here the somewhat aged, but commanding form of the Empress, and the still juvenile beauties of the fair historian, were seen to great advantage. In the front of a deep back–ground of spears and waving crests, stood the sounder of the sacred trumpet, conspicuous by his size and the richness of his apparel; he kept his post on a rock above the stone staircase, and, by an occasional note of his instrument, intimated to the squadrons beneath that they should stay their progress, and attend the motions

of the Empress and the wife of the Caesar.

The fair form of the Countess Brenhilda, and the fantastic appearance of her half masculine garb, attracted the attention of the ladies of Alexius' family, but was too extraordinary to command their admiration. Agelastes became sensible there was a necessity that he should introduce his guests to each other, if he desired they

should meet on satisfactory terms. "May I speak," he said, "and live? The armed strangers whom you find now with me are worthy companions of those myriads, whom zeal for the suffering

inhabitants of Palestine has brought from the western extremity of Europe, at once to enjoy the countenance of Alexius Comnenus, and to aid him, since it pleases him to accept their assistance, in
expelling the Paynims from the bounds of the sacred empire, and garrison those regions in their stead, as vassals of his Imperial Majesty."

"We are pleased," said the Empress, "worthy Agelastes, that you should be kind to those who are disposed to be so reverent to the Emperor. And We are rather disposed to talk with them ourselves, that our daughter (whom Apollo hath gifted with the choice talent of recording what she sees) may become acquainted with one of those female warriors of the West, of whom we have heard so much by common fame, and yet know so little with certainty."

"Madam," said the Count, "I can but rudely express to you what I have to find fault with in the explanation which this old man hath given of our purpose in coming hither. Certain it is, we neither owe Alexius fealty, nor had we the purpose of paying him any, when we took the vow upon ourselves which brought us against Asia. We came, because we understood that the Holy Land had been torn from the Greek Emperor by the Pagans, Saracens, Turks, and other infidels, from whom we are come to win it back. The wisest and most prudent among us have judged it necessary to acknowledge the Emperor's authority, since there was no such safe way of passing to the discharge of our vow, as that of acknowledging fealty to him, as the best mode of preventing quarrels among Christian States. We, though independent of any earthly king, do not pretend to be greater men than they, and therefore have condescended to pay the same homage."

The Empress coloured several times with indignation in the course of this speech, which, in more passages than one, was at variance with those imperial maxims of the Grecian court, which held its dignity so high, and plainly intimated a tone of opinion which was depreciating to the Emperor's power. But the Empress Irene had received instructions from her imperial spouse to beware how she gave, or even took, any ground of quarrel with the crusaders, who, though coming in the appearance of subjects, were, nevertheless, too punctilious and ready to take fire, to render them safe discussers of delicate differences. She made a graceful reverence accordingly, as if she had scarce understood what the Count of Paris had explained so bluntly.

At this moment the appearance of the principal persons on either hand attracted, in a wonderful degree, the attention of the other party, and there seemed to exist among them a general desire of further acquaintance, and, at the same time, a manifest difficulty in expressing such a wish.

Agelastes—to begin with the master of the house—had risen from the ground indeed, but without venturing to assume an upright posture; he remained before the Imperial ladies with his body and head still bent, his hand interposed between his eyes and their faces, like a man that would shade his eyesight from the level sun, and awaited in silence the commands of those to whom he seemed to think it disrespectful to propose the slightest action, save by testifying in general, that his house and his slaves were at their unlimited command. The Countess of Paris, on the other hand, and her warlike husband, were the peculiar objects of curiosity to Irene, and her accomplished daughter, Anna Comnena; and it occurred to both these Imperial ladies, that they had never seen finer specimens of human strength and beauty; but by a natural instinct, they preferred the manly bearing of the husband to that of the wife, which seemed to her own sex rather too haughty and too masculine to be altogether pleasing.

Count Robert and his lady had also their own object of attention in the newly arrived group, and, to speak truth, it was nothing else than the peculiarities of the monstrous animal which they now saw, for the first time, employed as a beast of burden in the service of the fair Irene and her daughter. The dignity and splendour of the elder Princess, the grace and vivacity of the younger, were alike lost in Brenhilda's earnest inquiries into the history of the elephant, and the use which it made of its trunk, tusks, and huge ears, upon different occasions.

Another person, who took a less direct opportunity to gaze on

Brenhilda with a deep degree of interest, was the Caesar, Nicephorus. This Prince kept his eye as steadily upon the Frankish Countess as he could well do, without attracting the attention, and exciting perhaps the suspicions, of his wife and mother–in–law; he therefore endeavoured to restore speech to an interview which would have been awkward without it. "It is possible," he said, "beautiful Countess, that this being your first visit to the Queen, of the world, you have never hitherto seen the singularly curious animal called the elephant."

"Pardon me," said the Countess, "I have been treated by this learned gentleman to a sight, and some account of that wonderful creature."

By all who heard this observation, the Lady Brenhilda was supposed to have made a satirical thrust at the philosopher himself, who, in the imperial court, usually went by the name of the elephant.

"No one could describe the beast more accurately than Agelastes," said the Princess, with a smile of intelligence, which went round her attendants.

"He knows its docility, its sensibility, and its fidelity," said the philosopher, in a subdued tone.

"True, good Agelastes," said the Princess; "we should not criticise the animal which kneels to take us up.—Come, lady of a foreign land," she continued, turning to the Frank Count, and especially his Countess— "and you her gallant lord! When you return to your native country, you shall say you have seen the imperial family partake of their food, and in so far acknowledge themselves to be of the same clay with other mortals, sharing their poorest wants, and relieving them in the same manner."

"That, gentle lady, I can well believe," said Count Robert; "my curiosity would be more indulged by seeing this strange animal at his food."

"You will see the elephant more conveniently at his mess within doors," answered the Princess, looking at Agelastes.

"Lady," said Brenhilda, "I would not willingly refuse an invitation given in courtesy, but the sun has waxed low unnoticed, and we must return to the city."

"Be not afraid," said the fair historian; "you shall have the advantage of our Imperial escort to protect you in your return."

"Fear?—afraid?—escort?—protect?—These are words I know not. Know, lady, that my husband, the noble Count of Paris, is my sufficient escort; and even were he not with me, Brenhilda de Aspramonte fears nothing, and can defend herself."

"Fair daughter," said Agelastes, "if I may be permitted to speak, you mistake the gracious intentions of the Princess, who expresses herself as to a lady of her own land. What she desires is to learn from you some of the most marked habits and manners of the Franks, of which you are so beautiful an example; and in return for such information the illustrious Princess would be glad to procure your entrance to those spacious collections, where animals from all corners of the habitable world have been assembled at the command of our Emperor Alexius, as if to satisfy the wisdom of those sages to whom all creation is known, from the deer so small in size that it is exceeded by an ordinary rat, to that huge and singular inhabitant of Africa that can browse on the tops of trees that are forty feet high, while the length of its hind– legs does not exceed the half of that wondrous height."

"It is enough," said the Countess, with some eagerness; but Agelastes had got a point of discussion after his own mind.

"There is also," he said, "that huge lizard, which, resembling in shape the harmless inhabitant of the moors of other countries, is in Egypt a monster thirty feet in length, clothed in impenetrable scales, and moaning over his prey when he catches it, with the hope and purpose of drawing others within his danger, by mimicking the lamentations of humanity."

"Say no more, father!" exclaimed the lady. "My Robert, we will go —will we not, where such objects are to be seen?"

"There is also," said Agelastes, who saw that he would gain his point by addressing himself to the curiosity of the strangers, "the huge animal, wearing on its back an invulnerable vestment, having on its nose a horn, and sometimes two, the folds of whose hide are of the most immense thickness, and which never knight was able to wound."

"We will go, Robert—will we not?" reiterated the Countess.

"Ay," replied the Count, "and teach, these Easterns how to judge of a knight's sword, by a single blow of my trusty Tranchefer."

"And who knows," said Brenhilda, "since this is a land of enchantment, but what some person, who is languishing in a foreign shape, may have their enchantment unexpectedly dissolved by a stroke of the good weapon?"

"Say no more, father!" exclaimed the Count. "We will attend this Princess, since such she is, were her whole escort bent to oppose our passage, instead of being by her command to be our guard. For know, all who hear me, thus much of the nature of the Franks, that when you tell us of danger and difficulties, you give us the same desire to travel the road where they lie, as other men have in seeking either pleasure or profit in the paths in which such are to be found."

As the Count pronounced these words, he struck his hand upon his Tranchefer, as an illustration of the manner in which he purposed upon occasion to make good his way. The courtly circle startled somewhat at the clash of steel, and the fiery look of the chivalrous Count Robert. The Empress indulged her alarm by retreating into the inner apartment of the pavilion.

With a grace, which was rarely deigned to any but those in close alliance with the Imperial family, Anna Comnena took the arm of the noble Count. "I see," she said, "that the Imperial Mother has honoured the house of the learned Agelastes, by leading the way; therefore, to teach you Grecian breeding must fall to my share." Saying this she conducted him to the inner apartment.

"Fear not for your wife," she said, as she noticed the Frank look round; "our husband, like ourselves, has pleasure in showing attention to the stranger, and will lead the Countess to our board. It is not the custom of the Imperial family to eat in company with strangers; but we thank Heaven for having instructed us in that civility, which can know no degradation in dispensing with ordinary rules to do honour to strangers of such merit as yours. I know it will be my mother's request, that you will take your places without ceremony; and also, although the grace be somewhat particular, I am sure that it will have my Imperial father's approbation.

"Be it as your ladyship lists," said Count Robert. "There are few men to whom I would yield place at the board, if they had not gone before me in the battle–field. To a lady, especially so fair a one, I willingly yield my place, and bend my knee, whenever I have the good hap to meet her."

The Princess Anna, instead of feeling herself awkward in the discharge of the extraordinary, and, as she might have thought it, degrading office of ushering a barbarian chief to the banquet, felt, on the contrary, flattered, at having bent to her purpose a heart so obstinate as that of Count Robert, and elated, perhaps, with a certain degree of satisfied pride while under his momentary protection.

The Empress Irene had already seated herself at the head of the table. She looked with some astonishment, when her daughter and son–in–law, taking their seats at her right and left hand, invited the Count and Countess of Paris, the former to recline, the latter to sit at the board, in the places next to themselves; but she had received the strictest orders from her husband to be deferential in every respect to the strangers, and did not think it right, therefore, to interpose any ceremonious scruples.

The Countess took her seat, as indicated, beside the Caesar; and the Count, instead of reclining in the mode of the Grecian men, also seated himself in the European fashion by the Princess.

"I will not lie prostrate," said he, laughing, "except in consideration of a blow weighty enough to compel me to do so; nor then either, if I am able to start up and return it."

The service of the table then began, and, to say truth, it appeared to be an important part of the business of the day. The officers who attended to perform their several duties of deckers of the table, sewers of the banquet, removers and tasters to the Imperial family, thronged into the banqueting room, and seemed to vie with each other in calling upon Agelastes for spices, condiments, sauces, and wines of various kinds, the variety and multiplicity of their demands being apparently devised *ex preposito*, for stirring the patience of the philosopher. But Agelastes, who had anticipated most of their requests, however unusual, supplied them completely, or in the greatest part, by the ready agency of his active slave Diogenes, to whom, at the same time, he contrived to transfer all blame for the absence of such articles as he was unable to provide.

"Be Homer my witness, the accomplished Virgil, and the curious felicity of Horace, that, trifling and unworthy as this banquet was, my note of directions to this thrice unhappy slave gave the instructions to procure every ingredient necessary to convey to each dish its proper gusto.—Ill—omened carrion that thou art, wherefore placedst thou the pickled cucumber so far apart from the boar's head? and why are these superb congers unprovided with a requisite quantity of fennel? The divorce betwixt the shell—fish and the Chian wine, in a presence like this, is worthy of the divorce of thine own soul from thy body; or, to say the least, of a lifelong residence in the Pistrinum." While thus the philosopher proceeded with threats, curses, and menaces against his slave, the stranger might have an opportunity of comparing the little torrent of his domestic eloquence, which the manners of the times did not consider as ill—bred, with the louder and deeper share of adulation towards his guests. They mingled like the oil with the vinegar and pickles which Diogenes mixed for the sauce. Thus the Count and Countess had an opportunity to estimate the happiness and the felicity reserved for those slaves, whom the Omnipotent Jupiter, in the plenitude of compassion for their state, and in guerdon of their good morals, had dedicated to the service of a philosopher. The share they themselves took in the banquet, was finished with a degree of speed which gave surprise not only to their host, but also to the Imperial guests.

The Count helped himself carelessly out of a dish which stood near

him, and partaking of a draught of wine, without enquiring whether
it was of the vintage which the Greeks held it matter of conscience to mingle
with that species of food, he declared himself satisfied; nor could the obliging
entreaties of his neighbour, Anna Comnena,
induce him to partake of other messes represented as being either delicacies
or curiosities. His spouse ate still more moderately of the food which seemed
most simply cooked, and stood nearest her at the board, and partook of a cup
of crystal water, which she slightly tinged with wine, at the persevering
entreaty of the Caesar. They
then relinquished the farther business of the banquet, and leaning back
upon their seats, occupied themselves in watching the liberal credit done to
the feast by the rest of the guests present.

A modern synod of gourmands would hardly have equalled the Imperial
family of Greece seated, at a philosophical banquet, whether in the critical
knowledge displayed of the science of eating in all its branches, or in the
practical cost and patience with which they exercised it. The ladies, indeed,
did not eat much of any one dish, but they tasted of almost all that were
presented to them, and their name was Legion. Yet, after a short time, in
Homeric phrase, the rage of thirst and hunger was assuaged, or, more
probably, the Princess Anna Comnena was tired of being an object of some
inattention to the guest who sat next her, and who, joining his high military
character to his very handsome presence, was a person by whom few ladies
would willingly be neglected. There is no new guise, says our father
Chaucer, but what resembles an old one; and
the address of Anna Comnena to the Frankish Count might resemble that of a
modern lady of fashion, in her attempts to engage in conversation the
exquisite, who sits by her side in an apparently absent fit. "We have piped
unto you," said the Princess, "and you have not danced! We have sung to you
the jovial chorus of *Evoe, evoe,* and you will neither worship Comus nor
Bacchus! Are we then to judge you a follower of the Muses, in whose service,
as well as in that of Phoebus, we ourselves pretend to be enlisted?"

"Fair lady," replied the Frank, "be not offended at my stating once for all, in
plain terms, that I am a Christian man, spitting at, and bidding defiance to
Apollo, Bacchus, Comus, and all other heathen deities whatsoever."

"O! cruel interpretation of my unwary words!" said the Princess; "I did but mention the gods of music, poetry, and eloquence, worshipped by our divine philosophers, and whose names are still used to distinguish the arts and sciences over which they presided— and the Count interprets it seriously into a breach of the second commandment! Our Lady preserve me, we must take care how we speak, when our words are so sharply interpreted."

The Count laughed as the Princess spoke. "I had no offensive meaning, madam," he said, "nor would I wish to interpret your words otherwise than as being most innocent and praiseworthy. I shall suppose that your speech contained all that was fair and blameless. You are, I have understood, one of those who, like our worthy host, express in composition the history and feats of the warlike time in which you live, and give to the posterity which shall succeed us, the knowledge of the brave deeds which have been achieved in our day. I respect the task to which you have dedicated yourself, and know not how a lady could lay after ages under an
obligation to her in the same degree, unless, like my wife, Brenhilda, she were herself to be the actress of deeds which she recorded. And, by the way, she now looks towards her neighbour at the table, as if she were about to rise and leave him; her inclinations are towards Constantinople, and, with your ladyship's permission, I cannot allow her to go thither alone."

"That you shall neither of you do," said Anna Comnena; "since we all go to the capital directly, and for the purpose of seeing those wonders of nature, of which numerous examples have been collected by the splendour of my Imperial father.—If my husband seems to have given offence to the Countess, do not suppose that it was intentionally dealt to her; on the contrary, you will find the good
man, when you are better acquainted with him, to be one of those simple persons who manage so unhappily what they mean for civilties, that those to whom they are addressed receive them frequently in another sense."

The Countess of Paris, however, refused again to sit down to the table from which she had risen, so that Agelastes and his Imperial guests saw themselves under the necessity either to permit the strangers to depart, which they seemed unwilling to do, or to detain them by force, to attempt which might not perhaps have been either safe or pleasant; or, lastly, to have waived the etiquette of rank and set out along with them, at the same time managing their dignity, so as to take the initiatory step, though the departure took place upon the motion of their wilful guests. Much tumult there was—bustling, disputing, and shouting—among the troops and officers who were thus moved from their repast, two hours at least sooner than had been experienced upon similar occasions in the memory of the oldest among them. A different arrangement of the Imperial party likewise seemed to take place by mutual consent.

Nicephorus Briennius ascended the seat upon the elephant, and remained there placed beside his august mother–in–law. Agelastes, on a sober– minded palfrey, which permitted him to prolong his philosophical harangues at his own pleasure, rode beside the Countess Brenhilda, whom he made the principal object of his oratory. The fair historian, though she usually travelled in a litter, preferred upon this occasion a spirited horse, which enabled her to keep pace with Count Robert of Paris, on whose imagination, if not his feelings, she seemed to have it in view to work a marked impression. The conversation of the Empress with her son–in–law requires no special detail. It was a tissue of criticisms upon the manners and behaviour of the Franks, and a hearty wish that they might be soon transported from the realms of Greece, never more to return. Such was at least the tone of the Empress, nor did the Caesar find it convenient to express any more tolerant opinion of the strangers. On the other hand, Agelastes made a long circuit ere he ventured to approach the subject which he wished to introduce. He spoke of the menagerie of the Emperor as a most superb collection of natural history; he extolled different persons at court for having encouraged Alexius Comnenus in this wise and philosophical amusement. But, finally, the praise of all others was abandoned that the philosopher might dwell upon that of Nicephorus Briennius, to whom the cabinet or collection of Constantinople was indebted, he said, for the principal treasures it contained.

"I am glad it is so," said the haughty Countess, without lowering her voice or affecting any change of manner; "I am glad that he understands some things better worth understanding than whispering with stranger young women. Credit me, if he gives much license to his tongue among such women of nay country as these stirring times may bring hither, some one or other of them will fling him into the cataract which dashes below."

"Pardon me, fair lady," said Agelastes; "no female heart could meditate an action so atrocious against so fine a form as that of the Caesar Nicephorus Briennius."

"Put it not on that issue, father," said the offended Countess; "for, by my patroness Saint, our Lady of the Broken Lances, had it not been for regard to these two ladies, who seemed to intend some respect to my husband and myself, that same Nicephorus should have been as perfectly a Lord of the Broken Bones as any Caesar who has borne the title since the great Julius!"

The philosopher, upon this explicit information, began to entertain some personal fear for himself, and hastened, by diverting the conversation, which he did with great dexterity, to the story of Hero and Leander, to put the affront received out of the head of this unscrupulous Amazon.

Meantime, Count Robert of Paris was engrossed, as it may be termed, by the fair Anna Comnena. She spoke on all subjects, on some better, doubtless, others worse, but on none did she suspect herself of any deficiency; while the good Count wished heartily within himself that his companion had been safely in bed with the enchanted Princess of Zulichium. She performed, right or wrong, the part of a panegyrist of the Normans, until at length the Count, tired
of hearing her prate of she knew not exactly what, broke in as
follows:—

"Lady," he said, "notwithstanding I and my followers are sometimes so named, yet we are not Normans, who come hither as a numerous and separate body of pilgrims, under the command of their Duke Robert, a valiant, though extravagant, thoughtless, and weak man. I say nothing against the fame of these Normans. They conquered, in our fathers' days, a kingdom far stronger than their own, which men call England; I see that you entertain some of the natives of which country in your pay, under the name of Varangians. Although defeated, as I said, by the Normans, they are, nevertheless, a brave race; nor would we think ourselves much dishonoured by mixing in battle with them. Still we are the valiant Franks, who had their dwelling on the eastern banks of the Rhine and of the Saale, who were converted to the Christian faith by the celebrated Clovis, and are sufficient, by our numbers and courage, to re–conquer the Holy Land, should all Europe besides stand neutral in the contest."

There are few things more painful to the vanity of a person like the Princess, than the being detected in an egregious error, at the moment she is taking credit to herself for being peculiarly accurately informed.

"A false slave, who knew not what he was saying, I suppose," said the Princess, "imposed upon me the belief that the Varangians were the natural enemies of the Normans. I see him marching there by the side of Achilles Tatius, the leader of his corps.—Call him hither, you officers!—Yonder tall man, I mean, with the battle–axe upon his shoulder."

Hereward, distinguished by his post at the head of the squadron, was summoned from thence to the presence of the Princess, where he made his military obeisance with a cast of sternness in his aspect, as his glance lighted upon the proud look of the Frenchman who rode beside Anna Comnena.

"Did I not understand thee, fellow," said Anna Comnena, "to have informed me, nearly a month ago, that the Normans and the Franks were the same people, and enemies to the race from which you spring?"

"The Normans are our mortal enemies, Lady," answered Hereward, "by whom we were driven from our native land. The Franks are subjects of the same Lord–Paramount with the Normans, and therefore they neither love the Varangians, nor are beloved by them."

"Good fellow," said the French Count, "you do the Franks wrong, and ascribe to the Varangians, although not unnaturally, an undue degree of importance, when you suppose that a race which has ceased to exist as an independent nation for more than a generation, can be either an object of interest or resentment to such as we are."

"I am no stranger," said the Varangian, "to the pride of your heart, or the precedence which you assume over those who have been less fortunate in war than yourselves. It is God who casteth down and who buildeth up, nor is there in the world a prospect to which the Varangians would look forward with more pleasure than that a hundred of their number should meet in a fair field, either with the oppressive Normans, or their modern compatriots, the vain Frenchmen, and let God be the judge which is most worthy of victory."

"You take an insolent advantage of the chance," said the Count of Paris, "which gives you an unlooked–for opportunity to brave a nobleman."

"It is my sorrow and shame," said the Varangian, "that that opportunity is not complete; and that there is a chain around me which forbids me to say, Slay me, or I'll kill thee before we part from this spot!"

"Why, thou foolish and hot–brained churl," replied the Count, "what right hast thou to the honour of dying by my blade? Thou art mad, or hast drained the ale–cup so deeply that thou knowest not what thou thinkest or sayest."

"Thou liest," said the Varangian; "though such a reproach be the utmost scandal of thy race."

The Frenchman motioned his hand quicker than light to his sword, but instantly withdrew it, and said with dignity, "thou canst not offend me."

"But thou," said the exile, "hast offended me in a matter which can only be atoned by thy manhood."

"Where and how?" answered the Count; "although it is needless to ask the question, which thou canst not answer rationally."

"Thou hast this day," answered the Varangian, "put a mortal affront upon a great prince, whom thy master calls his ally, and by whom thou hast been received with every rite of hospitality. Him thou hast affronted as one peasant at a merry–making would do shame to another, and this dishonour thou hast done to him in the very face of his own chiefs and princes, and the nobles from every court of Europe."

"It was thy master's part to resent my conduct," said the Frenchman, "if in reality he so much felt it as an affront."

"But that," said Hereward, "did not consist with the manners of his country to do. Besides that, we trusty Varangians esteem ourselves bound by our oath as much to defend our Emperor, while the service lasts, on every inch of his honour as on every foot of his territory; I therefore tell thee, Sir Knight, Sir Count, or whatever thou callest thyself, there is mortal quarrel between thee and the Varangian guard, ever and until thou hast fought it out in fair and manly battle, body to body, with one of the said Imperial Varangians, when duty and opportunity shall permit:—and so God schaw the right!"

As this passed in the French language, the meaning escaped the understanding of such Imperialists as were within hearing at the time; and the Princess, who waited with some astonishment till the Crusader and the Varangian had finished their conference, when it was over, said to him with interest, "I trust you feel that poor man's situation to be too much at a distance from your own, to admit of your meeting him in what is termed knightly battle?"

"On such a question," said the knight, "I have but one answer to any lady who does not, like my Brenhilda, cover herself with a shield, and bear a sword by her side, and the heart of a knight in her bosom."

"And suppose for once," said the Princess Anna Comnena, "that I possessed such titles to your confidence, what would your answer be to me?"

"There can be little reason for concealing it," said the Count. "The Varangian is a brave man, and a strong one; it is contrary to my vow to shun his challenge, and perhaps I shall derogate from my rank by accepting it; but the world is wide, and he is yet to be born who has seen Robert of Paris shun the face of mortal man. By means of some gallant officer among the Emperor's guards, this poor fellow, who nourishes so strange an ambition, shall learn that he shall have his wish gratified."

"And then?"—said Anna Comnena.

"Why, then," said the Count, "in the poor man's own language, God schaw the right!"

"Which is to say," said the Princess, "that if my father has an officer of his guards honourable enough to forward so pious and reasonable a purpose, the Emperor must lose an ally, in whose faith he puts confidence, or a most trusty and faithful soldier of his personal guard, who has distinguished himself upon many occasions?"

"I am happy to hear," said the Count, "that the man bears such a character. In truth, his ambition ought to have some foundation. The more I think of it, the rather am I of opinion that there is something generous, rather than derogatory, in giving to the poor exile, whose thoughts are so high and noble, those privileges of a man of rank, which some who were born in such lofty station are too cowardly to avail themselves of. Yet despond not, noble Princess; the challenge is not yet accepted of, and if it was, the issue is in the hand of God. As for me, whose trade is war, the sense that I have something so serious to transact with this resolute man, will keep me from other less honourable quarrels, in which a lack of occupation might be apt to involve me."

The Princess made no farther observation, being resolved, by private remonstrance to Achilles Tatius, to engage him to prevent a meeting which might be fatal to the one or the other of two brave men. The town now darkened before them, sparkling, at the same time, through its obscurity, by the many lights which illuminated the houses of the citizens. The royal cavalcade held their way to the

Golden Gate, where the trusty centurion put his guard under arms to receive them.

"We must now break off, fair ladies," said the Count, as the party, having now dismounted, were standing together at the private gate of the Blacquernal Palace, "and find as we can, the lodgings which we occupied last night."

"Under your favour, no," said the Empress. "You must be content to take your supper and repose in quarters more fitting your rank; and," added Irene, "with no worse quartermaster than one of the Imperial family who has been your travelling companion."

This the Count heard, with considerable inclination to accept the hospitality which was so readily offered. Although as devoted as a man could well be to the charms of his Brenhilda, the very idea never having entered his head of preferring another's beauty to hers, yet, nevertheless, he had naturally felt himself flattered by the
attentions of a woman of eminent beauty and very high rank; and the praises with which the Princess had loaded him, had not entirely fallen to the ground. He was no longer in the humour in which the morning had found him, disposed to outrage the feelings of the Emperor, and to insult his dignity; but, flattered by the adroit sycophancy which the old philosopher had learned from the schools, and the beautiful Princess had been gifted with by nature, he assented to the Empress's proposal; the more readily, perhaps, that the darkness did not permit him to see that there was distinctly a shade of displeasure on the brow of Brenhilda. Whatever the cause, she cared not to express it, and the married pair had just entered that labyrinth of passages through which Hereward had formerly wandered, when a chamberlain, and a female attendant, richly dressed, bent the knee before them, and offered them the means and place to adjust their attire, ere they entered the Imperial presence. Brenhilda looked upon her apparel and arms, spotted with the blood of the insolent Scythian, and, Amazon as she was, felt the shame of being carelessly and improperly dressed. The arms of the knight were also bloody, and in disarrangement.

"Tell my female squire, Agatha, to give her attendance," said the

Countess. "She alone is in the habit of assisting to unarm and to attire me."

"Now, God be praised," thought the Grecian lady of the bed– chamber, "that I am not called to a toilet where smiths' hammers and tongs are like to be the instruments most in request!"

"Tell Marcian, my armourer," said the Count, "to attend with the silver and blue suit of plate and mail which I won in a wager from the Count of Thoulouse." [Footnote: Raymond Count of Thoulouse, and St. Giles, Duke of Carboune, and Marquis of Provence, an aged warrior who had won high distinction in the contests against the Saracens in Spain, was the chief leader of the Crusaders from the south of France. His title of St. Giles is corrupted by Anna Comnena into *Sangles*, by which name she constantly mentions him in the Alexiad.]

"Might I not have the honour of adjusting your armour," said a splendidly drest courtier, with some marks of the armourer's profession, "since I have put on that of the Emperor himself?—may his name be sacred!"

"And how many rivets hast thou clenched upon the occasion with this hand," said the Count, catching hold of it, "which looks as if it had never been washed, save with milk of roses,—and with this childish toy?" pointing to a hammer with ivory haft and silver head, which, stuck into a milk–white kidskin apron, the official wore as badges of his duty. The armourer fell back in some confusion. "His grasp," he said to another domestic, "is like the seizure of a vice!"

While this little scene passed apart, the Empress Irene, her daughter, and her son–in–law, left the company, under pretence of making a necessary change in their apparel. Immediately after, Agelastes was required to attend the Emperor, and the strangers were conducted to two adjacent chambers of retirement, splendidly fitted up, and placed for the present at their disposal, and that of their attendants. There
we shall for a time leave them, assuming, with the assistance of their own attendants, a dress which their ideas regarded as most fit for a great occasion; those of the Grecian court willingly keeping apart

from a task which they held nearly as formidable as assisting at the lair of a royal tiger or his bride.

Agelastes found the Emperor sedulously arranging his most splendid court–dress; for, as in the court of Pekin, the change of ceremonial attire was a great part of the ritual observed at Constantinople.

"Thou hast done well, wise Agelastes," said Alexius to the philosopher, as he approached with abundance of prostrations and genuflexions—"Thou hast done well, and we are content with thee. Less than thy wit and address must have failed in separating from their company this tameless bull, and unyoked heifer, over whom, if we obtain influence, we shall command, by every account, no small interest among those who esteem them the bravest in the host."

"My humble understanding," said Agelastes, "had been infinitely inferior to the management of so prudent and sagacious a scheme, had it not been shaped forth and suggested by the inimitable wisdom of your most sacred Imperial Highness."

"We are aware," said Alexius, "that we had the merit of blocking forth the scheme of detaining these persons, either by their choice as allies, or by main force as hostages. Their friends, ere yet they have missed them, will be engaged in war with the Turks, and at no liberty, if the devil should suggest such an undertaking, to take arms against the sacred empire. Thus, Agelastes, we shall obtain hostages at least as important and as valuable as that Count of Vermandois, whose liberty the tremendous Godfrey of Bouillon extorted from us by threats of instant war."

"Pardon," said Agelastes, "if I add another reason to those which of themselves so heavily support your august resolution. It is possible that we may, by observing the greatest caution and courtesy towards these strangers, win them in good earnest to our side."

"I conceive you, I conceive you,"—said the Emperor; "and this very night I will exhibit myself to this Count and his lady in the royal presence chamber, in the richest robes which our wardrobe can furnish. The lions of Solomon shall roar, the golden tree of Comnenus shall display its wonders, and the feeble eyes of these

Franks shall be altogether dazzled by the splendour of the empire. These spectacles cannot but sink into their minds, and dispose them to become the allies and servants of a nation so much more powerful, skilful, and wealthy than their own—Thou hast something to say, Agelastes. Years and long study have made thee wise; though we have given our opinion, thou mayst speak thine own, and live."

Thrice three times did Agelastes press his brow against the hem of the Emperor's garment, and great seemed his anxiety to find such words as might intimate his dissent from his sovereign, yet save him from the informality of contradicting him expressly.

"These sacred words, in which your sacred Highness has uttered your most just and accurate opinions, are undeniable, and incapable of contradiction, were any vain enough to attempt to impugn them. Nevertheless, be it lawful to say, that men show the wisest arguments in vain to those who do not understand reason, just as you would in vain exhibit a curious piece of limning to the blind, or endeavour to bribe, as scripture saith, a sow by the offer of a precious stone. The fault is not, in such case, in the accuracy of your sacred reasoning, but in the obtuseness and perverseness of the barbarians to whom it is applied."

"Speak more plainly," said the Emperor; "how often must we tell thee, that in cases in which we really want counsel, we know we must be contented to sacrifice ceremony?"

"Then in plain words," said Agelastes, "these European barbarians are like no others under the cope of the universe, either on the things on which they look with desire, or on those which they consider as discouraging. The treasures of this noble empire, so far as they affected their wishes, would merely inspire them with the desire to go to war with a nation possessed of so much wealth, and who, in their self–conceited estimation, were less able to defend, than they themselves are powerful to assail. Of such a description, for instance, is Bohemond of Tarentum,—and such, a one is many a crusader less able and sagacious than he;—for I think I need not tell your Imperial Divinity, that he holds his own self–interest to be the devoted guide of his whole conduct through this extraordinary war;

and that, therefore, you can justly calculate his course, when once you are aware from which point of the compass the wind of avarice and self–interest breathes with respect to him. But there are spirits among the Franks of a very different nature, and who must be acted upon by very different motives, if we would make ourselves masters of their actions, and the principles by which they are governed. If it were lawful to do so, I would request your Majesty to look at the manner by which an artful juggler of your court achieves his imposition upon the eyes of spectators, yet needfully disguises the means by which he attains his object. This people—I mean the more lofty–minded of these crusaders, who act up to the pretences of the doctrines which they call chivalry— despise the thirst of gold, and gold itself, unless to hilt their swords, or to furnish forth some necessary expenses, as alike useless and contemptible. The man who can be moved by the thirst of gain, they contemn, scorn, and despise, and liken him, in the meanness of his objects, to the most paltry serf that ever followed the plough, or wielded the spade. On the other hand, if it happens that they actually need gold, they are sufficiently unceremonious in taking it where they can most easily find it. Thus, they are neither easily to be bribed by giving them sums of gold, nor to be starved into compliance by withholding what chance may render necessary for them. In the one case, they set no value upon
the gift of a little paltry yellow dross; in the other, they are
accustomed to take what they want."

"Yellow dross," interrupted Alexius. "Do they call that noble metal, equally respected by Roman and barbarian, by rich and poor, by great and mean, by churchmen and laymen, which all mankind are fighting for, plotting for, planning for, intriguing for, and damning themselves for, both soul and body—by the opprobrious name of yellow dross? They are mad, Agelastes, utterly mad. Perils and dangers, penalties and scourges, are the arguments to which men who are above the universal influence which moves all others, can possibly be accessible."

"Nor are they," said Agelastes, "more accessible to fear than they are to self–interest. They are indeed, from their boyhood, brought up to scorn those passions which influence ordinary minds, whether by means of avarice to impel, or of fear to hold back. So much is this

the case, that what is enticing to other men, must, to interest them, have the piquant sauce of extreme danger. I told, for instance, to this very hero, a legend of a Princess of Zulichium, who lay on an enchanted couch, beautiful as an angel, awaiting the chosen knight who should, by dispelling her enchanted slumbers, become master of her person, of her kingdom of Zulichium, and of her countless treasures; and, would your Imperial Majesty believe me, I could scarce get the gallant to attend to my legend or take any interest in
the adventure, till I assured him he would have to encounter a winged dragon, compared to which the largest of those in the Frank romances was but like a mere dragon–fly?"

"And did this move the gallant?" said the Emperor.

"So much so," replied the philosopher, "that had I not unfortunately, by the earnestness of my description, awakened the jealousy of his Penthesilea of a Countess, he had forgotten the crusade and all belonging to it, to go in quest of Zulichium and its slumbering sovereign."

"Nay, then," said the Emperor, "we have in our empire (make us sensible of the advantage!) innumerable tale–tellers who are not possessed in the slightest degree of that noble scorn of gold which is proper to the Franks, but shall, for a brace of besants, lie with the devil, and beat him to boot, if in that manner we can gain, as mariners say, the weathergage of the Franks."

"Discretion," said Agelastes, "is in the highest degree necessary. Simply to lie is no very great matter; it is merely a departure from the truth, which is little different from missing a mark at archery, where the whole horizon, one point alone excepted, will alike serve the shooter's purpose; but to move the Frank as is desired, requires a perfect knowledge of his temper and disposition, great caution and presence of mind, and the most versatile readiness in changing from one subject to another. Had I not myself been, somewhat alert, I might have paid the penalty of a false step in your Majesty's service, by being flung into my own cascade by the virago whom I offended."

"A perfect Thalestris!" said the Emperor; "I shall take care what offence I give her."

"If I might speak and live," said Agelastes, "the Caesar Nicephorus Briennius had best adopt the same precaution."

"Nicephorus," said the Emperor, "must settle that with our daughter. I have ever told her that she gives him too much of that history, of which a page or two is sufficiently refreshing; but by our own self we must swear it, Agelastes, that, night after night, hearing nothing else, would subdue the patience of a saint!—Forget, good Agelastes, that them hast heard me say such a thing—more especially, remember it not when thou art in presence of our Imperial wife and daughter."

"Nor were the freedoms taken by the Caesar beyond the bounds of an innocent gallantry," said Agelastes; "but the Countess, I must needs say, is dangerous. She killed this day the Scythian Toxartis, by what seemed a mere fillip on the head."

"Hah!" said the Emperor; "I knew that Toxartis, and he was like enough to deserve his death, being a bold unscrupulous marauder. Take notes, however, how it happened, the names of witnesses, etc., that, if necessary, we may exhibit the fact as a deed of aggression on the part of the Count and Countess of Paris, to the assembly of the crusaders."

"I trust," said Agelastes, "your Imperial Majesty will not easily resign the golden opportunity of gaining to your standard persons whose character stands so very high in chivalry. It would cost you but little to bestow upon them a Grecian island, worth a hundred of their own paltry lordship of Paris; and if it were given under the condition of their expelling the infidels or the disaffected who may have obtained the temporary possession, it would be so much the more likely to be an acceptable offer. I need not say that the whole knowledge, wisdom, and skill of the poor Agelastes is at your Imperial Majesty's disposal."

The Emperor paused for a moment, and then said, as if on full consideration, "Worthy Agelastes, I dare trust thee in this difficult and somewhat dangerous matter; but I will keep my purpose of exhibiting to them the lions of Solomon, and the golden tree of our Imperial house."

"To that there can be no objection," returned the philosopher; "only remember to exhibit few guards, for these Franks are like a fiery horse; when in temper he may be ridden with a silk thread, but when he has taken umbrage or suspicion, as they would likely do if they saw many armed men, a steel bridle would not restrain him."

"I will be cautious," said the Emperor, "in that particular, as well as others.—Sound the silver bell, Agelastes, that the officers of our wardrobe may attend."

"One single word, while your Highness is alone," said Agelastes. "Will your Imperial Majesty transfer to me the direction of your menagerie, or collection of extraordinary creatures?"

"You make me wonder," said the Emperor, taking a signet, bearing upon it a lion, with the legend, *Vicit Leo ex tribu Judae*. "This," he said, "will give thee the command of our dens. And now, be candid for once with thy master—for deception is thy nature even with me
—By what charm wilt thou subdue these untamed savages?"

"By the power of falsehood," replied Agelastes, with deep reverence. "I

believe thee an adept in it," said the Emperor. "And to which of their foibles wilt thou address it?"

"To their love of fame," said the philosopher; and retreated backwards out of the royal apartment, as the officers of the wardrobe entered to complete the investment of the Emperor in his Imperial habiliments.

Chapter the Fourteenth

I will converse with iron–witted fools, And
unrespective boys; none are for me, That look into
me with considerate eyes;—
High–reaching Buckingham grows circumspect.
RICHARD III.

As they parted from each other, the Emperor and philosopher had each their
own anxious thoughts on the interview which had passed between them;
thoughts which they expressed in broken sentences and ejaculations, though
for the better understanding of the degree of estimation in which they held
each other, we will give them a more regular and intelligible form.

"Thus, then," half muttered half said Alexius, but so low as to hide his
meaning from the officers of the wardrobe, who entered to do their office,—
"thus, then, this bookworm—this remnant of old heathen philosophy, who
hardly believes, so God save me, the truth of the Christian creed, has topp'd
his part so well that he forces his Emperor to dissemble in his presence.
Beginning by being the buffoon of the court, he has wormed himself into all
its secrets,
made himself master of all its intrigues, conspired with my own son–
in–law against me, debauched my guards,—indeed so woven his web of
deceit, that my life is safe no longer, than he believes me the imperial dolt
which I have affected to seem, in order to deceive him; fortunate that even so
can I escape his cautionary anticipation of my displeasure, by avoiding to
precipitate his measures of violence. But were this sudden storm of the
crusade fairly passed over, the ungrateful Caesar, the boastful coward
Achilles Tatius, and the bosom serpent Agelastes, shall know whether
Alexius Comnenus
has been born their dupe. When Greek meets Greek, comes the strife of
subtlety, as well as the tug of war." Thus saying, he resigned himself to the
officers of his wardrobe, who proceeded to ornament him as the solemnity
required,

"I trust him not," said Agelastes, the meaning of whose gestures and exclamations, we, in like manner, render into a connected meaning. "I cannot, and do not trust him—he somewhat overacts his part. He has borne himself upon other occasions with the shrewd wit of his family the Comneni; yet he now trusts to the effect of his trumpery lions upon such a shrewd people as the Franks and Normans, and seems to rely upon me for the character of men with whom he has been engaged in peace and war for many years. This can be but to gain my confidence; for there were imperfect looks, and broken sentences, which seemed to say, 'Agelastes, the Emperor knows thee and confides not in thee.' Yet the plot is successful and undiscovered, as far as can be judged; and were I to attempt to recede now, I were lost for ever. A little time to carry on this intrigue with the Frank, when possibly, by the assistance of this gallant, Alexius shall exchange the crown for a cloister, or a still narrower abode; and then, Agelastes, thou deservest to be blotted from the roll of philosophers, if thou canst not push out of the throne the conceited and luxurious Caesar, and reign in his stead, a second Marcus Antoninus, when the wisdom of thy rule, long unfelt in a world which has been guided by tyrants and voluptuaries, shall soon obliterate recollection of the manner in which thy power was acquired. To work then—be active, and be cautious. The time requires it, and the prize deserves it."

While these thoughts passed through his mind, he arrayed himself, by the assistance of Diogenes, in a clean suit of that simple apparel in which he always frequented the court; a garb as unlike that of a candidate for royalty, as it was a contrast to the magnificent robes with which Alexius was now investing himself,

In their separate apartments, or dressing–rooms, the Count of Paris and his lady put on the best apparel which they had prepared to meet such a chance upon their journey. Even in France, Robert was seldom seen in the peaceful cap and sweeping mantle, whose high plumes and flowing folds were the garb of knights in times of peace.
He was now arrayed in a splendid suit of armour, all except the head, which was bare otherwise than as covered by his curled locks. The rest of his person was sheathed in the complete mail of the time, richly inlaid with silver, which contrasted with the azure in which

the steel was damasked. His spurs were upon his heels—his sword was by his side, and his triangular shield was suspended round his neck, bearing, painted upon it, a number of *fleures–de–lis semees*, as it is called, upon the field, being the origin of those lily flowers
which after times reduced to three only; and which were the terror of Europe, until they suffered so many reverses in our own time.

The extreme height of Count Robert's person adapted him for a garb, which had a tendency to make persons of a lower stature appear rather dwarfish and thick when arrayed *cap–a–pie*. The features,
with their self–collected composure, and noble contempt of whatever could have astounded or shaken an ordinary mind, formed a well– fitted capital to the excellently proportioned and vigorous frame which they terminated. The Countess was in more peaceful attire;
but her robes were short and succinct, like those of one who might be called to hasty exercise. The upper part of her dress consisted of more than one tunic, sitting close to the body, while a skirt, descending from the girdle, and reaching to the ankles, embroidered elegantly but richly, completed an attire which a lady might have worn in much more modern times. Her tresses were covered with a light steel head–piece, though some of them, escaping, played round her face, and gave relief to those handsome features which might otherwise have seemed too formal, if closed entirely within the verge of steel. Over these undergarments was flung a rich velvet cloak of a deep green colour, descending from the head, where a species of
hood was loosely adjusted over the helmet, deeply laced upon its verges and seams, and so long as to sweep the ground behind. A dagger of rich materials ornamented a girdle of curious goldsmith's work, and was the only offensive weapon which, notwithstanding her military occupation, she bore upon this occasion.

The toilet—as modern times would say—of the Countess, was not nearly so soon ended as that of Count Robert, who occupied his time, as husbands of every period are apt to do, in little sub–acid complaints between jest and earnest, upon the dilatory nature of ladies, and the time which they lose in doffing and donning their garments. But when the Countess Brenhilda came forth in the pride of loveliness, from the inner chamber where she had attired herself, her husband, who was still her lover, clasped her to his breast and expressed his privilege by the kiss which he took as of right from a creature so beautiful. Chiding him for his folly, yet almost returning the kiss which she received, Brenhilda began now to wonder how they were to find their way to the presence of the Emperor.

The query was soon solved, for a gentle knock at the door announced Agelastes, to whom, as best acquainted with the Frankish manners, had been committed, by the Emperor, the charge of introducing the noble strangers. A distant sound, like that of the roaring of a lion, or not unsimilar to a large and deep gong of modern times, intimated the commencement of the ceremonial. The black slaves upon guard, who, as hath been observed, were in small numbers, stood ranged in their state dresses of white and gold, bearing in one hand a naked sabre, and in the other a torch of white wax, which served to guide the Count and Countess through the passages that led to the interior of the palace, and to the most secret hall of audience.

The door of this *sanctum sanctorum* was lower than usual, a simple stratagem devised by some superstitious officer of the Imperial household, to compel the lofty–crested Frank to lower his body, as he presented himself in the Imperial presence. Robert, when the door flew open, and he discovered in the background the Emperor seated upon his throne amidst a glare of light, which was broken and reflected in ten thousand folds by the jewels with which his vestments were covered, stopt short, and demanded the meaning of introducing him through so low an arch? Agelastes pointed to the Emperor by way of shifting from himself a question which he could not have answered. The mute, to apologize for his silence, yawned, and showed the loss of his tongue.

"Holy Virgin!" said the Countess, "what can these unhappy Africans have done, to have deserved a condemnation which involves so cruel a fate?"

"The hour of retribution is perhaps come," said the Count, in a displeased tone, while Agelastes, with such hurry as time and place permitted, entered, making his prostrations and genuflexions, little doubting that the Frank must follow him, and to do so must lower his body to the Emperor. The Count, however, in the height of displeasure at the trick which he conceived had been, intended him, turned himself round, and entered the presence–chamber with his back purposely turned to the sovereign, and did not face Alexius until he reached the middle of the apartment, when he was joined by

the Countess, who had made her approach in a more seemly manner. The Emperor, who had prepared to acknowledge the Count's expected homage in the most gracious manner, found himself now even more unpleasantly circumstanced than when this uncompromising Frank had usurped the royal throne in the course of the day.

The officers and nobles who stood around, though a very select number, were more numerous than usual, as the meeting was not held for counsel, but merely for state. These assumed such an appearance of mingled displeasure and confusion as might best suit with the perplexity of Alexius, while the wily features of the Norman–Italian, Bohemond of Tarentum, who was also present, had a singular mixture of fantastical glee and derision. It is the misfortune of the weaker on such occasions, or at least the more timid, to be obliged to take the petty part of winking hard, as if not able to see what they cannot avenge.

Alexius made the signal that the ceremonial of the grand reception should immediately commence. Instantly the lions of Solomon, which had been newly furbished, raised their heads, erected their manes, brandished their tails, until they excited the imagination of Count Robert, who, being already on fire at the circumstances of his

reception, conceived the bellowing of these automata to be the actual annunciation of immediate assault. Whether the lions, whose forms he beheld, were actually lords of the forest,—whether they were mortals who had suffered transformation,—whether they were productions of the skill of an artful juggler or profound naturalist,

the Count neither knew nor cared. All that he thought of the danger was, it was worthy of his courage; nor did his heart permit him a moment's irresolution. He strode to the nearest lion, which seemed in the act of springing up, and said, in a tone loud and formidable as its own, "How now, dog!" At the same time he struck the figure with

his clenched fist and steel gauntlet with so much force, that its head burst, and the steps and carpet of the throne were covered with wheels, springs, and other machinery, which had been the means of producing its mimic terrors.

On this display of the real nature of the cause of his anger, Count Robert could not but feel a little ashamed of having given way to passion on such an occasion. He was still more confused when Bohemond, descending from his station near the Emperor, addressed him in the Frank language;—"You have done a gallant deed, truly, Count Robert, in freeing the court of Byzantium from an object of fear which has long been used to frighten peevish children and
unruly barbarians!"

Enthusiasm has no greater enemy than ridicule. "Why, then," said Count Robert, blushing deeply at the same time, "did they exhibit its fantastic terrors to me? I am neither child nor barbarian."

"Address yourself to the Emperor, then, as an intelligent man," answered Bohemond. "Say something to him in excuse of your conduct, and show that our bravery has not entirely run away with our common sense. And hark you also, while I have a moment's speech of you,—do you and your wife heedfully follow my example at supper!" These words were spoken with a significant tone and corresponding look.

The opinion of Bohemond, from his long intercourse, both in peace and war, with the Grecian Emperor, gave him great influence with the other crusaders, and Count Robert yielded to his advice. He turned towards the Emperor with something liker an obeisance than he had hitherto paid. "I crave your pardon," he said, "for breaking that gilded piece of pageantry; but, in sooth, the wonders of sorcery, and the portents of accomplished and skilful jugglers, are so numerous in this country, that one does not clearly distinguish what is true from what is false, or what is real from what is illusory."

The Emperor, notwithstanding the presence of mind for which he was remarkable, and the courage in which he was not held by his countrymen to be deficient, received this apology somewhat awkwardly. Perhaps the rueful complaisance with which he accepted the Count's apology, might be best compared to that of a lady of the present day when an awkward guest has broken a valuable piece of china. He muttered something about the machines having been long preserved in the Imperial family, as being made on the model of those which guarded the throne of the wise King of Israel; to which the blunt plain–spoken Count expressed his doubt in reply, whether the wisest prince in the world ever condescended to frighten his subjects or guests by the mimic roarings of a wooden lion. "If," said he, "I too hastily took it for a living creature, I have had the worst, by damaging my excellent gauntlet in dashing to pieces its timber skull."

The Emperor, after a little more had been said, chiefly on the same subject, proposed that they should pass to the banquet–room. Marshalled, accordingly, by the grand sewer of the Imperial table, and attended by all present, excepting the Emperor and the immediate members of his family, the Frankish guests were guided through a labyrinth of apartments, each of which was filled with wonders of nature and art, calculated to enhance their opinion of the
wealth and grandeur which had assembled together so much that was wonderful. Their passage being necessarily slow and interrupted, gave the Emperor time to change his dress, according to the ritual of his court, which did not permit his appearing twice in the same vesture before the same spectators. He took the opportunity to summon Agelastes into his presence, and, that their conference
might be secret, he used, in assisting his toilet, the agency of some of the mutes destined for the service of the interior.

The temper of Alexius Comnenus was considerably moved, although it was one of the peculiarities of his situation to be ever under the necessity of disguising the emotions of his mind, and of affecting, in presence of his subjects, a superiority to human passion, which he was far from feeling. It was therefore with gravity, and even reprehension, that he asked, "By whose error it was that the wily Bohemond, half– Italian, and half–Norman, was present at this interview? Surely, if there be one in the crusading army likely to conduct that foolish youth and his wife behind the scenes of the exhibition by which we hoped to impose upon them, the Count of Tarentum, as he entitles himself, is that person."

"It was that old man," said Agelastes, "(if I may reply and live,) Michael Cantacuzene, who deemed that his presence was peculiarly desired; but he returns to the camp this very night."

"Yes," said Alexius, "to inform Godfrey, and the rest of the crusaders, that one of the boldest and most highly esteemed of their number is left, with his wife, a hostage in our Imperial city, and to bring back, perhaps, an alternative of instant war, unless they are delivered up!"

"If it is your Imperial Highness's will to think so," said Agelastes, "you can suffer Count Robert and his wife to return to the camp with the Italian–Norman."

"What?" answered the Emperor, "and so lose all the fruits of an enterprise, the preparations for which have already cost us so much in actual expense; and, were our heart made of the same stuff with that of ordinary mortals, would have cost us so much more in vexation and anxiety? No, no; issue warning to the crusaders, who are still on the hither side, that farther rendering of homage is dispensed with, and that they repair to the quays on the banks of the Bosphorus, by peep of light to–morrow. Let our admiral, as he values his head, pass every man of them over to the farther side before noon. Let there be largesses, a princely banquet on the farther bank— all that may increase their anxiety to pass. Then, Agelastes, we will trust to ourselves to meet this additional danger, either by bribing the venality of Bohemond, or by bidding defiance to the crusaders. Their forces are scattered, and the chief of them, with the leaders themselves, are all now—or by far the greater part—on the east side of the Bosphorus.—And now to the banquet! seeing that
the change of dress has been made sufficient to answer the statutes of the household; since our ancestors chose to make rules for exhibiting us to our subjects, as priests exhibit their images at their shrines!"

"Under grant of life," said Agelastes, "it was not done inconsiderately, but in order that the Emperor, ruled ever by the same laws from father to son, might ever be regarded as something beyond the common laws of humanity—the divine image of a saint, therefore, rather than a human being."

"We know it, good Agelastes," answered the Emperor, with a smile, "and we are also aware, that many of our subjects, like the worshippers of Bel in holy writ, treat us so far as an image, as to assist us in devouring the revenues of our provinces, which are gathered in our name, and for our use. These things we now only touch lightly, the time not suiting them."

Alexius left the secret council accordingly, after the order for the passage of the crusaders had been written out and subscribed in due form, and in the sacred ink of the Imperial chancery.

Meantime, the rest of the company had arrived in a hall, which, like the other apartments in the palace, was most tastefully as well as gorgeously fitted up, except that a table, which presented a princely banquet, might have been deemed faulty in this respect, that the dishes, which were most splendid, both in the materials of which they were composed, and in the viands which they held, were elevated by means of feet, so as to be upon a level with female guests as they sat, and with men as they lay recumbent at the banquet which it offered.

Around stood a number of black slaves richly attired, while the grand sewer, Michael Cantazucene, arranged the strangers with his golden wand, and conveyed orders to them, by signs, that all should remain standing around the table, until a signal should be given.

The upper end of the board, thus furnished, and thus surrounded,
was hidden by a curtain of muslin and silver, which fell from the top of the arch under which the upper part seemed to pass. On this curtain the sewer kept a wary eye; and when he observed it slightly shake, he waved his wand of office, and all expected the result.

As if self–moved, the mystic curtain arose, and discovered behind it a throne eight steps higher than the end of the table, decorated in the most magnificent manner, and having placed before it a small table of ivory inlaid with silver, behind which was seated Alexius
Comnenus, in a dress entirely different from what he had worn in the course of the day, and so much more gorgeous than his former

vestments, that it seemed not unnatural that his subjects should prostrate themselves before a figure so splendid. His wife, his daughter, and his son–in–law the Caesar, stood behind him with faces bent to the ground, and it was with deep humility, that, descending from the throne at the Emperor's command, they mingled with the guests of the lower table, and, exalted as they were, proceeded to the festive board at the signal of the grand sewer. So that they could not be said to partake of the repast with the Emperor, nor to be placed at the Imperial table, although they supped in his presence, and were encouraged by his repeated request to them to make good cheer. No dishes presented at the lower table were offered at the higher; but wines, and more delicate sorts of food, which arose before the Emperor as if by magic, and seemed designed for his own proper use, were repeatedly sent, by his special directions, to one or other of the guests whom Alexius delighted to honour— among these the Franks being particularly distinguished.

The behaviour of Bohemond was on this occasion particularly remarkable.

Count Robert, who kept an eye upon him, both from his recent words, and owing to an expressive look which he once or twice darted towards him, observed, that in no liquors or food, not even those sent from the Emperor's own table, did this astucious prince choose to indulge. A piece of bread, taken from the canister at random, and a glass of pure water, was the only refreshment of which he was pleased to partake. His alleged excuse was, the veneration due to the Holy Festival of the Advent, which chanced to occur that very night, and which both the Greek and Latin rule agree to hold sacred.

"I had not expected this of you, Sir Bohemond," said the Emperor, "that you should have refused my personal hospitality at my own board, on the very day on which you honoured me by entering into my service as vassal for the principality of Antioch."

"Antioch is not yet conquered," said Sir Bohemond; "and conscience, dread sovereign, must always have its exceptions, in whatever temporal contracts we may engage."

"Come, gentle Count," said the Emperor, who obviously regarded Bohemond's inhospitable humour as something arising more from suspicion than devotion, "we invite, though it is not our custom, our children, our noble guests, and our principal officers here present, to a general carouse. Fill the cups called the Nine Muses! let them be brimful of the wine which is said to be sacred to the Imperial lips!"

At the Emperor's command the cups were filled; they were of pure gold, and there was richly engraved upon each the effigy of the Muse to whom it was dedicated.

"You at least," said the Emperor, "my gentle Count Robert, you and your lovely lady, will not have any scruple to pledge your Imperial host?"

"If that scruple is to imply suspicion of the provisions with which we are here served, I disdain to nourish such," said Count Robert. "If it is a sin which I commit by tasting wine to–night, it is a venial one; nor shall I greatly augment my load by carrying it, with the rest of my trespasses, to the next confessional."

"Will you then, Prince Bohemond, not be ruled by the conduct of your friend?" said the Emperor.

"Methinks," replied the Norman–Italian, "my friend might have done better to have been, ruled by mine; but be it as his wisdom pleases. The flavour of such exquisite wine is sufficient for me."

"So saying, he emptied the wine into another goblet, and seemed alternately to admire the carving of the cup, and the flavour of what it had lately contained.

"You are right, Sir Bohemond," said the Emperor; "the fabric of that cup is beautiful; it was done by one of the ancient gravers of Greece. The boasted cup of Nestor, which Homer has handed down to us, was a good deal larger perhaps, but neither equalled these in the value of the material, nor the exquisite beauty of the workmanship. Let each one, therefore, of my stranger guests, accept of the cup which he either has or might have drunk out of, as a recollection of me; and may the expedition against the infidels be as propitious as their confidence and courage deserve!"

"If I accept your gift, mighty Emperor," said Bohemond, "it is only to atone for the apparent discourtesy, when my devotion, compels me to decline your Imperial pledge, and to show you that we part on the most intimate terms of friendship."

So saying, he bowed deeply to the Emperor, who answered him with a smile, into which was thrown, a considerable portion of sarcastic expression.

"And I," said the Count of Paris, "having taken upon my conscience the fault of meeting your Imperial pledge, may stand excused from incurring the blame of aiding to dismantle your table of these curious drinking cups. We empty them to your health, and we cannot in any other respect profit by them."

"But Prince Bohemond can," said the Emperor; "to whose quarters they shall be carried, sanctioned by your generous use. And we have still a set for you, and for your lovely Countess, equal to that of the Graces, though no longer matching in number the nymphs of Parnassus.—The evening bell rings, and calls us to remember the hour of rest, that we may be ready to meet the labours of to– morrow."

The party then broke up for the evening. Bohemond left the palace that night, not forgetting the Muses, of whom he was not in general a devotee. The result was, as the wily Greek had intended, that he had established between Bohemond and the Count, not indeed a quarrel, but a kind of difference of opinion; Bohemond feeling that the fiery Count of Paris must think his conduct sordid and avaricious, while Count Robert was far less inclined than before to rely on him as a counsellor.

CHAPTER THE FIFTEENTH

The Count of Paris and his lady were that night lodged in the Imperial Palace of the Blacquernal. Their apartments were contiguous, but the communication between them was cut off for the night by the mutual door being locked and barred. They marvelled somewhat at this precaution. The observance, however, of the
festival of the Church, was pleaded as an admissible, and not unnatural excuse for this extraordinary circumstance. Neither the Count nor his lady entertained, it may be believed, the slightest personal fear for any thing which could happen to them. Their attendants, Marcian and Agatha, having assisted their master and mistress in the performance of their usual offices, left them, in order to seek the places of repose assigned to them among persons of their degree.

The preceding day had been one of excitation, and of much bustle and interest; perhaps, also, the wine, sacred to the Imperial lips, of which Count Robert had taken a single, indeed, but a deep draught, was more potent than the delicate and high–flavoured juice of the Gascogne grape, to which he was accustomed; at any rate, it seemed to him that, from the time he felt that he had slept, daylight ought to have been broad in his chamber when he awaked, and yet it was still darkness almost palpable. Somewhat surprised, he gazed eagerly around, but could discern nothing, except two balls of red light which shone from among the darkness with a self–emitted brilliancy, like the eyes of a wild animal while it glares upon its prey. The
Count started from bed to put on his armour, a necessary precaution if what he saw should really be a wild creature and at liberty; but the instant he stirred, a deep growl was uttered, such as the Count had never heard, but which might be compared to the sound of a thousand monsters at once; and, as the symphony, was heard the clash of iron chains, and the springing of a monstrous creature towards the bedside, which appeared, however, to be withheld by some fastening from attaining the end of its bound. The roars which

it uttered now ran thick on each other. They were most tremendous, and must have been heard throughout the whole palace. The creature seemed to gather itself many yards nearer to the bed than by its glaring eyeballs it appeared at first to be stationed, and how much nearer, or what degree of motion, might place him within the monster's reach, the Count was totally uncertain. Its breathing was even heard, and Count Robert thought he felt the heat of its respiration, while his defenceless limbs might not be two yards distant from the fangs which he heard grinding against each other, and the claws which tore up fragments of wood from the oaken

floor. The Count of Paris was one of the bravest men who lived in a time when bravery was the universal property of all who claimed a drop of noble blood, and the knight was a descendant of Charlemagne. He was, however, a man, and therefore cannot be said to have endured unappalled a sense of danger so unexpected and so extraordinary. But his was not a sudden alarm or panic, it was a calm sense of extreme peril, qualified by a resolution to exert his faculties to the uttermost, to save his life if it were possible. He withdrew himself within the bed, no longer a place of rest, being thus a few

feet further from the two glaring eyeballs which remained so closely fixed upon him, that, in spite of his courage, nature painfully suggested the bitter imagination of his limbs being mangled, torn, and churned with their life–blood, in the jaws of some monstrous beast of prey. One saving thought alone presented itself—this might be a trial, an experiment of the philosopher Agelastes, or of the Emperor his master, for the purpose of proving the courage of which the Christians vaunted so highly, and punishing the thoughtless

insult which the Count had been misadvised enough to put upon the Emperor the preceding day.

"Well is it said," he reflected in his agony, "beard not the lion in his den! Perhaps even, now some base slave deliberates whether I have yet tasted enough of the preliminary agonies of death, and whether he shall yet slip the chain which keeps the savage from doing his work. But come death when it will, it shall never be said that Count Robert was heard to receive it with prayers for compassion, or with cries of pain or terror." He turned his face to the wall, and waited, with a strong mental exertion, the death which he conceived to be fast approaching.

His first feelings had been unavoidably of a selfish nature. The danger was too instant, and of a description too horrible, to admit of any which involved a more comprehensive view of his calamity; and other reflections of a more distant kind, were at first swallowed up in the all–engrossing thought of immediate death. But as his ideas became clearer, the safety of his Countess rushed upon his mind— what might she now be suffering! and, while he was subjected to a trial so extraordinary, for what were her weaker frame and female courage reserved? Was she still within a few yards of him, as when he lay down the last night? or had the barbarians, who had devised for him a scene so cruel, availed themselves of his and his lady's incautious confidence to inflict upon her some villany of the same kind, or even yet more perfidious? Did she sleep or wake, or could she sleep within the close hearing of that horrible cry, which shook all around? He resolved to utter her name, warning her, if possible, to be upon her guard, and to answer without venturing rashly into the apartment which contained a guest so horribly perilous.

He uttered, therefore, his wife's name, but in trembling accents, as if he had been afraid of the savage beast overhearing him.

"Brenhilda! Brenhilda!—there is danger–awake, and speak to me, but do not arise." There was no answer.—"What am I become," he said to himself, "that I call upon Brenhilda of Aspramonte, like a child on its sleeping nurse, and all because there is a wild–cat in the same room with me? Shame on thee, Count of Paris! Let thy arms be rent, and thy spurs be hacked from thy heels!—What ho!" he cried aloud, but still with a tremulous voice, "Brenhilda, we are beset, the foe are upon us! —Answer me, but stir not."

A deep growl from the monster which garrisoned his apartment was the only answer. The sound seemed to say, "Thou hast no hope!" and it ran to the knight's bosom as the genuine expression of despair.

"Perhaps, however, I am still too cold in making my misery known. What ho! my love! Brenhilda!"

A voice, hollow and disconsolate as that which might have served an inhabitant of the grave, answered as if from a distance. "What disconsolate wretch art thou, who expectest that the living can answer thee from the habitations of the dead?"

"I am a Christian man, a free noble of the kingdom of France," answered the Count. "Yesterday the captain of five hundred men, the bravest in France—the bravest, that is, who breathe mortal air—and
I am here without a glimpse of light, to direct me how to avoid the corner in which lies a wild tiger–cat, prompt to spring upon and to devour me."

"Thou art an example," replied the voice, "and wilt not long be the last, of the changes of fortune. I, who am now suffering in my third year, was that mighty Ursel, who rivalled Alexius Comnenus for the Crown of Greece, was betrayed by my confederates, and being deprived of that eyesight which is the chief blessing of humanity, I inhabit these vaults, no distant neighbour of the wild animals by whom they are sometimes occupied, and whose cries of joy I hear when unfortunate victims like thyself are delivered up to their fury."

"Didst thou not then hear," said Count Robert, in return, "a warlike guest and his bride conducted hither last night, with sounds as it might seem, of bridal music?—O, Brenhilda! hast thou, so young— so beautiful—been so treacherously done to death by means so unutterably horrible!"

"Think not," answered Ursel, as the voice had called its owner, "that the Greeks pamper their wild beasts on such lordly fare. For their enemies, which term includes not only all that are really such, but all those whom they fear or hate, they have dungeons whose locks
never revolve; hot instruments of steel, to sear the eyeballs in the head; lions and tigers, when it pleases them to make a speedy end of their captives—but these are only for the male prisoners. While for the women—if they be young and beautiful, the princes of the land have places in their bed and bower; nor are they employed like the captives of Agamemnon's host, to draw water from an Argive spring, but are admired and adored by those whom fate has made the lords
of their destiny."

"Such shall never be the doom of Brenhilda!" exclaimed Count

Robert; "her husband still lives to assist her, and should he die, she knows well how to follow him without leaving a blot in the epitaph of either."

The captive did not immediately reply, and a short pause ensued, which was broken by Ursel's voice. "Stranger," he said, "what noise is that I hear?"

"Nay, I hear nothing," said Count Robert.

"But I do," said Ursel. "The cruel deprivation of my eyesight renders my other senses more acute."

"Disquiet not thyself about the matter, fellow–prisoner," answered the Count, "but wait the event in silence."

Suddenly a light arose in the apartment, lurid, red, and smoky. The knight had bethought him of a flint and match which he usually carried about him, and with as little noise as possible had lighted the torch by the bedside; this he instantly applied to the curtains of the bed, which, being of thin muslin, were in a moment in flames. The knight sprung, at the same instant, from his bed. The tiger, for such it was, terrified at the flame, leaped backwards as far as his chain
would permit, heedless of any thing save this new object of terror. Count Robert upon this seized on a massive wooden stool, which was the only offensive weapon on which he could lay his hand, and, marking at those eyes which now reflected the blaze of fire, and which had recently seemed so appalling, he discharged against them this fragment of ponderous oak, with a force which less resembled human strength than the impetus with which an engine hurls a stone. He had employed his instant of time so well, and his aim was so
true, that the missile went right to the mark and with incredible force. The skull of the tiger, which might be, perhaps, somewhat exaggerated if described as being of the very largest size, was fractured by the blow, and with the assistance of his dagger, which had fortunately been left with him, the French Count despatched the monster, and had the satisfaction to see him grin his last, and roll, in the agony of death, those eyes which were lately so formidable.

Looking around him, he discovered, by the light of the fire which he had raised, that the apartment in which he now lay was different from that in which he had gone to bed overnight; nor could there be a stronger contrast between the furniture of both, than the flickering half–burnt remains of the thin muslin curtains, and the strong, bare, dungeon–looking walls of the room itself, or the very serviceable wooden stool, of which he had made such good use.

The knight had no leisure to form conclusions upon such a subject. He hastily extinguished the fire, which had, indeed, nothing that it could lay hold of, and proceeded, by the light of the flambeau, to examine the apartment, and its means of entrance. It is scarce necessary to say, that he saw no communication with the room of Brenhilda, which convinced him that they had been separated the evening before under pretence of devotional scruples, in order to accomplish some most villanous design upon one or both of them. His own part of the night's adventure we have already seen, and success, so far, over so formidable a danger, gave him a trembling hope that Brenhilda, by her own worth and valour, would be able to defend herself against all attacks of fraud or force, until he could find his way to her rescue. "I should have paid more regard," he said, "to Bohemond's caution last night, who, I think, intimated to me as plainly as if he had spoke it in direct terms, that that same cup of wine was a drugged potion. But then, fie upon him for an avaricious hound! How was it possible I should think he suspected any such thing, when he spoke not out like a man, but, for sheer coldness of heart, or base self–interest, suffered me to run the risk of being poisoned by the wily despot?"

Here he heard a voice from the same quarter as before. "Ho, there! Ho, stranger! Do you live, or have you been murdered? What means this stifling smell of smoke? For God's sake, answer him who can receive no information from eyes, closed, alas, for ever!"

"I am at liberty," said the Count, "and the monster destined to devour me has groaned its last. I would, my friend Ursel, since such is thy name, thou hadst the advantage of thine eyes, to have borne witness to yonder combat; it had been worth thy while, though thou shouldst have lost them a minute afterwards, and it would have greatly advantaged whoever shall have the task of compiling my history."

While he gave a thought to that vanity which strongly ruled him, he lost no time in seeking some mode of escape from the dungeon, for by that means only might he hope to recover his Countess. At last he found an entrance in the wall, but it was strongly locked and bolted. "I have found the passage,"— he called out; "and its direction is the same in which thy voice is heard—But how shall I undo the door?"

"I'll teach thee that secret," said Ursel. "I would I could as easily unlock each bolt that withholds us from the open air; but, as for thy seclusion within the dungeon, heave up the door by main strength, and thou shalt lift the locks to a place where, pushing then the door from thee, the fastenings will find a grooved passage in the wall, and the door itself will open. Would that I could indeed see thee, not
only because, being a gallant man, thou must be a goodly sight, but also because I should thereby know that I was not caverned in darkness for ever."

While he spoke thus, the Count made a bundle of his armour, from which he missed nothing except his sword, Tranchefer, and then proceeded to try what efforts he could make, according to the blind man's instructions, to open the door of his prison–house. Pushing in a direct line was, he soon found, attended with no effect; but when he applied his gigantic strength, and raised the door as high as it would go, he had the satisfaction to find that the bolts yielded, though reluctantly. A space had been cut so as to allow them to move out of the socket into which they had been forced; and without the turn of a key, but by a powerful thrust forwards, a small passage was left open. The knight entered, bearing his armour in his hand.

"I hear thee," said Ursel, "O stranger! and am aware thou art come into my place of captivity. For three years have I been employed in cutting these grooves, corresponding to the sockets which hold these iron bolts, and preserving the knowledge of the secret from the prison–keepers. Twenty such bolts, perhaps, must be sawn through, ere my steps shall approach the upper air. What prospect is there that I shall have strength of mind sufficient to continue the task? Yet, credit me, noble stranger, I rejoice in having been thus far aiding to thy deliverance; for if Heaven blesses not, in any farther degree, our aspirations after freedom, we may still be a comfort to each other, while tyranny permits our mutual life."

Count Robert looked around, and shuddered that a human being should talk of any thing approaching to comfort, connected with his residence in what seemed a living tomb. Ursel's dungeon was not above twelve feet square, vaulted in the roof, and strongly built in
the walls by stones which the chisel had morticed closely together. A bed, a coarse footstool, like that which Robert had just launched at the head of the tiger, and a table of equally massive materials, were its only articles of furniture. On a long stone, above the bed, were these few, but terrible words:—Zedekias Ursel, imprisoned here on the Ides of March, A.D.—. Died and interred on the spot"—A blank was left for filling up the period. The figure of the captive could hardly be discerned amid the wildness of his dress and dishabille.
The hair of his head, uncut and uncombed, descended in elf–locks, and mingled with a beard of extravagant length.

"Look on me," said the captive, "and rejoice that thou canst yet see the wretched condition to which iron–hearted tyranny can reduce a fellow–creature, both in mortal existence and in future hope."

"Was it thou," said Count Robert, whose blood ran cold in his veins, "that hadst the heart to spend thy time in sawing through the blocks of stone by which these bolts are secured?"

"Alas!" said Ursel, "what could a blind man do? Busy I must be, if I would preserve my senses. Great as the labour was, it was to me the task of three years; nor can you wonder that I should have devoted to it my whole time, when I had no other means of occupying it. Perhaps, and most likely, my dungeon does not admit the distinction of day and night; but a distant cathedral clock told me how hour after hour fled away, and found me expending them in rubbing one stone against another. But when the door gave way, I found I had only cut an access into a prison more strong than that which held me. I
rejoice, nevertheless, since it has brought us together, given thee an entrance to my dungeon, and me a companion in my misery."

"Think better than that," said Count Robert, "think of liberty—think of revenge! I cannot believe such unjust treachery will end successfully, else needs must I say, the heavens are less just than priests tell us of. How art thou supplied with food in this dungeon of thine?"

"A warder," said Ursel, "and who, I think, understands not the Greek language—at least he never either answers or addresses me—brings a loaf and a pitcher of water, enough to supply my miserable life till two days are past. I must, therefore, pray that you will retire for a space into the next prison, so that the warder may have no means of knowing that we can hold correspondence together."

"I see not," said Count Robert, "by what access the barbarian, if he is one, can enter my dungeon without passing through yours; but no matter, I will retire into the inner or outer room, whichever it happens to be, and be thou then well aware that the warder will have some one to grapple with ere he leaves his prison–work to–day. Meanwhile, think thyself dumb as thou art blind, and be assured that the offer of freedom itself would not induce me to desert the cause of a companion in adversity."

"Alas," said the old man, "I listen to thy promises as I should to those of the morning gale, which tells me that the sun is about to rise, although I know that I at least shall never behold it. Thou art one of those wild and undespairing knights, whom for so many years the west of Europe hath sent forth to attempt impossibilities, and from thee, therefore, I can only hope for such a fabric of relief as an idle boy would blow out of soap bubbles."

"Think better of us, old man," said Count Robert, retiring; "at least let me die with my blood warm, and believing it possible for me to be once more united to my beloved Brenhilda."

So saying, he retired into his own cell, and replaced the door, so that the operations of Ursel, which indeed were only such as three years' solitude could have achieved, should escape observation when again visited by the Warder. "It is ill luck," said he, when once more within his own prison—for that in which the tiger had been secured, he instinctively concluded to be destined for him—"It is ill luck that I had not found a young and able fellow–captive, instead of one decrepit by imprisonment, blind, and broken down past exertion. But God's will be done! I will not leave behind me the poor wretch whom I have found in such a condition, though he is perfectly unable to assist me in accomplishing my escape, and is rather more likely to retard it. Meantime, before we put out the torch, let us see, if, by close examination, we can discover any door in the wall save that to the blind man's dungeon. If not, I much suspect that my descent has been made through the roof. That cup of wine—that Muse, as they called it, had a taste more like medicine than merry companions' pledge."

He began accordingly a strict survey of the walls, which he resolved to conclude by extinguishing the torch, that he might take the person who should enter his dungeon darkling and by surprise, For a similar reason, he dragged into the darkest corner the carcass of the tiger, and covered it with the remains of the bed–clothes, swearing at the same time, that a half tiger should be his crest in future, if he had the fortune, which his bold heart would not suffer him to doubt, of getting through the present danger. "But," he added, "if these necromantic vassals of hell shall raise the devil upon, me, what shall I do then? And so great is the chance, that methinks I would fain dispense with extinguishing the flambeau. Yet it is childish for one dubbed in the chapel of Our Lady of the Broken Lances, to make much difference between a light room and a dark one. Let them come, as many fiends as the cell can hold, and we shall see if we receive them not as becomes a Christian knight; and surely, Our Lady, to whom I was ever a true votary, will hold it an acceptable sacrifice that I tore myself from my Brenhilda, even for a single moment, in honour of her advent, and thus led the way for our woful separation. Fiends! I defy ye in the body as in the spirit, and I retain the remains of this flambeau until some more convenient opportunity." He dashed it against the wall as he spoke, and then quietly sat down in a corner, to watch what should next happen.

Thought after thought chased each other through his mind. His confidence in his wife's fidelity, and his trust in her uncommon strength and activity, were the greatest comforts which he had; nor could her danger present itself to him in any shape so terrible, but that he found consolation in these reflections: "She is pure," he said, "as the dew of heaven, and heaven will not abandon its own."

CHAPTER THE SIXTEENTH

Strange ape of man! who loathes thee while he scorns thee.
Half a reproach to us and half a jest.
What fancies can be ours ere we have pleasure
In viewing our own form, our pride and passions,
Reflected in a shape grotesque as thine! ANONYMOUS.

Count Robert of Paris having ensconced himself behind the ruins of the bed, so that he could not well be observed, unless a strong light was at once flung upon the place of his retreat, waited with anxiety how and in what manner the warder of the dungeon, charged with the task of bringing food to the prisoners, should make himself visible; nor was it long ere symptoms of his approach began to be heard and observed.

A light was partially seen, as from a trap–door opening in the roof, and a voice was heard to utter these words in Anglo–Saxon, "Leap, sirrah; come, no delay; leap, my good Sylvan, show your honour's activity." A strange chuckling hoarse voice, in a language totally unintelligible to Count Robert, was heard to respond, as if disputing the orders which were received.

"What, sir," said his companion, "you must contest the point, must you? Nay, if thou art so lazy, I must give your honour a ladder, and perhaps a kick to hasten your journey." Something then, of very great size, in the form of a human being, jumped down from the trap–door, though the height might be above fourteen feet. This figure was gigantic, being upwards of seven feet high. In its left hand it held a torch, and in its right a skein of fine silk, which unwinding itself as it descended, remained unbroken, though it was easy to conceive it could not have afforded a creature so large any support in his descent from the roof. He alighted with perfect safety and activity upon his feet, and, as if rebounding from the floor, he sprung upwards again, so as almost to touch the roof. In this last gambaud the torch which he bore was extinguished; but this extraordinary warder whirled it round his head with infinite velocity, so that it again ignited. The bearer, who appeared to intend the accomplishment of this object, endeavoured to satisfy himself that it was really attained by approaching, as if cautiously, its left hand to the flame of the torch. This practical experiment seemed attended with consequences which the creature had not expected, for it howled with pain, shaking the burnt hand, and chattering as if bemoaning itself.

"Take heed there, Sylvanus!" said the same voice in Anglo–Saxon, and in a tone of rebuke. "Ho, there! mind thy duty, Sylvan! Carry food to the blind man, and stand not there to play thyself, lest I trust thee not again alone on such an errand!"

The creature—for it would have been rash to have termed it a man— turning its eye upwards to the place from whence the voice came, answered with a dreadful grin and shaking of its fist, yet presently began to undo a parcel, and rummage in the pockets of a sort of jerkin and pantaloons which it wore, seeking, it appeared, a bunch of keys, which at length it produced, while it took from the pocket a loaf of bread. Heating the stone of the wall, it affixed the torch to it by a piece of wax, and then cautiously looked out for the entrance to the old man's dungeon, which it opened with a key selected from the bunch. Within the passage it seemed to look for and discover the handle of a pump, at which it filled a pitcher that it bore, and bringing back the fragments of the former loaf, and remains of the pitcher of water, it ate a little, as if it were in sport, and very soon making a frightful grimace, flung the fragments away. The Count of Paris, in the meanwhile, watched anxiously the proceedings of this unknown animal. His first thought was, that the creature, whose limbs were so much larger than humanity, whose grimaces were so frightful, and whose activity seemed supernatural, could be no other than the Devil himself, or some of his imps, whose situation and office in those gloomy regions seemed by no means hard to conjecture. The human voice, however, which he had heard, was less that of a necromancer conjuring a fiend than that of a person giving commands to a wild animal, over whom he had, by training, obtained a great superiority.

"A shame on it," said the Count, "if I suffer a common jackanapes,— for such I take this devil–seeming beast to be, although twice as large as any of its fellows whom I have ever seen,—to throw an obstacle in the way of my obtaining daylight and freedom! Let us but watch, and the chance is that we make that furry gentleman our guide to the upper regions."

Meantime the creature, which rummaged about everywhere, at length. discovered the body of the tiger,—touched it, stirred it, with many strange motions, and seemed to lament and wonder at its death. At once it seemed struck with the idea that some one must have slain it, and Count Robert had the mortification to see it once more select the key, and spring towards the door of Ursel's prison with such alacrity, that had its intention been to strangle him, it would have accomplished its purpose before the interference of Count Robert could have prevented its revenge taking place. Apparently, however, it reflected, that for reasons which seemed satisfactory, the death of the tiger could not be caused by the unfortunate Ursel, but had been accomplished by some one concealed within the outer prison.

Slowly grumbling, therefore, and chattering to itself, and peeping anxiously into every corner, the tremendous creature, so like yet so very unlike to the human form, came stealing along the walls, moving whatever he thought could seclude a man from his observation. Its extended legs and arms were protruded forward with great strides, and its sharp eyes, on the watch to discover the object
of its search, kept prying, with the assistance of the torch, into every corner.

Considering the vicinity of Alexius's collection of animals, the reader, by this time, can have little doubt that the creature in question, whose appearance seemed to the Count of Paris so very problematical, was a specimen of that gigantic species of ape—if it is not indeed some animal more nearly allied to ourselves—to which, I believe, naturalists have given the name of the Ourang

Outang. This creature differs from the rest of its fraternity, in being comparatively more docile and serviceable: and though possessing the power of imitation which is common to the whole race, yet making use of it less in mere mockery, than in the desire of improvement and instruction perfectly unknown to his brethren. The aptitude which it possesses of acquiring information, is surprisingly great, and probably, if placed in a favourable situation, it might
admit of being domesticated in a considerable degree; but such advantages the ardour of scientific curiosity has never afforded this creature. The last we have heard of was seen, we believe, in the Island of Sumatra—it was of great size and strength, and upwards of seven feet high. It died defending desperately its innocent life
against a party of Europeans, who, we cannot help thinking, might have better employed the superiority which their knowledge gave them over the poor native of the forest. It was probably this creature, seldom seen, but when once seen never forgotten, which occasioned the ancient belief in the god Pan, with his sylvans and satyrs. Nay, but for the gift of speech, which we cannot suppose any of the
family to have attained, we should have believed the satyr seen by St. Anthony in the desert to have belonged to this tribe.

We can, therefore, the more easily credit the annals which attest that the collection of natural history belonging to Alexius Comnenus, preserved an animal of this kind, which had been domesticated and reclaimed to a surprising extent, and showed a degree of intelligence never perhaps to be attained in any other case. These explanations being premised, we return to the thread of our story.

The animal advanced with long noiseless steps; its shadow on the wall, when it held the torch so as to make it visible to the Frank, forming another fiend–resembling mimicry of its own large figure and extravagant–looking members. Count Robert remained in his lurking hole, in no hurry to begin a strife, of which it was impossible to foretell the end. In the meantime, the man of the woods came
nigh, and every step by which he approached, caused the Count's heart to vibrate almost audibly, at the idea of meeting danger of a nature so strange and new. At length the creature approached the bed
—his hideous eyes were fixed on those of the Count; and, as much surprised at seeing him as Robert was at the meeting, he skipped

about fifteen paces backwards at one spring, with a cry of instinctive terror, and then advanced on tiptoe, holding his torch as far forward as he could, between him and the object of his fears, as if to examine him at the safest possible distance. Count Robert caught up a fragment of the bedstead, large enough to form a sort of club, with which he menaced the native of the wilds.

Apparently this poor creature's education, like education of most kinds, had not been acquired without blows, of which the recollection was as fresh as that of the lessons which they enforced. Sir Robert of Paris was a man at once to discover and to avail himself of the advantage obtained by finding that he possessed a degree of ascendancy over his enemy, which he had not suspected. He erected his warlike figure, assumed a step as if triumphant in the lists, and advanced threatening his enemy with his club, as he would have menaced his antagonist with the redoutable Tranchefer. The man of the woods, on the other hand, obviously gave way, and converted his cautious advance into a retreat no less cautious. Yet apparently the creature had not renounced some plan of resistance; he chattered in an angry and hostile tone, held out his torch in opposition, and seemed about to strike the crusader with it. Count Robert, however, determined to take his opponent at advantage, while his fears influenced him, and for this purpose resolved, if possible, to deprive him of his natural superiority in strength and agility, which his singular form showed he could not but possess over the human species. A master of his weapon, therefore, the Count menaced his savage antagonist with a stroke on the right side of his head, but suddenly averting the blow, struck him with his whole force on the left temple, and in an instant was kneeling above him, when, drawing his dagger, he was about to deprive him of life.

The Ourang Outang, ignorant of the nature of this new weapon with which he was threatened, attempted at one and the same moment, to rise from the ground, overthrow his antagonist, and wrench the dagger from his grasp. In the first attempt, he would probably have succeeded; and as it was, he gained his knees, and seemed likely to prevail in the struggle, when he became sensible that the knight, drawing his poniard sharply through his grasp, had cut his paw severely, and seeing him aim the trenchant weapon at his throat, became probably aware that his enemy had his life at command. He suffered himself to be borne backwards without further resistance, with a deep wailing and melancholy cry, having in it something human, which excited compassion. He covered his eyes with the unwounded hand, as if he would have hid from his own sight the death which seemed approaching him.

Count Robert, notwithstanding his military frenzy, was, in ordinary matters, a calm–tempered and mild man, and particularly benevolent to the lower classes of creation. The thought rushed through his mind, "Why take from this unfortunate monster the breath which is
in its nostrils, after which it cannot know another existence? And then, may it not be some prince or knight changed to this grotesque shape, that it may help to guard these vaults, and the wonderful adventures that attach to them? Should I not, then, be guilty of a crime by slaying him, when he has rendered himself, rescue or no rescue, which he has done as completely as his transformed figure permits; and if he be actually a bestial creature, may he not have some touch of gratitude? I have heard the minstrels sing the lay of Androcles and the Lion. I will be on my guard with him.'"

So saying, he rose from above the man of the woods, and permitted him. also to arise. The creature seemed sensible of the clemency, for he muttered in a low and supplicating tone, which seemed at once to crave for mercy, and to return thanks for what he had already experienced. He wept too, as he saw the blood dropping from his wound, and with an anxious countenance, which had more of the human now that it was composed into an expression of pain and melancholy, seemed to await in terror the doom of a being more powerful than himself.

The pocket which the knight wore under his armour, capable of containing but few things, had, however, some vulnerary balsam, for which its owner had often occasion, a little lint, and a small roll of linen; these the knight took out, and motioned to the animal to hold forth his wounded hand. The man of the woods obeyed with hesitation and reluctance, and Count Robert applied the balsam and the dressings, acquainting his patient, at the same time, in a severe tone of voice, that perhaps he did wrong in putting to his use a balsam compounded for the service of the noblest knights; but that, if he saw the least sign of his making an ungrateful use of the benefit he had conferred, he would bury the dagger, of which he had felt the efficacy, to the very handle, in his body.

The Sylvan looked fixedly upon Count Robert, almost as if he understood the language used to him, and, making one of its native murmurs, it stooped to the earth, kissed the feet of the knight, and embracing his knees, seemed to swear to him eternal gratitude and fidelity. Accordingly, when the Count retired to the bed and assumed his armour, to await the re–opening of the trap–door, the animal sat down by his side, directing its eyes in the line with his, and seemed quietly to wait till the door should open. After waiting about an hour, a slight noise was heard in the upper chamber, and the wild man plucked the Frank by the cloak, as if to call his attention to what was about to happen. The same voice which had before spoken, was, after a whistle or two, heard to call, "Sylvan, Sylvan! where loiterest thou? Come instantly, or, by the rood, thou shalt abye thy sloth!"

The poor monster, as Trinculo might have called him, seemed perfectly aware of the meaning of this threat, and showed his sense of it by pressing close to the side of Count Robert, making at the same time a kind of whining, entreating, it would seem, the knight's protection. Forgetting the great improbability there was, even in his own opinion, that the creature could understand him, Count Robert said, "Why, my friend, thou hast already learned the principal court prayer of this country, by which men. entreat permission, to speak and live. Fear nothing, poor creature—I am thy protector."

"Sylvan! what, ho!" said the voice again; "whom hast thou got for a companion?—some of the fiends, or ghosts of murdered men, who they say are frequent in these dungeons? or dost thou converse with the old blind rebel Grecian?—or, finally, is it true what men say of thee, that thou canst talk intelligibly when thou wilt, and only gibberest and chatterest for fear thou art sent to work? Come, thou lazy rascal! thou shalt have the advantage of the ladder to ascend by, though thou needest it no more than a daw to ascend the steeple of the Cathedral of St. Sophia. [Footnote: Now the chief mosque of the Ottoman capital.] Come along then," he said, putting a ladder down the trap–door, "and put me not to the trouble of descending to fetch thee, else, by St. Swithin, it shall be the worse for thee. Come along, therefore, like a good fellow, and for once I shall spare the whip."

The animal, apparently, was moved by this rhetoric, for, with a doleful look, which Count Robert saw by means of the nearly extinguished torch, he seemed to bid him farewell, and to creep away towards the ladder with the same excellent good–will
wherewith a condemned criminal performs the like evolution. But no sooner did the Count look angry, and shake the formidable dagger, than the intelligent animal seemed at once to take his resolution, and clenching his hands firmly together in the fashion of one who has made up his mind, he returned from the ladder's foot, and drew up behind Count Robert,—with the air, however, of a deserter, who
feels himself but little at home when called into the field against his ancient commander.

In a short time the warder's patience was exhausted, and despairing of the Sylvan's voluntary return, he resolved to descend in quest of him. Down the ladder he came, a bundle of keys in one hand, the other assisting his descent, and a sort of dark lantern, whose bottom was so fashioned that he could wear it upon his head like a hat. He had scarce stept on the floor, when he was surrounded by the nervous arms of the Count of Paris. At first the warder's idea was, that he was seized by the recusant Sylvan.

"How now, villain!" he said; "let me go, or thou shalt die the death." "Thou

diest thyself," said the Count, who, between the surprise and his own skill in wrestling, felt fully his advantage in the struggle.

"Treason! treason!" cried the warder, hearing by the voice that a stranger had mingled in the contest; "help, ho! above there! help, Hereward— Varangian!—Anglo–Saxon, or whatever accursed name thou callest thyself!"

While he spoke thus, the irresistible grasp of Count Robert seized his throat, and choked his utterance. They fell heavily, the jailor undermost, upon the floor of the dungeon, and Robert of Paris, the necessity of whose case excused the action, plunged his dagger in the throat of the unfortunate. Just as he did so, a noise of armour was heard, and, rattling down the ladder, our acquaintance Hereward stood on the floor of the dungeon. The light, which had rolled from the head of the warder, continued to show him streaming with blood, and in the death–grasp of a stranger. Hereward hesitated not to fly to his assistance, and, seizing upon the Count of Paris at the same advantage which that knight had gained over his own adversary a moment before, held him forcibly down with his face to the earth. Count Robert was one of the strongest men of that military age; but then so was the Varangian; and save that the latter had obtained a decided advantage by having his antagonist beneath him, it could not certainly have been conjectured which way the combat was to go.

"Yield, as your own jargon goes, rescue or no rescue," said the Varangian, "or die on the point of my dagger!"

"A French Count never yields," answered Robert, who began to conjecture with what sort of person he was engaged, "above all to a vagabond slave like thee!" With this he made an effort to rise, so sudden, so strong, so powerful, that he had almost freed himself from the Varangian's grasp, had not Hereward, by a violent exertion of his great strength, preserved the advantage he had gained, and raised his poniard to end the strife for ever; but a loud chuckling laugh of an unearthly sound was at this instant heard. The Varangian's extended arm was seized with vigour, while a rough arm embracing his throat, turned him over on his back, and gave the French Count an opportunity of springing up.

"Death to thee, wretch!" said the Varangian, scarce knowing whom he threatened; but the man of the woods apparently had an awful recollection of the prowess of human beings. He fled, therefore, swiftly up the ladder, and left Hereward and his deliverer to fight it out with what success chance might determine between them.

The circumstances seemed to argue a desperate combat; both were tall, strong, and courageous, both had defensive armour, and the fatal and desperate poniard was their only offensive weapon. They paused facing each other, and examined eagerly into their respective means of defence before hazarding a blow, which, if it missed, its attaint would certainly be fatally requited. During this deadly pause, a gleam shone from the trapdoor above, as the wild and alarmed visage of the man of the woods was seen peering down by the light of a newly kindled torch which he held as low into the dungeon as he well could.

"Fight bravely, comrade," said Count Robert of Paris, "for we no longer battle in private; this respectable person, having chosen to constitute himself judge of the field."

Hazardous as his situation was, the Varangian looked up, and was so struck with the wild and terrified expression which the creature had assumed, and the strife between curiosity and terror which its grotesque features exhibited, that he could not help bursting into a fit of laughter.

"Sylvan is among those," said Hereward, "who would rather hold the candle to a dance so formidable than join in it himself."

"Is there then," said Count Robert, "any absolute necessity that thou and I perform this dance at all?"

"None but our own pleasure," answered Hereward; "for I suspect there is not between us any legitimate cause of quarrel demanding to be fought out in such a place, and before such a spectator. Thou art, if I mistake not, the bold Frank, who was yesternight imprisoned in this place with, a tiger, chained within no distant spring of his bed?"

"I am," answered the Count.

"And where is the animal who was opposed to thee?"

"He lies yonder," answered the Count, "never again to be the object of more terror than the deer whom he may have preyed on in his day." He pointed to the body of the tiger, which Hereward examined by the light of the dark lantern already mentioned.

"And this, then, was thy handiwork?" said the wondering Anglo– Saxon.

"Sooth to say it was," answered the Count, with indifference.

"And thou hast slain my comrade of this strange watch?" said the Varangian.

"Mortally wounded him at the least," said Count Robert.

"With your patience, I will be beholden to you for a moment's truce, while I examine his wound," said Hereward.

"Assuredly," answered the Count; "blighted be the arm which strikes a foul blow at an open antagonist!"

Without demanding further security, the Varangian quitted his posture of defence and precaution, and set himself, by the assistance of the dark lantern, to examine the wound of the first warder who appeared on the field, who seemed, by his Roman military dress, to be a soldier of the bands called Immortals. Pie found him in the death–agony, but still able to speak.

"So, Varangian, thou art come at last,—and is it to thy sloth or treachery that I am to impute my fate?—Nay, answer me not!—The stranger struck me over the collar–bone—had we lived long together, or met often, I had done the like by thee, to wipe out the memory of certain transactions at the Golden Gate.—I know the use of the knife too well to doubt the effect of a blow aimed over the collar–bone by so strong a hand—I feel it coming. The Immortal, so called, becomes now, if priests say true, an immortal indeed, and
Sebastes of Mytilene's bow is broken ere his quiver is half emptied."

The robber Greek sunk back in Hereward's arms, and closed his life with a groan, which was the last sound he uttered. The Varangian laid the body at length on the dungeon floor.

"This is a perplexed matter," he said; "I am certainly not called upon to put to death a brave man, although my national enemy, because he hath killed a miscreant who was privately meditating my own
murder. Neither is this a place or a light by which to fight as becomes the champions of two nations. Let that quarrel be still for the present.— How say you then, noble sir, if we adjourn the present

dispute till we effect your deliverance from the dungeons of the Blacquernal, and your restoration to your own friends and followers? If a poor Varangian should be of service to you in this matter, would you, when it was settled, refuse to meet him in fair fight, with your national weapons or his own?"

"If," said Count Robert, "whether friend or enemy, thou wilt extend thy assistance to my wife, who is also imprisoned somewhere in this inhospitable palace, be assured, that whatever be thy rank, whatever be thy country, whatever be thy condition, Robert of Paris will, at thy choice, proffer thee his right hand in friendship, or raise it against thee in fair and manly battle—a strife not of hatred, but of honour and esteem; and this I vow by the soul of Charlemagne, my ancestor, and by the shrine of my patroness, Our Lady of the Broken Lances."

"Enough said," replied Hereward. "I am as much bound to the assistance of your Lady Countess, being a poor exile, as if I were the first in the ranks of chivalry; for if any thing can make the cause of worth and bravery yet more obligatory, it must be its being united with that of a helpless and suffering female."

"I ought," said Count Robert, "to be here silent, without loading thy generosity with farther requests; yet thou art a man, whom, if fortune has not smiled at thy birth, by ordaining thee to be born within the ranks of noblesse and knighthood, yet Providence hath done thee more justice by giving thee a more gallant heart than is always possessed, I fear, by those who are inwoven in the gayest wreath of chivalry. There lingers here in these dungeons, for I cannot say he lives—a blind old man, to whom for three years every thing beyond his prison has been a universal blot. His food is bread and water, his intercourse limited to the conversation of a sullen warder, and if death can ever come as a deliverer, it must be to this dark old man. What sayst thou? Shall he, so unutterably miserable, not profit by perhaps the only opportunity of freedom that may ever occur to him?"

"By St. Dunstan," answered the Varangian, "thou keepest over truly the oath thou hast taken as a redresser of wrongs! Thine own case is well– nigh desperate, and thou art willing to make it utterly so by uniting with it that of every unhappy person whom fate throws in thy way!"

"The more of human misery we attempt to relieve," said Robert of Paris, "the more we shall carry with us the blessing of our merciful saints, and Our Lady of the Broken Lances, who views with so much pain every species of human suffering or misfortune, save that which occurs within the enclosure of the lists. But come, valiant Anglo– Saxon, resolve me on my request as speedily as thou canst. There is something in thy face of candour as well as sense, and it is with no small confidence that I desire to see us set forth in quest of my beloved Countess, who, when her deliverance is once achieved, will be a powerful aid to us in recovering that of others."

"So be it, then," said the Varangian; "we will proceed in quest of the Countess Brenhilda; and if, on recovering her, we find ourselves strong enough to procure the freedom of the dark old man, my cowardice, or want of compassion, shall never stop the attempt."

CHAPTER THE SEVENTEENTH

'Tis strange that, in the dark sulphureous mine, Where
wild ambition piles its ripening stores Of slumbering
thunder, Love will interpose
His tiny torch, and cause the stern explosion To burst,
when the deviser's least aware. ANONYMOUS.

About noon of the same day, Agelastes met with Achilles Tatius, the
commander of the Varangian guard, in those ruins of the Egyptian temple in
which we formerly mentioned Hereward having had an interview with the
philosopher. They met, as it seemed, in a very different humour. Tatius was
gloomy, melancholy, and downcast; while the philosopher maintained the
calm indifference which procured for him, and in some sort deserved, the title
of the
Elephant. "Thou blenchest, Achilles Tatius," said the philosopher, "now that
thou hast frankly opposed thyself to all the dangers which stood between thee
and greatness. Thou art like the idle boy who turned the mill–stream upon the
machine, and that done, instead of making a proper use of it, was terrified at
seeing it in motion."

"Thou dost me wrong, Agelastes," answered the Acolyte, "foul wrong; I am
but like the mariner, who although determined upon his voyage, yet cannot
forbear a sorrowing glance at the shore, before he parts with it, it may be, for
ever."

"It may have been right to think of this, but pardon me, valiant
Tatius, when I tell you the account should have been made up
before; and the grandson of Alguric the Hun ought to have computed chances
and consequences ere he stretched his hand to his master's diadem."

"Hush! for Heaven's sake," said Tatius, looking round; "that, thou knowest,
is a secret between our two selves; for if Nicephorus, the

Caesar, should learn it, where were we and our conspiracy?"

"Our bodies on the gibbet, probably," answered Agelastes, "and our souls divorced from them, and in the way of discovering the secrets which thou hast hitherto taken upon trust."

"Well," said Achilles, "and should not the consciousness of the possibility of this fate render us cautious?"

"Cautious *men*, if you will," answered Agelastes, "but not timid children."

"Stone walls can hear,"—said the Follower, lowering his voice. "Dionysius the tyrant, I have read, had an ear which conveyed to him the secrets spoken within his state–prison at Syracuse."

"And that Ear is still stationary at Syracuse," said the philosopher. "Tell me, my most simple friend, art thou afraid it has been transported hither in one night, as the Latins believe of Our Lady's house of Loretto?"

"No," answered Achilles, "but in an affair so important too much caution cannot be used."

"Well, thou most cautious of candidates for empire, and most cold of military leaders, know that the Caesar, deeming, I think, that there is no chance of the empire falling to any one but himself, hath taken in his head to consider his succession to Alexius as a matter of course, whenever the election takes place. In consequence, as matters of course are usually matters of indifference, he has left all thoughts of securing his interest upon, this material occasion to thee and to me, while the foolish voluptuary hath himself run mad—for what think you? Something between man and woman,—female in her lineaments, her limbs, and a part at least of her garments; but, so help me St. George, most masculine in the rest of her attire, in her propensities, and in her exercises."

"The Amazonian wife, thou meanest," said Achilles, "of that iron– handed Frank, who dashed to pieces last night the golden lion of Solomon with a blow of his fist? By St. George, the least which can come of such an amour is broken bones."

"That," said Agelastes, "is not quite so improbable as that Dionysius's Ear should fly hither from Syracuse in a single night; but he is presumptuous in respect of the influence which his supposed good looks have gained him among the Grecian dames."

"He was too presumptuous, I suppose," said Achilles Tatius, "to make a proper allowance for his situation as Caesar, and the prospect of his being Emperor."

"Meantime," said Agelastes, "I have promised him an interview with his Bradamante, who may perhaps reward his tender epithets of *Zoe kai psyche*, [Footnote: "Life and Soul."] by divorcing his amorous soul from his unrivalled person."

"Meantime," said the Follower, "thou obtainest, I conclude, such orders and warrants as the Caesar can give for the furtherance of our plot?"

"Assuredly," said Agelastes, "it is an opportunity not to be lost. This love fit, or mad fit, has blinded him; and without exciting too much attention to the progress of the plot, we can thus in safety conduct matters our own way, without causing malevolent remarks; and though I am conscious that, in doing so, I act somewhat at variance with my age and character, yet the end being to convert a worthy Follower into an Imperial Leader, I shame me not in procuring that interview with the lady, of which the Caesar, as they term him, is so desirous.—What progress, meanwhile, hast thou made with the Varangians, who are, in respect of execution, the very arm of our design?"

"Scarce so good as I could wish," said Achilles Tatius; "yet I have made sure of some two or three score of those whom I found most accessible; nor have I any doubt, that when the Caesar is set aside, their cry will be for Achilles Tatius."

"And what of the gallant who assisted at our prelections?" said Agelastes; "your Edward, as Alexius termed him?"

"I have made no impression upon him," said the Follower; "and I am sorry for it, for he is one whom his comrades think well of, and would gladly follow. Meantime I have placed him as an additional sentinel upon the iron–witted Count of Paris, whom, both having an inveterate love of battle, he is very likely to put to death; and if it is afterwards challenged by the crusaders as a cause of war, it is only delivering up the Varangian, whose personal hatred will needs be represented as having occasioned the catastrophe. All this being prepared beforehand, how and when shall we deal with the Emperor?"

"For that," said Agelastes, "we must consult the Caesar, who, although his expected happiness of to–day is not more certain than the state preferment that he expects to–morrow, and although his ideas are much more anxiously fixed upon his success with this said Countess than his succession to the empire, will, nevertheless, expect to be treated as the head of the enterprise for accelerating the latter. But, to speak my opinion, valiant Tatius, to–morrow will be the last day that Alexius shall hold the reins of empire."

"Let me know for certain," said the Follower, "as soon as thou canst, that I may warn our brethren, who are to have in readiness the insurgent citizens, and those of the Immortals who are combined with us, in the neighbourhood of the court, and in readiness to act— And, above all, that I may disperse upon distant guards such Varangians as I cannot trust."

"Rely upon me," said Agelastes, "for the most accurate information and instructions, so soon as I have seen Nicephorus Briennius. One word permit me to ask—in what manner is the wife of the Caesar to be disposed of?"

"Somewhere," said the Follower, "where I can never be compelled to hear more of her history. Were it not for that nightly pest of her lectures, I could be good–natured enough to take care of her destiny myself, and teach her the difference betwixt a real emperor and this Briennius, who thinks so much of himself." So saying, they separated; the Follower elated in look and manner considerably
above what he had been when they met.

Agelastes looked after his companion with a scornful laugh. "There," he said, "goes a fool, whose lack of sense prevents his eyes from being dazzled by the torch which cannot fail to consume them. A half–bred, half–acting, half–thinking, half–daring caitiff, whose poorest thoughts—and those which deserve that name must be poor indeed—are not the produce of his own understanding. He expects to circumvent the fiery, haughty, and proud Nicephorus Briennius! If

he does so, it will not be by his own policy, and still less by his valour. Nor shall Anna Comnena, the soul of wit and genius, be chained to such an unimaginative log as yonder half–barbarian. No

—she shall have a husband of pure Grecian extraction, and well stored with that learning which was studied when Rome was great, and Greece illustrious. Nor will it be the least charm of the Imperial throne, that it is partaken by a partner whose personal studies have taught her to esteem and value those of the Emperor." He took a step or two with conscious elevation, and then, as conscience–checked,

he added, in a suppressed voice, "But then, if Anna were destined for Empress, it follows of course that Alexius must die—no consent could be trusted.—And what then?—the death of an ordinary man is indifferent, when it plants on the throne a philosopher and a

historian; and at what time were possessors of the empire curious to enquire when or by whose agency their predecessors died?— Diogenes! Ho, Diogenes!" The slave did not immediately come, so that Agelastes, wrapt in the anticipation of his greatness, had time to add a few more words "Tush—I must reckon with Heaven, say the priests, for many things, so I will throw this also into the account. The death of the Emperor may be twenty ways achieved without my having the blame of it. The blood which we have shed may spot our hand, if closely regarded, but it shall scarce stain our forehead." Diogenes here entered—"Has the Frank lady been removed?" said the philosopher.

The slave signified his assent. "How did

she bear her removal?"

"As authorised by your lordship, indifferently well. She had resented her separation from her husband, and her being detained in the palace, and committed some violence upon the slaves of the

Household, several of whom were said to be slain, although we perhaps ought only to read sorely frightened. She recognised me at once, and when I told her that I came to offer her a day's retirement in your own lodgings, until it should be in your power to achieve the liberation of her husband, she at once consented, and I deposited her in the secret Cytherean garden– house."

"Admirably done, my faithful Diogenes," said the philosopher; "thou art like the genii who attended on the Eastern talisman; I have but to intimate my will to thee, and it is accomplished."

Diogenes bowed deeply, and withdrew.

"Yet remember, slave!" said Agelastes, speaking to himself; "there is danger in knowing too much—and should my character ever become questioned, too many of my secrets are in the power of Diogenes."

At this moment a blow thrice repeated, and struck upon one of the images without, which had been so framed as to return a tingling sound, and in so far deserved the praise of being vocal, interrupted his soliloquy.

"There knocks," said he, "one of our allies; who can it be that comes so late?" He touched the figure of Iris with his staff, and the Caesar Nicephorus Briennius entered in the full Grecian habit, and that graceful dress anxiously arranged to the best advantage. "Let me hope, my Lord," said Agelastes, receiving the Caesar with an apparently grave and reserved face, "your Highness comes to tell me that your sentiments are changed on reflection, and that whatever
you had to confer about with this Frankish lady, may be at least deferred until the principal part of our conspiracy has been successfully
executed."

"Philosopher," answered the Caesar, "no. My resolution, once taken, is not the sport of circumstances. Believe me, that I have not finished so many labours without being ready to undertake others. The favour of Venus is the reward of the labours of Mars, nor would I think it worth while to worship the god armipotent with the toil and risk attending his service, unless I had previously attained some decided proofs that I was wreathed with the myrtle, intimating the favour of his beautiful mistress."

"I beg pardon for my boldness," said Agelastes; "but has your Imperial Highness reflected, that you were wagering, with the wildest rashness, an empire, including thine own life, mine, and all who are joined with us, in a hardy scheme? And against what were they waged? Against the very precarious favour of a woman, who is altogether divided betwixt fiend and female, and in either capacity is most likely to be fatal to our present scheme, either by her good will, or by the offence which she may take. If she prove such as you wish, she will desire to keep her lover by her side, and to spare him the danger of engaging in a perilous conspiracy; and if she remains, as the world believe her, constant to her husband, and to the sentiments she vowed to him at the altar, you may guess what cause of offence you are likely to give, by urging a suit which she has already received so very ill."

"Pshaw, old man! Thou turnest a dotard, and in the great knowledge thou possessest of other things, hast forgotten the knowledge best worth knowing—that of the beautiful part of the creation. Think of the impression likely to be made by a gallant neither ignoble in situation, nor unacceptable in presence, upon a lady who must fear the consequences of refusal! Come, Agelastes, let me have no more of thy croaking, auguring bad fortune like the raven from the blasted oak on the left hand; but declaim, as well thou canst, how faint heart never won fair lady, and how those best deserve empire who can wreathe the myrtles of Venus with the laurels of Mars. Come, man, undo me the secret entrance which combines these magical ruins with groves that are fashioned rather like those of Cytheros or Naxos."

"It must be as you will!" said the philosopher, with a deep and somewhat affected sigh.

"Here, Diogenes!" called aloud the Caesar; "when thou art summoned, mischief is not far distant. Come, undo the secret entrance. Mischief, my trusty negro, is not so distant but she will answer the first clatter of the stones."

The negro looked at his master, who returned him a glance acquiescing in the Caesar's proposal. Diogenes then went to a part of the ruined wall which was covered by some climbing shrubs, all of which he carefully removed. This showed a little postern door,
closed irregularly, and filled up, from the threshold to the top, with large square stones, all of which the slave took out and piled aside,
as if for the purpose of replacing them. "I leave thee," said Agelastes to the negro, "to guard this door, and let no one enter, except he has the sign, upon the peril of thy life. It were dangerous it should be left open at this period of the day."

The obsequious Diogenes put his hand to his sabre and to his head, as if to signify the usual promise of fidelity or death, by which those in his condition generally expressed their answer to their master's commands. Diogenes then lighted a small lantern, and pulling out a key, opened an inner door of wood, and prepared to step forward.

"Hold, friend Diogenes," said the Caesar; "thou wantest not my lantern, to discern an honest man, whom, if thou didst seek, I must needs say thou hast come to the wrong place to find one. Nail thou up these creeping shrubs before the entrance of the place, and abide
thou there as already directed, till our return, to parry the curiosity of any who may be attracted by the sight of the private passage."

The black slave drew back as he gave the lamp to the Caesar, and Agelastes followed the light through a long, but narrow, arched passage, well supplied with air from space to space, and not neglected in the inside to the degree which its exterior would have implied.

"I will not enter with you into the Gardens," said Agelastes, "or to the bower of Cytherea, where I am too old to be a worshipper. Thou thyself, I think, Imperial Caesar, art well aware of the road, having travelled it divers times! and, if I mistake not, for the fairest reasons."

"The more thanks," said the Caesar, "are due to mine excellent friend Agelastes, who forgets his own age to accommodate the youth of his friends."

CHAPTER THE EIGHTEENTH

We must now return to the dungeon of the Blacquernal, where circumstances had formed at least a temporary union between the stout Varangian and Count Robert of Paris, who had a stronger resemblance to each other in their dispositions than probably either of them would have been willing to admit. The virtues of the Varangian were all of that natural and unrefined kind which Nature herself dictates to a gallant man, to whom a total want of fear, and the most prompt alacrity to meet danger, had been attributes of a life–long standing. The Count, on the other hand, had all that bravery, generosity, and love of adventure, which was possessed by the rude soldier, with the virtues, partly real, partly fantastic, which those of his rank and country acquired from the spirit of chivalry. The one might be compared to the diamond as it came from the mine, before it had yet received the advantages of cutting and

setting; the other was the ornamented gem, which, cut into facets and richly set, had lost perhaps a little of its original substance, yet still,

at the same time, to the eye of an inspector, had something more showy and splendid than when it was, according to the phrase of lapidaries, *en brut*. In the one case, the value was more artificial; in the other, it was the more natural and real of the two. Chance, therefore, had made a temporary alliance between two men, the foundation of whose characters bore such strong resemblance to each other, that they were only separated by a course of education, which had left rigid prejudices on both sides, and which prejudices were not unlikely to run counter to each other. The Varangian commenced his conversation with the Count in a tone of familiarity, approaching nearer to rudeness than the speaker was aware of, and much of which, though most innocently intended by Hereward,

might be taken amiss by his new brother in arms. The most offensive part of his deportment, however, was a blunt, bold disregard to the title of those whom he addressed, adhering thereby to the manners of the Saxons, from whom he drew his descent, and which was likely to be at least unpleasing to the Franks as well as Normans, who had already received and become very tenacious of the privileges of the feudal system, the mummery of heraldry, and the warlike claims assumed by knights, as belonging only to their own order.

Hereward was apt, it must be owned, to think too little of these distinctions; while he had at least a sufficient tendency to think enough of the power and wealth of the Greek empire which he served,—of the dignity inherent in Alexius Comnenus, and which he was also disposed to grant to the Grecian officers, who, under the Emperor, commanded his own corps, and particularly to Achilles Tatius. This man Hereward knew to be a coward, and half–suspected to be a villain. Still, however, the Follower was always the direct channel through which the Imperial graces were conferred on the Varangians in general, as well as upon Hereward himself; and he had always the policy to represent such favours as being more or less indirectly the consequence of his own intercession. He was supposed vigorously to espouse the quarrel of the Varangians, in all the disputes between them and the other corps; he was liberal and open– handed; gave every soldier his due; and, bating the trifling circumstance of valour, which was not particularly his forte, it would have been difficult for these strangers to have demanded a leader more to their wishes. Besides this, our friend Hereward was admitted by him into his society, attended him, as we have seen, upon secret expeditions, and shared, therefore, deeply, in what may be termed by an expressive, though vulgar phrase, the sneaking kindness entertained for this new Achilles by the greater part of his myrmidons. Their attachment might be explained, perhaps, as a liking to their commander, as strong as could well exist with a marvellous lack of honour and esteem. The scheme, therefore, formed by Hereward to effect the deliverance of the Count of Paris, comprehended as much faith to the Emperor, and his representative, the Acolyte or Follower, as was consistent with rendering justice to the injured Frank.

In furtherance of this plan, he conducted Count Robert from the subterranean vaults of the Blacquernal, of the intricacies of which he was master, having been repeatedly, of late, stationed sentinel there, for the purpose of acquiring that knowledge of which Tatius promised himself the advantage in the ensuing conspiracy. When they were in the open air, and at some distance from the gloomy towers of the Palace, he bluntly asked the Count of Paris whether he knew Agelastes the Philosopher. The other answered in the negative.

"Look you now, Sir Knight, you hurt yourself in attempting to impose upon me," said Hereward. "You must know him; for I saw you dined with him yesterday."

"O! with that learned old man?" said the Count. "I know nothing of him worth owning or disguising to thee or any one. A wily person he is, half herald and half minstrel."

"Half procurer and whole knave," subjoined the Varangian. "With the mask of apparent good–humour he conceals his pandering to the vices of others; with the specious jargon of philosophy, he has argued himself out of religious belief and moral principle; and, with the appearance of the most devoted loyalty, he will, if he is not checked in time, either argue his too confiding master out of life and empire, or, if he fails in this, reason his simple associates into death and misery."

"And do you know all this," said Count Robert, "and permit this man to go unimpeached?"

"O, content you, sir," replied the Varangian; "I cannot yet form any plot which Agelastes may not countermine; but the time will come, nay it is already approaching, when the Emperor's attention shall be irresistibly turned to the conduct of this man, and then let the philosopher sit fast, or by St. Dunstan the barbarian overthrows him! I would only fain, methinks, save from his clutches a foolish friend, who has listed to his delusions."

"But what have I to do," said the Count, "with this man, or with his plots?"

"Much," said Hereward, "although you know it not. The main supporter of this plot is no other than the Caesar, who ought to be the most faithful of men; but ever since Alexius has named a Sebastocrator, an officer that is higher in rank, and nearer to the throne than the Caesar himself, so long has Nicephorus Briennius been displeased and dissatisfied, though for what length of time he has joined the schemes of the astucious Agelastes it is more difficult to say. This I know, that for many months he has fed liberally, as his riches enable him to do, the vices and prodigality of the Caesar. He has encouraged him to show disrespect to his wife, although the Emperor's daughter; has put ill–will between him and the royal family. And if Briennius bears no longer the fame of a rational man, and the renown of a good leader, he is deprived of both by following the advice of this artful sycophant."

"And what is all this to me?" said, the Frank. "Agelastes may be a true man or a time–serving slave; his master, Alexius Comnenus, is not so much allied to me or mine that I should meddle in the intrigues of his court."

"You may be mistaken in that," said the blunt Varangian; "if these intrigues involve the happiness and virtue"'—

"Death of a thousand martyrs!" said the Frank, "doth paltry intrigues and quarrels of slaves involve a single thought of suspicion of the noble Countess of Paris? The oaths of thy whole generation were ineffectual to prove but that one of her hairs had changed its colour to silver!"

"Well imagined, gallant knight," said the Anglo–Saxon; "thou art a husband fitted for the atmosphere of Constantinople, which calls for little vigilance and a strong belief. Thou wilt find many followers and fellows in this court of ours."

"Hark thee, friend," replied the Frank, "let us have no more words, nor walk farther together than just to the most solitary nook of this bewildered city, and let us there set to that work which we left even now unfinished."

"If thou wert a Duke, Sir Count," replied the Varangian, "thou couldst not invite to a combat one who is more ready for it. Yet consider the odds on which we fight. If I fall, my moan is soon made; but will my death set thy wife at liberty if she is under restraint, or restore her honour if it is tarnished?—Will it do any thing more than remove from the world the only person who is willing to give thee aid, at his own risk and danger, and who hopes to unite thee to thy wife, and replace thee at the head of thy forces?"

"I was wrong," said the Count of Paris; "I was entirely wrong; but beware, my good friend, how thou couplest the name of Brenhilda of Aspramonte with the word of dishonour, and tell me, instead of this irritating discourse, whither go we now?"

"To the Cytherean gardens of Agelastes, from which we are not far distant," said the Anglo–Saxon; "yet he hath a nearer way to it than that by which we now travel, else I should be at a loss to account for the short space in which he could exchange the charms of his garden for the gloomy ruins of the Temple of Isis, and the Imperial palace
of the Blacquernal."

"And wherefore, and how long," said Count Robert, "dost thou conclude that my Countess is detained in these gardens?"

"Ever since yesterday," replied Hereward. "When both I, and several of my companions, at my request, kept close watch upon the Caesar and your lady, we did plainly perceive passages of fiery admiration on his part, and anger as it seemed on hers, which Agelastes, being Nicephorus's friend, was likely, as usual, to bring to an end, by a separation of you both from the army of the crusaders, that your
wife, like many a matron before, might have the pleasure of taking up her residence in the gardens of that worthy sage; while you, my Lord, might take up your own permanently in the castle of Blacquernal."

"Villain! why didst thou not apprize me of this yesterday?"

"A likely thing," said Hereward, "that I should feel myself at liberty to leave the ranks, and make such a communication to a man, whom, far from a friend, I then considered in the light of a personal enemy! Methinks, that instead of such language as this, you should be thankful that so many chance circumstances have at length brought me to befriend and assist you."

Count Robert felt the truth of what was said, though at the same time his fiery temper longed to avenge itself, according to its wont, upon the party which was nearest at hand.

But now they arrived at what the citizens of Constantinople called the Philosopher's Gardens. Here Hereward hoped to obtain entrance, for he had gained a knowledge of some part, at least, of the private signals of Achilles and Agelastes, since he had been introduced to the last at the ruins of the Temple of Isis. They had not indeed admitted him to their entire secret; yet, confident in his connexion with the Follower, they had no hesitation in communicating to him snatches of knowledge, such as, committed to a man of shrewd natural sense like the Anglo– Saxon, could scarce fail, in time and by degrees, to make him master of the whole. Count Robert and his companion stood before an arched door, the only opening in a high wall, and the Anglo– Saxon was about to knock, when, as if the idea had suddenly struck him,—

"What if the wretch Diogenes opens the gate? We must kill him, ere he can fly back and betray us. Well, it is a matter of necessity, and the villain has deserved his death by a hundred horrid crimes."

"Kill him then, thyself," retorted Count Robert; "he is nearer thy degree, and assuredly I will not defile the name of Charlemagne with the blood of a black slave."

"Nay, God–a–mercy!" answered the Anglo–Saxon, "but you must bestir yourself in the action, supposing there come rescue, and that I be over–borne by odds."

"Such odds," said the knight, "will render the action more like a *melee*, or general battle; and assure yourself, I will not be slack when I may, with my honour, be active."

"I doubt it not," said the Varangian; "but the distinction seems a strange one, that before permitting a man to defend himself, or annoy his enemy, requires him to demand the pedigree of his ancestor."

"Fear you not, sir," said Count Robert. "The strict rule of chivalry indeed bears what I tell thee, but when the question is, Fight or not? there is great allowance to be made for a decision in the affirmative."

"Let me give then the exorciser's rap," replied Hereward, "and see what fiend will appear."

So saying, he knocked in a particular manner, and the door opened inwards; a dwarfish negress stood in the gap—her white hair contrasted singularly with her dark complexion, and with the broad laughing look peculiar to those slaves. She had something in her physiognomy which, severely construed, might argue malice, and a delight in human misery.

"Is Agelastes"—said the Varangian; but he had not completed the sentence, when she answered him, by pointing down a shadowed walk.

The Anglo–Saxon and Frank turned in that direction, when the hag rather muttered, than said distinctly, "You are one of the initiated, Varangian; take heed whom you take with you, when you may hardly, peradventure, be welcomed even going alone."

Hereward made a sign that he understood her, and they were instantly out of her sight. The path winded beautifully through the shades of an Eastern garden, where clumps of flowers and labyrinths of flowering shrubs, and the tall boughs of the forest trees, rendered even the breath of noon cool and acceptable.

"Here we must use our utmost caution," said Hereward, speaking in a low tone of voice; "for here it is most likely the deer that we seek has found its refuge. Better allow me to pass before, since you are too deeply agitated to possess the coolness necessary for a scout. Keep concealed beneath yon oak, and let no vain scruples of honour
deter you from creeping beneath the underwood, or beneath the earth itself, if you should hear a footfall. If the lovers have agreed, Agelastes, it is probable, walks his round, to prevent intrusion."

"Death and furies! it cannot be!" exclaimed the fiery Frank.—"Lady of the Broken Lances, take thy votary's life, ere thou torment him with this agony!"

He saw, however, the necessity of keeping a strong force upon himself, and permitted, without further remonstrance, the Varangian to pursue his way, looking, however, earnestly after him.

By advancing forward a little, he could observe Hereward draw near to a pavilion which arose at no great distance from the place where they had parted. Here he observed him apply, first his eye, and then his ear, to one of the casements, which were in a great measure grown over, and excluded from the light, by various flowering shrubs. He almost thought he saw a grave interest take place in the countenance of the Varangian, and he longed to have his share of the information which he had doubtless obtained.

He crept, therefore, with noiseless steps, through the same labyrinth of foliage which had covered the approaches of Hereward; and so silent were his movements, that he touched the Anglo–Saxon, in order to make him aware of his presence, before he observed his approach.

Hereward, not aware at first by whom he was approached, turned on the intruder with a countenance like a burning coal. Seeing, however, that it was the Frank, he shrugged his shoulders, as if pitying the impatience which could not be kept under prudent restraint, and drawing himself back allowed the Count the privilege of a peeping place through plinths of the casement, which could not be discerned by the sharpest eye from the inner side. The sombre character of the light which penetrated into this abode of pleasure, was suited to that species of thought to which a Temple of Cytherea was supposed to be dedicated. Portraits and groups of statuary were also to be seen, in the taste of those which they had beheld at the Kiosk of the waterfall, yet something more free in the ideas which they conveyed than were to be found at their first resting–place. Shortly after, the door of the pavilion opened, and the Countess entered, followed by her attendant Agatha. The lady threw herself on a couch as she came in, while her attendant, who was a young and very handsome woman, kept herself modestly in the background, so much so as hardly to be distinguished.

"What dost thou think," said the Countess, "of so suspicious a friend as Agelastes? so gallant an enemy as the Caesar, as he is called?"

"What should I think," returned the damsel, "except that what the old man calls friendship is hatred, and what the Caesar terms a patriotic love for his country, which will not permit him to set its enemies at liberty, is in fact too strong an affection for his fair captive?"

"For such an affection," said the Countess, "he shall have the same requital as if it were indeed the hostility of which he would give it the colour.—My true and noble lord; hadst thou an idea of the calamities to which they have subjected me, how soon wouldst thou break through every restraint to hasten to my relief!"

"Art thou a man," said Count Robert to his companion; "and canst thou advise me to remain still and hear this?"

"I am one man," said the Anglo–Saxon; "you, sir, are another; but all our arithmetic will not make us more than two; and in this place, it is probable that a whistle from the Caesar, or a scream from Agelastes, would bring a thousand to match us, if we were as bold as Bevis of Hampton.—Stand still and keep quiet. I counsel this, less as respecting my own life, which, by embarking upon a wild–goose chase with so strange a partner, I have shown I put at little value,
than for thy safety, and that of the lady thy Countess, who shows herself as virtuous as beautiful."

"I was imposed on at first," said the Lady Brenhilda to her attendant. "Affectation of severe morals, of deep learning, and of rigid rectitude, assumed by this wicked old man, made me believe in part
the character which he pretended; but the gloss is rubbed off since he let me see into his alliance with the unworthy Caesar, and the ugly picture remains in its native loathsomeness. Nevertheless, if I can, by address or subtlety, deceive this arch–deceiver,—as he has taken
from me, in a great measure, every other kind of assistance,—I will not refuse that of craft, which he may find perhaps equal to his own?"

"Hear you that?" said the Varangian to the Count of Paris. "Do not let your impatience mar the web of your lady's prudence. I will weigh a woman's wit against a man's valour where there is aught to do! Let us not come in with our assistance until time shall show us that it is necessary for her safety and our success."

"Amen," said the Count of Paris; "but hope not, Sir Saxon, that thy prudence shall persuade me to leave this garden without taking full vengeance on that unworthy Caesar, and the pretended philosopher, if indeed he turns out to have assumed a character"—The Count was here beginning to raise his voice, when the Saxon, without ceremony, placed his hand on his mouth. "Thou takest a liberty,"
said Count Robert, lowering however his tones.

"Ay, truly," said Hereward; "when the house is on fire, I do not stop to ask whether the water which I pour on it be perfumed or no."

This recalled the Frank to a sense of his situation; and if not contented with the Saxon's mode of making an apology, he was at least silenced. A distant noise was now heard—the Countess listened, and changed colour. "Agatha," she said, "we are like champions in the lists, and here comes the adversary. Let us retreat into this side apartment, and so for a while put off an encounter thus alarming." So saying, the two females withdrew into a sort of anteroom, which opened from the principal apartment behind the seat which Brenhilda had occupied.

They had scarcely disappeared, when, as the stage direction has it, enter from the other side the Caesar and Agelastes. They had perhaps heard the last words of Brenhilda, for the Caesar repeated in a low tone—

"Militat omnis amans, habet et sua castra Cupido.

"What, has our fair opponent withdrawn her forces? No matter, it shows she thinks of the warfare, though the enemy be not in sight. Well, thou shalt not have to upbraid me this time, Agelastes, with precipitating my amours, and depriving myself of the pleasure of pursuit. By Heavens, I will be as regular in my progress as if in reality I bore on my shoulders the whole load of years which make the difference between us; for I shrewdly suspect that with thee, old man, it is that envious churl Time that hath plucked the wings of Cupid."

"Say not so, mighty Caesar," said the old man; "it is the hand of Prudence, which, depriving Cupid's wing of some wild feathers, leaves him still enough to fly with an equal and steady flight."

"Thy flight, however, was less measured, Agelastes, when thou didst collect that armoury—that magazine of Cupid's panoply, out of which thy kindness permitted me but now to arm myself, or rather to repair my accoutrements."

So saying, he glanced his eye over his own person, blazing with gems, and adorned with a chain of gold, bracelets, rings, and other ornaments, which, with a new and splendid habit, assumed since his arrival at these Cytherean gardens, tended to set off his very handsome figure.

"I am glad," said Agelastes, "if you have found among toys, which I now never wear, and seldom made use of even when life was young with me, anything which may set off your natural advantages. Remember only this slight condition, that such of these trifles as have made part of your wearing apparel on this distinguished day, cannot return to a meaner owner, but must of necessity remain the property of that greatness of which they had once formed the ornament."

"I cannot consent to this, my worthy friend," said the Caesar; "I know thou valuest these jewels only in so far as a philosopher may value them; that is, for nothing save the remembrances which attach to them. This large seal-ring, for instance, was—I have heard you say—the property of Socrates; if so, you cannot view it save with devout thankfulness, that your own philosophy has never been tried with the exercise of a Xantippe. These clasps released, in older times, the lovely bosom of Phryne; and they now belong to one who could do better homage to the beauties they concealed or discovered than could the cynic Diogenes. These buckles, too"—

"I will spare thy ingenuity, good youth," said Agelastes, somewhat nettled; "or rather, noble Caesar. Keep thy wit—thou wilt have ample occasion for it."

"Fear not me," said the Caesar. "Let us proceed, since you will, to exercise the gifts which we possess, such as they are, either natural or bequeathed to us by our dear and respected friend. Hah!" he said, the door opening suddenly, and the Countess almost meeting him, "our wishes are here anticipated."

He bowed accordingly with the deepest deference to the Lady Brenhilda, who, having made some alterations to enhance the splendour of her attire, now moved forward from the withdrawing– room into which she had retreated.

"Hail, noble lady," said the Caesar, "whom I have visited with the intention of apologizing for detaining you, in some degree against your will, in those strange regions in which yon unexpectedly find yourself."

"Not in some degree," answered the lady, "but entirely contrary to my inclinations, which are, to be with my husband, the Count of Paris, and the followers who have taken the cross under his banner."

"Such, doubtless, were your thoughts when you left the land of the west," said Agelastes; "but, fair Countess, have they experienced no change? You have left a shore streaming with human blood when the slightest provocation occurred, and thou hast come to one whose principal maxim is to increase the sum of human happiness by every mode which can be invented. In the west yonder, he or she is respected most who can best exercise their tyrannical strength in making others miserable, while, in these more placid realms, we reserve our garlands for the ingenious youth, or lovely lady, who can best make happy the person whose affection is fixed upon her."

"But, reverend philosopher," said the Countess, "who labourest so artificially in recommending the yoke of pleasure, know that you contradict every notion which I have been taught from my infancy. In the land where my nurture lay, so far are we from acknowledging your doctrines, that we match not, except like the lion and the
lioness, when the male has compelled the female to acknowledge his superior worth and valour. Such is our rule, that a damsel, even of mean degree, would think herself heinously undermatched, if
wedded to a gallant whose fame in arms was yet unknown."

"But, noble lady," said the Caesar, "a dying man may then find room for some faint hope. Were there but a chance that distinction in arms could gain those affections which have been stolen, rather than fairly conferred, how many are there who would willingly enter into the competition where the prize is so fair! What is the enterprise too
bold to be under–taken on such a condition! And where is the individual whose heart would not feel, that in baring his sword for
the prize, he made vow never to return it to the scabbard, without the proud boast, What I have not yet won, I have deserved!"

"You see, lady," said Agelastes, who, apprehending that the last speech of the Caesar had made some impression, hastened to follow it up with a suitable observation—"You see that the fire of chivalry burns as gallantly in the bosom of the Grecians as in that of the western nations."

"Yes," answered Brenhilda, "and I have heard of the celebrated siege of Troy, on which occasion a dastardly coward carried off the wife
of a brave man, shunned every proffer of encounter with the husband whom he had wronged, and finally caused the death of his numerous brothers, the destruction of his native city, with all the wealth which
it contained, and died himself the death of a pitiful poltroon, lamented only by his worthless leman, to show how well the rules of chivalry were understood by your predecessors."

"Lady, you mistake," said the Caesar; "the offences of Paris were those of a dissolute Asiatic; the courage which avenged them was that of the Greek Empire."

"You are learned, sir," said the lady; "but think not that I will trust your words until you produce before me a Grecian knight, gallant enough to look upon the armed crest of my husband without quaking."

"That, methinks, were not extremely difficult," returned the Caesar; "if they have not flattered me, I have myself been thought equal in battle to more dangerous men than him who has been strangely mated with the Lady Brenhilda."

"That is soon tried," answered the Countess. "You will hardly, I

think, deny, that my husband, separated from me by some unworthy trick, is still at thy command, and could be produced at thy pleasure. I will ask no armour for him save what he wears, no weapon but his good sword Tranchefer; then place him in this chamber, or any other lists equally narrow, and if he flinch, or cry craven, or remain dead under shield, let Brenhilda be the prize of the conqueror.—Merciful Heaven!" she concluded, as she sunk back upon her seat, "forgive
me for the crime of even imagining such a termination, which is equal almost to doubting thine unerring judgment!"

"Let me, however," said the Caesar, "catch up these precious words before they fall to the ground,—Let me hope that he, to whom the heavens shall give power and strength to conquer this highly- esteemed Count of Paris, shall succeed him in the affections of Brenhilda; and believe me, the sun plunges not through the sky to his resting–place, with the same celerity that I shall hasten to the encounter."

"Now, by Heaven!" said Count Robert, in an anxious whisper to Hereward, "it is too much to expect me to stand by and hear a contemptible Greek, who durst not stand even the rattling farewell which Tranchefer takes of his scabbard, brave me in my absence, and affect to make love to my lady *par amours!* And she, too— methinks Brenhilda allows more license than she is wont to do to yonder chattering popinjay. By the rood! I will spring into the apartment, front them with my personal appearance, and confute yonder braggart in a manner he is like to remember."

"Under favour," said the Varangian, who was the only auditor of this violent speech, "you shall be ruled by calm reason while I am with you. When we are separated, let the devil of knight–errantry, which has such possession of thee, take thee upon his shoulders, and carry thee full tilt wheresoever he lists."

"Thou art a brute," said the Count, looking at him with a contempt corresponding to the expression he made use of; "not only without humanity, but without the sense of natural honour or natural shame. The most despicable of animals stands not by tamely and sees another assail his mate. The bull offers his horns to a rival—the mastiff uses his jaws—and even the timid stag becomes furious, and gores."

"Because they are beasts," said the Varangian, "and their mistresses also creatures without shame or reason, who are not aware of the sanctity of a choice. But thou, too, Count, canst thou not see the obvious purpose of this poor lady, forsaken by all the world, to keep her faith towards thee, by eluding the snares with which wicked men have beset her? By the souls of my fathers! my heart is so much moved by her ingenuity, mingled as I see it is with the most perfect candour and faith, that I myself, in fault of a better champion, would willingly raise the axe in her behalf!"

"I thank thee, my good friend," said the Count; "I thank thee as heartily as if it were possible thou shouldst be left to do that good office for Brenhilda, the beloved of many a noble lord, the mistress of many a powerful vassal; and, what is more, much more than thanks, I crave thy pardon for the wrong I did thee but now."

"My pardon you cannot need" said the Varangian; "for I take no offence that is not seriously meant.—Stay, they speak again."

"It is strange it should be so," said the Caesar, as he paced the apartment; "but methinks, nay, I am almost certain, Agelastes, that I hear voices in the vicinity of this apartment of thy privacy." "It is impossible," said Agelastes; "but I will go and see." Perceiving him to leave the pavilion, the Varangian made the Frank sensible that they must crouch down among a little thicket of evergreens, where they lay completely obscured. The philosopher made his rounds with a heavy step, but a watchful eye; and the two listeners were obliged to observe the strictest silence, without motion of any kind, until he had completed an ineffectual search, and returned into the pavilion. "By my faith, brave man," said the Count, "ere we return to our skulking–place, I must tell thee in thine ear, that never, in my life, was temptation so strong upon me, as that which prompted me to beat out that old hypocrite's brains, provided I could have reconciled it with my honour; and heartily do I wish that thou, whose honour no way withheld thee, had experienced and given way to some impulse of a similar nature."

"Such fancies have passed through my head," said the Varangian; "but I will not follow them till they are consistent both with our own safety, and more particularly with that of the Countess."

"I thank thee again for thy good—will to her," said Count Robert; "and, by Heaven! if fight we must at length, as it seems likely, I will neither grudge thee an honourable antagonist, nor fair quarter if the combat goes against thee."

"Thou hast my thanks," was the reply of Hereward; "only, for Heaven's sake, be silent in this conjecture, and do what thou wilt afterwards." Before the Varangian and the Count had again resumed their posture of listeners, the parties within the pavilion, conceiving themselves unwatched, had resumed their conversation, speaking low, yet with considerable animation.

"It is in vain you would persuade me," said the Countess, "that you know not where my husband is, or that you have not the most absolute influence over his captivity. Who else could have an interest in banishing or putting to death the husband, but he that affects to admire the wife?" "You do me wrong, beautiful lady,"
answered the Caesar, "and forget that I can in no shape be termed the moving—spring of this empire; that my father—in—law, Alexius, is the Emperor; and that the woman who terms herself my wife, is jealous as a fiend can be of my slightest motion.—What possibility was there that I should work the captivity of your husband and your own? The open affront which the Count of Paris put upon the Emperor, was
one which he was likely to avenge, either by secret guile or by open force. Me it no way touched, save as the humble vassal of thy charms; and it was by the wisdom and the art of the sage Agelastes, that I was able to extricate thee from the gulf in which thou hadst else certainly perished. Nay, weep not, lady, for as yet we know not the fate of Count Robert; but, credit me, it is wisdom to choose a better protector, and consider him as no more."

"A better than him," said Brenhilda, "I can never have, were I to choose out of the knighthood of all the world!"

"This hand," said the Caesar, drawing himself into a martial attitude, "should decide that question, were the man of whom thou thinkest so much yet moving on the face of this earth and at liberty."

"Thou art," said Brenhilda, looking fixedly at him with the fire of indignation flashing from every feature—"thou art—but it avails not telling thee what is thy real name; believe me, the world shall one day ring with it, and be justly sensible of its value. Observe what I am about to say—Robert of Paris is gone—or captive, I know not where. He cannot fight the match of which thou seemest so desirous
—but here stands Brenhilda, born heiress of Aspramonte, by marriage the wedded wife of the good Count of Paris. She was never matched in the lists by mortal man, except the valiant Count, and since thou art so grieved that thou canst not meet her husband in battle, thou canst not surely object, if she is willing to meet thee in his stead!"

"How, madam?" said the Caesar, astonished; "do you propose yourself to hold the lists against me?"

"Against you!" said the Countess; "against all the Grecian Empire, if they shall affirm that Robert of Paris is justly used and lawfully confined."

"And are the conditions," said the Caesar, "the same as if Count Robert himself held the lists? The vanquished must then be at the pleasure of the conqueror for good or evil."

"It would seem so," said the Countess, "nor do I refuse the hazard; only, that if the other champion shall bite the dust, the noble Count Robert shall be set at liberty, and permitted to depart with all suitable honours."

"This I refuse not," said the Caesar, "provided it is in my power."

A deep growling sound, like that of a modern gong, here interrupted the conference.

CHAPTER THE NINETEENTH

The Varangian and Count Robert, at every risk of discovery, had remained so near as fully to conjecture, though they could not expressly overhear, the purport of the conversation.

"He has accepted her challenge!" said the Count of Paris. "And

with apparent willingness," said Hereward.

"O, doubtless, doubtless,"—answered the Crusader; "but he knows not the skill in war which a woman may attain; for my part, God knows I have enough depending upon the issue of this contest, yet such is my confidence, that I would to God I had more. I vow to our Lady of the Broken Lances, that I desire every furrow of land I possess—every honour which I can call my own, from the Countship of Paris, down to the leather that binds my spur, were dependent and at issue upon this fair field, between your Caesar, as men term him, and Brenhilda of Aspramonte."

"It is a noble confidence," said the Varangian, "nor durst I say it is a rash one; only I cannot but remember that the Caesar is a strong man, as well as a handsome, expert in the use of arms, and, above all, less strictly bound than you esteem yourself by the rules of honour. There are many ways in which advantage may be given and taken, which will not, in the Caesar's estimation, alter the character
of the field from an equal one, although it might do so in the opinion of the chivalrous Count of Paris, or even in that of the poor Varangian. But first let me conduct you to some place of safety, for your escape must be soon, if it is not already, detected. The sounds which we heard intimate that some of his confederate plotters have visited the garden on other than love affairs. I will guide thee to another avenue than that by which we entered. But you would hardly, I suppose, be pleased to adopt the wisest alternative?" "And

what may that be?" said the Count.

"To give thy purse, though it were thine all, to some poor ferryman to waft thee over the Hellespont, then hasten to carry thy complaint to Godfrey of Bouillon, and what friends thou mayst have among thy brethren crusaders, and determine, as thou easily canst, on a sufficient number of them to come back and menace the city with instant war, unless the Emperor should deliver up thy lady, most unfairly made prisoner, and prevent, by his authority, this absurd and unnatural combat."

"And would you have me, then," said Count Robert, "move the crusaders to break a fairly appointed field of battle? Do you think that Godfrey of Bouillon would turn back upon his pilgrimage for such an unworthy purpose; or that the Countess of Paris would accept as a service, means of safety which would stain her honour for ever, by breaking an appointment solemnly made on her own challenge?—Never!"

"My judgment is then at fault," said the Varangian, "for I see I can hammer out no expedient which is not, in some extravagant manner or another, controlled by your foolish notions. Here is a man who has been trapped into the power of his enemy, that he might not interfere to prevent a base stratagem upon his lady, involving both her life and honour; yet he thinks it a matter of necessity that he keeps faith as precisely with these midnight poisoners, as he would had it been pledged to the most honourable men!"

"Thou say'st a painful truth," said Count Robert; "but my word is the emblem of my faith; and if it pass to a dishonourable or faithless foe, it is imprudently done on my part; but if I break it, being once pledged, it is a dishonourable action, and the disgrace can never be washed from my shield."

"Do you mean, then," said the Varangian, "to suffer your wife's honour to remain pledged as it at present is, on the event of an unequal combat?"

"God and the saints pardon thee such a thought!" said the Count of Paris. "I will go to see this combat with a heart as firm, if not as light, as any time I ever saw spears splintered. If by the influence of any accident or treachery,—for fairly, and with such an antagonist, Brenhilda of Aspramonte cannot be overthrown,—I step into the lists, proclaim the Caesar as he is—a villain—show the falsehood of his conduct from beginning to end,—appeal to every noble heart that hears me, and then—God show the right!"

Hereward paused, and shook his head. "All this," he said, "might be feasible enough provided the combat were to be fought in the presence of your own countrymen, or even, by the mass! if the Varangians were to be guards of the lists. But treachery of every kind is so familiar to the Greeks, that I question if they would view the conduct of their Caesar as any thing else than a pardonable and natural stratagem of Dan Cupid, to be smiled at, rather than subjected to disgrace or punishment."

"A nation," said Count Robert, "who could smile at such a jest, may heaven refuse them sympathy at their utmost need, when their sword is broken in their hand, and their wives and daughters shrieking in the relentless grasp of a barbarous enemy!"

Hereward looked upon his companion, whose flushed cheeks and sparkling eyes bore witness to his enthusiasm.

"I see," he said, "you are resolved, and I know that your resolution can in justice be called by no other name than an act of heroic folly: —What then? it is long since life has been bitter to the Varangian exile. Morn has raised him from a joyless bed, which night has seen him lie down upon, wearied with wielding a mercenary weapon in the wars of strangers. He has longed to lay down his life in an honourable cause, and this is one in which the extremity and very essence of honour is implicated. It tallies also with my scheme of saving the Emperor, which will be greatly facilitated by the downfall of his ungrateful son–in– law." Then addressing himself to the Count, he continued, "Well, Sir Count, as thou art the person principally concerned, I am willing to yield to thy reasoning in this affair; but I hope you will permit me to mingle with your resolution some advices of a more everyday and less fantastic nature. For example, thy escape from the dungeons of the Blacquernal must soon be generally known. In prudence, indeed, I myself must be the first to communicate it, since otherwise the suspicion will fall on me —Where do you think of concealing yourself? for assuredly the search will be close and general."

"For that," said the Count of Paris, "I must be indebted to thy suggestion, with thanks for every lie which thou findest thyself obliged to make, to contrive, and produce in my behalf, entreating thee only to render them as few as possible, they being a coin which I myself never fabricate."

"Sir knight," answered Hereward, "let me begin first by saying, that no knight that ever belted sword is more a slave to truth, when truth is observed towards him, than the poor soldier who talks to thee; but when the game depends not upon fair play, but upon lulling men's cautiousness asleep by falsehood, and drugging their senses by opiate draughts, they who would scruple at no means of deceiving me, can hardly expect that I, who am paid in such base money, should pass nothing on my part but what is lawful and genuine. For the present thou must remain concealed within my poor apartment, in the barracks of the Varangians, which is the last place where they will think of seeking for thee. Take this, my upper cloak, and follow me; and now that we are about to leave these gardens, thou mayst follow me unsuspected as a sentinel attending his officer; for, take it along with you, noble Count, that we Varangians are a sort of persons upon whom the Greeks care not to look very long or fixedly."

They now reached the gate where they had been admitted by the negress, and Hereward, who was intrusted with the power, it seems, of letting himself out of the philosopher's premises, though not of entering without assistance from the portress, took out a key which turned the lock on the garden side, so that they soon found themselves at liberty. They then proceeded by by–paths through the city, Hereward leading the way, and the Count following, without speech or remonstrance, until they stood before the portal of the barracks of the Varangians.

"Make haste," said the sentinel who was on duty, "dinner is already begun." The communication sounded joyfully in the ears of

Hereward, who was much afraid that his companion might have been stopt and examined. By a side passage he reached his own quarters, and introduced the Count into a small room, the sleeping chamber of his squire, where he apologized for leaving him for some time; and, going out, locked the door, for fear, as he said, of intrusion.

The demon of suspicion was not very likely to molest a mind so frankly constituted as that of Count Robert, and yet the last action of Hereward did not fail to occasion some painful reflections.

"This man," he said, "had needs be true, for I have reposed in him a mighty trust, which few hirelings in his situation would honourably discharge. What is to prevent him to report to the principal officer of his watch, that the Frank prisoner, Robert, Count of Paris, whose wife stands engaged for so desperate a combat with the Caesar, has escaped, indeed, this morning, from the prisons of the Blacquernal, but has suffered himself to be trepanned at noon, and is again a captive in the barracks of the Varangian Guard?—what means of defence are mine, were I discovered to these mercenaries?—What man could do, by the favour of our Lady of the Broken Lances, I have not failed to achieve. I have slain a tiger in single combat—I have killed one warder, and conquered the desperate and gigantic creature by whom he was supported. I have had terms enough at command to bring over this Varangian to my side, in appearance at least; yet all this does not encourage me to hope that I could long keep at bay ten or a dozen such men as these beef–fed knaves appear to be, led in upon me by a fellow of thewes and sinews such as those of my late companion.—Yet for shame, Robert! such thoughts are unworthy a descendant of Charlemagne. When wert thou wont so curiously to count thine enemies, and when wert thou wont to be suspicious, since he, whose bosom may truly boast itself incapable of fraud, ought in honesty to be the last to expect it in another? The Varangian's look is open, his coolness in danger is striking, his speech is more frank and ready than ever was that of a traitor. If he is false, there is no faith in the hand of nature, for truth, sincerity, and courage are written upon his forehead."

While Count Robert was thus reflecting upon his condition, and combating the thick–coming doubts and suspicions which its uncertainties gave rise to, he began to be sensible that he had not eaten for many hours; and amidst many doubts and fears of a more heroic nature, he half entertained a lurking suspicion, that they meant to let hunger undermine his strength before they adventured into the apartment to deal with him.

We shall best see how far these doubts were deserved by Hereward, or how far they were unjust, by following his course after he left his barrack–room. Snatching a morsel of dinner, which he ate with an affectation of great hunger, but, in fact, that his attention to his food might be a pretence for dispensing with disagreeable questions, or with conversation of any kind, he pleaded duty, and immediately leaving his comrades, directed his course to the lodgings of Achilles Tatius, which were a part of the same building. A Syrian slave, who opened the door, after a deep reverence to Hereward, whom he knew as a favourite attendant of the Acolyte, said to him that his master was gone forth, but had desired him to say, that if he wished to see him, he would find him at the Philosopher's Gardens, so called, as belonging to the sage Agelastes.

Hereward turned about instantly, and availing himself of his knowledge of Constantinople to thread its streets in the shortest time possible, at length stood alone before the door in the garden–wall, at which he and the Count of Paris had previously been admitted in the earlier part of the day. The same negress appeared at the same
private signal, and when he asked for Achilles Tatius, she replied, with some sharpness, "Since you were here this morning, I marvel you did not meet him, or that, having business with him, you did not stay till he arrived. Sure I am, that not long after you entered the garden the Acolyte was enquiring for you."

"It skills not, old woman" said the Varangian; "I communicate the reason of my motions to my commander, but not to thee." He entered the garden accordingly, and avoiding the twilight path that led to the Bower of Love,— so was the pavilion named in which he had overheard the dialogue between the Caesar and the Countess of
Paris,—he arrived before a simple garden–house, whose humble and modest front seemed to announce that it was the abode of philosophy

and learning. Here, passing before the windows, he made some little noise, expecting to attract the attention either of Achilles Tatius, or his accomplice Agelastes, as chance should determine. It was the first who heard, and who replied. The door opened; a lofty plume stooped itself, that its owner might cross the threshold, and the stately form of Achilles Tatius entered the gardens. "What now," he
said, "our trusty sentinel? what hast thou, at this time of day, come to report to us? Thou art our good friend, and highly esteemed soldier, and well we wot thine errand must be of importance, since thou hast brought it thyself, and at an hour so unusual."

"Pray Heaven," said Hereward, "that the news I have brought deserve a welcome."

"Speak them instantly," said the Acolyte, "good or bad; thou speakest to a man to whom fear is unknown." But his eye, which quailed as he looked on the soldier—his colour, which went and came—his hands, which busied themselves in an uncertain manner in adjusting the belt of his sword,—all argued a state of mind very different from that which his tone of defiance would fain have implied. "Courage," he said, "my trusty soldier! speak the news to me. I can bear the worst thou hast to tell."

"In a word, then," said the Varangian, "your Valour directed me this morning to play the office of master of the rounds upon those dungeons of the Blacquernal palace, where last night the boisterous Count Robert of Paris was incarcerated"—

"I remember well," said Achilles Tatius.—"What then?"

"As I reposed me," said Hereward, "in an apartment above the vaults, I heard cries from beneath, of a kind which attracted my attention. I hastened to examine, and my surprise was extreme, when looking down into the dungeon, though I could see nothing
distinctly, yet, by the wailing and whimpering sounds, I conceived that the Man of the Forest, the animal called Sylvan, whom our soldiers have so far indoctrinated in our Saxon tongue as to make him useful in the wards of the prison, was bemoaning himself on account of some violent injury. Descending with a torch, I found the

bed on which the prisoner had been let down burnt to cinders; the tiger which had been chained within a spring of it, with its skull broken to pieces; the creature called Sylvan, prostrate, and writhing under great pain and terror, and no prisoner whatever in the dungeon. There were marks that all the fastenings had been withdrawn by a Mytilenian soldier, companion of my watch, when he visited the dungeon at the usual hour; and as, in my anxious search, I at length found his dead body, slain apparently by a stab in the throat, I was obliged to believe that while I was examining the cell, he, this Count Robert, with whose daring life the adventure is well consistent, had escaped into the upper air, by means, doubtless, of the ladder and trap–door by which I had descended."

"And wherefore didst thou not instantly call treason, and raise the hue and cry?" demanded the Acolyte.

"I dared not venture to do so," replied the Varangian, "till I had instructions from your Valour. The alarming cry of treason, and the various rumours likely at this moment to ensue, might have involved a search so close, as perchance would have discovered matters in which the Acolyte himself would have been rendered subject to suspicion."

"Thou art right," said Achilles Tatius, in a whisper: "and yet it will be necessary that we do not pretend any longer to conceal the flight of this important prisoner, if we would not pass for being his accomplices. Where thinkest thou this unhappy fugitive can have taken refuge?"

"That I was in hopes of learning from your Valour's greater wisdom," said Hereward.

"Thinkest thou not," said Achilles, "that he may have crossed the Hellespont, in order to rejoin his own countrymen and adherents?"

"It is much to be dreaded," said Hereward. "Undoubtedly, if the Count listened to the advice of any one who knew the face of the country, such would be the very counsel he would receive."

"The danger, then, of his return at the head of a vengeful body of

Franks," said the Acolyte, "is not so immediate as I apprehended at first, for the Emperor gave positive orders that the boats and galleys which yesterday transported the crusaders to the shores of Asia should recross the strait, and bring back no single one of them from the step upon their journey on which he had so far furthered them.— Besides, they all,—their leaders, that is to say,—made their vows before crossing, that they would not turn back so much as a foot's pace, now that they had set actually forth on the road to Palestine."

"So, therefore," said Hereward, "one of the two propositions is unquestionable; either Count Robert is on the eastern side of the strait, having no means of returning with his brethren to avenge the usage he has received, and may therefore be securely set, at defiance,—or else he lurks somewhere in Constantinople, without a friend or ally to take his part, or encourage him openly to state his supposed wrongs; in either case, there can, I think, be no tact in conveying to the palace the news that he has freed himself, since it would only alarm the court, and afford the Emperor ground for many suspicions.—But it is not for an ignorant barbarian like me to prescribe a course of conduct to your valour and wisdom, and methinks the sage Agelastes were a fitter counsellor than such as I am."

"No, no, no," said the Acolyte, in a hurried whisper; "the philosopher and I are right good friends, sworn good friends, very especially bound together; but should it come to this, that one of us must needs throw before the footstool of the Emperor the head of the other, I think thou wouldst not advise that I, whose hairs have not a trace of silver, should be the last in making the offering; therefore we will
say nothing of this mishap, but give thee full power, and the highest charge to seek for Count Robert of Paris, be he dead or alive, to secure him within the dungeons set apart for the discipline of our own corps, and when thou hast done so, to bring me notice. I may make him my friend in many ways, by extricating his wife from danger by the axes of my Varangians. What is there in this metropolis that they have to oppose them?"

"When raised in a just cause," answered Hereward, "nothing."

"Hah!—say'st thou?" said the Acolyte; "how meanest thou by that?
—but I know—Thou art scrupulous about having the just and lawful
command of thy officer in every action in which thou art engaged, and,
thinking in that dutiful and soldierlike manner, it is my duty as thine Acolyte
to see thy scruples satisfied. A warrant shalt thou have, with full powers, to
seek for and imprison this foreign Count of whom we have been speaking—
And, hark thee, my excellent
friend," he continued, with some hesitation, "I think thou hadst better begone,
and begin, or rather continue thy search. It is unnecessary to inform our friend
Agelastes of what has happened, until his advice
be more needful than as yet it is on the occasion. Home—home to the
barracks; I will account to him for thy appearance here, if he be curious on the
subject, which, as a suspicious old man, he is likely to be. Go to the barracks,
and act as if thou hadst a warrant in every respect full and ample. I will
provide thee with one when I come back to my quarters."

The Varangian turned hastily homewards.

"Now, is it not," he said, "a strange thing, and enough to make a man a rogue
for life—to observe how the devil encourages young beginners in falsehood! I
have told a greater lie—at least I have suppressed more truth—than on any
occasion before in my whole life—and what is the consequence? Why, my
commander throws almost at my head a warrant sufficient to guarantee and
protect me
in all I have done, or propose to do! If the foul fiend were thus regular in
protecting his votaries, methinks they would have little reason to complain
of him, or better men to be astonished at their number. But a time comes,
they say, when he seldom fails to desert them. Therefore, get thee behind
me, Satan! If I have seemed to be thy servant for a short time, it is but with
an honest and Christian purpose."

As he entertained these thoughts, he looked back upon the path, and was
startled at an apparition of a creature of a much greater size, and a stranger
shape than human, covered, all but the face, with a reddish dun fur; his
expression an ugly, and yet a sad melancholy; a cloth
was wrapped round one hand, and an air of pain and languor bespoke
suffering from a wound. So much was Hereward pre–

occupied with his own reflections, that at first he thought his imagination had actually raised the devil; but after a sudden start of surprise, he recognised his acquaintance Sylvan. "Hah! old friend," he said, "I am happy thou hast made thy escape to a place where them wilt find plenty of fruit to support thee. Take my advice—keep out of the way of discovery—Keep thy friend's counsel."

The Man of the Wood uttered a chattering noise in return to this address.

"I understand thee," said Hereward, "thou wilt tell no tales, thou sayest; and faith, I will trust thee rather than the better part of my own two–legged race, who are eternally circumventing or murdering each other."

A minute after the creature was out of sight, Hereward heard the shriek of a female, and a voice which cried for help. The accents must have been uncommonly interesting to the Varangian, since, forgetting his own dangerous situation, he immediately turned and flew to the suppliant's assistance.

Chapter the Twentieth

She comes! she comes! in all the charms of youth,
Unequall'd love, and unsuspected truth!

Hereward was not long in tracing the cry through the wooded walks, when a female rushed into his arms; alarmed, as it appeared, by Sylvan, who was pursuing her closely. The figure of Hereward, with his axe uplifted, put an instant stop to his career, and with a terrified note of his native cries, he withdrew into the thickest of the
adjoining foliage.

Relieved from his presence, Hereward had time to look at the female whom he had succoured: She was arrayed in a dress which consisted of several colours, that which predominated being a pale yellow; her tunic was of this colour, and, like a modern gown, was closely fitted to the body, which, in the present case, was that of a tall, but very well– formed person. The mantle, or upper garment, in which the whole figure was wrapped, was of fine cloth; and the kind of hood which was attached to it having flown back with the rapidity of her motion, gave to view the hair beautifully adorned and twisted into a natural head–dress. Beneath this natural head–gear appeared a face pale as death, from a sense of the supposed danger, but which preserved, even amidst its terrors, an exquisite degree of beauty.

Hereward was thunderstruck at this apparition. The dress was neither Grecian, Italian, nor of the costume of the Franks;—it was *Saxon!*— connected by a thousand tender remembrances with Hereward's childhood and youth. The circumstance was most extraordinary. Saxon women, indeed, there were in Constantinople, who had united their fortunes with those of the Varangians; and those often chose to wear their national dress in the city, because the character and conduct of their husbands secured them a degree of respect, which they might not have met with either as Grecian or as stranger females of a similar rank. But almost all these were personally known to Hereward. It was no time, however, for reverie—he was himself in danger—the situation of the young female might be no safe one. In every case, it was judicious to quit the more public part of the gardens; he therefore lost not a moment in conveying the fainting Saxon to a retreat he fortunately was acquainted with. A covered path, obscured by vegetation, led through a species of labyrinth to an artificial cave, at the bottom of which, half–paved with shells, moss, and spar, lay the gigantic and half–recumbent statue of a river deity, with its usual attributes—that is, its front crowned with water–lilies and sedges, and its ample hand half– resting upon an empty urn. The attitude of the whole figure corresponded with the motto,—"I SLEEP—AWAKE ME NOT."

"Accursed relic of paganism," said Hereward, who was, in proportion to his light, a zealous Christian—"brutish stock or stone that thou art! I will wake thee with a vengeance." So saying, he struck the head of the slumbering deity with his battle–axe, and deranged the play of the fountain so much that the water began to pour into the basin.

"Thou art a good block, nevertheless," said the Varangian, "to send succour so needful to the aid of my poor countrywoman. Thou shalt give her also, with thy leave, a portion of thy couch." So saying he arranged his fair burden, who was as yet insensible, upon the pedestal where the figure of the River God reclined. In doing this, his attention was recalled to her face, and again and again he was thrilled with an emotion of hope, but so excessively like fear, that it could only be compared to the flickering of a torch, uncertain whether it is to light up or be instantly extinguished. With a sort of mechanical attention, he continued to make such efforts as he could to recall the intellect of the beautiful creature before him. His feelings were those of the astronomical sage, to whom the rise of the moon slowly restores the contemplation of that heaven, which is at once, as a Christian, his hope of felicity, and, as a philosopher, the source of his knowledge. The blood returned to her cheek, and reanimation, and even recollection, took place in her earlier than in the astonished Varangian.

"Blessed Mary!" she said, "have I indeed tasted the last bitter cup, and is it here where thou reunitest thy votaries after death!—Speak, Hereward! if thou art aught but an empty creature of the imagination!— speak, and tell me, if I have but dreamed of that monstrous ogre!"

"Collect thyself, my beloved Bertha," said the Anglo–Saxon, recalled by the sound of her voice, "and prepare to endure what thou livest to witness, and thy Hereward survives to tell. That hideous thing exists— nay, do not start, and look for a hiding–place—thy own gentle hand with a riding rod is sufficient to tame its courage. And am I not here, Bertha? Wouldst thou wish another safeguard?"

"No—no," exclaimed she, seizing on the arm of her recovered lover. "Do I not know you now?"

"And is it but now you know me, Bertha?" said Hereward.

"I suspected before," she said, casting down her eyes; "but I know with certainty that mark of the boar's tusk."

Hereward suffered her imagination to clear itself from the shock it had received so suddenly, before he ventured to enter upon present events, in which there was so much both to doubt and to fear. He permitted her, therefore, to recall to her memory all the circumstances of the rousing the hideous animal, assisted by the tribes of both their fathers. She mentioned in broken words the flight of arrows discharged against the boar by young and old, male and female, and how her own well aimed, but feeble shaft, wounded him sharply; she forgot not how, incensed at the pain, the creature rushed upon her as the cause, laid her palfrey dead upon the spot, and would soon have slain her, had not Hereward, when every attempt failed to bring his horse up to the monster, thrown himself from his seat, and interposed personally between the boar and Bertha. The battle was not decided without a desperate struggle; the boar was slain, but Hereward received the deep gash upon his brow which she whom he had saved how recalled to her memory. "Alas!" she said, "what have we been to each other since that period? and what are we now, in this foreign land?"

"Answer for thyself, my Bertha," said the Varangian, "if thou canst;

— and if thou canst with truth say that thou art the same Bertha who vowed affection to Hereward, believe me, it were sinful to suppose that the saints have brought us together with a view of our being afterwards separated."

"Hereward," said Bertha, "you have not preserved the bird in your bosom safer than I have; at home or abroad, in servitude or in freedom, amidst sorrow or joy, plenty or want, my thought was always on the troth I had plighted to Hereward at the stone of Odin."

"Say no more of that," said Hereward; "it was an impious rite, and good could not come of it."

"Was it then so impious?" she said, the unbidden tear rushing into her large blue eyes.—"Alas! it was a pleasure to reflect that Hereward was mine by that solemn engagement!"

"Listen to me, my Bertha," said Hereward, taking her hand: "We were then almost children; and though our vow was in itself innocent, yet it was so far wrong, as being sworn in the presence of a dumb idol, representing one who was, while alive, a bloody and cruel magician. But we will, the instant an opportunity offers itself, renew our vow before a shrine of real sanctity, and promise suitable penance for our ignorant acknowledgment of Odin, to propitiate the real Deity, who can bear us through those storms of adversity which are like to surround us."

Leaving them for the time to their love–discourse, of a nature pure, simple, and interesting, we shall give, in a few words, all that the reader needs to know of their separate history between the boar's hunt and the time of their meeting in the gardens of Agelastes.

In that doubtful state experienced by outlaws, Waltheoff, the father of Hereward, and Engelred, the parent of Bertha, used to assemble their unsubdued tribes, sometimes in the fertile regions of Devonshire, sometimes in the dark wooded solitudes of Hampshire, but as much as possible within the call of the bugle of the famous Edric the Forester, so long leader of the insurgent Saxons. The chiefs we have mentioned were among the last bold men who asserted the independence of the Saxon race of England; and like their captain

Edric, they were generally known by the name of Foresters, as men who lived by hunting, when their power of making excursions was checked and repelled. Hence they made a step backwards in civilization, and became more like to their remote ancestors of German descent, than they were to their more immediate and civilized predecessors, who before the battle of Hastings, had advanced considerably in the arts of civilized life.

Old superstitions had begun to revive among them, and hence the practice of youths and maidens plighting their troth at the stone circles dedicated, as it was supposed, to Odin, in whom, however, they had long ceased to nourish any of the sincere belief which was entertained by their heathen ancestors.

In another respect these outlaws were fast resuming a striking peculiarity of the ancient Germans. Their circumstances naturally brought the youth of both sexes much together, and by early marriage, or less permanent connexions, the population would have increased far beyond the means which the outlaws had to maintain, or even to protect themselves. The laws of the Foresters, therefore, strictly enjoined that marriages should be prohibited until the bridegroom was twenty–one years complete. Future alliances were indeed often formed by the young people, nor was this discountenanced by their parents, provided that the lovers waited until the period when the majority of the bridegroom should permit them to marry. Such youths as infringed this rule, incurred the dishonourable epithet of *niddering*, or worthless,— an epithet of a nature so insulting, that men were known to have slain themselves, rather than endure life under such opprobrium. But the offenders were very few amidst a race trained in moderation and self– denial; and hence it was that woman, worshipped for so many years like something sacred, was received, when she became the head of a family, into the arms and heart of a husband who had so long expected her, was treated as something more elevated than the mere idol of the moment; and feeling the rate at which she was valued, endeavoured by her actions to make her life correspond with it.

It was by the whole population of these tribes, as well as their parents, that after the adventure of the boar hunt, Hereward and

Bertha were considered as lovers whose alliance was pointed out by Heaven, and they were encouraged to approximate as much as their mutual inclinations prompted them. The youths of the tribe avoided asking Martha's hand at the dance, and the maidens used no maidenly entreaty or artifice to detain Hereward beside them, if Bertha was present at the feast. They clasped each other's hands through the perforated stone, which they called the altar of Odin, though later ages have ascribed it to the Druids, and they implored that if they broke their faith to each other, their fault might be avenged by the twelve swords which were now drawn around them during the ceremony by as many youths, and that their misfortunes might be so many as twelve maidens, who stood around with their hair loosened, should be unable to recount, either in prose or verse.

The torch of the Saxon Cupid shone for some years as brilliant as when it was first lighted. The time, however, came when they were to be tried by adversity, though undeserved by the perfidy of either. Years had gone past, and Hereward had to count with anxiety how many months and weeks were to separate him from the bride, who was beginning already by degrees to shrink less shyly from the expressions and caresses of one who was soon to term her all his own. William Rufus, however, had formed a plan of totally extirpating the Foresters, whose implacable hatred, and restless love of freedom, had so often disturbed the quiet of his kingdom, and despised his forest laws. He assembled his Norman forces, and united to them a body of Saxons who had submitted to his rule. He thus brought an overpowering force upon the bands of Waltheoff and Engelred, who found no resource but to throw the females of
their tribe, and such as could, not bear arms, into a convent dedicated to St. Augustin, of which Kenelm their relation was prior, and then turning to the battle, vindicated their ancient valour by fighting it to the last. Both the unfortunate chiefs remained dead on the field, and Hereward and his brother had wellnigh shared their fate; but some Saxon inhabitants of the neighbourhood, who adventured on the
field of battle, which the victors had left bare of every thing save the booty of the kites and the ravens, found the bodies of the youths still retaining life. As they were generally well known and much beloved by these people, Hereward and his brother were taken care of till their wounds began to close, and their strength returned. Hereward

then heard the doleful news of the death of his father and Engelred. His next enquiry was concerning his betrothed bride and her mother. The poor inhabitants could give him little information. Some of the females who had taken refuge in the convent, the Norman knights and nobles had seized upon as their slaves, and the rest, with the monks who had harboured them, were turned adrift, and their place of retreat was completely sacked and burnt to the ground.

Half–dead himself at hearing these tidings, Hereward sallied out, and at every risk of death, for the Saxon Foresters were treated as outlaws, commenced enquiries after those so dear to him. He asked concerning the particular fate of Bertha and her mother, among the miserable creatures who yet hovered about the neighbourhood of the convent, like a few half–scorched bees about their smothered hive. But, in the magnitude of their own terrors, none had retained eyes for their neighbours, and all that they could say was, that the wife and daughter of Engelred were certainly lost; and their imaginations suggested so many heart–rending details to this conclusion, that Hereward gave up all thoughts of further researches, likely to terminate so uselessly and so horribly.

The young Saxon had been all his life bred up in a patriotic hatred to the Normans, who did not, it was likely, become dearer to his thoughts in consequence of this victory. He dreamed at first of crossing the strait, to make war against the hated enemy in their own country; but an idea so extravagant did not long retain possession of his mind. His fate was decided by his encountering an aged palmer, who knew or pretended to have known, his father, and to be a native of England. This man was a disguised Varangian, selected for the purpose, possessed of art and dexterity, and well provided with money. He had little difficulty in persuading Hereward, in the hopeless desolation of his condition, to join the Varangian Guard, at this moment at war with the Normans, under which name it suited Hereward's prepossessions to represent the Emperor's wars with Robert Guiscard, his son Bohemond, and other adventurers, in Italy, Greece, or Sicily. A journey to the East also inferred a pilgrimage, and gave the unfortunate Hereward the chance of purchasing pardon for his sins by visiting the Holy Land. In gaining Hereward, the recruiter also secured the services of his elder brother, who had vowed not to separate from him.

The high character of both brothers for courage, induced this wily agent to consider them as a great prize, and it was from the memoranda respecting the history and character of those whom he recruited, in which the elder had been unreservedly communicative, that Agelastes picked up the information respecting Hereward's family and circumstances, which, at their first secret interview, he made use of to impress upon the Varangian the idea of his supernatural knowledge. Several of his companions in arms were thus gained over; for it will easily be guessed, that these memorials were intrusted to the keeping of Achilles Tatius, and he, to further their joint purposes, imparted them to Agelastes, who thus obtained a general credit for supernatural knowledge among these ignorant
men. But Hereward's blunt faith and honesty enabled him to shun the snare.

Such being the fortunes of Hereward, those of Bertha formed the subject of a broken and passionate communication between the lovers, broken like an April day, and mingled with many a tender caress, such as modesty permits to lovers when they meet again unexpectedly after a separation, which threatened to be eternal. But the story may be comprehended in few words. Amid the general sack of the monastery, an old Norman knight seized upon Bertha as his prize. Struck with her beauty, he designed her as an attendant upon his daughter, just then come out of the years of childhood, and the very apple of her father's eye, being the only child of his beloved Countess, and sent late in life to bless their marriage–bed. It was in the order of things that the lady of Aspramonte, who was considerably younger than the knight, should govern her husband, and that Brenhilda, their daughter, should govern both her parents.

The Knight of Aspramonte, however, it may be observed, entertained some desire to direct his young offspring to more feminine amusements than those which began already to put her life frequently in danger. Contradiction was not to be thought of, as the good old knight knew by experience. The influence and example of
a companion a little older than herself might be of some avail, and it was with this view that, in the confusion of the sack, Aspramonte

seized upon the youthful Bertha. Terrified to the utmost degree, she clung to her mother, and the Knight of Aspramonte, who had a softer heart than was then usually found under a steel cuirass, moved by
the affliction of the mother and daughter, and recollecting that the former might also be a useful attendant upon his lady, extended his protection to both, and conveying them out of the press, paid the soldiers who ventured to dispute the spoil with him, partly in some small pieces of money, and partly in dry blows with the reverse of his lance.

The well–natured knight soon after returned to his own castle, and being a man of an orderly life and virtuous habits, the charming beauties of the Saxon virgin, and the more ripened charms of her mother, did not prevent their travelling in all honour as well as safety to his family fortress, the castle of Aspramonte. Here such masters as could be procured were got together to teach the young Bertha every sort of female accomplishment, In the hope that her mistress, Brenhilda, might be inspired with a desire to partake in her education; but although this so far succeeded, that the Saxon captive became highly skilled in such music, needle–work, and other female accomplishments as were known to the time, yet her young mistress, Brenhilda, retained the taste for those martial amusements which had so sensibly grieved her father, but to which her mother, who herself had nourished such fancies in her youth, readily gave sanction.

The captives, however, were kindly treated. Brenhilda became infinitely attached to the young Anglo–Saxon, whom she loved less for her ingenuity in arts, than for her activity in field sports, to which her early state of independence had trained her.

The Lady of Aspramonte was also kind to both the captives; but, in one particular, she exercised a piece of petty tyranny over them. She had imbibed an idea, strengthened by an old doting father–confessor, that the Saxons were heathens at that time, or at least heretics, and made a positive point with her husband that the bondswoman and
girl who were to attend on her person and that of her daughter, should be qualified for the office by being anew admitted into the Christian Church by baptism.

Though feeling the falsehood and injustice of the accusation, the mother had sense enough to submit to necessity, and received the name of Martha in all form at the altar, to which she answered during the rest of her life.

But Bertha showed a character upon this occasion inconsistent with the general docility and gentleness of her temper. She boldly refused to be admitted anew into the pale of the Church, of which her conscience told her she was already a member, or to exchange for another the name originally given her at the font. It was in vain that the old knight commanded, that the lady threatened, and that her mother advised and entreated. More closely pressed in private by her mother, she let her motive be known, which had not before been suspected. "I know," she said, with a flood of tears, "that my father would have died ere I was subjected to this insult; and then—who shall assure me that vows which were made to the Saxon Bertha, will be binding if a French Agatha be substituted in her stead? They may banish me," she said, "or kill me if they will, but if the son of Waltheoff should again meet with the daughter of Engelred, he shall meet that Bertha whom he knew in the forests of Hampton."

All argument was in vain; the Saxon maiden remained obstinate, and to try to break her resolution, the Lady of Aspramonte at length spoke of dismissing her from the service of her young mistress, and banishing her from the castle. To this also she had made up her mind, and she answered firmly though respectfully, that she would sorrow bitterly at parting with her young lady; but as to the rest, she would rather beg under her own name, than be recreant to the faith of her fathers and condemn it as heresy, by assigning one of Frank origin. The Lady Brenhilda, in the meantime, entered the chamber, where her mother was just about to pass the threatened doom of banishment.—"Do not stop for my entrance, madam," said the dauntless young lady; "I am as much concerned in the doom which you are about to pass as is Bertha; If she crosses the drawbridge of Aspramonte as an exile, so will I, when she has dried her tears, of which even my petulance could never wring one from her eyes. She shall be my squire and body attendant, and Launcelot, the bard, shall follow with my spear and shield."

"And you will return, mistress," said her mother, "from so foolish an expedition, before the sun sets?"

"So heaven further me in my purpose, lady," answered the young heiress, "the sun shall neither rise nor set that sees us return, till this name of Bertha, and of her mistress, Brenhilda, are wafted as far as the trumpet of fame can sound them.—Cheer up, my sweetest Bertha!" she said, taking her attendant by the hand, "If heaven hath torn thee from thy country and thy plighted troth, it hath given thee a sister and a friend, with whom thy fame shall be forever blended."

The Lady of Aspramonte was confounded: She knew that her daughter was perfectly capable of the wild course which she had announced, and that she herself, even with her husband's assistance, would be unable to prevent her following it. She passively listened, therefore, while the Saxon matron, formerly Urica, but now Martha, addressed her daughter. "My child," she said, "as you value honour, virtue, safety, and gratitude, soften your heart towards your master and mistress, and follow the advice of a parent, who has more years and more judgment than you. And you, my dearest young lady, let not your lady–mother think that an attachment to the exercises you excel in, has destroyed in your bosom filial affection, and a regard to the delicacy of your sex!—As they seem both obstinate, madam," continued the matron, after watching the influence of this advice upon the young woman, "perhaps, if it may be permitted me. I could state an alternative, which might, in the meanwhile, satisfy your ladyship's wishes, accommodate itself to the wilfulness of my obstinate daughter, and answer the kind purpose of her generous mistress." The Lady of Aspramonte signed to the Saxon matron to proceed. She went on accordingly: "The Saxons, dearest lady, of the present day, are neither pagans nor heretics; they are, in the time of keeping Easter, as well as in all other disputable doctrine, humbly obedient to the Pope of Rome; and this our good Bishop well knows, since he upbraided some of the domestics for calling me an old heathen. Yet our names are uncouth in the ears of the Franks, and bear, perhaps, a heathenish sound. If it be not exacted that my daughter submit to a new rite of baptism, she will lay aside her Saxon name of Bertha upon all occasions while in your honourable household. This will cut short a debate which, with forgiveness, I think is scarce of importance enough to break the peace of this castle. I will engage that, in gratitude for this indulgence of a trifling scruple, my daughter, if possible, shall double the zeal and assiduity of her service to her young lady."

The Lady of Aspramonte was glad to embrace the means which this offer presented, of extricating herself from the dispute with as little compromise of dignity as could well be. "If the good Lord Bishop approved of such a compromise," she said, "she would for herself withdraw her opposition." The prelate approved accordingly, the more readily that he was informed that the young heiress desired earnestly such an agreement. The peace of the castle was restored, and Bertha recognized her new name of Agatha as a name of service, but not a name of baptism.

One effect the dispute certainly produced, and that was, increasing in an enthusiastic degree the love of Bertha for her young mistress. With that amiable failing of attached domestics and humble friends, she endeavoured to serve her as she knew she loved to be served; and therefore indulged, her mistress in those chivalrous fancies which distinguished her even in her own age, and in ours would have rendered her a female Quixote. Bertha, indeed, never caught the frenzy of her mistress; but, strong, willing, and able–bodied, she readily qualified herself to act upon occasion as a squire of the body to a Lady Adventuress; and, accustomed from her childhood to see blows dealt, blood flowing, and men dying, she could look with an undazzled eye upon the dangers which her mistress encountered, and seldom teased her with remonstrances, unless when those were unusually great. This compliance on most occasions, gave Bertha a right of advice upon some, which, always given with the best intentions and at fitting times, strengthened her influence with her mistress, which a course of conduct savouring of diametrical opposition would certainly have destroyed.

A few more words serve to announce the death of the Knight of Aspramonte—the romantic marriage of the young lady with the Count of Paris—their engagement in the crusade—and the detail of events with which the reader is acquainted.

Hereward did not exactly comprehend some of the later incidents of the story, owing to a slight strife which arose between Bertha and him during the course of her narrative. When she avowed the girlish simplicity with which she obstinately refused to change her name, because, in her apprehension, the troth–plight betwixt her and her lover might be thereby prejudiced, it was impossible for Hereward not to acknowledge her tenderness, by snatching her to his bosom, and impressing his grateful thanks upon her lips. She extricated herself immediately from his grasp, however, with cheeks more crimsoned in modesty than in anger, and gravely addressed her lover thus: "Enough, enough, Hereward! this may be pardoned to so unexpected a meeting; but we must in future remember, that we are probably the last of our race; and let it not be said, that the manners of their ancestors were forgotten by Hereward and by Bertha; think, that though we are alone, the shades of our fathers are not far off,
and watch to see what use we make of the meeting, which, perhaps, their intercession has procured us."

"You wrong me, Bertha," said Hereward, "if you think me capable of forgetting my own duty and yours, at a moment when our thanks are due to Heaven, to be testified very differently than by infringing on its behests, or the commands of our parents. The question is now, How we shall rejoin each other when we separate? since separate, I fear, we must."

"O! do not say so!" exclaimed the unfortunate Bertha.

"It must be so," said Hereward, "for a time; but I swear to thee by the hilt of my sword, and the handle of my battle–axe, that blade was never so true to shaft as I will be to thee!"

"But wherefore, then, leave me, Hereward?" said the maiden; "and oh! wherefore not assist me in the release of my mistress?"

"Of thy mistress!" said Hereward. "Shame! that thou canst give that name to mortal woman!"

"But she *is* my mistress," answered Bertha, "and by a thousand kind ties which cannot be separated so long as gratitude is the reward of kindness."

"And what is her danger," said Hereward; "what is it she wants, this accomplished lady whom thou callest mistress?"

"Her honour, her life, are alike in danger," said Bertha. "She has agreed to meet the Caesar in the field, and he will not hesitate, like a baseborn miscreant, to take every advantage in the encounter, which, I grieve to say, may in all likelihood be fatal to my mistress."

"Why dost thou think so?" answered Hereward. "This lady has won many single combats, unless she is belied, against adversaries more formidable than the Caesar."

"True," said the Saxon maiden; "but you speak of things that passed in a far different land, where faith and honour are not empty sounds; as, alas! they seem but too surely to be here. Trust me, it is no girlish terror which sends me out in this disguise of my country dress, which, they say, finds respect at Constantinople: I go to let the chiefs of the Crusade know the peril in which the noble lady stands, and trust to their humanity, to their religion, to their love of honour, and fear of disgrace, for assistance in this hour of need; and now that I have had the blessing of meeting with thee, all besides will go well —all will go well—and I will back to my mistress and report whom I have seen."

"Tarry yet another moment, my recovered treasure!" said Hereward, "and let me balance this matter carefully. This Frankish lady holds the Saxons like the very dust that thou brushest from the hem of her garment. She treats—she regards—the Saxons as pagans and heretics. She has dared to impose slavish tasks upon thee, born in freedom. Her father's sword has been embrued to the hilt with Anglo–Saxon blood— perhaps that of Waltheoff and Engelred has added death to the stain! She has been, besides, a presumptuous fool, usurping for herself the trophies and warlike character which belong to the other sex. Lastly, it will be hard to find a champion to fight in her stead, since all the crusaders have passed over to Asia, which is the land, they say, in which they have come to war; and by orders of the Emperor, no means of return to the hither shore will be permitted to any of them."

"Alas! alas!" said Bertha, "how does this world change us! The son of Waltheoff I once knew brave, ready to assist distress, bold and generous. Such was what I pictured him to myself during his absence. I have met him again, and he is calculating, cold, and selfish!"

"Hush, damsel," said the Varangian, "and know him of whom thou speakest, ere thou judgest him. The Countess of Paris is such as I have said; yet let her appear boldly in the lists, and when the trumpet shall sound thrice, another shall reply, which shall announce the arrival of her own noble lord to do battle in her stead; or should he fail to appear— I will requite her kindness to thee, Bertha, and be ready in his place."

"Wilt thou? wilt thou indeed?" said the damsel; "that was spoken like the son of Waltheoff—like the genuine stock! I will home, and comfort my mistress; for surely if the judgment of God ever directed the issue of a judicial combat, its influence will descend upon this. But you hint that the Count is here—that he is at liberty—she will enquire about that."

"She must be satisfied," replied Hereward, "to know that her husband is under the guidance of a friend, who will endeavour to protect him from his own extravagances and follies; or, at all events, of one who, if he cannot properly be called a friend, has certainly not acted, and will not act, towards him the part of an enemy.—And
now, farewell, long lost—long loved!"—Before he could say more, the Saxon maiden, after two or three vain attempts to express her gratitude, threw herself into her lover's arms, and despite the coyness which she had recently shown, impressed upon his lips the thanks which she could not speak.

They parted, Bertha returning to her mistress at the lodge, which she had left both with trouble and danger, and Hereward by the portal kept by the negro–portress, who, complimenting the handsome Varangian on his success among the fair, intimated, that she had
been in some sort a witness of his meeting with the Saxon damsel. A piece of gold, part of a late largesse, amply served to bribe her tongue; and the soldier, clear of the gardens of the philosopher, sped

back as he might to the barrack—judging that it was full time to carry some supply to Count Robert, who had been left without food the whole day.

It is a common popular saying, that as the sensation of hunger is not connected with any pleasing or gentle emotion, so it is particularly remarkable for irritating those of anger and spleen. It is not, therefore, very surprising that Count Robert, who had been so unusually long without sustenance, should receive Hereward with a degree of impatience beyond what the occasion merited, and injurious certainly to the honest Varangian, who had repeatedly exposed his life that day for the interest of the Countess and the Count himself.

"Soh, sir!" he said, in that accent of affected restraint by which a superior modifies his displeasure against his inferior into a cold and scornful expression—"You have played a liberal host to us!—Not that it is of consequence; but methinks a Count of the most Christian kingdom dines not every day with a mercenary soldier, and might expect, if not the ostentatious, at least the needful part of
hospitality."

"And methinks," replied the Varangian, "O most Christian Count, that such of your high rank as, by choice or fate, become the guests of such as I, may think themselves pleased, and blame not their
host's niggardliness, but the difficulty of his circumstances, if dinner should not present itself oftener than once in four–and–twenty hours." So saying, he clapt his hands together, and his domestic Edric entered. His guest looked astonished at the entrance of this third party into their retirement. "I will answer for this man," said Hereward, and addressed him in the following words:—"What food hast thou, Edric, to place before the honourable Count?"

"Nothing but the cold pasty," replied the attendant, "marvellously damaged by your honour's encounter at breakfast."

The military domestic, as intimated, brought forward a large pasty, but which had already that morning sustained a furious attack, insomuch, that Count Robert of Paris, who, like all noble Normans, was somewhat nice and delicate in his eating, was in some doubt whether his scrupulousness should not prevail over his hunger; but on looking more closely, sight, smell, and a fast of twenty hours, joined to convince him that the pasty was an excellent one, and that the charger on which it was presented possessed corners yet untouched. At length, having suppressed his scruples, and made bold inroad upon the remains of the dish, he paused to partake of a flask of strong red wine which stood invitingly beside him, and a lusty draught increased the good–humour which had begun to take place towards Hereward, in exchange for the displeasure with which he had received him.

"Now, by heaven!" he said, "I myself ought to be ashamed to lack the courtesy which I recommend to others! Here have I, with the manners of a Flemish boor, been devouring the provisions of my gallant host, without even asking him to sit down at his own table, and to partake of his own good cheer!"

"I will not strain courtesies with you for that," said Hereward; and thrusting his hand into the pasty, he proceeded with great speed and dexterity to devour the miscellaneous contents, a handful of which was enclosed in his grasp. The Count now withdrew from the table, partly in disgust at the rustic proceedings of Hereward, who, however, by now calling Edric to join him in his attack upon the pasty, showed that he had, in fact, according to his manners, subjected himself previously to some observance of respect towards his guest; while the assistance of his attendant enabled him to make a clear cacaabulum of what was left. Count Robert at length summoned up courage sufficient to put a question, which had been trembling upon his lips ever since Hereward had returned.

"Have thine enquiries, my gallant friend, learned more concerning my unfortunate wife, my faithful Brenhilda?"

"Tidings I have," said the Anglo–Saxon, "but whether pleasing or not, yourself must be the judge. This much I have learned;—she hath, as you know, come under an engagement to meet the Caesar in arms in the lists, but under conditions which you may perhaps think strange; these, however, she hath entertained without scruple."

"Let me know these terms,", said the Count of Paris; "they will, I think, appear less strange in my eyes than in thine."

But while he affected to speak with the utmost coolness, the husband's sparkling eye and crimsoned cheek betrayed the alteration which had taken place in his feelings. "The lady and the Caesar," said Hereward, "as you partly heard yourself, are to meet in fight; if the Countess wins, of course she remains the wife of the noble Count of Paris; if she loses, she becomes the paramour of the Caesar Nicephorus Briennius."

"Saints and angels forbid!" said Count Robert; "were they to permit such treason to triumph, we might be pardoned for doubting their divinity!"

"Yet methinks," said the Anglo–Saxon, "it were no disgraceful precaution that both you and I, with other friends, if we can obtain such, should be seen under shield in the lists on the morning of the conflict. To triumph, or to be defeated, is in the hand of fate; but what we cannot fail to witness is, whether or not the lady receives that fair play which is the due of an honourable combatant, and which, as you have yourself seen, can be sometimes basely transgressed in this Grecian empire."

"On that condition," said the Count, "and protesting, that not even the extreme danger of my lady shall make me break through the rule of a fair fight, I will surely attend the lists, if thou, brave Saxon, canst find me any means of doing so.—Yet stay," he continued, after reflecting for a moment, "thou shalt promise not to let her know that her Count is on the field, far less to point him out to her eye among the press of warriors. O, thou dost not know that the sight of the beloved will sometimes steal from us our courage, even when it has most to achieve!"

"We will endeavour," said the Varangian, "to arrange matters according to thy pleasure, so that thou findest out no more fantastical difficulties; for, by my word, an affair so complicated in itself, requires not to be confused by the fine–spun whims of thy national gallantry. Meantime, much must be done this night; and while I go about it, thou, Sir Knight, hadst best remain here, with such disguise of garments, and such food, as Edric may be able to procure for thee. Fear nothing from intrusion on the part of thy neighbours. We Varangians respect each other's secrets, of whatever nature they may chance to be."

CHAPTER THE TWENTY-FIRST

But for our trusty brother–in–law–and the Abbot, With all
the rest of that consorted crew,— Destruction straight shall
dog them at the heels:— Good uncle, help to order several
powers
To Oxford, or where'er these traitors are: They shall
not live within this world, I swear. RICHARD II.

As Hereward spoke the last words narrated in the foregoing chapter, he left
the count in his apartment, and proceeded to the Blacquernal Palace. We
traced his first entrance into the court, but since then he had frequently been
summoned, not only by order of the Princess Anna Comnena, who delighted
in asking him questions concerning the customs of his native country, and
marking down the replies in her own inflated language; but also by the direct
command of the Emperor himself, who had the humour of many princes, that
of desiring to obtain direct information from persons in a very inferior station
in their Court. The ring which the Princess had given to the Varangian, served
as a pass– token more than once, and was now so generally known by the
slaves of the palace, that Hereward had only to slip it into the hand of a
principal person among them, and was introduced into a small chamber, not
distant from the saloon already mentioned, dedicated to the Muses. In this
small apartment, the Emperor, his spouse Irene, and their accomplished
daughter Anna Comnena, were seated together, clad in very ordinary apparel,
as indeed the furniture of the room itself was of the kind used by respectable
citizens, saving that mattrasses, composed of eiderdown, hung before each
door to prevent the risk of eavesdropping.

"Our trusty Varangian," said the Empress.

"My guide and tutor respecting the manners of those steel–clad men," said
the Princess Anna Comnena, "of whom it is so necessary

that I should form an accurate idea."

"Your Imperial Majesty," said the Empress, "will not, I trust, think your consort and your muse–inspired daughter, are too many to share with you the intelligence brought by this brave and loyal man?"

"Dearest wife and daughter," returned the Emperor, "I have hitherto spared you the burden of a painful secret, which I have locked in my own bosom, at whatever expense of solitary sorrow and unimparted anxiety. Noble daughter, you in particular will feel this calamity, learning, as you must learn, to think odiously of one, of whom it has hitherto been your duty to hold a very different opinion."

"Holy Mary!" exclaimed the Princess.

"Rally yourself," said the Emperor; "remember you are a child of the purple chamber, born, not to weep for your father's wrongs, but to avenge them,— not to regard even him who has lain by your side as half so important as the sacred Imperial grandeur, of which you are yourself a partaker."

"What can such words preface?" said Anna Comnena, in great agitation.

"They say," answered the Emperor, "that the Caesar is an ungrateful man to all my bounties, and even to that which annexed him to my own. house, and made him by adoption my own son. He hath consorted himself with a knot of traitors, whose very names are enough to raise the foul fiend, as if to snatch his assured prey!"

"Could Nicephorus do this?" said the astonished and forlorn Princess; "Nicephorus, who has so often called my eyes the lights by which he steered his path? Could he do this to my father, to whose exploits he has listened hour after hour, protesting that he knew not whether it was the beauty of the language, or the heroism of the action, which most enchanted him? Thinking with the same thought, seeing with the same eye, loving with the same heart,—O, my father! it is impossible that he could be so false. Think of the neighbouring Temple of the Muses!"

"And if I did," murmured Alexius in his heart, "I should think of the only apology which could be proposed for the traitor. A little is well enough, but the full soul loatheth the honey–comb." Then speaking aloud, "My daughter," he said, "be comforted; we ourselves were unwilling to believe the shameful truth; but our guards have been debauched; their commander, that ungrateful Achilles Tatius, with the equal traitor, Agelastes, have been seduced to favour our imprisonment or murder; and, alas for Greece in the very moment when she required the fostering care of a parent, she was to be deprived of him by a sudden and merciless blow!"

Here the Emperor wept, whether for the loss to be sustained by his subjects, or of his own life, it is hard to say.

"Methinks," said Irene, "your Imperial Highness is slow in taking measures against the danger."

"Under your gracious permission, mother," answered the Princess, "I would rather say he was hasty in giving belief to it. Methinks the evidence of a Varangian, granting him to be ever so stout a man–at– arms, is but a frail guarantee against the honour of your son–in–law —the approved bravery and fidelity of the captain of your guards— the deep sense, virtue, and profound wisdom, of the greatest of your philosophers"—

"And the conceit of an over–educated daughter," said the Emperor, "who will not allow her parent to judge in what most concerns him. I will tell thee, Anna, I know every one of them, and the trust which may be reposed in them; the honour of your Nicephorus—the bravery and fidelity of the Acolyte—and the virtue and wisdom of Agelastes—have I not had them all in my purse? And had my purse continued well filled, and my arm strong as it was of late, there they would have still remained. But the butterflies went off as the weather became cold, and I must meet the tempest without their assistance. You talk of want of proof? I have proof sufficient when I see danger; this honest soldier brought me indications which corresponded with my own private remarks, made on purpose. Varangian he shall be of Varangians; Acolyte he shall be named, in place of the present traitor; and who knows what may come thereafter?"

"May it please your Highness," said the Varangian, who had been hitherto silent, "many men in this empire rise to dignity by the fall of their original patrons, but it is a road to greatness to which I cannot reconcile my conscience; moreover, having recovered a friend, from whom I was long ago separated, I shall require, in short space, your Imperial license for going hence, where I shall leave thousands of enemies behind me, and spending my life, like many of my countrymen, under the banner of King William of Scotland"—

"Part with *thee*, most inimitable man!" cried the Emperor, with emphasis; "where shall I get a soldier—a champion—a friend—so faithful?"

"Noble sir," replied the Anglo–Saxon, "I am every way sensible to your goodness and munificence; but let me entreat you to call me by my own name, and to promise me nothing but your forgiveness, for my having been the agent of such confusion among your Imperial servants. Not only is the threatened fate of Achilles Tatius, my benefactor; of the Caesar, whom I think my well–wisher; and even of Agelastes himself, painful, so far as it is of my bringing round; but also I have known it somehow happen, that those on whom your Imperial Majesty has lavished the most valuable expressions of your favour one day, were the next day food to fatten the chough and crow. And this, I acknowledge, is a purpose, for which I would not willingly have it said I had brought my English limbs to these Grecian shores."

"Call thee by thine own name, my Edward," said the Emperor, (while he muttered aside—"by Heaven, I have again forgot the name of the barbarian!")—"by thine own name certainly for the present, but only until we shall devise one more fitted for the trust we repose in thee. Meantime, look at this scroll, which contains, I think, all the particulars which we have been able to learn of this plot, and give it to these unbelieving women, who will not credit that an Emperor is in danger, till the blades of the conspirators' poniards are clashing within his ribs."

Hereward did as he was commanded, and having looked at the scroll, and signified, by bending his head, his acquiescence in its contents, he presented it to Irene, who had not read long, ere, with a countenance so embittered that she had difficulty in pointing out the cause of her displeasure to her daughter, she bade her, with animation, "Read that— read that, and judge of the gratitude and affection of thy Caesar!"

The Princess Anna Comnena awoke from a state of profound and overpowering melancholy, and looked at the passage pointed out to her, at first with an air of languid curiosity, which presently deepened into the most intense interest. She clutched the scroll as a falcon does his prey, her eye lightened with indignation; and it was with the cry of the bird when in fury that she exclaimed, "Bloody- minded, double–hearted traitor! what wouldst thou have? Yes, father," she said, rising in fury, "it is no longer the voice of a deceived princess that shall intercede to avert from the traitor Nicephorus the doom he has deserved! Did he think that one born in the purple chamber could be divorced—murdered, perhaps—with the petty formula of the Romans, 'Restore the keys—be no longer my domestic drudge?'[Footnote: The laconic form of the Roman divorce.] Was a daughter of the blood of Comnenus liable to such insults as the meanest of Quirites might bestow on a family housekeeper!"

So saying, she dashed the tears from her eyes, and her countenance, naturally that of beauty and gentleness, became animated with the expression of a fury. Hereward looked at her with a mixture of fear, dislike and compassion. She again burst forth, for nature having given her considerable abilities, had lent her at the same time an energy of passion, far superior in power to the cold ambition of Irene, or the wily, ambidexter, shuffling policy of the Emperor.

"He shall abye it," said the Princess; "he shall dearly abye it! False, smiling, cozening traitor!—and for that unfeminine barbarian! Something of this I guessed, even at that old fool's banqueting- house; and yet if this unworthy Caesar submits his body to the chance of arms, he is less prudent than I have some reason to believe. Think you he will have the madness to brand us with such open neglect, my father? and will you not invent some mode of ensuring our revenge?"

"Soh!" thought the Emperor, "this difficulty is over; she will run down hill to her revenge, and will need the snaffle and curb more than the lash. If every jealous dame in Constantinople were to pursue her fury as unrelentingly, our laws should be written, like Draco's, not in ink, but in blood.—Attend to me now," he said aloud, "my wife, my daughter, and thou, dear Edward, and you shall learn, and you three only, my mode of navigating the vessel of the state through these shoals."

"Let us see distinctly," continued Alexius, "the means by which they propose to act, and these shall instruct us how to meet them. A certain number of the Varangians are unhappily seduced, under pretence of wrongs, artfully stirred up by their villanous general. A part of them are studiously to be arranged nigh our person—the traitor Ursel, some of them suppose, is dead, but if it were so, his name is sufficient to draw together his old factionaries—I have a means of satisfying them on that point, on which I shall remain silent for the present.—A considerable body of the Immortal Guards have also given way to seduction; they are to be placed to support the handful of treacherous Varangians, who are in the plot to attack our person.—Now. a slight change in the stations of the soldiery, which thou, my faithful Edward —or—a—a— whatever thou art named,— for which thou, I say, shalt have full authority, will derange the plans of the traitors, and place the true men in such position around them as to cut them to pieces with little trouble." "And the

combat, my lord?" said the Saxon.

"Thou hadst been no true Varangian hadst thou not enquired after that," said the Emperor, nodding good–humouredly towards him. "As to the combat, the Caesar has devised it, and it shall be my care that he shall not retreat from the dangerous part of it. He cannot in honour avoid fighting with this woman, strange as the combat is; and however it ends, the conspiracy will break forth, and as assuredly as it comes against persons prepared, and in arms, shall it be stifled in the blood of the conspirators!"

"My revenge does not require this," said the Princess; "and your Imperial honour is also interested that this Countess shall be protected."

"It is little business of mine," said the Emperor. "She comes here with her husband altogether uninvited. He behaves with insolence in my presence, and deserves whatever may be the issue to himself or his lady of their mad adventure. In sooth, I desired little more than to give him a fright with those animals whom their ignorance judged enchanted, and to give his wife a slight alarm about the impetuosity of a Grecian lover, and there my vengeance should have ended. But
it may be that his wife may be taken under my protection, now that little revenge is over."

"And a paltry revenge it was," said the Empress, "that you, a man past middle life, and with a wife who might command some attention, should constitute yourself the object of alarm to such a handsome man as Count Robert, and the Amazon his wife."

"By your favour, dame Irene, no," said the Emperor. "I left that part of the proposed comedy to my son–in–law the Caesar."

But when the poor Emperor had in some measure stopt one floodgate, he effectually opened another, and one which was more formidable. "The more shame to your Imperial wisdom, my father!" exclaimed the Princess Anna Comnena; "it is a shame, that with wisdom and a beard like yours, you should be meddling in such indecent follies as admit disturbance into private families, and that family your own daughter's! Who can say that the Caesar Nicephorus Briennius ever looked astray towards another woman than his wife, till the Emperor taught him to do so, and involved him in a web of intrigue and treachery, in which he has endangered the life of his father–in–law?"

"Daughter! daughter! daughter!"—said the Empress; "daughter of a she–wolf, I think, to goad her parent at such an unhappy time, when all the leisure he has is too little to defend his life!"

"Peace, I pray you, women both, with your senseless clamours," answered Alexius, "and let me at least swim for my life undisturbed with your folly. God knows if I am a man to encourage, I will not say the reality of wrong, but even its mere appearance!"

These words he uttered, crossing himself, with a devout groan. His wife Irene, in the meantime, stept before him, and said, with a bitterness in her looks and accent, which only long–concealed nuptial hatred breaking forth at once could convey,—"Alexius,
terminate this affair how it will, you have lived a hypocrite, and thou wilt not fail to die one." So saying, with an air of noble indignation, and carrying her daughter along with her, she swept out of the apartment.

The Emperor looked after her in some confusion. He soon, however, recovered his self–possession, and turning to Hereward, with a look of injured majesty, said, "Ah! my dear Edward,"—for the word had become rooted in his mind, instead of the less euphonic name of Hereward,— "thou seest how it is even with the greatest, and that the Emperor, in moments of difficulty, is a subject of misconstruction,
as well as the meanest burgess of Constantinople; nevertheless, my trust is so great in thee, Edward, that I would have thee believe, that my daughter, Anna Comnena, is not of the temper of her mother, but rather of my own; honouring, thou mayst see, with religious fidelity, the unworthy ties which I hope soon to break, and assort her with other fetters of Cupid, which shall be borne more lightly. Edward,
my main trust is in thee. Accident presents us with an opportunity, happy of the happiest, so it be rightly improved, of having all the traitors before us assembled on one fair field. Think, *then*, on that day, as the Franks say at their tournaments, that fair eyes behold thee. Thou canst not devise a gift within my power, but I will gladly load thee with it."

"It needs not," said the Varangian, somewhat coldly; "my highest ambition is to merit the epitaph upon my tomb, 'Hereward was faithful.' I am about, however, to demand a proof of your imperial confidence, which, perhaps, you may think a startling one."

"Indeed!" said the Emperor. "What, in one word, is thy demand?"

"Permission," replied Hereward, "to go to the Duke of Bouillon's encampment, and entreat his presence in the lists, to witness this extraordinary combat."

"That he may return with his crusading madmen," said the Emperor, "and sack Constantinople, under pretence of doing justice to his Confederates? This, Varangian, is at least speaking thy mind openly."

"No, by Heavens!" said Hereward suddenly; "the Duke of Bouillon shall come with no more knights than may be a reasonable guard, should treachery be offered to the Countess of Paris."

"Well, even in this," said the Emperor, "will I be conformable; and if thou, Edward, betrayest my trust, think that thou forfeitest all that my friendship has promised, and dost incur, besides, the damnation that is due to the traitor who betrays with a kiss."

"For thy reward, noble sir," answered the Varangian, "I hereby renounce all claim to it. When the diadem is once more firmly fixed upon thy brow, and the sceptre in thy hand, if I am then alive, if my poor services should deserve so much, I will petition thee for the means of leaving this court, and returning to the distant island in which I was born. Meanwhile, think me not unfaithful, because I have for a time the means of being so with effect. Your Imperial Highness shall learn that Hereward is as true as is your right hand to your left."—So saying, he took his leave with a profound obeisance.

The Emperor gazed after him with a countenance in which doubt was mingled with admiration.

"I have trusted him," he said, "with all he asked, and with the power of ruining me entirely, if such be his purpose. He has but to breathe a whisper, and the whole mad crew of crusaders, kept in humour at the expense of so much current falsehood, and so much more gold, will return with fire and sword to burn down Constantinople, and sow with salt the place where it stood. I have done what I had resolved never to do,—I have ventured kingdom and life on the faith of a man born of woman. How often have I said, nay, sworn, that I would not hazard myself on such peril, and yet, step by step, I have done so! I cannot tell—there is in that man's looks and words a good faith which overwhelms me; and, what is almost incredible, my belief in him has increased in proportion to his showing me how slight my

power was over him. I threw, like the wily angler, every bait I could devise, and some of them such as a king would scarcely have disdained; to none of these would he rise; but yet he gorges, I may say, the bare hook, and enters upon my service without a shadow of self–interest.—Can this be double–distilled treachery?—or can it be what men call disinterestedness?—If I thought him false, the
moment is not yet past—he has not yet crossed the bridge—he has not passed the guards of the palace, who have no hesitation, and know no disobedience—But no—I were then alone in the land, and without a friend or confidant.—I hear the sound of the outer gate unclose, the sense of danger certainly renders my ears more acute than usual.—It shuts again—the die is cast. He is at liberty—and Alexius Comnenus must stand or fall, according to the uncertain faith of a mercenary Varangian." He clapt his hands; a slave appeared, of whom he demanded wine. He drank, and his heart was cheered within him. "I am decided," he said, "and will abide with resolution the cast of the throw, for good or for evil."

So saying, he retired to his apartment, and was not again seen during that night.

CHAPTER THE TWENTY-SECOND

And aye, as if for death, some lonely trumpet peal'd.
CAMPBELL.

The Varangian, his head agitated with the weighty matters which imposed on him, stopt from time to time as he journeyed through the moonlight streets, to arrest passing ideas as they shot through his mind, and consider them with accuracy in all their bearings. His thoughts were such as animated or alarmed him alternately, each followed by a confused throng of accompaniments which it suggested, and banished again in its turn by reflections of another description. It was one of those conjunctures when the minds of ordinary men feel themselves unable to support a burden which is suddenly flung upon them, and when, on the contrary, those of uncommon fortitude, and that best of Heaven's gifts, good sense, founded on presence of mind, feel their talents awakened and regulated for the occasion, like a good steed under the management of a rider of courage and experience.

As he stood in one of those fits of reverie, which repeatedly during that night arrested his stern military march, Hereward thought that his ear caught the note of a distant trumpet. This surprised him; a trumpet blown at that late hour, and in the streets of Constantinople, argued something extraordinary; for as all military movements were the subject of special ordinance, the etiquette of the night could hardly have been transgressed without some great cause. The question was, what that cause could be?

Had the insurrection broken out unexpectedly, and in a different manner from what the conspirators proposed to themselves?—If so, his meeting with his plighted bride, after so many years' absence, was but a delusive preface to their separating for ever. Or had the crusaders, a race of men upon whose motions it was difficult to calculate, suddenly taken arms and returned from the opposite shore

to surprise the city? This might very possibly be the case; so numerous had been the different causes of complaint afforded to the crusaders, that, when they were now for the first time assembled into one body, and had heard the stories which they could reciprocally
tell concerning the perfidy of the Greeks, nothing was so likely, so natural, even perhaps so justifiable, as that they should study revenge.

But the sound rather resembled a point of war regularly blown, than the tumultuous blare of bugle–horns and trumpets, the accompaniments at once, and the annunciation, of a taken town, in which the horrid circumstances of storm had not yet given place to such stern peace as the victors' weariness of slaughter and rapine allows at length to the wretched inhabitants. Whatever it was, it was necessary that Hereward should learn its purport, and therefore he made his way into a broad street near the barracks, from, which the sound seemed to come, to which point, indeed, his way was directed for other reasons.

The inhabitants of that quarter of the town did not appear violently startled by this military signal. The moonlight slept on the street, crossed by the gigantic shadowy towers of Sancta Sophia. No human being appeared in the streets, and such as for an instant looked from their doors or from their lattices, seemed to have their curiosity quickly satisfied, for they withdrew their heads, and secured the opening through which they had peeped.

Hereward could not help remembering the traditions which were recounted by the fathers of his tribe, in the deep woods, of Hampshire, and which spoke of invisible huntsmen, who were heard to follow with viewless horses and hounds the unseen chase through the depths of the forests of Germany. Such it seemed were the sounds with which these haunted woods were wont to ring while the wild chase was up; and with such apparent terror did the hearers listen to their clamour.

"Fie!" he said, as he suppressed within him a tendency to the same superstitious fears; "do such childish fancies belong to a man trusted with so much, and from whom so much is expected?" He paced down the street, therefore, with his battle–axe over his shoulder, and the first person whom he saw venturing to look out of his door, he questioned concerning the cause of this military music at such an unaccustomed hour.

"I cannot tell, so please you, my lord," said the citizen, unwilling, it appeared, to remain in the open air, or to enter into conversation, and greatly disposed to decline further questioning. This was the political citizen of Constantinople whom we met with at the beginning of this history, and who, hastily stepping into his habitation, eschewed all further conversation.

The wrestler Stephanos showed himself at the next door, which was garlanded with oak and ivy leaves, in honour of some recent victory. He stood unshrinking, partly encouraged by the consciousness of personal strength, and partly by a rugged surliness of temper, which is often mistaken among persons of this kind for real courage. His admirer and flatterer, Lysimachus, kept himself ensconced behind
his ample shoulders.

As Hereward passed, he put the same question as he did to the
former citizen,—"Know you the meaning of these trumpets sounding so late?"

"You should know best yourself," answered Stephanos, doggedly; "for, to judge by your axe and helmet, they are your trumpets, and not ours, which disturb honest men in their first sleep."

"Varlet!" answered the Varangian, with an emphasis which made the prizer start,—"but—when that trumpet sounds, it is no time for a soldier to punish insolence as it deserves."

The Greek started back and bolted into his house, nearly overthrowing in the speed of his retreat the artist Lysimachus, who was listening to what passed.

Hereward passed on to the barracks, where the military music had seemed to halt; but on the Varangian crossing the threshold of the ample courtyard, it broke forth again with a tremendous burst, whose clangour almost stunned him, though well accustomed to the sounds.

"What is the meaning of this, Engelbrecht?" he said to the Varangian sentinel, who paced axe in hand before the entrance.

"The proclamation of a challenge and combat," answered Engelbrecht. "Strange things towards, comrade; the frantic crusaders have bit the Grecians, and infected them with their humour of tilting, as they say dogs do each other with madness."

Hereward made no reply to the sentinel's speech, but pressed forward into a knot of his fellow–soldiers who were assembled in the court, half–armed, or, more properly, in total disarray, as just arisen from their beds, and huddled around the trumpets of their corps, which were drawn out in full pomp. He of the gigantic instrument, whose duty it was to intimate the express commands of the Emperor, was not wanting in his place, and the musicians were supported by a band of the Varangians in arms, headed by Achilles Tatius himself. Hereward could also notice, on approaching nearer, as his comrades made way for him, that six of the Imperial heralds were on duty on this occasion; four of these (two acting at the same time) had already made proclamation, which was to be repeated for the third time by the two last, as was the usual fashion in Constantinople with Imperial mandates of great consequence. Achilles Tatius, the moment he saw his confidant, made him a sign, which Hereward understood as conveying a desire to speak with him after the proclamation was over. The herald, after the flourish of trumpets was finished, commenced in. these words:

"By the authority of the resplendent and divine Prince Alexius Comnenus, Emperor of the most holy Roman Empire, his Imperial Majesty desires it to be made known to all and sundry the subjects of his empire, whatever their race of blood may be, or at whatever shrine of divinity they happen, to bend—Know ye, therefore, that upon the second day after this is dated, our beloved son–in–law, the much esteemed Caesar, hath taken upon, him to do battle with our sworn enemy, Robert, Count of Paris, on account of his insolent conduct, by presuming publicly to occupy our royal seat, and no less by breaking, in our Imperial presence, those curious specimens of art, ornamenting our throne, called by tradition the Lions of Solomon. And that there may not remain a man in Europe who shall dare to say that the Grecians are behind other parts of the world in any of the manly exercises which Christian nations use, the said noble enemies, renouncing all assistance from falsehood, from spells, or from magic, shall debate this quarrel in three courses with grinded spears, and three passages of arms with sharpened swords; the field to be at the judgment of the honourable Emperor, and to be decided at his most gracious and unerring pleasure. And so God show the right!"

Another formidable flourish of the trumpets concluded the ceremony. Achilles then dismissed the attendant troops, as well as the heralds and musicians, to their respective quarters; and having got Hereward close to his side, enquired of him whether he had learned any thing of the prisoner, Robert, Count of Paris.

"Nothing," said the Varangian, "save the tidings your proclamation contains."

"You think, then," said Achilles, "that the Count has been a party to it."

"He ought to have been so," answered the Varangian. "I know no one but himself entitled to take burden for his appearance in the lists."

"Why, look you," said the Acolyte, "my most excellent, though blunt– witted Hereward, this Caesar of ours hath had the extravagance to venture his tender wit in comparison to that of Achilles Tatius. He stands upon his honour, too, this ineffable fool, and is displeased with the idea of being supposed either to challenge a woman, or to receive a challenge at her hand. He has substituted, therefore, the name of the lord instead of the lady. If the Count fail to appear, the Caesar walks forward challenger and successful combatant at a cheap rate, since no one has encountered him, and claims that the lady should be delivered up to him as a captive of his dreaded bow and spear. This will be the signal for a general tumult, in which, if the Emperor be not slain on the spot, he will be conveyed to the dungeon of his own Blacquernal, there to endure the doom which his cruelty has inflicted upon so many others."

"But"—said the Varangian.

"But—but—but," said his officer; "but thou art a fool. Canst thou not see that this gallant Caesar is willing to avoid the risk of encountering with this lady, while he earnestly desires to be supposed willing to meet her husband? It is our business to fix the combat in such a shape as to bring all who are prepared for insurrection together in arms to play their parts. Do thou only see that our trusty friends are placed near to the Emperor's person, and in such a manner as to keep from him the officious and meddling portion of guards, who may be disposed to assist him; and whether the Caesar fights a combat with lord or lady, or whether there be any combat at all or not, the revolution shall be accomplished, and the Tatii shall replace the Comneni upon the Imperial throne of Constantinople. Go, my trusty Hereward. Thou wilt not forget that the signal word of the insurrection is Ursel, who lives in the affections of the people, although his body, it is said, has long lain a corpse in the dungeons of the Blacquernal."

"What was this Ursel," said Hereward, "of whom I hear men talk so variously?"

"A competitor for the crown with Alexius Comnenus—good, brave, and honest; but overpowered by the cunning, rather than the skill or bravery of his foe. He died, as I believe, in the Blacquernal; though when, or how, there are few that can say. But, up and be doing, my Hereward! Speak encouragement to the Varangians—Interest whomsoever thou canst to join us. Of the Immortals, as they are called, and of the discontented citizens, enough are prepared to fill up the cry, and follow in the wake of those on whom we must rely as the beginners of the enterprise. No longer shall Alexius's cunning, in avoiding popular assemblies, avail to protect him; he cannot, with regard to his honour, avoid being present at a combat to be fought beneath his own eye; and Mercury be praised for the eloquence which inspired him, after some hesitation, to determine for the proclamation!"

"You have seen him, then, this evening?" said the Varangian.

"Seen him! Unquestionably," answered the Acolyte. "Had I ordered these trumpets to be sounded without his knowledge, the blast had blown the head from my shoulders."

"I had wellnigh met you at the palace," said Hereward; while his heart throbbed almost as high as if he had actually had such a dangerous encounter.

"I heard something of it," said Achilles; "that you came to take the parting orders of him who now acts the sovereign. Surely, had I seen you there, with that steadfast, open, seemingly honest countenance, cheating the wily Greek by very dint of bluntness, I had not forborne laughing at the contrast between that and the thoughts of thy heart."

"God alone," said Hereward, "knows the thoughts of our hearts; but I take him to witness, that I am faithful to my promise, and will discharge the task intrusted to me."

"Bravo! mine honest Anglo–Saxon," said Achilles. "I pray thee to call my slaves to unarm me; and when thou thyself doffest those weapons of an ordinary life–guardsman, tell them they never shall above twice more enclose the limbs of one for whom fate has much more fitting garments in store."

Hereward dared not intrust his voice with an answer to so critical a speech; he bowed profoundly, and retired to his own quarters in the building.

Upon entering the apartment, he was immediately saluted by the voice of Count Robert, in joyful accents, not suppressed by the fear of making himself heard, though prudence should have made that uppermost in his mind.

"Hast thou heard it, my dear Hereward," he said—"hast thou heard the proclamation, by which this Greek antelope hath defied me to tilting with grinded spears, and fighting three passages of arms with sharpened swords? Yet there is something strange, too, that he should not think it safer to hold my lady to the encounter! He may think, perhaps, that the crusaders would not permit such a battle to be fought. But, by our Lady of the Broken Lances! he little knows that the men of the West hold their ladies' character for courage as jealously as they do their own. This whole night have I been considering in what armour I shall clothe me; what shift I shall make for a steed; and whether I shall not honour him sufficiently by using Tranchefer, as my only weapon, against his whole armour, offensive and defensive."

"I shall take care, however," said Hereward, "that, thou art better provided in case of need.—Thou knowest not the Greeks."

CHAPTER THE TWENTY-THIRD

The Varangian did not leave the Count of Paris until the latter had in his hands his signet–ring, *semee*, (as the heralds express it,) *with lances splintered*, and bearing the proud motto, "Mine yet unscathed." Provided with this symbol of confidence, it was now his business to take order for communicating the approaching solemnity to the leader of the crusading army, and demanding from him, in the name of Robert of Paris, and the Lady Brenhilda, such a detachment of western cavaliers as might ensure strict observance of honour and honesty in the arrangement of the lists, and during the progress of
the combat. The duties imposed on Hereward were such as to render it impossible for him to proceed personally to the camp of Godfrey: and though there were many of the Varangians in whose fidelity he could have trusted, he knew of none among those under his immediate command whose intelligence, on so novel an occasion, might be entirely depended on. In this perplexity, he strolled,
perhaps without well knowing why, to the gardens of Agelastes, where fortune once more produced him an interview with Bertha.

No sooner had Hereward made her aware of his difficulty, than the faithful bower–maiden's resolution was taken.

"I see," said she, "that the peril of this part of the adventure must rest with me; and wherefore should it not? My mistress, in the bosom of prosperity, offered herself to go forth into the wide world for my sake; I will for hers go to the camp of this Frankish lord. He is an honourable man, and a pious Christian, and his followers are faithful pilgrims. A woman can have nothing to fear who goes to such men upon such an errand."

The Varangian, however, was too well acquainted with the manners of camps to permit the fair Bertha to go alone. He provided, therefore, for her safe– guard a trusty old soldier, bound to his person by long kindness and confidence, and having thoroughly possessed her of the particulars of the message she was to deliver, and desired her to be in readiness without the enclosure at peep of dawn, returned once more to his barracks.

With the earliest light, Hereward was again at the spot where he had parted overnight with Bertha, accompanied by the honest soldier to whose care he meant to confide her. In a short time, he had seen them safely on board of a ferry–boat lying in the harbour; the master of which readily admitted them, after some examination of their license, to pass to Scutari, which was forged in the name of the Acolyte, as authorised by that foul conspirator, and which agreed with the appearance of old Osmund and his young charge.

The morning was lovely; and erelong the town of Scutari opened on the view of the travellers, glittering, as now, with a variety of architecture, which, though it might be termed fantastical, could not be denied the praise of beauty. These buildings rose boldly out of a thick grove of cypresses, and other huge trees, the larger, probably, as they were respected for filling the cemeteries, and being the guardians of the dead.

At the period we mention, another circumstance, no less striking than beautiful, rendered doubly interesting a scene which must have been at all times greatly so. A large portion of that miscellaneous army which came to regain the holy places of Palestine, and the blessed Sepulchre itself, from the infidels, had established themselves in a camp within a mile, or thereabouts, of Scutari. Although, therefore, the crusaders were destitute in a great measure
of the use of tents, the army (excepting the pavilions of some leaders of high rank) had constructed for themselves temporary huts, not unpleasing to the eye, being decorated with leaves and flowers,
while the tall pennons and banners that floated over them with various devices, showed that the flower of Europe were assembled at that place. A loud and varied murmur, resembling that of a thronged hive, floated from the camp of the crusaders to the neighbouring
town of Scutari, and every now and then the deep tone was broken by some shriller sound, the note of some musical instrument, or the treble scream of some child or female, in fear or in gaiety.

The party at length landed in safety; and as they approached one of the gates of the camp, there sallied forth a brisk array of gallant cavaliers, pages, and squires, exercising their masters' horses or their own. From the noise they made, conversing at the very top of their voices, galloping, curvetting, and prancing their palfreys, it seemed as if their early discipline had called them to exercise ere the fumes of last night's revel were thoroughly dissipated by repose. So soon as they saw Bertha and her party, they approached them with cries which marked their country was Italy—"Al'erta! al'erta!—Roba de guadagno, cameradi!" [Footnote: That is—"Take heed! take heed! there is booty, comrades!"]

They gathered round the Anglo–Saxon maiden and her companions, repeating their cries in a manner which made Bertha tremble. Their general demand was, "What was her business in their camp?"

"I would to the general–in–chief, cavaliers," answered Bertha, "having a secret message to his ear."

"For whose ear?" said a leader of the party, a handsome youth of about eighteen years of age, who seemed either to have a sounder brain than his fellows, or to have overflowed it with less wine. "Which of our leaders do you come hither to see?" he demanded.

"Godfrey of Bouillon."

"Indeed!" said the page who had spoken first; "can nothing of less consequence serve thy turn? Take a look amongst us; young are we all, and reasonably wealthy. My Lord of Bouillon is old, and if he has any sequins, he is not like to lavish them in this way."

"Still I have a token to Godfrey of Bouillon," answered Bertha, "an assured one; and he will little thank any who obstructs my free passage to him;" and therewithal showing a little case, in which the signet of the Count of Paris was enclosed, "I will trust it in your hands," she said, "if you promise not to open it, but to give me free access to the noble leader of the crusaders."

"I will," said the youth, "and if such be the Duke's pleasure, thou shalt be admitted to him."

"Ernest the Apulian, thy dainty Italian wit is caught in a trap," said one of his companions.

"Thou art an ultramontane fool, Polydore," returned Ernest; "there may be more in this than either thy wit or mine is able to fathom. This maiden and one of her attendants wear a dress belonging to the Varangian Imperial guard. They have perhaps been intrusted with a message from the Emperor, and it is not irreconcilable with Alexius's politics to send it through such messengers as these. Let us, therefore, convey them in all honour to the General's tent."

"With all my heart," said Polydore. "A blue–eyed wench is a pretty thing, but I like not the sauce of the camp–marshal, nor his taste in attiring men who gave way to temptation. [Footnote: Persons among the Crusaders found guilty of certain offences, did penance in a dress of tar and feathers though it is supposed a punishment of modern invention.] Yet, ere I prove a fool like my companion, I would ask who or what this pretty maiden is, who comes to put noble princes and holy pilgrims in mind that they have in their time had the follies of men?"

Bertha advanced and whispered in the ear of Ernest. Meantime joke followed jest, among Polydore and the rest of the gay youths, in riotous and ribald succession, which, however characteristic of the rude speakers, may as well be omitted here. Their effect was to shake in some degree the fortitude of the Saxon maiden, who had some difficulty in mustering courage to address them. "As you have mothers, gentlemen," she said, "as you have fair sisters, whom you would protect from dishonour with your best blood—as you love and honour those holy places which you are sworn to free from the infidel enemy, have compassion on me, that you may merit success in your undertaking!"

"Fear nothing, maiden," said Ernest, "I will be your protector; and you, my comrades, be ruled by me. I have, during your brawling, taken a view, though somewhat against my promise, of the pledge which she bears, and if she who presents it is affronted or maltreated, be assured Godfrey of Bouillon will severely avenge the wrong done her."

"Nay, comrade, if thou canst warrant us so much," said Polydore, "I will myself be most anxious to conduct the young woman in honour and safety to Sir Godfrey's tent."

"The Princes," said Ernest, "must be nigh meeting there in council. What I have said I will warrant and uphold with hand and life. More I might guess, but I conclude this sensible young maiden can speak for herself."

"Now, Heaven bless thee, gallant squire," said Bertha, "and make thee alike brave and fortunate! Embarrass yourself no farther about me, than to deliver me safe to your leader, Godfrey."

"We spend time," said Ernest, springing from his horse. "You are no soft Eastern, fair maid, and I presume you will find yourself under no difficulty in managing a quiet horse?"

"Not the least," said Bertha, as, wrapping herself in her cassock, she sprung from the ground, and alighted upon the spirited palfrey, as a linnet stoops upon a rose–bush. "And now, sir, as my business really brooks no delay, I will be indebted to you to show me instantly to the tent of Duke Godfrey of Bouillon."

By availing herself of this courtesy of the young Apulian, Bertha imprudently separated herself from the old Varangian; but the intentions of the youth were honourable, and he conducted her through the tents and huts to the pavilion of the celebrated General– in–chief of the Crusade.

"Here," he said, "you must tarry for a space, under the guardianship of my companions," (for two or three of the pages had accompanied them, out of curiosity to see the issue,) "and I will take the commands of the Duke of Bouillon upon the subject."

To this nothing could be objected, and Bertha had nothing better to do, than to admire the outside of the tent, which, in one of Alexius's fits of generosity and munificence, had been presented by the Greek Emperor to the Chief of the Franks. It was raised upon tall spear– shaped poles, which had the semblance of gold; its curtains were of thick stuff, manufactured of silk, cotton, and gold thread. The warders who stood round, were (at least during the time that the council was held) old grave men, the personal squires of the body, most of them, of the sovereigns who had taken the Cross, and who could, therefore, be trusted as a guard over the assembly, without danger of their blabbing what they might overhear. Their appearance was serious and considerate, and they looked like men who had

taken upon them the Cross, not as an idle adventure of arms, but as a purpose of the most solemn and serious nature. One of these stopt

the Italian, and demanded what business authorized him to press forward into the council of the crusaders, who were already taking their seats. The page answered by giving his name, "Ernest of Otranto, page of Prince Tancred;" and stated that he announced a young woman, who bore a token to the Duke of Bouillon, adding that it was accompanied by a message for his own ear.

Bertha, meantime, laid aside her mantle, or upper garment, and disposed the rest of her dress according to the Anglo–Saxon costume. She had hardly completed this task, before the page of Prince Tancred returned, to conduct her into the presence of the council of the Crusade. She followed his signal; while the other young men who had accompanied her, wondering at the apparent ease with which she gained admittance, drew back to a respectful distance from the tent, and there canvassed the singularity of their morning's adventure.

In the meanwhile, the ambassadress herself entered the council chamber, exhibiting an agreeable mixture of shamefacedness and reserve, together with a bold determination to do her duty at all events. There were about fifteen of the principal crusaders

assembled in council, with their chieftain Godfrey. He himself was a tall strong man, arrived at that period of life in—which men are supposed to have lost none of their resolution, while they have acquired a wisdom and circumspection unknown to their earlier years. The countenance of Godfrey bespoke both prudence and boldness, and resembled his hair, where a few threads of silver were already mingled with his raven locks.

Tancred, the noblest knight of the Christian chivalry, sat at no great distance from him, with Hugh, Earl of Vermandois, generally called the Great Count, the selfish and wily Bohemond, the powerful Raymond of Provence, and others of the principal crusaders, all more or less completely sheathed in armour.

Bertha did not allow her courage to be broken down, but advancing with a timid grace towards Godfrey, she placed in his hands the signet which had been restored to her by the young page, and after a deep obeisance, spoke these words: "Godfrey, Count of Bouillon, Duke of Lorraine the Lower, Chief of the Holy Enterprise called the Crusade, and you, his gallant comrades, peers, and companions, by whatever titles you may be honoured, I, an humble maiden of England, daughter of Engelred, originally a franklin of Hampshire, and since Chieftain of the Foresters, or free Anglo–Saxons, under the command of the celebrated Edric, do claim what credence is due to the bearer of the true pledge which I put into your hand, on the part of one not the least considerable of your own body, Count Robert of Paris"—

"Our most honourable confederate," said Godfrey, looking at the ring. "Most of you, my lords, must, I think, know this signet—a field sown with the fragments of many splintered lances." The signet was handed from one of the Assembly to another, and generally recognised.

When Godfrey had signified so much, the maiden resumed her message. "To all true crusaders, therefore, comrades of Godfrey of Bouillon, and especially to the Duke himself,—to all, I say, excepting Bohemond of Tarentum, whom he counts unworthy of his notice"—

"Hah! me unworthy of his notice," said Bohemond. "What mean you by that, damsel?—But the Count of Paris shall answer it to me."

"Under your favour, Sir Bohemond," said Godfrey, "no. Our articles renounce the sending of challenges among ourselves, and the matter, if not dropt betwixt the parties, must be referred to the voice of this honourable council."

"I think I guess the business now, my lord," said Bohemond. "The Count of Paris is disposed to turn and tear me, because I offered him good counsel on the evening before we left Constantinople, when he neglected to accept or be guided by it"—

"It will be the more easily explained when we have heard his message," said Godfrey.—"Speak forth Lord Robert of Paris's charge, damsel, that we may take some order with that which now seems a perplexed business."

Bertha resumed her message; and, having briefly narrated the recent events, thus concluded:—"The battle is to be done to–morrow, about two hours after daybreak, and the Count entreats of the noble Duke of Lorraine that he will permit some fifty of the lances of France to attend the deed of arms, and secure that fair and honourable conduct which he has otherwise some doubts of receiving at the hands of his adversary. Or if any young and gallant knight should, of his own free will, wish to view the said combat, the Count will feel his presence as an honour; always he desires that the name of such knight be numbered carefully with the armed crusaders who shall attend in the lists, and that the whole shall be limited, by Duke Godfrey's own inspection, to fifty lances only, which are enough to obtain the protection required, while more would be considered as a preparation for aggression upon the Grecians, and occasion the revival of disputes which are now happily at rest."

Bertha had no sooner finished delivering her manifesto, and made with great grace her obeisance to the council, than a sort of whisper took place in the assembly, which soon assumed a more lively tone.

Their solemn vow not to turn their back upon Palestine, now that they had set their hands to the plough, was strongly urged by some of the elder knights of the council, and two or three high prelates, who had by this time entered to take share in the deliberations. The young knights, on the other hand, were fired with indignation on hearing the manner in which their comrade had been trepanned; and few of them could think of missing a combat in the lists in a country in which such sights were so rare, and where one was to be fought so near them.

Godfrey rested his brow on his hand, and seemed in great perplexity.

To break with the Greeks, after having suffered so many injuries in order to maintain the advantage of keeping the peace with them, seemed very impolitic, and a sacrifice of all he had obtained by a long course of painful forbearance towards Alexius Comnenus. On the other hand, he was bound as a man of honour to resent the injury offered to Count Robert of Paris, whose reckless spirit of chivalry made him the darling of the army. It was the cause, too, of a beautiful lady, and a brave one: every knight in the host would think himself bound, by his vow, to hasten to her defence. When Godfrey spoke, it was to complain of the difficulty of the determination, and the short time there was to consider the case.

"With submission to my Lord Duke of Lorraine," said Tancred, "I was a knight ere I was a crusader, and took on me the vows of chivalry, ere I placed this blessed, sign upon my shoulder: the vow first made must be first discharged. I will therefore do penance for neglecting, for a space, the obligations of the second vow, while I observe that which recalls me to the first duty of knighthood,—the relief of a distressed lady in the hands of men whose conduct towards her, and towards this host, in every respect entitles me to call them treacherous faitours."

"If my kinsman Tancred," said Bohemond, "will check his impetuosity, and you, my lords, will listen, as you have sometimes deigned to do, to my advice, I think I can direct you how to keep clear of any breach of your oath, and yet fully to relieve our distressed fellow–pilgrims.—I see some suspicious looks are cast towards me, which are caused perhaps by the churlish manner in which this violent, and, in this case, almost insane young warrior, has protested against receiving my assistance. My great offence is the having given him warning, by precept and example, of the treachery which was about to be practised against him, and instructed him to use forbearance and temperance. My warning he altogether contemned—my example he neglected to follow, and fell
into the snare which was spread, as it were, before his very eyes. Yet the Count of Paris, in rashly contemning me, has acted only from a temper which misfortune and disappointment have rendered
irrational and frantic. I am so far from bearing him ill–will, that, with your lordship's permission, and that of the present council, I will

haste to the place of rendezvous with fifty lances, making up the retinue which attends upon each to at least ten men, which will make the stipulated auxiliary force equal to five hundred; and with these I can have little doubt of rescuing the Count and his lady."

"Nobly proposed," said the Duke of Bouillon; "and with a charitable forgiveness of injuries which becomes our Christian expedition. But thou hast forgot the main difficulty, brother Bohemond, that we are sworn never to turn back upon the sacred journey."

"If we can elude that oath upon the present occasion," said Bohemond, "it becomes our duty to do so. Are we such bad horsemen, or are our steeds so awkward, that we cannot rein them back from this to the landing–place at Scutari? We can get them on shipboard in the same retrograde manner, and when we arrive in Europe, where our vow binds us no longer, the Count and Countess of Paris are rescued, and our vow remains entire in the Chancery of Heaven."

A general shout arose—"Long life to the gallant Bohemond!— Shame to us if we do not fly to the assistance of so valiant a knight, and a lady so lovely, since we can do so without breach of our vow."

"The question," said Godfrey, "appears to me to be eluded rather than solved; yet such evasions have been admitted by the most learned and scrupulous clerks; nor do I hesitate to admit of Bohemond's expedient, any more than if the enemy had attacked our rear, which might have occasioned our countermarching to be a case of absolute necessity."

Some there were in the assembly, particularly the churchmen, inclined to think that the oath by which the crusaders had solemnly bound themselves, ought to be as literally obeyed. But Peter the Hermit, who had a place in the council, and possessed great weight, declared it as his opinion, "That since the precise observance of their vow would tend to diminish the forces of the crusade, it was in fact unlawful, and should not be kept according to the literal meaning, if, by a fair construction, it could be eluded."

He offered himself to back the animal which he bestrode—that is, his ass; and though he was diverted from showing this example by the remonstrances of Godfrey of Bouillon, who was afraid of his becoming a scandal in the eyes of the heathen, yet he so prevailed by his arguments, that the knights, far from scrupling to countermarch, eagerly contended which should have the honour of making one of the party which should retrograde to Constantinople, see the combat, and bring back to the host in safety the valorous Count of Paris, of whose victory no one doubted, and his Amazonian Countess.

This emulation was also put an end to by the authority of Godfrey, who himself selected the fifty knights who were to compose the party. They were chosen from different nations, and the command of the whole was given to young Tancred of Otranto. Notwithstanding the claim of Bohemond, Godfrey detained the latter, under the
pretext that his knowledge of the country and people was absolutely necessary to enable the council to form the plan of the campaign in Syria; but in reality he dreaded the selfishness of a man of great ingenuity as well as military skill, who, finding himself in a separate command, might be tempted, should opportunities arise, to enlarge his own power and dominion, at the expense of the pious purposes of the crusade in general. The younger men of the expedition were chiefly anxious to procure such horses as had been thoroughly trained, and could go through with ease and temper the manoeuvre of equitation, by which it was designed to render legitimate the movement which they had recourse to. The selection was at length made, and the detachment ordered to draw up in the rear, or upon the eastward line of the Christian encampment. In the meanwhile, Godfrey charged Bertha with a message for the Count of Paris, in which, slightly censuring him for not observing more caution in his intercourse with the Greeks, he informed him that he had sent a detachment of fifty lances, with the corresponding squires, pages, men–at–arms, and cross–bows, five hundred in number, commanded by the valiant Tancred, to his assistance. The Duke also informed him, that he had added a suit of armour of the best temper Milan could afford, together with a trusty war–horse, which he entreated him to use upon the field of battle; for Bertha had not omitted to intimate Count Robert's want of the means of knightly equipment. The horse was brought before the pavilion accordingly, completely barbed or armed in steel, and laden with armour for the knight's

body. Godfrey himself put the bridle into Bertha's hand.

"Thou need'st not fear to trust thyself with this steed, he is as gentle and docile as he is fleet and brave. Place thyself on his back, and take heed thou stir not from the side of the noble Prince Tancred of Otranto, who will be the faithful defender of a maiden that has this day shown dexterity, courage, and fidelity."

Bertha bowed low, as her cheeks glowed at praise from one whose talents and worth were in such general esteem, as to have raised him to the distinguished situation of leader of a host which numbered in
it the bravest and most distinguished captains of Christendom.

"Who are yon two persons?" continued Godfrey, speaking of the companions of Bertha, whom he saw in the distance before the tent.

"The one," answered the damsel, "is the master of the ferry–boat which brought me over; and the other an old Varangian who came hither as my protector."

"As they may come to employ their eyes here, and their tongues on the opposite side," returned the general of the crusaders, "I do not think it prudent to let them accompany you. They shall remain here for some short time. The citizens of Scutari will not comprehend for some space what our intention is, and I could wish Prince Tancred and his attendants to be the first to announce their own arrival."

Bertha accordingly intimated the pleasure of the French general to the parties, without naming his motives; when the ferryman began to exclaim on the hardship of intercepting him in his trade; and
Osmund to complain of being detained from his duties. But Bertha, by the orders of Godfrey, left them, with the assurance that they would be soon at liberty. Finding themselves thus abandoned, each applied himself to his favourite amusement. The ferryman occupied himself in staring about at all that was new; and Osmund, having in the meantime accepted an offer of breakfast from some of the domestics, was presently engaged with a flask of such red wine as would have reconciled him to a worse lot than that which he at present experienced.

The detachment of Tancred, fifty spears and their armed retinue, which amounted fully to five hundred men, after having taken a short and hasty refreshment, were in arms and mounted before the sultry hour of noon. After some manoeuvres, of which the Greeks of Scutari, whose curiosity was awakened by the preparations of the detachment, were at a loss to comprehend the purpose, they formed into a single column, having four men in front. When the horses were in this position, the whole riders at once began to rein back. The action was one to which both the cavaliers and their horses were well accustomed, nor did it at first afford much surprise to the spectators; but when the same retrograde evolution was continued, and the body of crusaders seemed about to enter the town of Scutari in so extraordinary a fashion, some idea of the truth began to occupy the citizens. The cry at length was general, when Tancred and a few others, whose horses were unusually well–trained, arrived at the port, and possessed themselves of a galley, into which they led their horses, and, disregarding all opposition from the Imperial officers of the haven, pushed the vessel off from the shore.

Other cavaliers did not accomplish their purpose so easily; the riders, or the horses, were less accustomed to continue in the constrained pace for such a considerable length of time, so that many of the knights, having retrograded for one or two hundred yards, thought their vow was sufficiently observed by having so far deferred to it, and riding in the ordinary manner into the town, seized without farther ceremony on some vessels, which, notwithstanding the orders of the Greek Emperor, had been allowed to remain on the Asiatic side of the strait. Some less able horsemen met with various accidents; for though it was a proverb of the time, that nothing was so bold as a blind horse, yet from this mode of equitation, where neither horse nor rider saw the way he was going, some steeds were overthrown, others backed upon dangerous obstacles; and the bones of the cavaliers themselves suffered much more than would have been the case in an ordinary march.

Those horsemen, also, who met with falls, incurred the danger of being slain by the Greeks, had not Godfrey, surmounting his religious scruples, despatched a squadron to extricate them—a task which they performed with great ease. The greater part of Tancred's followers succeeded in embarking, as was intended, nor was there more than a score or two finally amissing. To accomplish their voyage, however, even the Prince of Otranto himself, and most of his followers, were obliged to betake themselves to the unknightly labours of the oar. This they found extremely difficult, as well from the state both of the tide and the wind, as from the want of practice at the exercise. Godfrey in person viewed their progress anxiously, from a neighbouring height, and perceived with regret the difficulty which they found in making their way, which was still more increased by the necessity for their keeping in a body, and waiting for the slowest and worst manned vessels, which considerably detained those that were more expeditious. They made some progress, however; nor had the commander–in–chief the least doubt, that before sunset they would safely reach the opposite side of the strait.

He retired at length from his post of observation, having placed a careful sentinel in his stead, with directions to bring him word the instant that the detachment reached the opposite shore. This the soldier could easily discern by the eye, if it was daylight at the time; if, on the contrary, it was night before they could arrive, the Prince of Otranto had orders to show certain lights, which, in case of their meeting resistance from the Greeks, should be arranged in a peculiar manner, so as to indicate danger.

Godfrey then explained to the Greek authorities of Scutari, whom he summoned before him, the necessity there was that he should keep in readiness such vessels as could be procured, with which, in case of need, he was determined to transport a strong division from his army to support those who had gone before. He then rode back to his camp, the confused murmurs of which, rendered more noisy by the various discussions concerning the events of the day, rolled off from the numerous host of the crusaders, and mingled with the hoarse sound of the many–billowed Hellespont.

CHAPTER THE TWENTH-FOURTH

All is prepared—the chambers of the mine
Are cramm'd with the combustible, which, harmless
While yet unkindled, as the sable sand, Needs but
a spark to change its nature so,
That he who wakes it from its slumbrous mood, Dreads
scarce the explosion less than he who knows That 'tis his
towers which meet its fury. ANONYMOUS.

When the sky is darkened suddenly, and the atmosphere grows thick and stifling, the lower ranks of creation entertain the ominous sense of a coming tempest. The birds fly to the thickets, the wild creatures retreat to the closest covers which their instinct gives them the habit of frequenting, and domestic animals show their apprehension of the approaching thunderstorm by singular actions and movements inferring fear and disturbance.

It seems that human nature, when its original habits are cultivated and attended to, possesses, on similar occasions, something of that prescient foreboding, which announces the approaching tempest to the inferior ranks of creation. The cultivation of our intellectual powers goes perhaps too far, when it teaches us entirely to suppress and disregard those natural feelings, which were originally designed as sentinels by which nature warned us of impending danger.

Something of the kind, however, still remains, and that species of feeling which announces to us sorrowful or alarming tidings, may be said, like the prophecies of the weird sisters, to come over us like a sudden cloud.

During the fatal day which was to precede the combat of the Caesar with the Count of Paris, there were current through the city of Constantinople the most contradictory, and at the same time the most terrific reports. Privy conspiracy, it was alleged, was on the very eve of breaking out; open war, it was reported by others, was about to shake her banners over the devoted city; the precise cause was not agreed upon, any more than the nature of the enemy. Some said that the barbarians from the borders of Thracia, the Hungarians, as they were termed, and the Comani, were on their march from the frontiers to surprise the city; another report stated that the Turks, who, during this period, were established in Asia, had resolved to prevent the threatened attack of the crusaders upon Palestine, by surprising not only the Western Pilgrims, but the Christians of the East, by one of their innumerable invasions, executed with their characteristic rapidity.

Another report, approaching more near to the truth, declared that the crusaders themselves, having discovered their various causes of complaint against Alexius Comnenus, had resolved to march back their united forces to the capital, with a view of dethroning or chastising him; and the citizens were dreadfully alarmed for the consequences of the resentment of men so fierce in their habits and so strange in their manners. In short, although they did not all agree on the precise cause of danger, it was yet generally allowed that something of a dreadful kind was impending, which appeared to be in a certain degree confirmed by the motions that were taking place among the troops. The Varangians, as well as the Immortals, were gradually assembled, and placed in occupation of the strongest parts of the city, until at length the fleet of galleys, row–boats, and transports, occupied by Tancred and his party, were observed to put
themselves in motion from Scutari, and attempt to gain such a height in the narrow sea, as upon the turn of the tide should transport them to the port of the capital.

Alexius Comnenus was himself struck at this unexpected movement on the part of the crusaders. Yet, after some conversation with Hereward, on whom he had determined to repose his confidence,
and had now gone too far to retreat, he became reassured, the more especially by the limited size of the detachment which seemed to meditate so bold a measure as an attack upon his capital. To those around him he said with carelessness, that it was hardly to be supposed that a trumpet could blow to the charge, within hearing of

the crusaders' camp, without some out of so many knights coming forth to see the cause and the issue of the conflict.

The conspirators also had their secret fears when the little armament of Tancred had been seen on the straits. Agelastes mounted a mule, and went to the shore of the sea, at the place now called Galata. He met Bertha's old ferryman, whom Godfrey had set at liberty, partly in contempt, and partly that the report he was likely to make, might serve to amuse the conspirators in the city. Closely examined by Agelastes, he confessed that the present detachment, so far as he understood, was despatched at the instance of Bohemond, and was under the command of his kinsman Tancred, whose well–known banner was floating from the headmost vessel. This gave courage to Agelastes, who, in the course of his intrigues, had opened a private
communication with the wily and ever mercenary Prince of Antioch. The object of the philosopher had been to obtain from Bohemond a body of his followers to co–operate in the intended conspiracy, and fortify the party of insurgents. It is true, that Bohemond had returned no answer, but the account now given by the ferryman, and the sight of Tancred the kinsman of Bohemond's banner displayed on the straits, satisfied the philosopher that his offers, his presents, and his promises, had gained to his side the avaricious Italian, and that this band had been selected by Bohemond, and were coming to act in his favour.

As Agelastes turned to go off, he almost jostled a person, as much muffled up, and apparently as unwilling to be known, as the philosopher himself. Alexius Comnenus, however—for it was the Emperor himself— knew Agelastes, though rather from his stature and gestures, than his countenance; and could not forbear whispering in his ear, as he passed, the well–known lines, to which the
pretended sage's various acquisitions gave some degree of point:—

"Grammaticus, rhetor, geometres, pictor, aliptes, Augur, schoenobates, medicus, magus; omnia novit. Graeculus esuriens in caelum, jusseris, ibit."
[Footnote: The lines of Juvenal imitated by Johnson in his *London*— "All sciences a fasting Monsieur knows, And bid him go to hell—to hell he goes."]

Agelastes first started at the unexpected sound of the Emperor's voice, yet immediately recovered presence of mind, the want of which had made him suspect himself betrayed; and without taking notice of the rank of the person to whom he spoke, he answered by a quotation which should return the alarm he had received. The speech that suggested itself was said to be that which the Phantom of Cleonice dinned into the ears of the tyrant who murdered her:—

"Tu cole justitiam; toque atque alios manet ultor." [Footnote: "Do thou cultivate justice: for thee and for others there remains an avenger."—*Ovid. Met.*]

The sentence, and the recollections which accompanied it, thrilled through the heart of the Emperor, who walked on, however, without any notice or reply.

"The vile conspirator," he said, "had his associates around him, otherwise he had not hazarded that threat. Or it may have been worse — Agelastes himself, on the very brink of this world, may have obtained that singular glance into futurity proper to that situation, and perhaps speaks less from his own reflection than from a strange spirit of prescience, which dictates his words. Have I then in earnest sinned so far in my imperial duty, as to make it just to apply to me the warning used by the injured Cleonice to her ravisher and murderer? Methinks I have not. Methinks that at less expense than that of a just severity, I could ill have kept my seat in the high place where Heaven has been pleased to seat me, and where, as a ruler, I am bound to maintain my station. Methinks the sum of those who have experienced my clemency may be well numbered with that of such as have sustained the deserved punishments of their guilt—But has that vengeance, however deserved in itself, been always taken in a legal or justifiable manner? My conscience, I doubt, will hardly answer so home a question; and where is the man, had he the virtues of Antoninus himself, that can hold so high and responsible a place, yet sustain such an interrogation as is implied in that sort of warning which I have received from this traitor? *Tu cole justitiam*—we all need to use justice to others—*Teque atque alios manet ultor*—we are all amenable to an avenging being—I will see the Patriarch—instantly will I see him; and by confessing my transgressions to the

Church, I will, by her plenary indulgence, acquire the right of spending the last day of my reign in a consciousness of innocence, or at least of pardon—a state of mind rarely the lot of those whose lines have fallen in lofty places."

So saying, he passed to the palace of Zosimus the Patriarch, to whom he could unbosom himself with more safety, because he had long considered Agelastes as a private enemy to the Church, and a man attached to the ancient doctrines of heathenism. In the councils of the state they were also opposed to each other, nor did the Emperor doubt, that in communicating the secret of the conspiracy to the Patriarch, he was sure to attain a loyal and firm supporter in
the defence which he proposed to himself. He therefore gave a signal by a low whistle, and a confidential officer, well mounted, approached him, who attended him in his ride, though unostentatiously, and at some distance.

In this manner, therefore, Alexius Comnenus proceeded to the palace of the Patriarch, with as much speed as was consistent with his purpose of avoiding to attract any particular notice as he passed through the street. During the whole ride, the warning of Agelastes repeatedly occurred to him, and his conscience reminded him of too many actions of his reign which could only be justified by necessity, emphatically said to be the tyrant's plea, and which were of themselves deserving the dire vengeance so long delayed.

When he came in sight of the splendid towers which adorned the front of the patriarchal palace, he turned aside from the lofty gates, repaired to a narrow court, and again giving his mule to his attendant, he stopt before a postern, whose low arch and humble architrave seemed to exclude the possibility of its leading to any place of importance. On knocking, however, a priest of an inferior order opened the door, who, with a deep reverence, received the
Emperor so soon as he had made himself known, and conducted him into the interior of the palace. Demanding a secret interview with the Patriarch, Alexius was then ushered into his private library, where he was received by the aged priest with the deepest respect, which the nature of his communication soon changed into horror and astonishment.

Although Alexius was supposed by many of his own court, and particularly by some members of his own family, to be little better than a hypocrite in his religious professions, yet such severe observers were unjust in branding him with a name so odious. He was indeed aware of the great support which he received from the good opinion of the clergy, and to them he was willing to make sacrifices for the advantage of the Church, or of individual prelates who manifested fidelity to the crown; but though, on the one hand, such sacrifices were rarely made by Alexius, without a view to temporal policy, yet, on the other, he regarded them as recommended by his devotional feelings, and took credit to himself
for various grants and actions, as dictated by sincere piety, which, in another aspect, were the fruits of temporal policy. His mode of looking on these measures was that of a person with oblique vision, who sees an object in a different manner, according to the point from which he chances to contemplate it.

The Emperor placed his own errors of government before the Patriarch in his confession, giving due weight to every branch of morality as it occurred, and stripping from them the lineaments and palliative circumstances which had in his own imagination lessened their guilt. The Patriarch heard, to his astonishment, the real thread of many a court intrigue, which had borne a very different appearance, till the Emperor's narrative either justified his conduct
upon the occasion, or left it totally unjustifiable. Upon the whole, the balance was certainly more in favour of Alexius than the Patriarch had supposed likely in that more distant view he had taken of the intrigues of the court, when, as usual, the ministers and the courtiers endeavoured to make up for the applause which they had given in council in the most blameable actions of the absolute monarch, by elsewhere imputing to his motives greater guilt than really belonged to them. Many men who had fallen sacrifices, it was supposed to the personal spleen or jealousy of the Emperor, appeared to have been in fact removed from life, or from liberty, because their enjoying either was inconsistent with the quiet of the state and the safety of the monarch.

Zosimus also learned, what he perhaps already suspected, that amidst the profound silence of despotism which seemed to pervade the Grecian empire, it heaved frequently with convulsive throes, which ever and anon made obvious the existence of a volcano under the surface. Thus, while smaller delinquencies, or avowed discontent with the Imperial government, seldom occurred, and were severely punished when they did, the deepest and most mortal conspiracies against the life and the authority of the Emperor were cherished by those nearest to his person; and he was often himself aware of them, though it was not until they approached an explosion that he dared

act upon his knowledge, and punish the conspirators.

The whole treason of the Caesar, with his associates, Agelastes and Achilles Tatius, was heard by the Patriarch with wonder and astonishment, and he was particularly surprised at the dexterity with which the Emperor, knowing the existence of so dangerous a conspiracy at home, had been able to parry the danger from the crusaders occurring at the same moment.

"In that respect," said the Emperor, to whom indeed the churchman hinted his surprise, "I have been singularly unfortunate. Had I been secure of the forces of my own empire, I might have taken one out of two manly and open courses with these frantic warriors of the west

—I might, my reverend father, have devoted the sums paid to Bohemond and other of the more selfish among the crusaders, to the honest and open support of the army of western Christians, and safely transported them to Palestine, without exposing them to the great loss which they are likely to sustain by the opposition of the Infidels; their success would have been in fact my own, and a Latin kingdom in Palestine, defended by its steel–clad warriors, would have been a safe and unexpugnable barrier of the empire against the Saracens, Or, if it was thought more expedient for the protection of the empire and the holy Church, over which you are ruler, we might at once, and by open force, have defended the frontiers of our states, against a host commanded by so many different and discording chiefs, and advancing upon us with such equivocal intentions. If the first swarm of these locusts, under him whom they called Walter the Penniless, was thinned by the Hungarians, and totally destroyed by the Turks, as the pyramids of bones on the frontiers of the country still keep in memory, surely the united forces of the Grecian empire would have had little difficulty in scattering this second flight, though commanded by these Godfreys, Bohemonds, and Tancreds."

The Patriarch was silent, for though he disliked, or rather detested the crusaders, as members of the Latin Church, he yet thought it highly doubtful that in feats of battle they could have been met and overcome by the Grecian forces.

"At any rate," said Alexius, rightly interpreting his silence, "if vanquished, I had fallen under my shield as a Greek emperor should, nor had I been forced into these mean measures of attacking men by stealth, and with forces disguised as infidels; while the lives of the faithful soldiers of the empire, who have fallen in obscure
skirmishes, had better, both for them and me, been lost bravely in their ranks, avowedly fighting for their native emperor and their native country. Now, and as the matter stands, I shall be handed down to posterity as a wily tyrant, who engaged his subjects in fatal feuds for the safety of his own obscure life. Patriarch! these crimes rest not with me, but with the rebels whose intrigues compelled me into such courses—What, reverend father, will be my fate hereafter?
—and in what light shall I descend to posterity, the author of so many disasters?"

"For futurity," said the Patriarch, "your grace hath referred yourself to the holy Church, which hath power to bind and loose; your means of propitiating her are ample, and I have already indicated such as she may reasonably expect, in consequence of your repentance and forgiveness."

"They shall be granted," replied the Emperor, "in their fullest extent; nor will I injure you in doubting their effect in the next world. In this present state of existence, however, the favourable opinion of the Church may do much for me during this important crisis. If we understand each other, good Zosimus, her doctors and bishops are to thunder in my behalf, nor is my benefit from her pardon, to be deferred till the funeral monument closes upon me?"

"Certainly not," said Zosimus; "the conditions which I have already stipulated being strictly attended to."

"And my memory in history," said Alexius, "in what manner is that to be preserved?"

"For that," answered the Patriarch, "your Imperial Majesty must trust to the filial piety and literary talents of your accomplished daughter, Anna Comnena."

The Emperor shook his head. "This unhappy Caesar," he said, "is like to make a quarrel between us; for I shall scarce pardon so ungrateful a rebel as he is, because my daughter clings to him with a woman's fondness. Besides, good Zosimus, it is not, I believe, the page of a historian such as my daughter that is most likely to be received without challenge by posterity. Some Procopius, some philosophical slave, starving in a garret, aspires to write the life of an Emperor whom he durst not approach; and although the principal merit of his production be, that it contains particulars upon the subject which no man durst have promulgated while the prince was living, yet no man hesitates to admit such as true when he has passed from the scene."

"On that subject," said Zosimus, "I can neither afford your Imperial Majesty relief or protection. If, however, your memory is unjustly slandered upon earth, it will be a matter of indifference to your Highness, who will be then, I trust, enjoying a state of beatitude which idle slander cannot assail. The only way, indeed, to avoid it while on this side of time, would be to write your Majesty's own memoirs while you are yet in the body; so convinced am I that it is in your power to assign legitimate excuses for those actions of your life, which, without your doing so, would seem most worthy of censure."

"Change we the subject," said the Emperor; "and since the danger is imminent, let us take care for the present, and leave future ages to judge for themselves.—What circumstance is it, reverend father, in your opinion, which encourages these conspirators to make so audacious an appeal to the populace and the Grecian soldiers?"

"Certainly," answered the Patriarch, "the most irritating incident of your highness's reign was the fate of Ursel, who, submitting, it is said, upon capitulation, for life, limb, and liberty, was starved to death by your orders, in the dungeons of the Blacquernal, and whose courage, liberality, and other popular virtues, are still fondly remembered by the citizens of this metropolis, and by the soldiers of the guard, called Immortal."

"And this," said the Emperor, fixing his eye upon his confessor, "your reverence esteems actually the most dangerous point of the popular tumult?"

"I cannot doubt," said the Patriarch, "that his very name, boldly pronounced, and artfully repeated, will be the watchword, as has been plotted, of a horrible tumult."

"I thank Heaven!" said the Emperor; "on that particular I will be on my guard. Good–night to your reverence! and, believe me, that all in this scroll, to which I have set my hand, shall be with the utmost fidelity accomplished. Be not, however, over–impatient in this business;—such a shower of benefits falling at once upon the Church, would make men suspicious that the prelates and ministers proceeded rather as acting upon a bargain between the Emperor and Patriarch, than as paying or receiving an atonement offered by a sinner in excuse of his crimes. This would be injurious, father, both to yourself and me."

"All regular delay," said the Patriarch, "shall be interposed at your highness's pleasure; and we shall trust to you for recollection that the bargain, if it could be termed one, was of your own seeking, and that the benefit to the Church was contingent upon the pardon and the support which she has afforded to your majesty."

"True," said the Emperor—"most true—nor shall I forget it. Once more adieu, and forget not what I have told thee. This is a night, Zosimus, in which the Emperor must toil like a slave, if he means not to return to the humble Alexius Comnenus, and even then there were no resting– place."

So saying, he took leave of the Patriarch, who was highly gratified with the advantages he had obtained for the Church, which many of his predecessors had struggled for in vain. He resolved, therefore, to support the staggering Alexius.

CHAPTER THE TWENTY-FIFTH

Heaven knows its time; the bullet has its billet, Arrow
and javelin each its destined purpose; The fated beasts
of Nature's lower strain
Have each their separate task. OLD
PLAY.

Agelastes, after crossing the Emperor in the manner we have already
described, and after having taken such measures as occurred to him to ensure
the success of the conspiracy, returned to the lodge of his garden, where the
lady of the Count of Paris still remained, her only companion being an old
woman named Vexhelia, the wife of the soldier who accompanied Bertha to
the camp of the Crusaders; the kind–hearted maiden having stipulated that,
during her absence, her mistress was not to be left without an attendant, and
that attendant
connected with the Varangian guard. He had been all day playing the part of
the ambitious politician, the selfish time–server, the dark and subtle
conspirator; and now it seemed, as if to exhaust the catalogue of his various
parts in the human drama, he chose to exhibit himself in the character of the
wily sophist, and justify, or seem to justify,
the arts by which he had risen to wealth and eminence, and hoped even
now to arise to royalty itself.

"Fair Countess," he said, "what occasion is there for your wearing this veil
of sadness over a countenance so lovely?"

"Do you suppose me," said Brenhilda, "a stock, or stone, or a creature
without the feelings of a sensitive being, that I should endure mortification,
imprisonment, danger and distress, without expressing the natural feelings of
humanity? Do you imagine that to a lady like me, as free as the unreclaimed
falcon, you can offer the insult of captivity, without my being sensible to the
disgrace, or incensed against the authors of it? And dost thou think that I will
receive consolation at thy hands—at thine—one of the most active

artificers in this web of treachery in which I am so basely entangled?"

"Not entangled certainly by my means"—answered Agelastes; "clap your hands, call for what you wish, and the slave who refuses instant obedience had better been unborn. Had I not, with reference to your safety and your honour, agreed for a short time to be your keeper, that office would have been usurped by the Caesar, whose object you know, and may partly guess the modes by which it would be pursued. Why then dost thou childishly weep at being held for a short space in an honourable restraint, which the renowned arms of your husband will probably put an end to long ere to–morrow at noon?"

"Canst thou not comprehend," said the Countess, "thou man of many words, but of few honourable thoughts, that a heart like mine, which has been trained in the feelings of reliance upon my own worth and valour, must be necessarily affected with shame at being obliged to accept, even from the sword of a husband, that safety which I would gladly have owed only to my own?"

"Thou art misled, Countess," answered the philosopher, "by thy pride, a failing predominant in woman. Thinkest thou there has been no offensive assumption in laving aside the character of a mother and a wife, and adopting that of one of those brain–sick female fools, who, like the bravoes of the other sex, sacrifice every thing that is honourable or useful to a frantic and insane affectation of courage? Believe me, fair lady, that the true system of virtue consists in filling thine own place gracefully in society, breeding up thy children, and delighting those of the other sex, and any thing beyond this, may well render thee hateful or terrible, but can add nothing to thy amiable qualities."

"Thou pretendest," said the Countess, "to be a philosopher; methinks thou shouldst know, that the fame which hangs its chaplet on the tomb of a brave hero or heroine, is worth all the petty engagements in which ordinary persons spend the current of their time. One hour of life, crowded to the full with glorious action, and filled with noble risks, is worth whole years of those mean observances of paltry decorum, in which men steal through existence, like sluggish waters through a marsh, without either honour or observation."

"Daughter," said Agelastes, approaching near to the lady, "it is with pain I see you bewildered in errors which a little calm reflection might remove. We may flatter ourselves, and human vanity usually does so, that beings infinitely more powerful than those belonging to mere humanity, are employed daily in measuring out the good and evil of this world, the termination of combats, or the fate of empires, according to their own ideas of what is right or wrong, or, more properly, according to what we ourselves conceive to be such. The Greek heathens, renowned for their wisdom, and glorious for their actions, explained to men of ordinary minds the supposed existence of Jupiter and his Pantheon, where various deities presided over various virtues and vices, and regulated the temporal fortune and future happiness of such as practised them. The more learned and wise of the ancients rejected such the vulgar interpretation, and wisely, although affecting a deference to the public faith, denied before their disciples in private, the gross fallacies of Tartarus and Olympus, the vain doctrines concerning the gods themselves, and the extravagant expectations which the vulgar entertained of an immortality, supposed to be possessed by creatures who were in every respect mortal, both in the conformation of their bodies, and in the internal belief of their souls. Of these wrise and good men some granted the existence of the supposed deities, but denied that they cared about the actions of mankind any more than those of the inferior animals. A merry, jovial, careless life, such as the followers of Epicurus would choose for themselves, was what they assigned for those gods whose being they admitted. Others, more bold or more consistent, entirely denied the existence of deities who apparently had no proper object or purpose, and believed that such of them, whose being and attributes were proved to us by no supernatural appearances, had in reality no existence whatever."

"Stop, wretch!" said the Countess, "and know that thou speakest not to one of those blinded heathens, of whose abominable doctrines you are detailing the result. Know, that if an erring, I am nevertheless a sincere daughter of the Church, and this cross displayed on my shoulder, is a sufficient emblem of the vows I have undertaken in its cause. Bo therefore wary, as thou art wily; for, believe me, if thou scoffest or utterest reproach against my holy religion, what I am unable to answer in language, I will reply to, without hesitation, with the point of my dagger."

"To that argument" said Agelastes, drawing back from the neighbourhood of Brenhilda, "believe me, fair lady, I am very willing to urge your gentleness. But although I shall not venture to say any thing of those superior and benevolent powers to whom you ascribe the management of the world, you will surely not take offence at my noticing those base superstitions which have been adopted in explanation of what is called by the Magi, the Evil Principle. Was there ever received into a human creed, a being so mean— almost so ridiculous—as the Christian Satan? A goatish figure and limbs, with grotesque features, formed to express the most execrable passions; a degree of power scarce inferior to that of the Deity; and a talent at the same time scarce equal to that of the stupidest of the lowest order! What is he, this being, who is at least the second arbiter of the human race, save an immortal spirit, with the petty spleen and spite of a vindictive old man or old woman?"

Agelastes made a singular pause in this part of his discourse. A mirror of considerable size hung in the apartment, so that the philosopher could see in its reflection the figure of Brenhilda, and remark the change of her countenance, though she had averted her face from him in hatred of the doctrines which he promulgated. On this glass the philosopher had his eyes naturally fixed, and he was confounded at perceiving a figure glide from behind the shadow of a curtain, and glare at him with the supposed mien and expression of the Satan of monkish mythology, or a satyr of the heathen age.

"Man!" said Brenhilda, whose attention was attracted by this extraordinary apparition, as it seemed, of the fiend, "have thy wicked words, and still more wicked thoughts, brought the devil amongst us? If so, dismiss him instantly, else, by Our Lady of the Broken Lances! thou shalt know better than at present, what is the temper of a Frankish maiden, when in presence of the fiend himself, and those who pretend skill to raise him! I wish not to enter into a contest unless compelled; but if I am obliged to join battle with an enemy so horrible, believe me, no one shall say that Brenildha feared him."

Agelastes, after looking with surprise and horror at the figure as reflected in the glass, turned back his head to examine the substance, of which the reflection was so strange. The object, however, had disappeared behind the curtain, under which it probably lay hid, and it was after a minute or two that the half–gibing, half–scowling countenance showed itself again in the same position in the mirror.

"By the gods!" said Agelastes—

"In whom but now," said the Countess, "you professed unbelief." "By the

gods!" repeated Agelastes, in part recovering himself, "it is Sylvan! that singular mockery of humanity, who was said to have been brought from Taprobana. I warrant he also believes in his jolly god Pan, or the veteran Sylvanus. He is to the uninitiated a creature whose appearance is full of terrors, but he shrinks before the philosopher like ignorance before knowledge." So saying, he with one hand pulled down the curtain, under which the animal had nestled itself when it entered from the garden–window of the pavilion, and with the other, in which he had a staff uplifted, threatened to chastise the creature, with the words,—"How now, Sylvanus! what insolence is this?—To your place!"

As, in uttering these words, he struck the animal, the blow unluckily lighted upon his wounded hand, and recalled its bitter smart. The wild temper of the creature returned, unsubdued for the moment by any awe of man; uttering a fierce, and, at the same time, stifled cry, it flew on the philosopher, and clasped its strong and sinewy arms about his throat with the utmost fury. The old man twisted and struggled to deliver himself from the creature's grasp, but in vain. Sylvan kept hold of his prize, compressed his sinewy arms, and abode by his purpose of not quitting his hold of the philosopher's throat till he had breathed his last. Two more bitter yells, accompanied each with a desperate contortion of the countenance, and squeeze of the hands, concluded, in less than five minutes, the dreadful strife. Agelastes lay dead upon the ground, and his assassin Sylvan, springing from the body as if terrified and alarmed at what he had done, made his escape by the window. The Countess stood in astonishment, not knowing exactly whether she had witnessed a supernatural display of the judgment of Heaven, or an instance of its vengeance by mere mortal means. Her new attendant Vexhelia was no less astonished, though her acquaintance with the animal was considerably more intimate.

"Lady," she said, "that gigantic creature is an animal of great strength, resembling mankind in form, but huge in its size, and, encouraged by its immense power, sometimes malevolent in its intercourse with mortals. I have heard the Varangians often talk of it as belonging to the Imperial museum. It is fitting we remove the body of this unhappy man, and hide it in a plot of shrubbery in the garden. It is not likely that he will be missed to–night, and to– morrow there will be other matter astir, which will probably prevent much enquiry about him." The Countess Brenhilda assented, for she was not one of those timorous females to whom the countenances of the dead are objects of terror.

Trusting to the parole which she had given, Agelastes had permitted the Countess and her attendant the freedom of his gardens, of that part at least adjacent to the pavilion. They therefore were in little risk of interruption as they bore forth the dead body between them, and without much trouble disposed of it in the thickest part of one of the bosquets with which the garden was studded.

As they returned to their place of abode or confinement, the Countess, half speaking to herself, half addressing Vexhelia, said, "I am sorry for this; not that the infamous wretch did not deserve the full punishment of Heaven coming upon him in the very moment of blasphemy and infidelity, but because the courage and truth of the unfortunate Brenhilda may be brought into suspicion, as his slaughter took place when he was alone with her and her attendant, and as no one was witness of the singular manner in which the old blasphemer met his end.—Thou knowest," she added, addressing herself to Heaven—"thou! blessed Lady of the Broken Lances, the protectress both of Brenhilda and her husband, well knowest, that whatever faults may be mine, I am free from the slightest suspicion of treachery; and into thy hands I put my cause, with a perfect reliance upon thy wisdom and bounty to bear evidence in my favour." So saying, they returned to the lodge unseen, and with pious and submissive prayers, the Countess closed that eventful evening.

CHAPTER THE TWENTY-SIXTH

Will you hear of a Spanish lady, How she
wooed an Englishman? Garments gay, as
rich as may be, Deck'd with jewels she had
on.
Of a comely countenance and grace was she, And by
birth and parentage of high degree. OLD BALLAD.

We left Alexius Comnenus after he had unloaded his conscience in the ears of
the Patriarch, and received from him a faithful assurance of the pardon and
patronage of the national Church. He took leave of the dignitary with some
exulting exclamations, so unexplicitly expressed, however, that it was by no
means easy to conceive the meaning of what he said. His first enquiry, when
he reached the Blacquernal, being for his daughter, he was directed to the
room encrusted with beautifully carved marble, from which she herself, and
many of her race, derived the proud appellation of *Porphyrogenita*, or born in
the purple. Her countenance was clouded with anxiety, which, at the sight of
her father, broke out into open
and uncontrollable grief.

"Daughter," said the Emperor, with a harshness little common to his manner,
and a seriousness which he sternly maintained, instead of sympathizing with
his daughter's affliction, "as you would prevent the silly fool with whom you
are connected, from displaying himself to the public both as an ungrateful
monster and a traitor, you will not fail to exhort him, by due submission, to
make his petition for pardon, accompanied with a full confession of his
crimes, or, by my sceptre and my crown, he shall die the death! Nor will I
pardon any who rushes upon his doom in an open tone of defiance, under such
a standard of rebellion as my ungrateful son–in–law has hoisted.

"What can you require of me, father?" said the Princess. "Can you expect that I am to dip my own hands in the blood of this unfortunate man; or wilt thou seek a revenge yet more bloody than that which was exacted by the deities of antiquity, upon those criminals who offended against their divine power?"

"Think not so, my daughter!" said the Emperor; "but rather believe that thou hast the last opportunity afforded by my filial affection, of rescuing, perhaps from death, that silly fool thy husband, who has so richly deserved it."

"My father," said the Princess, "God knows it is not at your risk that I would wish to purchase the life of Nicephorus; but he has been the father of my children, though they are now no more, and women cannot forget that such a tie has existed, even though it has been broken by fate. Permit me only to hope that the unfortunate culprit shall have an opportunity of retrieving his errors; nor shall it, believe me, be my fault, if he resumes those practices, treasonable at once, and unnatural, by which his life is at present endangered."

"Follow me, then, daughter," said the Emperor, "and know, that to thee alone I am about to intrust a secret, upon which the safety of my life and crown, as well as the pardon of my son–in–law's life, will be found eventually to depend."

He then assumed in haste the garment of a slave of the Seraglio, and commanded his daughter to arrange her dress in a more succinct form, and to take in her hand a lighted lamp.

"Whither are we going, my father?" said Anna Comnena.

"It matters not," replied her father, "since my destiny calls me, and since thine ordains thee to be my torch–bearer. Believe it, and record it, if thou darest, in thy book, that Alexius Comnenus does not, without alarm, descend into those awful dungeons—which his predecessors built for men, even when his intentions are innocent, and free from harm.—Be silent, and should we meet any inhabitant of those inferior regions, speak not a word nor make any observation upon his appearance."

Passing through the intricate apartments of the palace, they now came to that large hall through which Hereward had passed on the first night of his introduction to the place of Anna's recitation called the Temple of the Muses. It was constructed, as we have said, of black marble, dimly illuminated. At the upper end of the apartment was a small altar, on which was laid some incense, while over the smoke was suspended, as if projecting from the wall, two imitations of human hands and arms, which were but imperfectly seen.

At the bottom of this hall, a small iron door led to a narrow and winding staircase, resembling a draw—well in shape and size, the steps of which were excessively steep, and which the Emperor, after a solemn gesture to his daughter commanding her attendance, began to descend with the imperfect light, and by the narrow and difficult steps by which those who visited the under regions of the Blacquernal seemed to bid adieu to the light of day. Door after door they passed in their descent, leading, it was probable, to different ranges of dungeons, from which was obscurely heard the stifled voice of groans and sighs, such as attracted Hereward's attention on a former occasion. The Emperor took no notice of these signs of human misery, and three stories or ranges of dungeons had been already passed, ere the father and daughter arrived at the lowest story of the building, the base of which was the solid rock, roughly carved, upon which were erected the side—walls and arches of solid but unpolished marble.

"Here," said Alexius Comnenus, "all hope, all expectation takes farewell, at the turn of a hinge or the grating of a lock. Yet shall not this be always the case—the dead shall revive and resume their right, and the disinherited of these regions shall again prefer their claim to inhabit the upper world. If I cannot entreat Heaven to my assistance, be assured, my daughter, that rather than be the poor animal which I have stooped to be thought, and even to be painted in thy history, I would sooner brave every danger of the multitude which now erect themselves betwixt me and safety. Nothing is resolved save that I
will live and die an Emperor; and thou, Anna, be assured, that if there is power in the beauty or in the talents, of which so much has been boasted, that power shall be this evening exercised to the advantage of thy parent, from whom it is derived."

"What is it that you mean, Imperial father?—Holy Virgin! is this the promise you made me to save the life of the unfortunate Nicephorus?"

"And so I will," said the Emperor; "and I am now about that action of benevolence. But think not I will once more warm in my bosom the household snake which had so nearly stung me to death. No, daughter, I have provided for thee a fitting husband, in one who is able to maintain and defend the rights of the Emperor thy father;— and beware how thou opposest an obstacle to what is my pleasure! for behold these walls of marble, though unpolished, and recollect it is as possible to die within the marble as to be born there."

The Princess Anna Comnena was frightened at seeing her father in a state of mind entirely different from any which she had before witnessed. "O, heaven! that my mother were here!" she ejaculated, in the terror of something she hardly knew what.

"Anna," said the Emperor, "your fears and your screams are alike in vain. I am one of those, who, on ordinary occasions, hardly nourish a wish of my own, and account myself obliged to those who, like my wife and daughter, take care to save me all the trouble of free judgment. But when the vessel is among the breakers, and the master is called to the helm, believe that no meaner hand shall be permitted to interfere with him, nor will the wife and daughter, whom he indulged in prosperity, be allowed to thwart his will while he can yet call it his own. Thou couldst scarcely fail to understand that I was almost prepared to have given thee, as a mark of my sincerity, to yonder obscure Varangian, without asking question of either birth or blood. Thou mayst hear when I next promise thee to a three years' inhabitant of these vaults, who shall be Caesar in Briennius's stead, if I can move him to accept a princess for his bride, and an imperial crown for his inheritance, in place of a starving dungeon."

"I tremble at your words, father," said Anna Comnena; "how canst thou trust a man who has felt thy cruelty?—How canst thou dream that aught can ever in sincerity reconcile thee to one whom thou hast deprived of his eyesight?"

"Care not for that," said Alexius; "he becomes mine, or he shall never know what it is to be again his own.—And thou, girl, mayst rest assured that, if I will it, thou art next day the bride of my present captive, or thou retirest to the most severe nunnery, never again to mix with society. Be silent, therefore, and await thy doom, as it shall come, and hope not that thy utmost endeavours can avert the current of thy destiny."

As he concluded this singular dialogue, in which he had assumed a tone to which his daughter was a stranger, and before which she trembled, he passed on through more than one strictly fastened door, while his daughter, with a faltering step, illuminated him on the obscure road. At length he found admittance by another passage into the cell in which Ursel was confined, and found him reclining in hopeless misery,—all those expectations having faded from his heart which the Count of Paris had by his indomitable gallantry for a time excited. He turned his sightless eyes towards the place where he heard the moving of bolts and the approach of steps.

"A new feature," he said, "in my imprisonment—a man comes with a heavy and determined step, and a woman or a child with one that scarcely presses the floor!—is it my death that you bring?—Believe me, that I have lived long enough in these dungeons to bid my doom welcome."

"It is not thy death, noble Ursel," said the Emperor, in a voice somewhat disguised. Life, liberty, whatever the world has to give, is placed by the Emperor Alexius at the feet of his noble enemy, and he trusts that many years of happiness and power, together with the command of a large share of the empire, will soon obliterate the recollection of the dungeons of the Blacquernal."

"It cannot be," said Ursel, with a sigh. "He upon whose eyes the sun has set even at middle day, can have nothing left to hope from the most advantageous change of circumstances."

"You are not entirely assured of that," said the Emperor; "allow us to convince you that what is intended towards you is truly favourable and liberal, and I hope you will be rewarded by finding that there is more possibility of amendment in your case, than your first apprehensions are willing to receive. Make an effort, and try whether your eyes are not sensible of the light of the lamp."

"Do with, me," said Ursel, "according to your pleasure; I have neither strength to remonstrate, nor the force of mind equal to make me set your cruelty at defiance. Of something like light I am sensible; but whether it is reality or illusion, I cannot determine. If you are come to deliver me from this living sepulchre, I pray God to requite you; and if, under such deceitful pretence, you mean to take my life, I can only commend my soul to Heaven, and the vengeance due to my death to Him who can behold the darkest places in which injustice can shroud itself."

So saying, and the revulsion of his spirits rendering him unable to give almost any other signs of existence, Ursel sunk back upon his seat of captivity, and spoke not another word during the time that Alexius disembarrassed him of those chains which had so long hung about him, that they almost seemed to make a part of his person.

"This is an affair in which thy aid can scarce be sufficient, Anna," said the Emperor; "it would have been well if you and I could have borne him into the open air by our joint strength, for there is little wisdom in showing the secrets of this prison–house to those to whom they are not yet known; nevertheless, go, my child, and at a short distance from the head of the staircase which we descended, thou wilt find Edward, the bold and trusty Varangian, who on your communicating to him my orders, will come hither and render his assistance; and see that you send also the experienced leech, Douban." Terrified, half– stifled, and half struck with horror, the lady yet felt a degree of relief from the somewhat milder tone in which her father addressed her. With tottering steps, yet in some measure encouraged by the tenor of her instructions, she ascended the staircase which yawned upon these infernal dungeons. As she
approached the top, a large and strong figure threw its broad shadow between the lamp and the opening of the hall. Frightened nearly to death at the thoughts of becoming the wife of a squalid wretch like Ursel, a moment of weakness seized upon the Princess's mind, and, when she considered the melancholy option which her father had

placed before her, she could not but think that the handsome and gallant Varangian, who had already rescued the royal family from such imminent danger, was a fitter person with whom to unite herself, if she must needs make a second choice, than the singular and disgusting being whom her father's policy had raked from the bottom of the Blacquernal dungeons.

I will not say of poor Anna Comnena, who was a timid but not an unfeeling woman, that she would have embraced such a proposal, had not the life of her present husband Nicephorus Briennius been in extreme danger; and it was obviously the determination of the Emperor, that if he spared him, it should be on the sole condition of unloosing his daughter's hand, and binding her to some one of better faith, and possessed of a greater desire to prove an affectionate son– in–law. Neither did the plan of adopting the Varangian as a second husband, enter decidedly into the mind of the Princess. The present was a moment of danger, in which her rescue to be successful must be sudden, and perhaps, if once achieved, the lady might have had an opportunity of freeing herself both from Ursel and the Varangian, without disjoining either of them from her father's assistance, or of herself losing it. At any rate, the surest means of safety were to secure, if possible, the young soldier, whose features and appearance were of a kind which rendered the task no way disagreeable to a beautiful woman. The schemes of conquest are so natural to the fair sex, and the whole idea passed so quickly through Anna Comnena's mind, that having first entered while the soldier's shadow was interposed between her and the lamp, it had fully occupied her quick imagination, when, with deep reverence and great surprise at her sudden appearance on the ladder of Acheron, the Varangian advancing, knelt down, and lent his arm to the assistance of the fair lady, in order to help her out of the dreary staircase.

"Dearest Hereward," said the lady, with a degree of intimacy which seemed unusual, "how much do I rejoice, in this dreadful night, to have fallen under your protection! I have been in places which the spirit of hell appears to have contrived for the human race." The alarm of the Princess, the familiarity of a beautiful woman, who, while in mortal fear, seeks refuge, like a frightened dove, in the bosom of the strong and the brave, must be the excuse of Anna

Comnena for the tender epithet with which she greeted Hereward; nor, if he had chosen to answer in the same tone, which, faithful as he was, might have proved the case if the meeting had chanced before he saw Bertha, would the daughter of Alexius have been, to say the truth, irreconcilably offended. Exhausted as she was, she suffered herself to repose upon, the broad breast and shoulder of the Anglo–Saxon; nor did she make an attempt to recover herself, although the decorum of her sex and station seemed to recommend such an exertion. Hereward was obliged himself to ask her, with the unimpassioned and reverential demeanour of a private soldier to a princess, whether he ought to summon her female attendants? to which she faintly uttered a negative. "No, no," said she, "I have a duty to execute for my father, and I must not summon eye– witnesses;—he knows me to be in safety, Hereward, since he knows I am with thee; and if I am a burden to you in my present state of weakness, I shall soon recover, if you will set me down upon the marble steps."

"Heaven forbid, lady," said Hereward, "that I were thus neglectful of your Highness's gracious health! I see your two young ladies, Astarte and Violante, are in quest of you—Permit me to summon them
hither, and I will keep watch upon you, if you are unable to retire to your chamber, where, methinks, the present disorder of your nerves will be most properly treated."

"Do as thou wilt, barbarian," said the Princess, rallying herself, with a certain degree of pique, arising perhaps from her not thinking more *dramatis personae* were appropriate to the scene, than the two who were already upon the stage. Then, as if for the first time, appearing to recollect the message with which she had been commissioned, she exhorted the Varangian to repair instantly to her father.

On such occasions, the slightest circumstances have their effect on the actors. The Anglo–Saxon was sensible that the Princess was somewhat offended, though whether she was so, on account of her being actually in Hereward's arms, or whether the cause of her anger was the being nearly discovered there by the two young maidens, the sentinel did not presume to guess, but departed for the gloomy vaults to join Alexius, with the never–failing double–edged axe, the bane of many a Turk, glittering upon his shoulder.

Astarte and her companion had been despatched by the Empress Irene in search of Anna Comnena, through those apartments of the palace which she was wont to inhabit. The daughter of Alexius could nowhere be found, although the business on which they were
seeking her was described by the Empress as of the most pressing nature. Nothing, however, in a palace, passes altogether unespied, so that the Empress's messengers at length received information that their mistress and the Emperor had been seen to descend that gloomy access to the dungeons, which, by allusion to the classical infernal regions, was termed the Pit of Acheron. They came thither, accordingly, and we have related the consequences. Hereward thought it necessary to say that her Imperial Highness had swooned upon being suddenly brought into the upper air. The Princess, on the other part, briskly shook off her juvenile attendants, and declared herself ready to proceed to the chamber of her mother. The obeisance which she made Hereward at parting, had something in it of haughtiness, yet evidently qualified by a look of friendship and regard. As she passed an apartment in which some of the royal slaves were in waiting, she addressed to one of them, an old respectable man, of medical skill, a private and hurried order, desiring him to go to the assistance of her father, whom he would find at the bottom of the staircase called the Pit of Acheron, and to
take his scimitar along with him. To hear, as usual, was to obey, and Douban, for that was his name, only replied by that significant sign which indicates immediate acquiescence. In the meantime, Anna Comnena herself hastened onward to her mother's apartments, in which she found the Empress alone.

"Go hence, maidens," said Irene, "and do not let any one have access to these apartments, even if the Emperor himself should command it. Shut the door," she said, "Anna Comnena; and if the jealousy of the stronger sex do not allow us the masculine privileges of bolts and bars, to secure the insides of our apartments, let us avail ourselves,
as quickly as may be, of such opportunities as are permitted us; and remember, Princess, that however implicit your duty to your father, it is yet more so to me, who am of the same sex with thyself, and may truly call thee, even according to the letter, blood of my blood,

and bone of my bone. Be assured thy father knows not, at this moment, the feelings of a woman. Neither he nor any man alive can justly conceive the pangs of the heart which beats under a woman's robe. These men, Anna, would tear asunder without scruple the tenderest ties of affection, the whole structure of domestic felicity, in which lie a woman's cares, her joy, her pain, her love, and her despair. Trust, therefore, to me, my daughter, and believe me, I will at once save thy father's crown and thy happiness. The conduct of thy husband has been wrong, most cruelly wrong; but, Anna, he is a man— and in calling him such, I lay to his charge, as natural frailties, thoughtless treachery, wanton infidelity, every species of folly and inconsistency, to which his race is subject. You ought not, therefore, to think of his faults, unless it be to forgive them."

"Madam," said Anna Comnena, "forgive me if I remind you that you recommend to a princess, born in the purple itself, a line of conduct which would hardly become the female who carries the pitcher for the needful supply of water to the village well. All who are around me have been taught to pay me the obeisance due to my birth, and while this Nicephorus Briennius crept on his knees to your
daughter's hand, which you extended towards him, he was rather receiving the yoke of a mistress than accepting a household alliance with a wife. He has incurred his doom, without a touch even of that temptation which may be pled by lesser culprits in his condition; and if it is the will of my father that he should die, or suffer banishment, or imprisonment, for the crime he has committed, it is not the business of Anna Comnena to interfere, she being the most injured among the imperial family, who have in so many, and such gross respects, the right to complain of his falsehood."

"Daughter," replied the Empress, "so far I agree with you, that the treason of Nicephorus towards your father and myself has been in a great degree unpardonable; nor do I easily see on what footing, save that of generosity, his life could be saved. But still you are yourself in different circumstances from me, and may, as an affectionate and fond wife, compare the intimacies of your former habits with the bloody change which is so soon to be the consequence and the conclusion of his crimes. He is possessed of that person and of those features which women most readily recall to their memory, whether alive or dead. Think what it will cost you to recollect that the rugged executioner received his last salute,—that the shapely neck had no better repose than the rough block—that the tongue, the sound of which you used to prefer to the choicest instruments of music, is silent in the dust!"

Anna, who was not insensible to the personal graces of her husband, was much affected by this forcible appeal. "Why distress me thus, mother?" she replied in a weeping accent. "Did I not feel as acutely as you would have me to do, this moment, however awful, would be easily borne. I had but to think of him as he is, to contrast his personal qualities with those of the mind, by which they are more than overbalanced, and resign myself to his deserved fate with unresisting submission to my father's will."

"And that," said the Empress, "would be to bind thee, by his sole fiat, to some obscure wretch, whose habits of plotting and intriguing had, by some miserable chance, given him the opportunity of becoming of importance to the Emperor, and who is, therefore, to be rewarded by the hand of Anna Comnena."

"Do not think so meanly of me, madam," said the Princess—"I know, as well as ever Grecian maiden did, how I should free myself from dishonour; and, you may trust me, you shall never blush for your daughter."

"Tell me not that," said the Empress, "since I shall blush alike for the relentless cruelty which gives up a once beloved husband to an ignominious death, and for the passion, for which I want a name, which would replace him by an obscure barbarian from the extremity of Thule, or some wretch escaped from the Blacquernal dungeons."

The Princess was astonished to perceive that her mother was acquainted with the purposes, even the most private, which her father had formed for his governance during this emergency. She was ignorant that Alexius and his royal consort, in other respects living together with a decency ever exemplary in people of their rank, had, sometimes, on interesting occasions, family debates, in which the husband, provoked by the seeming unbelief of his partner, was tempted to let her guess more of his real purposes than he would have coolly imparted of his own calm choice.

The Princess was affected at the anticipation of the death of her husband, nor could this have been reasonably supposed to be otherwise; but she was still more hurt and affronted by her mother taking it for granted that she designed upon the instant to replace the Caesar by an uncertain, and at all events an unworthy successor. Whatever considerations had operated to make Hereward her choice, their effect was lost when the match was placed in this odious and degrading point of view; besides which is to be remembered, that women almost instinctively deny their first thoughts in favour of a suitor, and seldom willingly reveal them, unless time and circumstance concur to favour them. She called Heaven therefore passionately to witness, while she repelled the charge.

"Bear witness," she said, "Our Lady, Queen of Heaven! Bear witness, saints and martyrs all, ye blessed ones, who are, more than ourselves, the guardians of our mental purity! that I know no passion which I dare not avow, and that if Nicephorus's life depended on my entreaty to God and men, all his injurious acts towards me disregarded and despised, it should be as long as Heaven gave to those servants whom it snatched from the earth without suffering the pangs of mortality!"

"You have sworn boldly," said the Empress. "See, Anna Comnena, that you keep your word, for believe me it will be tried."

"What will be tried, mother?" said the Princess; "or what have I to do to pronounce the doom of the Caesar, who is not subject to my power?"

"I will show you," said the Empress, gravely; and, leading her towards a sort of wardrobe, which formed a closet in the wall, she withdrew a curtain which hung before it, and placed before her her unfortunate husband, Nicephorus Briennius, half–attired, with his sword drawn in his hand. Looking upon him as an enemy, and conscious of some schemes with respect to him which had passed through her mind in the course of these troubles, the Princess screamed faintly, upon perceiving him so near her with a weapon in his hand.

"Be more composed," said the Empress, "or this wretched man, if discovered, falls no less a victim to thy idle fears than to thy baneful revenge."

Nicephorus at this speech seemed to have adopted his cue, for, dropping the point of his sword, and falling on his knees before the Princess, he clasped his hands to entreat for mercy.

"What hast thou to ask from me?" said his wife, naturally assured, by her husband's prostration, that the stronger force was upon her own side—"what hast thou to ask from me, that outraged gratitude, betrayed affection, the most solemn vows violated, and the fondest ties of nature torn asunder like the spider's broken web, will permit thee to put in words for very shame?"

"Do not suppose, Anna," replied the suppliant, "that I am at this eventful period of my life to play the hypocrite, for the purpose of saving the wretched remnant of a dishonoured existence. I am but desirous to part in charity with thee, to make my peace with Heaven, and to nourish the last hope of making my way, though burdened with many crimes, to those regions in which alone I can find thy beauty, thy talents, equalled at least, if not excelled."

"You hear him, daughter?" said Irene; "his boon is for forgiveness alone; thy condition is the more godlike, since thou mayst unite the safety of his life with the pardon of his offences."

"Thou art deceived, mother," answered Anna. "It is not mine to pardon his guilt, far less to remit his punishment. You have taught me to think of myself as future ages shall know me; what will they say of me, those future ages, when I am described as the unfeeling daughter, who pardoned the intended assassin of her father, because she saw in him her own unfaithful husband?"

"See there," said the Caesar, "is not that, most serene Empress, the very point of despair? and have I not in vain offered my life–blood to wipe out the stain of parricide and ingratitude? Have I not also vindicated myself from the most unpardonable part of the accusation, which charged me with attempting the murder of the godlike Emperor? Have I not sworn by all that is sacred to man, that my purpose went no farther than to sequestrate Alexius for a little time from the fatigues of empire, and place him where he should quietly enjoy ease and tranquillity? while, at the same time, his empire should be as implicitly regulated by himself, his sacred pleasure being transmitted through me, as in any respect, or at any period, it had ever been?"

"Erring man!" said the Princess, "hast thou approached so near to the footstool of Alexius Comnenus, and durst thou form so false an estimate of him, as to conceive it possible that he would consent to
be a mere puppet by whose intervention you might have brought his empire into submission? Know that the blood of Comnenus is not so poor; my father would have resisted the treason in arms; and by the death of thy benefactor only couldst thou have gratified the suggestions of thy criminal ambition."

"Be such your belief," said the Caesar; "I have said enough for a life which is not and ought not to be dear to me. Call your guards, and let them take the life of the unfortunate Briennius, since it has become hateful to his once beloved Anna Comnena. Be not afraid that any resistance of mine shall render the scene of my apprehension
dubious or fatal. Nicephorus Briennius is Caesar no longer, and he thus throws at the feet of his Princess and spouse, the only poor means which he has of resisting the just doom which is therefore at her pleasure to pass."

He cast his sword before the feet of the Princess, while Irene exclaimed, weeping, or seeming to weep bitterly, "I have indeed read of such scenes! but could I ever have thought that my own daughter would have been the principal actress in one of them—could I ever have thought that her mind, admired by every one as a palace for the occupation of Apollo and the Muses, should not have had room enough for the humbler, but more amiable virtue of feminine charity and compassion, which builds itself a nest in the bosom of the lowest village girl? Do thy gifts, accomplishments, and talents, spread hardness as well as polish over thy heart? If so, a hundred times better renounce them all, and retain in their stead those gentle and domestic virtues which are the first honours of the female heart. A woman who is pitiless, is a worse monster than one who is unsexed by any other passion."

"What would you have me do?" said Anna. "You, mother, ought to know better than I, that the life of my father is hardly consistent with the existence of this bold and cruel man. O, I am sure he still meditates his purpose of conspiracy! He that could deceive a woman in the manner he has done me, will not relinquish a plan which is founded upon the death of his benefactor."

"You do me injustice, Anna," said Briennius, starting up, and imprinting a kiss upon her lips ere she was aware. "By this caress, the last that will pass between us, I swear, that if in my life I have yielded to folly, I have, notwithstanding, never been guilty of a treason of the heart towards a woman as superior to the rest of the
female world in talents and accomplishments, as in personal beauty."

The Princess, much softened, shook her head, as she replied—"Ah, Nicephorus!—such were once your words! such, perhaps, were then your thoughts! But who, or what, shall now warrant to me the veracity of either?"

"Those very accomplishments, and that very beauty itself," replied Nicephorus.

"And if more is wanting," said Irene, "thy mother will enter her security for him. Deem her not an insufficient pledge in this affair; she is thy mother, and the wife of Alexius Comnenus, interested beyond all human beings in the growth and increase of the power and dignity of her husband and her child; and one who sees on this occasion an opportunity for exercising generosity, for soldering up the breaches of the Imperial house, and reconstructing the frame of government upon a basis, which, if there be faith and gratitude in man, shall never be again exposed to hazard."

"To the reality of that faith and gratitude, then," said the Princess, "we must trust implicitly, as it is your will, mother; although even my own knowledge of the subject, both through study and experience of the world, has called me to observe the rashness of such confidence. But although we two may forgive Nicephorus's errors, the Emperor is still the person to whom the final reference must be had, both as to pardon and favour."

"Fear not Alexius," answered her mother; "he will speak determinedly and decidedly; but, if he acts not in the very moment of forming the resolution, it is no more to be relied on than an icicle in time of thaw. Do thou apprize me, if thou canst, what the Emperor is at present doing, and take my word I will find means to bring him round to our opinion."

"Must I then betray secrets which my father has intrusted to me?" said the Princess; "and to one who has so lately held the character of his avowed enemy?"

"Call it not betray," said Irene, "since it is written thou shalt betray no one, least of all thy father, and the father of the empire. Yet again it is written, by the holy Luke, that men shall be betrayed, both by parents and brethren, and kinsfolk and friends, and therefore surely also by daughters; by which I only mean thou shalt discover to us thy father's secrets, so far as may enable us to save the life of thy husband. The necessity of the case excuses whatever may be otherwise considered as irregular."

"Be it so then, mother. Having yielded my consent perhaps too easily, to snatch this malefactor from my father's justice, I am sensible I must secure his safety by such means as are in my power. I left my father at the bottom of those stairs, called the Pit of Acheron, in the cell of a blind man, to whom he gave the name of Ursel."

"Holy Mary!" exclaimed the Empress, "thou hast named a name which has been long unspoken in the open air."

"Has the Emperor's sense of his danger from the living," said the Caesar, "induced him to invoke the dead?—for Ursel has been no living man for the space of three years."

"It matters not," said Anna Comnena; "I tell you true. My father even now held conference with a miserable–looking prisoner, whom he so named."

"It is a danger the more," said the Caesar; "he cannot have forgotten the zeal with which I embraced the cause of the present Emperor against his own; and so soon as he is at liberty, he will study to avenge it. For this we must endeavour to make some provision, though it increases our difficulties.—Sit down then, my gentle, my beneficent mother; and thou, my wife, who hast preferred thy love
for an unworthy husband to the suggestions of jealous passion and of headlong revenge, sit down, and let us see in what manner it may be in our power, consistently with your duty to the Emperor, to bring
our broken vessel securely into port."

He employed much natural grace of manner in handing the mother and daughter to their seats; and, taking his place confidentially between them, all were soon engaged in concerting what measures should be taken for the morrow, not forgetting such as should at once have the effect of preserving the Caesar's life, and at the same time of securing the Grecian empire against the conspiracy of which he had been the chief instigator. Briennius ventured to hint, that
perhaps the best way would be to suffer the conspiracy to proceed as originally intended, pledging his own faith that the rights of Alexius should be held inviolate during the struggle; but his influence over the Empress and her daughter did not extend to obtaining so great a trust. They plainly protested against permitting him to leave the palace, or taking the least share in the confusion which to–morrow was certain to witness.

"You forget, noble ladies," said the Caesar, "that my honour is concerned in meeting the Count of Paris."

"Pshaw! tell me not of your honour, Briennius," said Anna Comnena; "do I not well know, that although the honour of the western knights be a species of Moloch, a flesh–devouring, blood– quaffing demon, yet that which is the god of idolatry to the eastern warriors, though equally loud and noisy in the hall, is far less implacable in the field? Believe not that I have forgiven great injuries and insults, in order to take such false coin as *honour* in

payment; your ingenuity is but poor, if you cannot devise some excuse which will satisfy the Greeks; and in good sooth, Briennius, to this battle you go not, whether for your good or for your ill. Believe not that I will consent to your meeting either Count or
Countess, whether in warlike combat or amorous parley. So you may at a word count upon remaining prisoner here until the hour
appointed for such gross folly be past and over."

The Caesar, perhaps, was not in his heart angry that his wife's pleasure was so bluntly and resolutely expressed against the intended combat. "If," said he, "you are determined to take my honour into your own keeping, I am here for the present your prisoner, nor have I the means of interfering with your pleasure. When once at liberty,
the free exercise of my valour and my lance is once more my own."

"Be it so, Sir Paladin," said the Princess, very composedly. "I have good hope that neither of them will involve you with any of yon dare– devils of Paris, whether male or female, and that we will regulate the pitch to which your courage soars, by the estimation of Greek philosophy, and the judgment of our blessed Lady of Mercy, not her of the Broken Lances."

At this moment an authoritative knock at the door alarmed the consultation of the Caesar and the ladies.

CHAPTER THE TWENTY-SEVENTH

Physician. Be comforted, good madam; the great rage, You see
is cured in him: and yet it is danger
To make him even o'er the time he has lost. Desire
him to go in: trouble him no more, Till further
settling.
KING LEAR.

We left the Emperor Alexius Comnenus at the bottom of a subterranean
vault, with a lamp expiring, and having charge of a prisoner, who seemed
himself nearly reduced to the same extremity. For the first two or three
moments, he listened after his daughter's retiring footsteps. He grew
impatient, and began to long for her return before it was possible she could
have traversed the path betwixt him and the summit of these gloomy stairs. A
minute or two he endured with patience the absence of the assistance which
he had sent her to summon; but strange suspicions began to cross his
imagination. Could it be possible? Had she changed her purpose on account
of the hard words which he had used towards her? Had she resolved to leave
her father to his fate in his hour of utmost need? and was he to rely no longer
upon the assistance which he had implored her to send?

The short time which the Princess trifled away in a sort of gallantry with the
Varangian Hereward, was magnified tenfold by the impatience of the
Emperor, who began to think that she was gone to fetch the accomplices of
the Caesar to assault their prince in his defenceless condition, and carry into
effect their half–disconcerted conspiracy.

After a considerable time, filled up with this feeling of agonizing
uncertainty, he began at length, more composedly, to recollect the little
chance there was that the Princess would, even for her own sake, resentful
as she was in the highest degree of her husband's ill

behaviour, join her resources to his, to the destruction of one who had so generally showed himself an indulgent and affectionate father. When he had adopted this better mood, a step was heard upon the staircase, and after a long and unequal descent, Hereward, in his heavy armour, at length coolly arrived at the bottom of the steps. Behind him, panting and trembling, partly with cold and partly with terror, came Douban, the slave well skilled in medicine.

"Welcome, good Edward! Welcome, Douban!" he said, "whose medical skill is sufficiently able to counterbalance the weight of years which hang upon him."

"Your Highness is gracious," said Douban—but what he would have farther said was cut off by a violent fit of coughing, the consequence of his age, of his feeble habit, of the damps of the dungeon, and the rugged exercise of descending the long and difficult staircase.

"Thou art unaccustomed to visit thy patients in so rough an abode," said Alexius; "and, nevertheless, to the damps of these dreary regions state necessity obliges us to confine many, who are no less our beloved subjects in reality than they are in title."

The medical man continued his cough, perhaps as an apology for not giving that answer of assent, with which his conscience did not easily permit him to reply to an observation, which, though stated by one who should know the fact, seemed not to be in itself altogether likely.

"Yes, my Douban," said the Emperor, "in this strong case of steel and adamant have we found it necessary to enclose the redoubted Ursel, whose fame is spread through the whole world, both for military skill, political wisdom, personal bravery, and other noble gifts, which we have been obliged to obscure for a time, in order that we might, at the fittest conjuncture, which is now arrived, restore them to the world in their full lustre. Feel his pulse, therefore, Douban—consider him as one who hath suffered severe confinement, with all its privations, and is about to be suddenly restored to the full enjoyment of life, and whatever renders life valuable."

"I will do my best," said Douban; "but your Majesty must consider, that we work upon a frail and exhausted subject, whose health seems already wellnigh gone, and may perhaps vanish in an instant—like this pale and trembling light, whose precarious condition the life– breath of this unfortunate patient seems closely to resemble."

"Desire, therefore, good Douban, one or two of the mutes who serve in the interior, and who have repeatedly been thy assistants in such cases—or stay—Edward, thy motions will be more speedy; do thou go for the mutes—make them bring some kind of litter to transport the patient; and, Douban, do thou superintend the whole. Transport him instantly to a suitable apartment, only taking care that it be secret, and let him enjoy the comforts of the bath, and whatever else may tend to restore his feeble animation—keeping in mind, that he must, if possible, appear to–morrow in the field."

"That will be hard," said Douban, "after having been, it would appear. subjected to such fare and such usage as his fluctuating pulse intimates but too plainly."

"'Twas a mistake of the dungeon–keeper, the inhuman villain, who should not go without his reward," continued the Emperor, "had not Heaven already bestowed it by the strange means of a sylvan man, or native of the woods, who yesterday put to death the jailor who meditated the death of his prisoner—Yes, my dear Douban, a private sentinel of our guards called the Immortal, had wellnigh annihilated this flower of our trust, whom for a time we were compelled to immure in secret. Then, indeed, a rude hammer had dashed to pieces an unparalleled brilliant, but the fates have arrested such a misfortune."

The assistance having arrived, the physician, who seemed more accustomed to act than to speak, directed a bath to be prepared with medicated herbs, and gave it as his opinion, that the patient should not be disturbed till to–morrow's sun was high in the heavens. Ursel accordingly was assisted to the bath, which was employed according to the directions of the physician; but without affording any material symptoms of recovery. From thence he was transferred to a cheerful bedchamber, opening by an ample window to one of the terraces of the palace, which commanded an extensive prospect. These operations were performed upon a frame so extremely stupified by previous suffering, so dead to the usual sensations of existence, that it was not till the sensibility should be gradually restored by friction of the stiffened limbs, and other means, that the leech hoped the mists of the intellect should at length begin to clear away.

Douban readily undertook to obey the commands of the Emperor, and remained by the bed of the patient until the dawn of morning, ready to support nature as far as the skill of leechcraft admitted.

From the mutes, much more accustomed to be the executioners of the Emperor's displeasure than of his humanity, Douban selected one man of milder mood, and by Alexius's order, made him understand, that the ask in which he was engaged was to be kept most strictly secret, while the hardened slave was astonished to find that the attentions paid to the sick were to be rendered with yet more mystery than the bloody offices of death and torture.

The passive patient received the various acts of attention which were rendered to him in silence; and if not totally without consciousness, at least without a distinct comprehension of their object. After the soothing operation of the bath, and the voluptuous exchange of the rude and musty pile of straw, on which he had stretched himself for years, for a couch of the softest down, Ursel was presented with a sedative draught, slightly tinctured with an opiate. The balmy
restorer of nature came thus invoked, and the captive sunk into a delicious slumber long unknown to him, and which seemed to occupy equally his mental faculties and his bodily frame, while the features were released from their rigid tenor, and the posture of the limbs, no longer disturbed by fits of cramp, and sudden and agonizing twists and throes, seemed changed for a placid state of the most perfect ease and tranquillity.

The morn was already colouring the horizon, and the freshness of the breeze of dawn had insinuated itself into the lofty halls of the palace of the Blacquernal, when a gentle tap at the door of the chamber awakened Douban, who, undisturbed from the calm state of his patient, had indulged himself in a brief repose. The door opened, and a figure appeared, disguised in the robes worn by an officer of the palace, and concealed, beneath an artificial beard of great size, and of a white colour, the features of the Emperor himself. "Douban," said Alexius, "how fares it with thy patient, whose safety is this day of such consequence to the Grecian state?"

"Well, my lord," replied the physician, "excellently well; and if he is not now disturbed, I will wager whatever skill I possess, that nature, assisted by the art of the physician, will triumph over the damps and the unwholesome air of the impure dungeon. Only be prudent, my lord, and let not an untimely haste bring this Ursel forward into the contest ere he has arranged the disturbed current of his ideas, and recovered, in some degree, the spring of his mind, and the powers of his body."

"I will rule my impatience," said the Emperor, "or rather, Douban, I will be ruled by thee. Thinkest thou he is awake?"

"I am inclined to think so," said the leech, "but he opens not his eyes, and seems to me as if he absolutely resisted the natural impulse to rouse himself and look around him."

"Speak to him," said the Emperor, "and let us know what is passing in his mind."

"It is at some risk," replied the physician, "but you shall be obeyed. —Ursel," he said, approaching the bed of his blind patient, and then, in a louder tone, he repeated again, "Ursel! Ursel!"

"Peace—Hush!" muttered the patient; "disturb not the blest in their ecstacy—nor again recall the most miserable of mortals to finish the draught of bitterness which his fate had compelled him to commence."

"Again, again," said the Emperor, aside to Douban, "try him yet again; it is of importance for me to know in what degree he possesses his senses, or in what measure they have disappeared from him."

"I would not, however," said the physician, "be the rash and guilty person, who, by an ill–timed urgency, should produce a total alienation of mind and plunge him back either into absolute lunacy, or produce a stupor in which he might remain for a long period."

"Surely not," replied the Emperor: "my commands are those of one Christian to another, nor do I wish them farther obeyed than as they are consistent with the laws of God and man."

He paused for a moment after this declaration, and yet but few minutes had elapsed ere he again urged the leech to pursue the interrogation of his patient. "If you hold me not competent," said Douban, somewhat vain of the trust necessarily reposed in him, "to judge of the treatment of my patient, your Imperial Highness must take the risk and the trouble upon yourself."

"Marry, I shall," said the Emperor, "for the scruples of leeches are not to be indulged, when the fate of kingdoms and the lives of monarchs are placed against them in the scales.—Rouse thee, my noble Ursel! hear a voice, with which thy ears were once well acquainted, welcome thee back to glory and command! Look around thee, and see how the world smiles to welcome thee back from imprisonment to empire!"

"Cunning fiend!" said Ursel, "who usest the most wily baits in order to augment the misery of the wretched! Know, tempter, that I am conscious of the whole trick of the soothing images of last night— thy baths—thy beds— and thy bowers of bliss.—But sooner shalt thou be able to bring a smile upon the cheek of St. Anthony the Eremite, than induce me to curl mine after the fashion of earthly voluptuaries."

"Try it, foolish man," insisted the Emperor, "and trust to the evidence of thy senses for the reality of the pleasures by which thou art now surrounded; or, if thou art obstinate in thy lack of faith, tarry as thou art for a single moment, and I will bring with me a being so unparalleled in her loveliness, that a single glance of her were worth the restoration of thine eyes, were it only to look upon her for a moment." So saying he left the apartment.

"Traitor," said Ursel, "and deceiver of old, bring no one hither! and strive not, by shadowy and ideal forms of beauty, to increase the delusion that gilds my prison–house for a moment, in order, doubtless, to destroy totally the spark of reason, and then exchange this earthly hell for a dungeon in the infernal regions themselves."

"His mind is somewhat shattered," mused the physician, "which is often the consequence of a long solitary confinement. I marvel much," was his farther thought, "if the Emperor can shape out any rational service which this man can render him, after being so long immured in so horrible a dungeon.—Thou thinkest, then," continued he, addressing the patient, "that the seeming release of last night, with its baths and refreshments, was only a delusive dream, without any reality?"

"Ay—what else?" answered Ursel.

"And that the arousing thyself, as we desire thee to do, would be but a resigning to a vain temptation, in order to wake to more unhappiness than formerly?"

"Even so," returned the patient.

"What, then, are thy thoughts of the Emperor by whose command thou sufferest so severe a restraint?"

Perhaps Douban wished he had forborne this question, for, in the very moment when he put it, the door of the chamber opened, and the Emperor entered, with his daughter hanging upon his arm,
dressed with simplicity, yet with becoming splendour. She had found time, it seems, to change her dress for a white robe, which resembled a kind of mourning, the chief ornament of which was a diamond chaplet, of inestimable value, which surrounded and bound the long sable tresses, that reached from her head to her waist. Terrified
almost to death, she had been surprised by her father in the company of her husband the Caesar, and her mother; and the same thundering mandate had at once ordered Briennius, in the character of a more than suspected traitor, under the custody of a strong guard of Varangians, and commanded her to attend her father to the bedchamber of Ursel, in which she now stood; resolved, however, that she would stick by the sinking fortunes of her husband, even in

the last extremity, yet no less determined that she would not rely upon her own entreaties or remonstrances, until she should see whether her father's interference was likely to reassume a resolved and positive character. Hastily as the plans of Alexius had been formed, and hastily as they had been disconcerted by accident, there remained no slight chance that he might be forced to come round to the purpose on which his wife and daughter had fixed their heart, the forgiveness, namely, of the guilty Nicephorus Briennius. To his astonishment, and not perhaps greatly to his satisfaction, he heard the patient deeply engaged with the physician in canvassing his own character.

"Think not," said Ursel in reply to him, "that though I am immured in this dungeon, and treated as something worse than an outcast of humanity—and although I am, moreover, deprived of my eyesight, the dearest gift of Heaven—think not, I say, though I suffer all this by the cruel will of Alexius Comnenus, that therefore I hold him to be mine enemy; on the contrary, it is by his means that the blinded and miserable prisoner has been taught to seek a liberty far more unconstrained than this poor earth can afford, and a vision far more clear than any Mount Pisgah on this wretched side of the grave can give us: Shall I therefore account the Emperor among mine enemies? He who has taught me the vanity of earthly things—the nothingness of earthly enjoyments—and the pure hope of a better world, as a certain exchange for the misery of the present? No!"

The Emperor had stood somewhat disconcerted at the beginning of this speech, but hearing it so very unexpectedly terminate, as he was willing to suppose, much in his own favour, he threw himself into an attitude which was partly that of a modest person listening to his own praises, and partly that of a man highly struck with the commendations heaped upon him by a generous adversary.

"My friend," he said aloud, "how truly do you read my purpose, when you suppose that the knowledge which men of your disposition can extract from evil, was all the experience which I wished you to derive from a captivity protracted by adverse circumstances, far, very far, beyond my wishes! Let me embrace the generous man who knows so well how to construe the purpose of a perplexed, but still faithful friend." The

patient raised himself in his bed.

"Hold there!" he said, "methinks my faculties begin to collect themselves. Yes," he muttered, "that is the treacherous voice which first bid me welcome as a friend, and then commanded fiercely that I should be deprived of the sight of my eyes!—Increase thy rigour if thou wilt, Comnenus—add, if thou canst, to the torture of my confinement—but since I cannot see thy hypocritical and inhuman features, spare me, in mercy, the sound of a voice, more distressing
to mine ear than toads, than serpents,—than whatever nature has most offensive and disgusting!"

This speech was delivered with so much energy, that it was in vain that the Emperor strove to interrupt its tenor; although he himself, as well as Douban and his daughter, heard a great deal more of the language of unadorned and natural passion than he had counted upon.

"Raise thy head, rash man," he said, "and charm thy tongue, ere it proceed in a strain which may cost thee dear. Look at me, and see if
I have not reserved a reward capable of atoning for all the evil which thy folly may charge to my account."

Hitherto the prisoner had remained with his eyes obstinately shut, regarding the imperfect recollection he had of sights which had been before his eyes the foregoing evening, as the mere suggestion of a deluded imagination, if not actually presented by some seducing spirit. But now when his eyes fairly encountered the stately figure of the Emperor, and the graceful form of his lovely daughter, painted in the tender rays of the morning dawn, he ejaculated faintly, "I see!—I see!"—And with that ejaculation fell back on the pillow in a swoon, which instantly found employment for Douban and his restoratives.

"A most wonderful cure indeed!" exclaimed the physician; "and the height of my wishes would be to possess such another miraculous restorative."

"Fool!" said the Emperor; "canst thou not conceive that what has

never been taken away is restored with little difficulty? He was made," he said, lowering his voice, "to undergo a painful operation, which led him to believe that the organs of sight were destroyed; and as light scarcely ever visited him, and when it did, only in doubtful and invisible glimmerings, the prevailing darkness, both physical
and mental, that surrounded him, prevented him from being sensible of the existence of that precious faculty, of which he imagined himself bereft. Perhaps thou wilt ask my reason for inflicting upon him so strange a deception?—Simply it was, that being by it conceived incapable of reigning, his memory might pass out of the minds of the public, while, at the same time, I reserved his eyesight, that in case occasion should call, it might be in my power once more to liberate him from his dungeon, and employ, as I now propose to do, his courage and talents in the service of the empire, to counterbalance those of other conspirators."

"And can your imperial Highness," said Douban, "hope that you have acquired this man's duty and affection by the conduct you have observed to him?"

"I cannot tell," answered the Emperor; "that must be as futurity shall determine. All I know is, that it is no fault of mine, if Ursel does not reckon freedom and a long course of Empire—perhaps sanctioned
by an alliance with our own blood—and the continued enjoyment of the precious organs of eyesight, of which a less scrupulous man would have deprived him, against a maimed and darkened existence."

"Since such is your Highness's opinion and resolution," said Douban, "it is for me to aid, and not to counteract it. Permit me, therefore, to pray your Highness and the Princess to withdraw, that I may use
such remedies as may confirm a mind which has been so strangely shaken, and restore to him fully the use of those eyes, of which he has been so long deprived."

"I am content, Douban," said the Emperor; "but take notice, Ursel is not totally at liberty until he has expressed the resolution to become actually mine. It may behove both him and thee to know, that although there is no purpose of remitting him to the dungeons of the

Blacquernal palace, yet if he, or any on his part, should aspire to head a party in these feverish times,—by the honour of a gentleman, to swear a Frankish oath, he shall find that he is not out of the reach of the battle–axes of my Varangians. I trust to thee to communicate this fact, which concerns alike him and all who have interest in his fortunes.— Come, daughter, we will withdraw, and leave the leech with his patient —Take notice, Douban, it is of importance that you acquaint me the very first moment when the patient can hold rational communication with me."

Alexius and his accomplished daughter departed accordingly.

CHAPTER THE TWENTY-EIGHTH

Sweet are the uses of adversity,
Which, like the toad, ugly and venomous, Bears
yet a precious jewel in its head.
AS YOU LIKE IT.

From a terraced roof of the Blacquernal palace, accessible by a sash– door, which opened from the bed–chamber of Ursel, there was commanded one of the most lovely and striking views which the romantic neighbourhood of Constantinople afforded.

After suffering him to repose and rest his agitated faculties, it was to this place that the physician led his patient; for when somewhat composed, he had of himself requested to be permitted to verify the truth of his restored eyesight, by looking out once more upon the majestic face of nature.

On the one hand, the scene which he beheld was a masterpiece of human art. The proud city, ornamented with stately buildings, as became the capital of the world, showed a succession of glittering spires and orders of architecture, some of them chaste and simple, like those the capitals of which were borrowed from baskets–full of acanthus; some deriving the fluting of their shafts from the props made originally to support the lances of the earlier Greeks—forms simple, yet more graceful in their simplicity, than any which human ingenuity has been able since to invent. With the most splendid specimens which ancient art could afford of those strictly classical models were associated those of a later age, where more modern taste had endeavoured at improvement, and, by mixing the various orders, had produced such as were either composite, or totally out of rule. The size of the buildings in which they were displayed, however, procured them respect; nor could even the most perfect judge of architecture avoid being struck by the grandeur of their extent and effect, although hurt by the incorrectness of the taste in

which they were executed. Arches of triumph, towers, obelisks, and spires, designed for various purposes, rose up into the air in confused magnificence; while the lower view was filled by the streets of the city, the domestic habitations forming long narrow alleys, on either side of which the houses arose to various and unequal heights, but, being generally finished with terraced coverings, thick set with
plants and flowers, and fountains, had, when seen from an eminence, a more noble and interesting aspect than is ever afforded by the sloping and uniform roofs of streets in the capitals of the north of Europe.

It has taken us some time to give, in words, the idea which was at a single glance conveyed to Ursel, and affected him at first with great pain. His eyeballs had been long strangers to that daily exercise, which teaches us the habit of correcting the scenes as they appear to our sight, by the knowledge which we derive from the use of our other senses. His idea of distance was so confused, that it seemed as if all the spires, turrets, and minarets which he beheld, were crowded forward upon his eyeballs, and almost touching them. With a shriek of horror, Ursel turned himself to the further side, and cast his eyes upon a different scene. Here also he saw towers, steeples, and turrets, but they were those of the churches and public buildings beneath his feet, reflected from the dazzling piece of water which formed the harbour of Constantinople, and which, from the abundance of wealth which it transported to the city, was well termed the Golden Horn. In one place, this superb basin was lined with quays, where stately dromonds and argosies unloaded their wealth, while, by the shore of the haven, galleys, feluccas, and other small craft, idly flapped the singularly shaped and snow–white pinions which served them for sails. In other places the Golden Horn lay shrouded in a verdant mantle of trees, where the private gardens of wealthy or distinguished individuals, or places of public recreation, shot down upon and were bounded by the glassy waters.

On the Bosphorus, which might be seen in the distance, the little fleet of Tancred was lying in the same station they had gained during the night, which was fitted to command the opposite landing; this their general had preferred to a midnight descent upon Constantinople, not knowing whether, so coming, they might be

received as friends or enemies. This delay, however, had given the Greeks an opportunity, either by the orders of Alexius, or the equally powerful mandates of some of the conspirators, to tow six ships of war, full of armed men, and provided with the maritime offensive weapons peculiar to the Greeks at that period, which they had
moored so as exactly to cover the place where the troops of Tancred must necessarily land.

This preparation gave some surprise to the valiant Tancred, who did not know that such vessels had arrived in the harbour from Lemnos on the preceding night. The undaunted courage of that prince was, however, in no respect to be shaken by the degree of unexpected danger with which his adventure now appeared to be attended.

This splendid view, from the description of which we have in some degree digressed, was seen by the physician and Ursel from a terrace, the loftiest almost on the palace of the Blacquernal. To the city–ward, it was bounded by a solid wall, of considerable height, giving a resting–place for the roof of a lower building, which, sloping outward, broke to the view the vast height unobscured
otherwise save by a high and massy balustrade, composed of bronze, which, to the havenward, sunk sheer down upon an uninterrupted precipice.

No sooner, therefore, had Ursel turned his eyes that way, than, though placed far from the brink of the terrace, he exclaimed, with a shriek, "Save me— save me! if you are not indeed the destined executors of the Emperor's will."

"We are indeed such," said Douban, "to save, and if possible to bring you to complete recovery; but by no means to do you injury, or to suffer it to be offered by others."

"Guard me then from myself," said Ursel, "and save me from the reeling and insane desire which I feel to plunge myself into the abyss, to the edge of which you have guided me."

"Such a giddy and dangerous temptation is," said the physician, "common to those who have not for a long time looked down from precipitous heights, and are suddenly brought to them. Nature, however bounteous, hath not provided for the cessation of our faculties for years, and for their sudden resumption in full strength and vigour. An interval, longer or shorter, must needs intervene. Can you not believe this terrace a safe station while you have my support and that of this faithful slave?"

"Certainly," said Ursel; "but permit me to turn my face towards this stone wall, for I cannot bear to look at the flimsy piece of wire, which is the only battlement of defence that interposes betwixt me and the precipice." He spoke of the bronze balustrade, six feet high, and massive in proportion. Thus saying, and holding fast by the physician's arm, Ursel, though himself a younger and more able
man, trembled, and moved his feet as slowly as if made of lead, until he reached the sashed–door, where stood a kind of balcony–seat, in which he placed himself.—"Here," he said, "will I remain."

"And here," said Douban, "will I make the communication of the Emperor, which it is necessary you should be prepared to reply to. It places you, you will observe, at your own disposal for liberty or captivity, but it conditions for your resigning that sweet but sinful morsel termed revenge, which, I must not conceal from you, chance appears willing to put into your hand. You know the degree of rivalry in which you have been held by the Emperor, and you know the measure of evil you have sustained at his hand. The question is, Can you forgive what has taken place?"

"Let me wrap my head round with my mantle," said Ursel, "to dispel this dizziness which still oppresses my poor brain, and as soon as the power of recollection is granted me, you shall know my sentiments."

He sunk upon the seat, muffled in the way which he described, and after a few minutes' reflection, with a trepidation which argued the patient still to be under the nervous feeling of extreme horror mixed with terror, he addressed Douban thus: "The operation of wrong and cruelty, in the moment when they are first inflicted, excites, of course, the utmost resentment of the sufferer; nor is there, perhaps, a passion which lives so long in his bosom as the natural desire of revenge. If, then, during the first month, when I lay stretched upon my bed of want and misery, you had offered me an opportunity of revenge upon my cruel oppressor, the remnant of miserable life which remained to me should have been willingly bestowed to purchase it. But a suffering of weeks, or even months, must not be compared in effect with that of years. For a short space of endurance, the body, as well as the mind, retains that vigorous habit

which holds the prisoner still connected with life, and teaches him to thrill at the long–forgotten chain of hopes, of wishes, of disappointments, and mortifications, which affected his former existence. But the wounds become callous as they harden, and other and better feelings occupy their place, while they gradually die away in forgetfulness. The enjoyments, the amusements of this world, occupy no part of his time upon whom the gates of despair have once closed. I tell thee, my kind physician, that for a season, in an insane attempt to effect my liberty, I cut through a large portion of the living rock. But Heaven cured me of so foolish an idea; and if I did not actually come to love Alexius Comnenus—for how could

that have been a possible effect in any rational state of my intellects? —yet as I became convinced of my own crimes, sins, and follies, the more and more I was also persuaded that Alexius was but the agent through whom Heaven exercised a dearly–purchased right of punishing me for my manifold offences and transgressions; and that it was not therefore upon the Emperor that my resentment ought to visit itself. And I can now say to thee, that so far as a man who has undergone so dreadful a change can be supposed to know his own mind, I feel no desire either to rival Alexius in a race for empire, or to avail myself of any of the various proffers which he proposes to me as the price of withdrawing my claim. Let him keep unpurchased the crown, for which he has paid, in my opinion, a price which it is not worth."

"This is extraordinary stoicism, noble Ursel," answered the physician Douban. "Am I then to understand that you reject the fair offers of Alexius, and desire, instead of all which he is willing—nay, anxious to bestow—to be committed safely back to thy old blinded dungeon in the Blacquernal, that you may continue at ease those pietistic meditations which have already conducted thee to so extravagant a conclusion?"

"Physician," said Ursel, while a shuddering fit that affected his whole body testified his alarm at the alternative proposed—"one would imagine thine own profession might have taught thee, that no mere mortal man, unless predestined to be a glorified saint, could ever prefer darkness to the light of day; blindness itself to the enjoyment of the power of sight; the pangs of starving to competent sustenance, or the damps of a dungeon to the free air of God's creation. No!—it may be virtue to do so, but to such a pitch mine does not soar. All I require of the Emperor for standing by him with all the power my name can give him at this crisis is, that he will provide for my reception as a monk in some of those pleasant and well endowed seminaries of piety, to which his devotion, or his fears, have given rise. Let me not be again the object of his suspicion, the operation of which is more dreadful than that of being the object of his hate. Forgotten by power, as I have myself lost the remembrance of those that wielded it, let me find my way to the grave, unnoticed, unconstrained, at liberty, in possession of my dim and disused organs of sight, and, above all, at peace."

"If such be thy serious and earnest wish, noble Ursel," said the physician, "I myself have no hesitation to warrant to thee the full accomplishment of thy religious and moderate desires. But, bethink thee, thou art once more an inhabitant of the court, in which thou mayst obtain what thou wilt to–day; while to–morrow, shouldst thou regret thy indifference, it may be thy utmost entreaty will not suffice to gain for thee the slightest extension of thy present conditions."

"Be it so," said Ursel; "I will then stipulate for another condition, which indeed has only reference to this day. I will solicit his Imperial Majesty, with all humility, to spare me the pain of a personal treaty between himself and me, and that he will be satisfied with the solemn assurance that I am most willing to do in his favour all that he is desirous of dictating; while, on the other hand, I desire only the execution of those moderate conditions of my future aliment which I have already told thee at length."

"But wherefore," said Douban, "shouldst thou be afraid of announcing to the Emperor thy disposition to an agreement, which cannot be esteemed otherwise than extremely moderate on thy part? Indeed, I fear the Emperor will insist on a brief personal conference."

"I am not ashamed," said Ursel, "to confess the truth. It is true, that I have, or think I have, renounced what the Scripture calls the pride of life; but the old Adam still lives within us, and maintains against the better part of our nature an inextinguishable quarrel, easy to be aroused from its slumber, but as difficult to be again couched in peace. While last night I but half understood that mine enemy was in my presence, and while my faculties performed but half their duty in recalling his deceitful and hated accents, did not my heart throb in my bosom with all the agitation of a taken bird, and shall I again have to enter into a personal treaty with the man who, be his general conduct what it may, has been, the constant and unprovoked cause of my unequalled misery? Douban, no!—to listen to his voice again, were to hear an alarm sounded to every violent and vindictive passion, of my heart; and though, may Heaven so help me as my intentions towards him are upright, yet it is impossible for me to listen to his professions with a chance of safety either to him or to myself."

"If you be so minded," replied Douban, "I shall only repeat to him your stipulation, and you must swear to him that you will strictly observe it. Without this being done, it must be difficult, or perhaps impossible, to settle the league of which both are desirous."

"Amen!" said Ursel; "and as I am pure in my purpose, and resolved to keep it to the uttermost, so may Heaven guard me from the influence of precipitate revenge, ancient grudge, or new quarrel!"

An authoritative knock at the door of the sleeping chamber was now heard, and Ursel, relieved by more powerful feelings, from the giddiness of which he had complained, walked firmly into the bedroom, and seating himself, waited with averted eyes the entrance of the person who demanded admittance, and who proved to be no other than Alexius Comnenus.

The Emperor appeared at the door in a warlike dress, suited for the decoration of a prince who was to witness a combat in the lists fought out before him.

"Sage Douban," he said, "has our esteemed prisoner, Ursel, made his choice between our peace and enmity?"

"He hath, my lord," replied the physician, "embraced the lot of that happy portion of mankind, whose hearts and lives are devoted to the service of your Majesty's government."

"He will then this day," continued the Emperor, "render me the office of putting down all those who may pretend to abet insurrection in his name, and under pretext of his wrongs?"

"He will, my lord," replied the physician, "act to the fullest the part which you require."

"And in what way," said the Emperor, adopting his most gracious tone of voice, "would our faithful Ursel desire that services like these, rendered in the hour of extreme need; should be acknowledged by the Emperor?"

"Simply," answered Douban, "by saying nothing upon the subject. He desires only that all jealousies between you and him may be henceforth forgotten, and that he may be admitted into one of your Highness's monastic institutions, with leave to dedicate the rest of his life to the worship of Heaven and its saints."

"Hath he persuaded thee of this, Douban?"—said the Emperor, in a low and altered voice. "By Heaven! when I consider from what prison he was brought, and in what guise he inhabited it, I cannot believe in this gall–less disposition. He must at least speak to me himself, ere I can believe, in some degree, the transformation of the fiery Ursel into a being so little capable of feeling the ordinary impulses of mankind."

"Hear me, Alexius Comnenus," said the prisoner; "and so may thine own prayers to Heaven find access and acceptation, as thou believest the words which I speak to thee in simplicity of heart. If thine empire of Greece were made of coined gold, it would hold out no bait for my acceptance; nor, I thank Heaven, have even the injuries I have experienced at thy hand, cruel and extensive as they have been, impressed upon me the slightest desire of requiting treachery with treachery. Think of me as thou wilt, so thou seek'st not again to exchange words with me; and believe me, that when thou hast put me under the most rigid of thy ecclesiastical foundations, the discipline, the fare, and the vigils, will be far superior to the existence falling to the share of those whom the King delights to honour, and who therefore must afford the King their society whenever they are summoned to do so."

"It is hardly for me," said the physician, "to interpose in so high a matter; yet, as trusted both by the noble Ursel, and by his Highness the Emperor, I have made a brief abstract of these short conditions to be kept by the high parties towards each other, *sub crimine falsi.*"

The Emperor protracted the intercourse with Ursel, until he more fully explained to him the occasion which he should have that very day for his services. When they parted, Alexius, with a great show of affection, embraced his late prisoner, while it required all the self– command and stoicism of Ursel to avoid expressing in plain terms
the extent to which he abhorred the person who thus caressed him.

CHAPTER THE TWENTY-NINTH

* * * * O, Conspiracy!
Sham'st thou to show thy dangerous brow by night, When
evils are most free? O, then, by day,
Where wilt thou find a cavern dark enough
To mask thy monstrous visage? Seek none, Conspiracy; Hide it
in smiles and affability;
For if thou path thy native semblance on, Not
Erebus itself were dim enough
To hide thee from prevention. JULIUS
CAESAR

The important morning at last arrived, on which, by the Imperial proclamation, the combat between the Caesar and Count Robert of Paris was appointed to take place. This was a circumstance in a great measure foreign to the Grecian manners, and to which, therefore, the people annexed different ideas from those which were associated with the same solemn decision of God, as the Latins called it, by the Western nations. The consequence was a vague, but excessive agitation among the people, who connected the extraordinary strife which they were to witness, with the various causes which had been whispered abroad as likely to give occasion to some general insurrection of a great and terrible nature.

By the Imperial order, regular lists had been prepared for the combat, with opposite gates, or entrances, as was usual, for the admittance of the two champions; and it was understood that the appeal was to be made to the Divinity by each, according to the forms prescribed by the Church of which the combatants were respectively members. The situation of these lists was on the side of the shore adjoining on the west to the continent. At no great distance, the walls of the city were seen, of various architecture, composed of lime and of stone, and furnished with no less than four–

and–twenty gates, or posterns, five of which regarded the land, and nineteen the water. All this formed a beautiful prospect, much of which is still visible. The town itself is about nineteen miles in circumference; and as it is on all sides surrounded with lofty cypresses, its general appearance is that of a city arising out of a stately wood of these magnificent trees, partly shrouding the pinnacles, obelisks, and minarets, which then marked the site of many noble Christian temples; but now, generally speaking, intimate the position of as many Mahomedan mosques.

These lists, for the convenience of spectators, were surrounded on all sides by long rows of seats, sloping downwards. In the middle of these seats, and exactly opposite the centre of the lists, was a high throne, erected for the Emperor himself; and which was separated from the more vulgar galleries by a circuit of wooden barricades, which an experienced eye could perceive, might, in case of need, be made serviceable for purposes of defence.

The lists were sixty yards in length, by perhaps about forty in breadth, and these afforded ample space for the exercise of the combat, both on horseback and on foot. Numerous bands of the Greek citizens began, with the very break of day, to issue from the gates and posterns of the city, to examine and wonder at the construction of the lists, pass their criticisms upon the purposes of
the peculiar parts of the fabric, and occupy places, to secure them for the spectacle. Shortly after arrived a large band of those soldiers who were called the Roman Immortals. These entered without ceremony, and placed themselves on either hand of the wooden barricade which fenced the Emperor's seat. Some of them took even a greater liberty; for, affecting to be pressed against the boundary, there were individuals who approached the partition itself, and seemed to meditate climbing over it, and placing themselves on the same side with the Emperor. Some old domestic slaves of the household now showed themselves, as if for the purpose of preserving this sacred circle for Alexius and his court; and, in proportion as the Immortals began to show themselves encroaching and turbulent, the strength of the defenders of the prohibited precincts seemed gradually to increase.

There was, though scarcely to be observed, besides the grand access to the Imperial seat from without, another opening also from the outside, secured by a very strong door, by which different persons received admission beneath the seats destined for the Imperial party. These persons, by their length of limb, breadth of shoulders, by the fur of their cloaks, and especially by the redoubted battle–axes
which all of them bore, appeared to be Varangians; but, although neither dressed in their usual habit of pomp, nor in their more effectual garb of war, still, when narrowly examined, they might be seen to possess their usual offensive weapons. These men, entering in separate and straggling parties, might be observed to join the slaves of the interior of the palace in opposing the intrusion of the Immortals upon the seat of the Emperor, and the benches around. Two or three Immortals, who had actually made good their frolic, and climbed over the division, were flung back again, very unceremoniously, by the barbaric strength and sinewy arms of the Varangians.

The people around, and in the adjacent galleries, most of whom had the air of citizens in their holyday dresses, commented a good deal on these proceedings, and were inclined strongly to make part with the Immortals. "It was a shame to the Emperor," they said, "to encourage these British barbarians to interpose themselves by violence between his person and the Immortal cohorts of the city, who were in some sort his own children."

Stephanos, the gymnastic, whose bulky strength and stature rendered him conspicuous amid this party, said, without hesitation, "If there are two people here who will join in saying that the Immortals are unjustly deprived of their right of guarding the Emperor's person, here is the hand that shall place them beside the Imperial chair."

"Not so," quoth a centurion of the Immortals, whom we have already introduced to our readers by the name of Harpax; "Not so,
Stephanos; that happy time may arrive, but it is not yet come, my gem of the circus. Thou knowest that on this occasion it is one of these Counts, or western Franks, who undertakes the combat; and the Varangians, who call these people their enemies, have some
reason to claim a precedency in guarding the lists, which it might not

at this moment be convenient to dispute with them. Why, man, if
thou wert half so witty as thou art long, thou wouldst be sensible that it were
bad woodmanship to raise the hollo upon the game, ere it had been driven
within compass of the nets."

While the athlete rolled his huge grey eyes as if to conjure out the sense of
this intimation, his little friend Lysimachus, the artist, putting himself to pain
to stand upon his tiptoe, and look intelligent, said, approaching as near as he
could to Harpax's ear, "Thou mayst trust me, gallant centurion, that this man.
of mould and muscle shall neither start like a babbling hound on a false scent,
nor become mute and inert, when the general signal is given. But tell me,"
said he, speaking very low, and for that purpose mounting a bench, which
brought him on a level with the centurion's ear, "would it not have been better
that a strong guard of the valiant Immortals had been placed in this wooden
citadel, to ensure the object of the day?"

"Without question," said the centurion, "it was so meant; but these strolling
Varangians have altered their station of their own authority."

"Were it not—well," said Lysimachus, "that you, who are greatly more
numerous than the barbarians, should begin a fray before more of these
strangers arrive?"

"Content ye, friend," said the centurion, coldly, "we know our time. An attack
commenced too early would be worse than thrown away, nor would an
opportunity occur of executing our project in the fitting time, if an alarm were
prematurely given at this moment."

So saying, he shuffled off among his fellow–soldiers, so as to avoid
suspicious intercourse with such persons as were only concerned with the
civic portion of the conspirators.

As the morning advanced, and the sun took a higher station in the horizon,
the various persons whom curiosity, or some more decided motive, brought
to see the proposed combat, were seen streaming from different parts of the
town, and rushing to occupy such accommodation as the circuit round the
lists afforded them. In their road to the place where preparation for combat
was made, they had

to ascend a sort of cape, which, in the form of a small hill, projected into the Hellespont, and the butt of which, connecting it with the shore, afforded a considerable ascent, and of course a more commanding view of the strait between Europe and Asia, than either the immediate vicinity of the city, or the still lower ground upon which the lists were erected. In passing this height, the earlier visitants of the lists made little or no halt; but after a time, when it became obvious that those who had hurried forward to the place of combat were lingering there without any object or occupation, they that followed them in the same route, with natural curiosity, paid a tribute to the landscape, bestowing some attention on its beauty, and paused to see what auguries could be collected from the water,

which were likely to have any concern in indicating the fate of the events that were to take place. Some straggling seamen were the first who remarked that a squadron of the Greek small craft (being that of Tancred) were in the act of making their way from Asia, and threatening a descent upon Constantinople.

"It is strange," said a person, by rank the captain of a galley, "that these small vessels, which were ordered to return to Constantinople as soon as they disembarked the Latins, should have remained so long at Scutari, and should not be rowing back to the imperial city until this time, on the second day after their departure from thence."

"I pray to Heaven," said another of the same profession, "that these seamen may come alone. It seems to me as if their ensign–staffs, bowsprits, and topmasts were decorated with the same ensigns, or nearly the same, with those which the Latins displayed upon them, when, by the Emperor's order, they were transported towards Palestine; so methinks the voyage back again resembles that of a fleet of merchant vessels, who have been prevented from discharging their cargo at the place of their destination."

"There is little good," said one of the politicians whom we formerly noticed, "in dealing with such commodities, whether they are imported or exported. Yon ample banner which streams over the foremost galley, intimates the presence of a chieftain of no small rank among the Counts, whether it be for valour or for nobility."

The seafaring leader added, with the voice of one who hints alarming tidings, "They seem to have got to a point in the straits as high as will enable them to run down—with the tide, and clear the cape which we stand on, although with what purpose they aim to land so close beneath the walls of the city, he is a wiser man than I who pretends to determine."

"Assuredly," returned his comrade, "the intention is not a kind one. The wealth of the city has temptations to a poor people, who only value the iron which they possess as affording them the means of procuring the gold which they covet."

"Ay, brother," answered Demetrius the politician, "but see you not, lying at anchor within this bay which is formed by the cape, and at the very point where these heretics are likely to be carried by the tide, six strong vessels, having the power of sending forth, not merely showers of darts and arrows, but of Grecian fire, as it is called, from their hollow decks? If these Frank gentry continue directing their course upon the Imperial city, being, as they are,

——'propago Contemptrix Superum sane, saevaeque
avidissima caedis Et violenta;' [Footnote: Ovid, Met.]

we shall speedily see a combat better worth witnessing than that announced by the great trumpet of the Varangians. If you love me,
let us sit down here for a moment, and see how this matter is to end."

"An excellent motion, my ingenious friend," said Lascaris, which was the name of the other citizen; "but bethink you, shall we not be in danger from the missiles with which the audacious Latins will not fail to return the Greek fire, if, according to your conjecture, it shall be poured upon them by the Imperial squadron?"

"That is not ill argued, my friend," said Demetrius; "but know that you have to do with a man who has been in such extremities before now; and if such a discharge should open from the sea, I would propose to you to step back some fifty yards inland, and thus to interpose the very crest of the cape between us and the discharge of missiles; a mere child might thus learn to face them without any alarm."

"You are a wise man, neighbour," said Lascaris, "and possess such a mixture of valour and knowledge as becomes a man whom a friend might be supposed safely to risk his life with. There be those, for instance, who cannot show you the slightest glimpse of what is going on, without bringing you within peril of your life; whereas you, my worthy friend Demetrius, between your accurate knowledge of military affairs, and your regard for your friend, are sure to show him all that is to be seen without the least risk to a person, who is naturally unwilling to think of exposing himself to injury. But, Holy Virgin! what is the meaning of that red flag which the Greek Admiral has this instant hoisted?"

"Why, you see, neighbour," answered Demetrius, "yonder western heretic continues to advance without minding the various signs which our Admiral has made to him to desist, and now he hoists the bloody colours, as if a man should clench his fist and say, If you persevere in your uncivil intention, I will do so and so."

"By St. Sophia," said Lascaris, "and that is giving him fair warning. But what is it the Imperial Admiral is about to do?"

"Run! run! friend Lascaris," said Demetrius, "or you will see more of that than perchance you have any curiosity for."

Accordingly, to add the strength of example to precept, Demetrius himself girt up his loins, and retreated with the most edifying speed to the opposite side of the ridge, accompanied by the greater part of the crowd, who had tarried there to witness the contest which the newsmonger promised, and were determined to take his word for their own safety. The sound and sight which had alarmed Demetrius, was the discharge of a large portion of Greek fire, which perhaps may be best compared to one of those immense Congreve rockets of the present day, which takes on its shoulders a small grapnel or anchor, and proceeds groaning through the air, like a fiend overburdened by the mandate of some inexorable magician, and of which the operation was so terrifying, that the crews of the vessels attacked by this strange weapon frequently forsook every means of defence, and ran themselves ashore. One of the principal ingredients of this dreadful fire was supposed to be naphtha, or the bitumen

which is collected on the banks of the Dead Sea, and which, when in a state of ignition, could only be extinguished by a very singular mixture, and which it was not likely to come in contact with. It produced a thick smoke and loud explosion, and was capable, says Gibbon, of communicating its flames with equal vehemence in descent or lateral progress, [Footnote: For a full account of the
Greek five, see Gibbon, chapter 53] In sieges, it was poured from the ramparts, or launched like our bombs, in red—hot balls of stone or iron, or it was darted in flax twisted round arrows and in javelins. It was considered as a state secret of the greatest importance; and for wellnigh four centuries it was unknown to the Mahomedans. But at length the composition was discovered by the Saracens, and used by them for repelling the crusaders, and overpowering the Greeks, upon whose side it had at one time been the most formidable implement of defence. Some exaggeration—we must allow for a barbarous period; but there seems no doubt that the general description of the crusader Joinville should be admitted as correct:—"It came flying through the air," says that good knight, "like a winged dragon, about the
thickness of a hogshead, with the report of thunder and the speed of lightning, and the darkness of the night was dispelled by this horrible illumination."

Not only the bold Demetrius and his pupil Lascaris, but all the crowd whom they influenced, fled manfully when the commodore of the Greeks fired the first discharge; and as the other vessels in the squadron followed his example, the heavens were filled with the unusual and outrageous noise, while the smoke was so thick as to darken the very air. As the fugitives passed the crest of the hill, they saw the seaman, whom we formerly mentioned as a spectator, snugly reclining under cover of a dry ditch, where he managed so as to secure himself as far as possible from any accident. He could not, however, omit breaking his jest on the politicians.

"What, ho!" he cried, "my good friends," without raising himself above the counterscarp of his ditch, "will you not remain upon your station long enough to finish that hopeful lecture upon battle by sea and land, which you had so happy an opportunity of commencing? Believe me, the noise is more alarming than hurtful; the fire is all pointed in a direction opposite to yours, and if one of those dragons which you see does happen to fly landward instead of seaward, it is but the mistake of some cabin–boy, who has used his linstock with more willingness than ability."

Demetrius and Lascaris just heard enough of the naval hero's harangue, to acquaint them with the new danger with which they might be assailed by the possible misdirection of the weapons, and, rushing clown towards the lists at the head of a crowd half–desperate with fear, they hastily propagated the appalling news, that the Latins were coming back from Asia with the purpose of landing in arms, pillaging, and burning the city. The uproar, in the meantime, of this unexpected occurrence, was such as altogether to vindicate, in public opinion, the reported cause, however exaggerated. The thunder of the Greek fire came successively, one hard upon the other, and each, in its turn, spread a blot of black smoke upon the face of the landscape, which, thickened by so many successive clouds, seemed at last, like that raised by a sustained fire of modern artillery to overshadow the whole horizon.

The small squadron of Tancred were completely hid from view in the surging volumes of darkness, which the breath of the weapons of the enemy had spread around him; and it seemed by a red light, which began to show itself among the thickest of the veil of darkness, that one of the flotilla at least had caught fire. Yet the Latins resisted, with an obstinacy worthy of their own courage, and the fame of their celebrated leader. Some advantage they had, on account of their small size, and their lowness in the water, as well as the clouded state of the atmosphere, which rendered them difficult marks for the fire of the Greeks.

To increase these advantages, Tancred, as well by boats as by the kind of rude signals made use of at the period, dispersed orders to his fleet, that each bark, disregarding the fate of the others, should press forward individually, and that the men from each should be put on shore wheresoever and howsoever they could effect that manoeuvre. Tancred himself set a noble example; he was on board a stout vessel, fenced in some degree against the effect of the Greek fire by being in a great measure covered with raw hides, which hides had also been recently steeped in water. This vessel contained upwards of a hundred valiant warriors, several of them of knightly order, who had all night toiled at the humble labours of the oar, and now in the morning applied their chivalrous hands to the arblast and to the bow, which were in general accounted the weapons of persons of a lower rank. Thus armed, and thus manned. Prince Tancred bestowed upon his bark the full velocity which wind, and tide, and oar, could enable her to obtain, and placing her in the situation to profit by them as much as his maritime skill could direct, he drove with the speed of lightning among the vessels of Lemnos, plying on either side, bows, crossbows, javelins, and military missiles of every kind, with the greater advantage that the Greeks, trusting to their artificial fire, had omitted arming themselves with other weapons; so that when the valiant Crusader bore down on them with so much fury, repaying the terrors of their fire with a storm of bolts and arrows no less formidable, they began to feel that their own advantage was much less than they had supposed, and that, like most other dangers, the maritime fire of the Greeks, when undauntedly confronted, lost at least one–half of its terrors. The Grecian sailors, too, when they observed the vessels approach so near, filled with the steel–clad Latins, began to shrink from a contest to be maintained hand to hand with so terrible an enemy.

By degrees, smoke began to issue from the sides of the great Grecian argosy, and the voice of Tancred announced to his soldiers that the Grecian Admiral's vessel had taken fire, owing to negligence in the management of the means of destruction she possessed, and that all they had now to do was to maintain such a distance as to avoid sharing her fate. Sparkles and flashes of flame were next seen
leaping from place to place on board of the great hulk, as if the element had had the sense and purpose of spreading wider the consternation, and disabling the few who still paid attention to the commands of their Admiral, and endeavoured to extinguish the fire. The consciousness of the combustible nature of the freight, began to add despair to terror; from the boltsprit, the rigging, the yards, the sides, and every part of the vessel, the unfortunate crew were seen dropping themselves, to exchange for the most part a watery death for one by the more dreadful agency of fire. The crew of Tancred's bark, ceasing, by that generous prince's commands, to offer any additional annoyance to an enemy who was at once threatened by the

perils of the ocean and of conflagration, ran their vessel ashore in a smooth part of the bay, and jumping into the shallow sea, made the land without difficulty; many of their steeds being, by the exertions of the owners, and the docility of the animals, brought ashore at the same time with their masters. Their commander lost no time in forming their serried ranks into a phalanx of lancers, few indeed at first, but perpetually increasing as ship after ship of the little flotilla ran ashore, or, having more deliberately moored their barks, landed their men, and joined their companions.

The cloud which had been raised by the conflict was now driven to leeward before the wind, and the strait exhibited only the relics of the combat. Here tossed upon the billows the scattered and broken remains of one or two of the Latin vessels which had been burnt at the commencement of the combat, though their crews, by the exertions of their comrades, had in general been saved. Lower down were seen the remaining five vessels of the Lemnos squadron,
holding a disorderly and difficult retreat, with the purpose of gaining the harbour of Constantinople. In the place so late the scene of combat, lay moored the hulk of the Grecian Admiral, burnt to the water's edge, and still sending forth a black smoke from its scathed beams and planks. The flotilla of Tancred, busied in discharging its troops, lay irregularly scattered along the bay, the men making
ashore as they could, and taking their course to join the standard of their leader. Various black substances floated on the surface of the water, nearer, or more distant to the shore; some proved to be the wreck of the vessels which had been destroyed, and others, more ominous still, the lifeless bodies of mariners who had fallen in the conflict.

The standard had been borne ashore by the Prince's favourite page, Ernest of Apulia, so soon as the keel of Tancred's galley had grazed upon the sand. It was then pitched on the top of that elevated cape between Constantinople and the lists, where Lascaris, Demetrius,
and other gossips, had held their station at the commencement of the engagement, but from which all had fled, between the mingled dread of the Greek fire and the missiles of the Latin crusaders.

Chapter the Thirtieth

Sheathed in complete armour, and supporting with his right hand the standard of his fathers, Tancred remained with his handful of warriors like so many statues of steel, expecting some sort of attack from the Grecian party which had occupied the lists, or from the numbers whom the city gates began now to pour forth—soldiers some of them, and others citizens, many of whom were arrayed as if for conflict. These persons, alarmed by the various accounts which were given of the combatants, and the progress of the fight, rushed towards the standard of Prince Tancred, with the intention of beating it to the earth, and dispersing the guards who owed it homage and defence. But if the reader shall have happened to have ridden at any time through a pastoral country, with a clog of a noble race
following him, he must have remarked, in the deference ultimately paid to the high–bred animal by the shepherd's cur as he crosses the lonely glen, of which the latter conceives himself the lord and guardian, something very similar to the demeanour of the incensed Greeks, when they approached near to the little band of Franks. At the first symptom of the intrusion of a stranger, the dog of the shepherd starts from his slumbers, and rushes towards the noble intruder with a clamorous declaration of war; but when the diminution of distance between them shows to the aggressor the size and strength of his opponent, he becomes like a cruiser, who, in a chase, has, to his surprise and alarm, found two tier of guns opposed to him instead of one. He halts— suspends his clamorous yelping, and, in fine, ingloriously retreats to his master, with, all the dishonourable marks of positively declining the combat.

It was in this manner that the troops of the noisy Greeks, with much hallooing and many a boastful shout, hastened both from the town and from the lists, with the apparent intention of sweeping from the field the few companions of Tancred. As they advanced, however, within the power of remarking the calm and regular order of those men who had landed, and arranged themselves under this noble chieftain's banner, their minds were altogether changed as to the resolution of instant combat; their advance became an uncertain and staggering gait, their heads were more frequently turned back to the point from which they came, than towards the enemy; and their desire to provoke an instant scuffle vanished totally, when there did not appear the least symptom that their opponents cared about the matter.

It added to the extreme confidence with which the Latins kept their ground, that they were receiving frequent, though small reinforcements from their comrades, who were landing by detachments all along the beach; and that, in the course of a short hour, their amount had been raised, on horseback and foot, to a number, allowing for a few casualties, not much less than that which set sail from Scutari.

Another reason why the Latins remained unassailed, was certainly the indisposition of the two principal armed parties on shore to enter into a quarrel with them. The guards of every kind, who were faithful to the Emperor, more especially the Varangians, had their orders to remain firm at their posts, some in the lists, and others at various places of rendezvous in Constantinople, where their presence was necessary to prevent the effects of the sudden insurrection which Alexius knew to be meditated against him. These, therefore, made no hostile demonstration towards the band of Latins, nor was it the purpose of the Emperor they should do so.

On the other hand, the greater part of the Immortal Guards, and those citizens who were prepared to play a part in the conspiracy, had been impressed by the agents of the deceased Agelastes with the opinion, that this band of Latins, commanded by Tancred, the relative of Bohemond, had been despatched by the latter to their assistance. These men, therefore, stood still, and made no attempt to guide or direct the popular efforts of such as inclined to attack these unexpected visitors; in which purpose, therefore, no very great party were united, while the majority were willing enough to find an apology for remaining quiet.

In the meantime, the Emperor, from his palace of Blacquernal, observed what passed upon the straits, and beheld his navy from Lemnos totally foiled in their attempt, by means of the Greek fire, to check, the intended passage of Tancred and his men. He had no sooner seen the leading ship of the squadron, begin to beacon the darkness with its own fire, than the Emperor formed a secret resolution to disown the unfortunate Admiral, and make peace with the Latins, if that should be absolutely necessary, by sending them his head. He had hardly, therefore, seen the flames burst forth, and the rest of the vessels retreat from their moorings, than in his own mind, the doom of the unfortunate Phraortes, for such was the name of the Admiral, was signed and sealed.

Achilles Tatius, at the same instant, determining to keep a close eye upon the Emperor at this important crisis, came precipitately into the palace, with an appearance of great alarm.

"My Lord!—my Imperial Lord! I am unhappy to be the messenger of such unlucky news; but the Latins have in great numbers succeeded in crossing the strait from Scutari. The Lemnos squadron endeavoured to stop them, as was last night determined upon in the Imperial Council of War. By a heavy discharge of the Greek fire, one or two of the crusaders' vessels were consumed, but by far the greater number of them pushed on their course, burnt the leading ship of the unfortunate Phraortes, and It is strongly reported he has himself perished, with almost all his men. The rest have cut their cables, and abandoned the defence of the passage of the Hellespont."

"And you, Achilles Tatius," said the Emperor, "with what purpose is it that you now bring me this melancholy news, at a period so late, when I cannot amend the consequences!"

"Under favour, most gracious Emperor," replied the conspirator, not without colouring and stammering, "such was not my intention—I had hoped to submit a plan, by which I might easily have prepared the way for correcting this little error."

"Well, your plan, sir?" said the Emperor, dryly.

"With your sacred Majesty's leave," said the Acolyte, "I would myself have undertaken instantly to lead against this Tancred and his

Italians the battle–axes of the faithful Varangian guard, who will make no more account of the small number of Franks who have come ashore, than the farmer holds of the hordes of rats and mice, and such like mischievous vermin, who have harboured in his granaries."

"And what mean you," said the Emperor, "that I am to do, while my Anglo–Saxons fight for my sake?"

"Your Majesty," replied Achilles, not exactly satisfied with the dry and caustic manner in which the Emperor addressed him, "may put yourself at the head of the Immortal cohorts of Constantinople; and I am your security, that you may either perfect the victory over the Latins, or at least redeem the most distant chance of a defeat, by advancing at the head of this choice body of domestic troops, should the day appear doubtful."

"You, yourself, Achilles Tatius," returned the Emperor, "have repeatedly assured us, that these Immortals retain a perverse attachment to our rebel Ursel. How is it, then, you would have us intrust our defence to these bands, when we have engaged our valiant Varangians in the proposed conflict with the flower of the western army?—Did you think of this risk, Sir Follower?"

Achilles Tatius, much alarmed at an intimation indicative of his purpose being known, answered, "That in his haste he had been more anxious to recommend the plan which should expose his own person to the greater danger, than that perhaps which was most attended
with personal safety to his Imperial Master."

"I thank you for so doing," said the Emperor; "you have anticipated my wishes, though it is not in my power at present to follow the advice you have given me. I would have been well contented, undoubtedly, had these Latins measured their way over the strait again, as suggested by last night's council; but since they have arrived, and stand embattled on our shores, it is better that we pay them with money and with spoil, than with the lives of our gallant subjects. We cannot, after all, believe that they come with any serious intention of doing us injury; it is but the insane desire of witnessing feats of battle and single combat, which is to them the breath of their nostrils, that can have impelled them to this partial countermarch. I impose upon you, Achilles Tatius, combining the Protospathaire in the same commission with you, the duty of riding up to yonder standard, and learning of their chief, called the Prince Tancred, if he is there in person, the purpose of his return, and the cause of his entering into debate with Phraortes and the Lemnos squadron. If they send us any reasonable excuse, we shall not be averse to receive it at their hands; for we have not made so many sacrifices for the preservation of peace, to break forth into war, if, after all, so great an evil can be avoided. Thou wilt receive, therefore, with a candid and complacent mind, such apologies as they may incline to bring forward; and, be assured, that the sight of this puppet–show of a single combat, will be enough of itself to banish every other consideration from the reflection of these giddy crusaders."

A knock was at this moment heard at the door of the Emperor's apartment; and upon the word being given to enter, the Protospathaire made his appearance. He was arrayed in a splendid suit of ancient Roman fashioned armour. The want of a visor left his countenance entirely visible; which, pale and anxious as it was, did not well become the martial crest and dancing plume with which it was decorated. He received the commission already mentioned with the less alacrity, because the Acolyte was added to him as his colleague; for, as the reader may have observed, these two officers were of separate factions in the army, and on indifferent terms with each other. Neither did the Acolyte consider his being united in commission with the Protospathaire, as a mark either of the Emperor's confidence, or of his own safety. He was, however, in the meantime, in the Blacquernal, where the slaves of the interior made not the least hesitation, when ordered, to execute any officer of the court. The two generals had, therefore, no other alternative, than that which is allowed to two greyhounds who are reluctantly coupled together. The hope of Achilles Tatius was, that he might get safely through his mission to Tancred, after which he thought the successful explosion of the conspiracy might take place and have its course, either as a matter desired and countenanced by those Latins, or passed over as a thing in which they took no interest on either side.

By the parting order of the Emperor, they were to mount on horseback at the sounding of the great Varangian trumpet, put themselves at the head of those Anglo–Saxon guards in the court– yard of their barrack, and await the Emperor's further orders.

There was something in this arrangement which pressed hard on the conscience of Achilles Tatius, yet he was at a loss to justify his apprehensions to himself, unless from a conscious feeling of his own guilt, he felt, however, that in being detained, under pretence of an honourable mission, at the head of the Varangians, he was deprived of the liberty of disposing of himself, by which he had hoped to communicate with the Caesar and Hereward, whom he reckoned upon as his active accomplices, not knowing that the first was at this moment a prisoner in the Blacquernal, where Alexius had arrested him in the apartments of the Empress, and that the second was the most important support of Comnenus during the whole of that eventful day.

When the gigantic trumpet of the Varangian guards sent forth its deep signal through the city, the Protospathaire hurried Achilles along with him to the rendezvous of the Varangians, and on the way said to him, in an easy and indifferent tone, "As the Emperor is in the field in person, you, his representative, or Follower, will of course transmit no orders to the body guard, except such as shall receive their origin from himself, so that you will consider your authority as this day suspended."

"I regret," said Achilles, "that there should have seemed any cause for such precautions; I had hoped my own truth and fidelity—but—I am obsequious to his imperial pleasure in all things."

"Such are his orders," said the other officer, "and you know under what penalty obedience is enforced."

"If I did not," said Achilles, "the composition of this body of guards would remind me, since it comprehends not only great part of those Varangians, who are the immediate defenders of the Emperor's throne, but those slaves of the interior, who are the executioners of his pleasure." To this the Protospathaire returned no answer, while the more closely the Acolyte looked upon the guard which attended, to the unusual number of nearly three thousand men, the more had he reason to believe that he might esteem himself fortunate, if, by the intervention of either the Caesar, Agelastes, or Hereward, he could pass to the conspirators a signal to suspend the intended explosion, which seemed to be provided against by the Emperor with unusual caution. He would have given the full dream of empire, with which he had been for a short time lulled to sleep, to have seen but a glimpse of the azure plume of Nicephorus, the white mantle of the philosopher, or even a glimmer of Hereward's battle–axe. No such objects could be seen anywhere, and not a little was the faithless Follower displeased to see that whichever way he turned his eyes, those of the Protospathaire, but especially of the trusty domestic officers of the empire, seemed to follow and watch their occupation.

Amidst the numerous soldiers whom he saw on all sides, his eye did not recognise a single man with whom he could exchange a friendly or confidential glance, and he stood in all that agony of terror, which is rendered the more discomfiting, because the traitor is conscious that, beset by various foes, his own fears are the most likely of all to betray him. Internally, as the danger seemed to increase, and as his alarmed imagination attempted to discern new reasons for it, he could only conclude that either one of the three principal conspirators, or at least some of the inferiors, had turned informers; and his doubt was, whether he should not screen his own share of what had been premeditated, by flinging himself at the feet of the Emperor, and making a full confession. But still the fear of being premature in having recourse to such base means of saving himself, joined to the absence of the Emperor, united to keep within his lips a secret, which concerned not only all his future fortunes, but life itself. He was in the meantime, therefore, plunged as it were in a sea of trouble and uncertainty, while the specks of land, which seemed to promise him refuge, were distant, dimly seen, and extremely difficult of attainment.

CHAPTER THE THIRTY-FIRST

To–morrow—oh, that's sudden! Spare him, spare him! He's not
prepared to die.
SHAKSPEARE.

At the moment when Achilles Tatius, with a feeling of much insecurity,
awaited the unwinding of the perilous skein of state politics, a private council
of the Imperial family was held in the hall termed the Temple of the Muses,
repeatedly distinguished as the apartment in which the Princess Anna
Comnena was wont to make her evening recitations to those who were
permitted the honour of hearing prelections of her history. The council
consisted of the Empress Irene, the Princess herself, and the Emperor, with
the Patriarch of the Greek Church, as a sort of mediator between a course of
severity and a dangerous degree of lenity.

"Tell not me, Irene," said the Emperor, "of the fine things attached to the
praise of mercy. Here have I sacrificed my just revenge over my rival Ursel,
and what good do I obtain by it? Why, the old obstinate man, instead of being
tractable, and sensible of the generosity which has spared his life and eyes,
can be with difficulty brought to exert himself in favour of the Prince to whom
he owes them. I used to
think that eyesight and the breath of life were things which one would
preserve at any sacrifice; but, on the contrary, I now believe men value them
like mere toys. Talk not to me, therefore, of the gratitude to be excited by
saving this ungrateful cub; and believe me, girl," turning to Anna, "that not
only will all my subjects, should I follow your advice, laugh at me for sparing
a man so predetermined to work my ruin, but even thou thyself wilt be the
first to upbraid me with the foolish kindness thou art now so anxious to extort
from
me."

"Your Imperial pleasure, then," said the Patriarch, "is fixed that your
unfortunate son–in–law shall suffer death for his accession to this

conspiracy, deluded by that heathen villain Agelastes, and the traitorous Achilles Tatius?"

"Such is my purpose," said the Emperor; "and in evidence that I mean not again to pass over a sentence of this kind with a seeming execution only, as in the case of Ursel, this ungrateful traitor of ours shall be led from the top of the staircase, or ladder of Acheron, as it is called, through the large chamber named the Hall of Judgment, at the upper end of which are arranged the apparatus for execution, by which I swear"—

"Swear not at all!" said the Patriarch; "I forbid thee, in the name of that Heaven whose voice (though unworthy) speaks in my person, to quench the smoking flax, or destroy the slight hope which there may remain, that you may finally be persuaded to alter your purpose respecting your misguided son–in–law, within the space allotted to him to sue for your mercy. Remember, I pray you, the remorse of Constantine."

"What means your reverence?" said Irene.

"A trifle," replied the Emperor, "not worthy being quoted from such a mouth as the Patriarch's, being, as it probably is, a relic of paganism."

"What is it?" exclaimed the females anxiously, in the hope of hearing something which might strengthen their side of the argument, and something moved, perhaps, by curiosity, a motive which seldom slumbers in a female bosom, even when the stronger passions are in arms.

"The Patriarch will tell you," answered Alexius, "since you must needs know; though I promise you, you will not receive any assistance in your argument from a silly legendary tale."

"Hear it, however," said the Patriarch; "for though it is a tale of the olden time, and sometimes supposed to refer to the period when heathenism predominated, it is no less true, that it was a vow made and registered in the chancery of the rightful Deity, by an Emperor of Greece."

"What I am now to relate to you," continued he, "is, in truth, a tale not only of a Christian Emperor, but of him who made the whole empire Christian; and of that very Constantine, who was also the
first who declared Constantinople to be the metropolis of the empire. This hero, remarkable alike for his zeal for religion and for his warlike achievements, was crowned by Heaven with repeated
victory, and with all manner of blessings, save that unity in his family which wise men are most ambitious to possess. Not only was the blessing of concord among brethren denied to the family of this triumphant Emperor, but a deserving son of mature age, who had been supposed to aspire to share the throne with his father, was suddenly, and at midnight, called upon to enter his defence against a capital charge of treason. You will readily excuse my referring to the arts by which the son was rendered guilty in the eyes of the father.
Be it enough to say, that the unfortunate young man fell a victim to the guilt of his step–mother, Fausta, and that he disdained to exculpate himself from a charge so gross and so erroneous. It is said, that the anger of the Emperor was kept up against his son by the sycophants who called upon Constantine to observe that the culprit disdained even to supplicate for mercy, or vindicate his innocence from so foul a charge.

"But the death–blow had no sooner struck the innocent youth, than his father obtained proof of the rashness with which he had acted. He had at this period been engaged in constructing the subterranean
parts of the Blacquernal palace, which his remorse appointed to contain a record of his paternal grief and contrition. At the upper part of the staircase, called the Pit of Acheron, he caused to be
constructed a large chamber, still called the Hall of Judgment, for the purpose of execution. A passage through an archway in the upper wall leads from the hall to the place of misery, where the axe, or
other engine, is disposed for the execution of state prisoners of consequence. Over this archway was placed a species of marble altar, surmounted by an image of the unfortunate Crispus—the materials were gold, and it bore the memorable inscription, TO MY SON, WHOM I RASHLY CONDEMNED, AND TOO HASTILY EXECUTED. When constructing this passage, Constantine made a vow, that he himself and his posterity, being reigning Emperors, would stand beside the statue of Crispus, at the time when any

individual of their family should be led to execution, and before they suffered him to pass from the Hall of Judgment to the Chamber of Death, that they should themselves be personally convinced of the truth of the charge under which he suffered.

"Time rolled on—the memory of Constantine was remembered almost like that of a saint, and the respect paid to it threw into shadow the anecdote of his son's death. The exigencies of the state rendered it difficult to keep so large a sum in specie invested in a statue, which called to mind the unpleasant failings of so great a
man. Your Imperial Highness's predecessors applied the metal which formed the statue to support the Turkish wars; and the remorse and penance of Constantine died away in an obscure tradition of the Church or of the palace. Still, however, unless your Imperial Majesty has strong reasons to the contrary, I shall give it as my opinion, that you will hardly achieve what is due to the memory of the greatest of your predecessors, unless you give this unfortunate criminal, being
so near a relation of your own, an opportunity of pleading his cause before passing by the altar of refuge; being the name which is commonly given to the monument of the unfortunate Crispus, son of Constantine, although now deprived both of the golden letters which composed the inscription, and the golden image which represented the royal sufferer."

A mournful strain of music was now heard to ascend the stair so often mentioned.

"If I must hear the Caesar Nicephorus Briennius, ere he pass the altar of refuge, there must be no loss of time," said the Emperor; "for these melancholy sounds announce that he has already approached the Hall of Judgment."

Both the Imperial ladies began instantly, with the utmost earnestness, to deprecate the execution of the Caesar's doom, and to conjure Alexius, as he hoped for quiet in his household, and the everlasting gratitude of his wife and daughter, that he would listen to their entreaties in behalf of an unfortunate man, who had been seduced into guilt, but not from his heart.

"I will at least see him," said the Emperor, "and the holy vow of Constantine shall be in the present instance strictly observed. But remember, you foolish women, that the state of Crispus and the present Caesar, is as different as guilt from innocence, and that their fates, therefore, may be justly decided upon opposite principles, and with opposite results. But I will confront this criminal; and you, Patriarch, may be present to render what help is in your power to a dying man; for you, the wife and mother of the traitor, you will, methinks, do well to retire to the church, and pray God for the soul of the deceased, rather than disturb his last moments with unavailing lamentations."

"Alexius," said the Empress Irene, "I beseech you to be contented; be assured that we will not leave you in this dogged humour of blood–shedding, lest you make such materials for history as are fitter for the time of Nero than of Constantine."

The Emperor, without reply, led the way into the Hall of Judgment, where a much stronger light than usual was already shining up the stair of Acheron, from which were heard to sound, by sullen and intermitted fits, the penitential psalms which the Greek Church has appointed to be sung at executions. Twenty mute slaves, the pale colour of whose turbans gave a ghastly look to the withered cast of their features, and the glaring whiteness of their eyeballs, ascended two by two, as it were from the bowels of the earth, each of them bearing in one hand a naked sabre, and in the other a lighted torch. After these came the unfortunate Nicephorus; his looks were those of a man half–dead from the terror of immediate dissolution, and what he possessed of remaining attention, was turned successively to two black–stoled monks, who were anxiously repeating religious passages to him alternately from the Greek scripture, and the form of devotion adopted by the court of Constantinople. The Caesar's dress also corresponded to his mournful fortunes: His legs and arms were bare, and a simple white tunic, the neck of which was already open, showed that ho had assumed the garments which were to serve his last turn. A tall muscular Nubian slave, who considered himself obviously as the principal person in the procession, bore on his shoulder a large heavy headsman's axe, and, like a demon waiting on a sorcerer, stalked step for step after his victim. The rear of the procession was closed by a band of four priests, each of whom chanted from time to time the devotional psalm which was thundered forth on the occasion; and another of slaves, armed with bows and quivers, and with lances, to resist any attempt at rescue, if such should be offered.

It would have required a harder heart than that of the unlucky princess to have resisted this gloomy apparatus of fear and sorrow, surrounding, at the same time directed against, a beloved object, the lover of her youth, and the husband of her bosom, within a few minutes of the termination of his mortal career.

As the mournful train approached towards the altar of refuge, half– encircled as it now was by the two great and expanded arms which projected from the wall, the Emperor, who stood directly in the passage, threw upon the flame of the altar some chips of aromatic wood, steeped in spirit of wine, which, leaping at once into a blaze, illuminated the doleful procession, the figure of the principal culprit, and the slaves, who had most of them extinguished their flambeaux so soon as they had served the purpose of lighting them up the staircase.

The sudden light spread from the altar failed not to make the Emperor and the Princess visible to the mournful group which approached through the hall. All halted—all were silent. It was a meeting, as the Princess has expressed herself in her historical work, such as took place betwixt Ulysses and the inhabitants of the other world, who, when they tasted of the blood of his sacrifices, recognised him indeed, but with empty lamentations, and gestures feeble and shadowy. The hymn of contrition sunk also into silence; and, of the whole group, the only figure rendered more distinct, was the gigantic executioner, whose high and furrowed forehead, as well as the broad steel of his axe, caught and reflected back the bright gleam from the altar. Alexius saw the necessity of breaking the silence which ensued, lest it should, give the intercessors for the prisoner an opportunity of renewing their entreaties.

"Nicephorus Briennius," he said, with a voice which, although generally interrupted by a slight hesitation, which procured him,

among his enemies, the nickname of the Stutterer, yet, upon important occasions like the present, was so judiciously tuned and balanced in its sentences, that no such defect was at all visible
—"Nicephorus Briennius," he said, "late Caesar, the lawful doom hath been spoken, that, having conspired against the life of thy rightful sovereign and affectionate father, Alexius Comnenus, thou shalt suffer the appropriate sentence, by having thy head struck from thy body. Here, therefore, at the last altar of refuge, I meet thee, according to the vow of the immortal Constantine, for the purpose of demanding whether thou hast any thing to allege why this doom should not be executed? Even at this eleventh hour, thy tongue is unloosed to speak with freedom what may concern thy life. All is prepared in this world and in the next. Look forward beyond yon archway—the block is fixed. Look behind thee, thou seest the axe already sharpened—thy place for good or evil in the next world is already determined—time flies—eternity approaches. If thou hast aught to say, speak it freely—if nought, confess the justice of thy sentence, and pass on to death."

The Emperor commenced this oration, with those looks described by his daughter as so piercing, that they dazzled like lightning, and his periods, if not precisely flowing like burning lava, were yet the accents of a man having the power of absolute command, and as
such produced an effect not only on the criminal, but also upon the Prince himself, whose watery eyes and faltering voice acknowledged his sense and feeling of the fatal import of the present moment.

Rousing himself to the conclusion of what he had commenced, the Emperor again demanded whether the prisoner had any thing to say in his own defence.

Nicephorus was not one of those hardened criminals who may be termed the very prodigies of history, from the coolness with which they contemplated the consummation of their crimes, whether in their own punishment, or the misfortunes of others. "I have been tempted," he said, dropping on his knees, "and I have fallen. I have nothing to allege in excuse of my folly and ingratitude; but I stand prepared to die to expiate my guilt," A deep sigh, almost amounting to a scream, was here heard, close behind the Emperor, and its cause

assigned by the sudden exclamation of Irene,—"My lord! my lord! your daughter is gone!" And in fact Anna Comnena had sunk into her mother's arms without either sense or motion. The father's attention was instantly called to support his swooning child, while the unhappy husband strove with the guards to be permitted to go to the assistance of his wife. "Give me but five minutes of that time
which the law has abridged—let my efforts but assist in recalling her to a life which should be as long as her virtues and her talents deserve; and then let me die at her feet, for I care not to go an inch beyond."

The Emperor, who in fact had been more astonished at the boldness and rashness of Nicephorus, than alarmed by his power, considered him as a man rather misled than misleading others, and felt, therefore, the full effect of this last interview. He was, besides, not naturally cruel, where severities were to be enforced under his own eye.

"The divine and immortal Constantine," he said, "did not, I am persuaded, subject his descendants to this severe trial, in order further to search out the innocence of the criminals, but rather to give to those who came after him an opportunity of generously forgiving a crime which could not, without pardon—the express
pardon of the Prince—escape unpunished. I rejoice that I am born of the willow rather than of the oak, and I acknowledge my weakness, that not even the safety of my own life, or resentment of this unhappy man's treasonable machinations, have the same effect with me as the tears of my wife, and the swooning of my daughter. Rise up, Nicephorus Briennius, freely pardoned, and restored even to the rank of Caesar. We will direct thy pardon to be made out by the
great Logothete, and sealed with the golden bull. For four–and– twenty hours thou art a prisoner, until an arrangement is made for preserving the public peace. Meanwhile, thou wilt remain under the charge of the Patriarch, who will be answerable for thy forthcoming.
—Daughter and wife, you must now go hence to your own apartment; a future time will come, during which you may have enough of weeping and embracing, mourning and rejoicing. Pray Heaven that I, who, having been trained on till I have sacrificed justice and true policy to uxorious compassion and paternal

tenderness of heart, may not have cause at last for grieving in good earnest for all the events of this miscellaneous drama."

The pardoned Caesar, who endeavoured to regulate his ideas according to this unexpected change, found it as difficult to reconcile himself to the reality of his situation as Ursel to the face of nature, after having been long deprived of enjoying it; so much do the dizziness and confusion of ideas, occasioned by moral and physical causes of surprise and terror, resemble each other in their effects on the understanding.

At length he stammered forth a request that he might be permitted to go to the field with the Emperor, and divert, by the interposition of his own body, the traitorous blows which some desperate man might aim against that of his Prince, in a day which was too likely to be one of danger and bloodshed.

"Hold there!" said Alexius Comnenus;—"we will not begin thy newly–redeemed life by renewed doubts of thine allegiance; yet it is but fitting to remind thee, that thou art still the nominal and ostensible head of those who expect to take a part in this day's insurrection, and it will be the safest course to trust its pacification to others than to thee. Go, sir, compare notes with the Patriarch, and merit your pardon by confessing to him any traitorous intentions concerning this foul conspiracy with which we may be as yet unacquainted.—Daughter and wife, farewell! I must now depart for the lists, where I have to speak with the traitor Achilles Tatius and the heathenish infidel Agelastes, if he still lives, but of whose providential death I hear a confirmed rumour."

"Yet do not go, my dearest father!" said the Princess; "but let me rather go to encourage the loyal subjects in your behalf. The extreme kindness which you have extended towards my guilty husband, convinces me of the extent of your affection towards your unworthy daughter, and the greatness of the sacrifice which you have made to her almost childish affection for an ungrateful man who put your life in danger."

"That is to say, daughter," said the Emperor, smiling, "that the

pardon of your husband is a boon which has lost its merit when it is granted. Take my advice, Anna, and think otherwise; wives and their husbands ought in prudence to forget their offences towards each other as soon as human nature will permit them. Life is too short,
and conjugal tranquillity too uncertain, to admit of dwelling long upon such irritating subjects. To your apartments, Princesses, and prepare the scarlet–buskins, and the embroidery which is displayed on the cuffs and collars of the Caesar's robe, indicative of his high rank. He must not be seen without them on the morrow.—Reverend father, I remind you once more that the Caesar is in your personal custody from this moment until to–morrow at the same hour."

They parted; the Emperor repairing to put himself at the head of his Varangian guards—the Caesar, under the superintendence of the Patriarch, withdrawing into the interior of the Blacquernal Palace, where Nicephorus Briennius was under the necessity of "unthreading the rude eye of rebellion," and throwing such lights as were in his power upon the progress of the conspiracy.

"Agelastes," he said, "Achilles Tatius, and Hereward the Varangian, were the persons principally entrusted in its progress. But whether they had been all true to their engagements, he did not pretend to be assured."

In the female apartments, there was a violent discussion betwixt Anna Comnena and her mother. The Princess had undergone during the day many changes of sentiment and feeling; and though they had finally united themselves into one strong interest in her husband's favour, yet no sooner was the fear of his punishment removed, than the sense of his ungrateful behaviour began to revive. She became sensible also that a woman of her extraordinary attainments, who
had been by a universal course of flattery disposed to entertain a very high opinion of her own consequence, made rather a poor figure when she had been the passive subject of a long series of
intrigues, by which she was destined to be disposed of in one way or the other, according to the humour of a set of subordinate conspirators, who never so much as dreamed of regarding her as a being capable of forming a wish in her own behalf, or even yielding or refusing a consent. Her father's authority over her, and right to

dispose of her, was less questionable; but even then it was something derogatory to the dignity of a Princess born in the purple— an authoress besides, and giver of immortality—to be, without her own consent, thrown, as it were, at the head now of one suitor, now of another, however mean or disgusting, whose alliance could for the time benefit the Emperor. The consequence of these moody reflections, was that Anna Comnena deeply toiled in spirit for the discovery of some means by which she might assert her sullied dignity, and various were the expedients which she revolved.

CHAPTER THE THIRTY-SECOND

But now the hand of fate is on the curtain, And
brings the scene to light.
DON SEBASTIAN.

The gigantic trumpet of the Varangians sounded its loudest note of march,
and the squadrons of the faithful guards, sheathed in complete mail, and
enclosing in their centre the person of their
Imperial master, set forth upon their procession through the streets of
Constantinople. The form of Alexius, glittering in his splendid armour,
seemed no unmeet central point for the force of an empire; and while the
citizens crowded in the train of him and his escort,
there might be seen a visible difference between those who came with the
premeditated intention of tumult, and the greater part, who, like the multitude
of every great city, thrust each other and shout for rapture on account of any
cause for which a crowd may be collected together. The hope of the
conspirators was lodged chiefly in the Immortal Guards, who were levied
principally for the defence of Constantinople, partook of the general
prejudices of the citizens, and had been particularly influenced by those in
favour of Ursel, by whom, previous to his imprisonment, they had themselves
been commanded. The conspirators had determined that those of this body
who were considered as most discontented, should early in the morning take
possession of the posts in the lists most favourable for their purpose of
assaulting the Emperor's person. But, in spite of all efforts short of actual
violence, for which the time did not seem to be come, they found themselves
disappointed in this purpose, by parties of the Varangian guards, planted with
apparent carelessness, but in fact, with perfect skill, for the prevention of their
enterprise. Somewhat confounded at perceiving that a design, which they
could not suppose to be suspected, was, nevertheless, on every part controlled
and counter–checked, the conspirators began to look for the principal persons
of their own party, on whom they depended for orders in this emergency; but
neither the Caesar nor Agelastes was to

be seen, whether in the lists or on the military march from Constantinople: and though Achilles Tatius rode in the latter assembly, yet it might be clearly observed that he was rather attending upon the Protospathaire, than, assuming that independence as an officer which he loved to affect.

In this manner, as the Emperor with his glittering bands approached the phalanx of Tancred and his followers, who were drawn up, it will be remembered, upon a rising cape between the city and the lists, the main body of the Imperial procession deflected in some degree from the straight road, in order to march past them without interruption; while the Protospathaire and the Acolyte passed under the escort of a band of Varangians, to bear the Emperor's inquiries to Prince Tancred, concerning the purpose of his being there with his band.

The short march was soon performed—the large trumpet which attended the two officers sounded a parley, and Tancred himself, remarkable for that personal beauty which Tasso has preferred to any of the crusaders, except Rinaldo d'Este, the creatures of his own poetical imagination, advanced to parley with them.

"The Emperor of Greece," said the Protospathaire to Tancred, "requires the Prince of Otranto to show, by the two high officers who shall deliver him this message, with what purpose he has returned, contrary to his oath, to the right side of these straits; assuring Prince Tancred at the same time, that nothing will so much please the Emperor, as to receive an answer not at variance with his treaty with the Duke of Bouillon, and the oath which was taken by the crusading nobles and their soldiers; since that would enable the Emperor, in conformity to his own wishes, by his kind reception of Prince Tancred and his troop, to show how high is his estimation of the dignity of the one, and the bravery of both—We wait an answer."

The tone of the message had nothing in it very alarming, and its substance cost Prince Tancred very little trouble to answer. "The cause," he said, "of the Prince of Otranto appearing here with fifty lances, is this cartel, in which a combat is appointed betwixt Nicephorus Briennius, called the Caesar, a high member of this empire, and a worthy knight of great fame, the partner of the Pilgrims who have taken the Cross, in their high vow to rescue

Palestine from the infidels. The name of the said Knight is the redoubted Robert of Paris. It becomes, therefore, an obligation, indispensable upon the Holy Pilgrims of the Crusade, to send one chief of their number, with a body of men–at–arms, sufficient to see, as is usual, fair play between the combatants. That such is their intention, may be seen from, their sending no more than fifty lances, with their furniture and following; whereas it would have cost them no trouble to have detached ten times the number, had they nourished any purpose of interfering by force, or disturbing the fair combat which is about to take place. The Prince of Otranto, therefore, and his followers, will place themselves at the disposal of the Imperial Court, and witness the proceedings of the combat, with the most perfect confidence that the rules of fair battle will be punctually observed."

The two Grecian officers transmitted this reply to the Emperor, who heard it with pleasure, and immediately proceeding to act upon the principle which he had laid down, of maintaining peace, if possible, with the crusaders, named Prince Tancred with the Protospathaire as Field Marshals of the lists, fully empowered, under the Emperor, to decide all the terms of the combat, and to have recourse to Alexius himself where their opinions disagreed. This was made known to the assistants, who were thus prepared for the entry into the lists of the Grecian officer and the Italian Prince in full armour, while a proclamation announced to all the spectators their solemn office.
The same annunciation commanded the assistants of every kind to clear a convenient part of the seats which surrounded the lists on one side, that it might serve for the accommodation of Prince Tancred's followers.

Achilles Tatius, who was a heedful observer of all these passages, saw with alarm, that by the last collocation the armed Latins were interposed between the Immortal Guards and the discontented citizens, which made it most probable that the conspiracy was discovered, and that Alexius found he had a good right to reckon upon the assistance of Tancred and his forces in the task of suppressing it. This, added to the cold and caustic manner in which the Emperor communicated his commands to him, made the Acolyte of opinion, that his best chance of escape from the danger in which he was now placed, was, that the whole conspiracy should fall to the ground, and that the day should pass without the least attempt to shake the throne of Alexius Comnenus. Even then it continued highly doubtful, whether a despot, so wily and so suspicious as the Emperor, would think it sufficient to rest satisfied with the private knowledge of the undertaking, and its failure, with which he appeared to be possessed, without putting into exercise the bow–strings and the blinding–irons of the mutes of the interior. There was, however, little possibility either of flight or of resistance. The least attempt to withdraw himself from the neighbourhood of those faithful followers of the Emperor, personal foes of his own, by whom he was gradually and more closely surrounded, became each moment more perilous, and more certain to provoke a rupture, which it was the interest of the weaker party to delay, with whatever difficulty. And while the soldiers under Achilles's immediate authority seemed still to treat him as their superior officer, and appeal to him for the word of command, it became more and more evident that the slightest degree of suspicion which should be excited, would be the instant signal for his being placed under arrest. With a trembling heart, therefore, and eyes dimmed by the powerful idea of soon parting with the light of day, and all that it made visible, the Acolyte saw himself condemned to watch the turn of circumstances over which he could have no influence, and to content himself with waiting the result of a drama, in which his own life was concerned, although the piece was played by others. Indeed, it seemed as if through the whole assembly some signal was waited for, which no one was in readiness to give.

The discontented citizens and soldiers looked in vain for Agelastes and the Caesar, and when they observed the condition of Achilles Tatius, it seemed such as rather to express doubt and consternation, than to give encouragement to the hopes they had entertained. Many of the lower classes, however, felt too secure in their own insignificance to fear the personal consequences of a tumult, and were desirous, therefore, to provoke the disturbance, which seemed hushing itself to sleep.

A hoarse murmur, which attained almost the importance of a shout, exclaimed,—"Justice, justice!—Ursel, Ursel!—The rights of the

Immortal Guards!" etc. At this the trumpet of the Varangians awoke, and its tremendous tones were heard to peal loudly over the whole assembly, as the voice of its presiding deity. A dead silence
prevailed in the multitude, and the voice of a herald announced, in the name of Alexius Comnenus, his sovereign will and pleasure.

"Citizens of the Roman Empire, your complaints, stirred up by factious men, have reached the ear of your Emperor; you shall yourselves be witness to his power of gratifying his people. At your request, and before your own sight, the visual ray which hath been quenched shall be re–illumined—the mind whose efforts were restricted to the imperfect supply of individual wants shall be again extended, if such is the owner's will, to the charge of an ample Theme or division of the empire. Political jealousy, more hard to receive conviction than the blind to receive sight, shall yield itself conquered, by the Emperor's paternal love of his people, and his desire to give them satisfaction. Ursel, the darling of your wishes, supposed to be long dead, or at least believed to exist in blinded seclusion, is restored to you well in health, clear in eyesight, and possessed of every faculty necessary to adorn the Emperor's favour, or merit the affection of the people."

As the herald thus spoke, a figure, which had hitherto stood shrouded behind some officers of the interior, now stepped forth,
and flinging from him a dusky veil, in which he was wrapt, appeared in a dazzling scarlet garment, of which the sleeves and buskins displayed those ornaments which expressed a rank nearly adjacent to that of the Emperor himself. He held in his hand a silver truncheon, the badge of delegated command over the Immortal Guards, and kneeling before the Emperor, presented it to his hands, intimating a virtual resignation of the command which it implied. The whole assembly were electrified at the appearance of a person long
supposed either dead, or by cruel means rendered incapable of public trust. Some recognised the man, whose appearance and features were not easily forgot, and gratulated him upon his most unexpected
return to the service of his country. Others stood suspended in amazement, not knowing whether to trust their eyes, while a few determined malecontents eagerly pressed upon the assembly an allegation that the person presented as Ursel was only a counterfeit,

and the whole a trick of the Emperor.

"Speak to them, noble Ursel," said the Emperor. "Tell them, that if I have sinned against thee, it has been because I was deceived, and that my disposition to make thee amends is as ample as ever was my purpose of doing thee wrong."

"Friends and countrymen," said Ursel, turning himself to the assembly, "his Imperial Majesty permits me to offer my assurance, that if in any former part of my life I have suffered at his hand, it is more than wiped out by the feelings of a moment so glorious as this; and that I am well satisfied, from the present instant, to spend what remains of my life in the service of the most generous and beneficent of sovereigns, or, with his permission, to bestow it in preparing, by devotional exercises, for an infinite immortality to be spent in the society of saints and angels. Whichever choice I shall make, I reckon that you, my beloved countrymen, who have remembered me so kindly during years of darkness and captivity, will not fail to afford me the advantage of your prayers."

This sudden apparition of the long–lost Ursel had too much of that which elevates and surprises not to captivate the multitude, and they sealed their reconciliation with three tremendous shouts, which are said to have shaken the air, that birds, incapable of sustaining themselves, sunk down exhausted out of their native element.

CHAPTER THE THIRTY-THIRD

"What, leave the combat out!" exclaimed the knight. "Yea! or
we must renounce the Stagyrite.
So large a crowd the stage will ne'er contain."
—"Then build a new, or act it on a plain." POPE.

The sounds of the gratulating shout had expanded over the distant shores of
the Bosphorus by mountain and forest, and died at length in the farthest
echoes, when the people, in the silence which ensued, appeared to ask each
other what next scene was about to adorn a pause so solemn and a stage so
august. The pause would probably have soon given place to some new
clamour, for a multitude, from whatever cause assembled, seldom remains
long silent, had not a new signal from the Varangian trumpet given notice of
a fresh purpose to solicit their attention. The blast had something in its tone
spirit–stirring and yet melancholy, partaking both of the character of a point
of war, and of the doleful sounds which might be chosen to
announce an execution of peculiar solemnity. Its notes were high and widely
extended, and prolonged and long dwelt upon, as if the
brazen clamour had been waked by something more tremendous than the
lungs of mere mortals.

The multitude appeared to acknowledge these awful sounds, which were
indeed such as habitually solicited their attention to Imperial edicts, of
melancholy import, by which rebellions were announced, dooms of treason
discharged, and other tidings of a great and affecting import intimated to the
people of Constantinople. When the trumpet had in its turn ceased, with its
thrilling and doleful notes, to agitate the immense assembly, the voice of the
herald again
addressed them.

It announced in a grave and affecting strain, that it sometimes chanced how
the people failed in their duty to a sovereign, who was

unto them as a father, and how it became the painful duty of the prince to use the rod of correction rather than the olive sceptre of mercy.

"Fortunate," continued the herald, "it is, when the supreme Deity having taken on himself the preservation of a throne, in beneficence and justice resembling his own, has also assumed the most painful task of his earthly delegate, by punishing those whom his unerring judgment acknowledges as most guilty, and leaving to his substitute the more agreeable task of pardoning such of those as art has misled, and treachery hath involved in its snares.

"Such being the case, Greece and its accompanying Themes are called upon to listen and learn that a villain, namely Agelastes, who had insinuated himself into the favour of the Emperor, by affection of deep knowledge and severe virtue, had formed a treacherous plan for the murder of the Emperor Alexius Comnenus, and a revolution in the state. This person, who, under pretended wisdom, hid the doctrines of a heretic and the vices of a sensualist, had found
proselytes to his doctrines even among the Emperor's household, and those persons who were most bound to him, and down to the lower order, to excite the last of whom were dispersed a multitude of
forged rumours, similar to those concerning Ursol's death and blindness, of which your own eyes have witnessed the falsehood."

The people, who had hitherto listened in silence, upon this appeal broke forth in a clamorous assent. They had scarcely been again silent, ere the iron–voiced herald continued his proclamation.

"Not Korah, Dathan, and Abiram," he said, "had more justly, or more directly fallen under the doom of an offended Deity, than this villain, Agelastes. The steadfast earth gaped to devour the apostate sons of Israel, but the termination of this wretched man's existence has been, as far as can now be known, by the direct means of an evil spirit, whom his own arts had evoked into the upper air. By the
spirit, as would appear by the testimony of a noble lady, and other females, who witnessed the termination of his life, Agelastes was strangled, a fate well–becoming his odious crimes. Such a death, even of a guilty man, must, indeed, be most painful to the humane

feelings of the Emperor, because it involves suffering beyond this world. But the awful catastrophe carries with it this comfort, that it absolves the Emperor from the necessity of carrying any farther a vengeance which Heaven itself seems to have limited to the exemplary punishment of the principal conspirator. Some changes of offices and situations shall be made, for the sake of safety and good order; but the secret who had or who had not, been concerned in this awful crime, shall sleep in the bosoms of the persons themselves implicated, since the Emperor is determined to dismiss their offence from his memory, as the effect of a transient delusion. Let all, therefore, who now hear me, whatever consciousness they may possess of a knowledge of what was this day intended, return to their houses, assured that their own thoughts will be their only

punishment. Let them rejoice that Almighty goodness has saved them from the meditations of their own hearts, and, according to the affecting language of Scripture,—'Let them repent and sin no more, lest a worse thing befall them.'"

The voice of the herald then ceased, and was again answered by the shouts of the audience. These were unanimous; for circumstances contributed to convince the malecontent party that they stood at the Sovereign's mercy, and the edict that they heard having shown his acquaintance with their guilt, it lay at his pleasure to let loose upon them the strength of the Varangians, while, from the terms on which it had pleased him to receive Tancred, it was probable that the Apuleian forces were also at his disposal.

The voices, therefore, of the bulky Stephanos, of Harpax the centurion, and other rebels, both of the camp and city, were the first to thunder forth their gratitude for the clemency of the Emperor, and their thanks to Heaven for his preservation.

The audience, reconciled to the thoughts of the discovered and frustrated conspiracy, began meantime, according to their custom, to turn themselves to the consideration of the matter which had more avowedly called them together, and private whispers, swelling by degrees into murmurs, began to express the dissatisfaction of the citizens at being thus long assembled, without receiving any communication respecting the announced purpose of their meeting.

Alexius was not slow to perceive the tendency of their thoughts; and, on a signal from his hand, the trumpets blew a point of war, in sounds far more lively than those which had prefaced the Imperial edict. "Robert, Count of Paris," then said a herald, "art thou here in thy place, or by knightly proxy, to answer the challenge brought against thee by his Imperial Highness Nicephorus Briennius, Caesar of this empire?"

The Emperor conceived himself to have equally provided against the actual appearance at this call of either of the parties named, and had prepared an exhibition of another kind, namely, certain cages, tenanted by wild animals, which being now loosened should do their pleasure with each other in the eyes of the assembly. His astonishment and confusion, therefore, were great, when, as the last note of the proclamation died in the echo, Count Robert of Paris stood forth, armed cap–a–pie, his mailed charger led behind him from within the curtained enclosure, at one end of the lists, as if ready to mount at the signal of the marshal.

The alarm and the shame that were visible in every countenance near the Imperial presence when no Caesar came forth in like fashion to confront the formidable Frank, were not of long duration. Hardly had the style and title of the Count of Paris been duly announced by the heralds, and their second summons of his antagonist uttered in due form, when a person, dressed like one of the Varangian Guards, sprung into the lists, and announced himself as ready to do battle in the name and place of the Caesar Nicephorus Briennius, and for the honour of the empire.

Alexius, with the utmost joy, beheld this unexpected assistance, and readily gave his consent to the bold soldier who stood thus forward in the hour of utmost need, to take upon himself the dangerous office of champion. He the more readily acquiesced, as, from the size and appearance of the soldier, and the gallant bearing he displayed, he had no doubt of his individual person, and fully confided in his valour. But Prince Tancred interposed his opposition.

"The lists," he said, "were only open to knights and nobles; or, at any rate, men were not permitted to meet therein who were not of some equality of birth and blood; nor could he remain a silent witness where the laws of chivalry are in such respects forgotten."

"Let Count Robert of Paris," said the Varangian, "look upon my countenance, and say whether he has not, by promise, removed all objection to our contest which might be founded upon an inequality of condition, and let him be judge himself, whether, by meeting me in this field, he will do more than comply with a compact which he has long since become bound by."

Count Robert, upon this appeal, advanced and acknowledged, without further debate, that, notwithstanding their difference of rank, he held himself bound by his solemn word to give this valiant soldier a meeting in the field. That he regretted, on account of this gallant man's eminent virtues, and the high services he had received at his hands, that they should now stand upon terms of such bloody arbitration; but since nothing was more common, than that the fate
of war called on friends to meet each other in mortal combat, he would not shrink from the engagement he had pledged himself to; nor did he think his quality in the slightest degree infringed or diminished, by meeting in battle a warrior so well known and of
such good account as Hereward, the brave Varangian. He added, that "he willingly admitted that the combat should take place on foot, and with the battle–axe, which was the ordinary weapon of the
Varangian guard."

Hereward had stood still, almost like a statue, while this discourse passed; but when the Count of Paris had made this speech, he inclined himself towards him with a grateful obeisance, and expressed himself honoured and gratified by the manly manner in which the Count acquitted himself, according to his promise, with complete honour and fidelity.

"What we are to do," said Count Robert, with a sigh of regret, which even his love of battle could not prevent, "let us do quickly; the heart may be affected, but the hand must do its duty."

Hereward assented, with the additional remark, "Let us then lose no more time, which is already flying fast." And, grasping his axe, he stood prepared for combat.

"I also am ready," said Count Robert of Paris, taking the same weapon from a Varangian soldier, who stood by the lists. Both were immediately upon the alert, nor did further forms or circumstances put off the intended duel.

The first blows were given and parried with great caution, and Prince Tancred and others thought that on the part of Count Robert the caution was much greater than usual; but, in combat as in food, the appetite increases with the exercise. The fiercer passions began, as usual, to awaken with the clash of arms and the sense of deadly blows, some of which were made with great fury on either side, and parried with considerable difficulty, and not so completely but that blood flowed on both their parts. The Greeks looked with astonishment on a single combat, such as they had seldom witnessed, and held their breath as they beheld the furious blows dealt by either warrior, and expected with each stroke the annihilation of one or other of the combatants. As yet their strength and agility seemed somewhat equally matched, although those who judged with more pretension to knowledge, were of opinion, that Count Robert spared putting forth some part of the military skill for which he was celebrated; and the remark was generally made and allowed that he had surrendered a great advantage by not insisting
upon his right to fight upon horseback. On the other hand, it was the general opinion that the gallant Varangian omitted to take advantage of one or two opportunities afforded him by the heat of Count Robert's temper, who obviously was incensed at the duration of the combat.

Accident at length seemed about to decide what had been hitherto an equal contest. Count Robert, making a feint on one side of his antagonist, struck him on the other, which was uncovered, with the edge of his weapon, so that the Varangian reeled, and seemed in the act of falling to the earth. The usual sound made by spectators at the sight of any painful or unpleasant circumstance, by drawing the breath between the teeth, was suddenly heard to pass through the assembly, while a female voice loud and eagerly exclaimed, —"Count Robert of Paris!—forget not this day that thou owest a life to Heaven and me." The Count was in the act of again seconding his blow, with what effect could hardly be judged, when this cry reached his ears, and apparently took away his disposition for farther combat.

"I acknowledge the debt," he said, sinking his battle–axe, and retreating two steps from his antagonist, who stood in astonishment, scarcely recovered from the stunning effect of the blow by which he was so nearly prostrated. He sank the blade of his battle–axe in imitation of his antagonist, and seemed to wait in suspense what was to be the next process of the combat. "I acknowledge my debt," said the valiant Count of Paris, "alike to Bertha of Britain and to the Almighty, who has preserved me from the crime of ungrateful blood–guiltiness.—You have seen the fight, gentlemen," turning to Tancred and his chivalry, "and can testify, on your honour, that it has been maintained fairly on both sides, and without advantage on
either. I presume my honourable antagonist has by this time satisfied the desire which brought me under his challenge, and which
certainly had no taste in it of personal or private quarrel. On my part, I retain towards him such a sense of personal obligation as would render my continuing this combat, unless compelled to it by self– defence, a shameful and sinful action."

Alexius gladly embraced the terms of truce, which he was far from expecting, and threw down his warder, in signal that the duel was ended. Tancred, though somewhat surprised, and perhaps even scandalized, that a private soldier of the Emperor's guard should have so long resisted the utmost efforts of so approved a knight, could not but own that the combat had been fought with perfect fairness and equality, and decided upon terms dishonourable to neither party. The Count's character being well known and established amongst the crusaders, they were compelled to believe that some motive of a most potent nature formed the principle upon which, very contrary to his general practice, he had proposed a cessation of the combat before it was brought to a deadly, or at least to a decisive conclusion. The edict of the Emperor upon the occasion, therefore, passed into a law, acknowledged by the assent of the chiefs present, and especially affirmed and gratulated by the shouts of the assembled spectators.

But perhaps the most interesting figure in the assembly was that of the bold Varangian, arrived so suddenly at a promotion of military renown, which the extreme difficulty he had experienced in keeping his ground against Count Robert had prevented him from anticipating, although his modesty had not diminished the indomitable courage with which he maintained the contest. He stood in the middle of the lists, his face ruddy with the exertion of the combat, and not less so from the modest consciousness proper to the plainness and simplicity of his character, which was disconcerted by finding himself the central point of the gaze of the multitude.

"Speak to me, my soldier," said Alexius, strongly affected by the gratitude which he felt was due to Hereward upon so singular an occasion, "speak to thine Emperor as his superior, for such thou art at this moment, and tell him if there is any manner, even at the expense of half his kingdom, to atone for his own life saved, and, what is yet dearer, for the honour of his country, which thou hast so manfully defended and preserved?"

"My Lord," answered Hereward, "your Imperial Highness values my poor services over highly, and ought to attribute them to the noble Count of Paris, first, for his condescending to accept of an antagonist so mean in quality as myself; and next, in generously relinquishing victory when he might have achieved it by an additional blow; for I here confess before your Majesty, my brethren, and the assembled Grecians, that my power of protracting the combat was ended, when the gallant Count, by his generosity, put a stop to it."

"Do not thyself that wrong, brave man," said Count Robert; "for I vow to our Lady of the Broken Lances, that the combat was yet within the undetermined doom of Providence, when the pressure of my own feelings rendered me incapable of continuing it, to the necessary harm, perhaps to the mortal damage, of an antagonist to whom I owe so much kindness. Choose, therefore, the recompense which the generosity of thy Emperor offers in a manner so just and grateful, and fear not lest mortal voice pronounces that reward unmerited which Robert of Paris shall avouch with his sword to have been gallantly won upon his own crest."

"You are too great, my lord, and too noble," answered the Anglo– Saxon, "to be gainsaid by such as I am, and I must not awaken new strife between us by contesting the circumstances under which our combat so suddenly closed, nor would it be wise or prudent in me further to contradict you. My noble Emperor generously offers me the right of naming what he calls my recompense; but let not his generosity be dispraised, although it is from you, my lord, and not from his Imperial Highness, that I am to ask a boon, to me the dearest to which my voice can give utterance."

"And that," said the Count, "has reference to Bertha, the faithful attendant of my wife?"

"Even so," said Hereward; "it is my proposal to request my discharge from the Varangian guard, and permission to share in your lordship's pious and honourable vow for the recovery of Palestine, with liberty to fight under your honoured banner, and permission from time to time to recommend my love–suit to Bertha, the attendant of the Countess of Paris, and the hope that it may find favour in the eyes of her noble lord and lady. I may thus finally hope to be restored to a country, which I have never ceased to love over the rest of the world."

"Thy service, noble soldier," said the Count, "shall be as acceptable to me as that of a born earl; nor is there an opportunity of acquiring honour which I can shape for thee, to which, as it occurs, I will not gladly prefer thee. I will not boast of what interest I have with the King of England, but something I can do with him, and it shall be strained to the uttermost to settle thee in thine own beloved native country."

The Emperor then spoke. "Bear witness, heaven and earth, and you my faithful subjects, and you my gallant allies; above all, you my bold and true Varangian Guard, that we would rather have lost the brightest jewel from our Imperial crown, than have relinquished the service of this true and faithful Anglo–Saxon. But since go he must and will, it shall be my study to distinguish him by such marks of beneficence as may make it known through his future life, that he is the person to whom the Emperor Alexius Comnenus acknowledged a debt larger than his empire could discharge. You, my Lord Tancred, and your principal leaders, will sup with us this evening, and to–morrow resume your honourable and religious purpose of pilgrimage. We trust both the combatants will also oblige us by their presence.—Trumpets, give the signal for dismission."

The trumpets sounded accordingly, and the different classes of spectators, armed and unarmed, broke up into various parties, or formed into their military ranks, for the purpose of their return to the city.

The screams of women suddenly and strangely raised, was the first thing that arrested the departure of the multitude, when those who glanced their eyes back, saw Sylvan, the great ourang–outang, produce himself in the lists, to their surprise and astonishment. The women, and many of the men who were present, unaccustomed to the ghastly look and savage appearance of a creature so extraordinary, raised a yell of terror so loud, that it discomposed the animal who was the occasion of its being raised. Sylvan, in the course of the night, having escaped over the garden–wall of Agelastes, and clambered over the rampart of the city, found no difficulty in hiding himself in the lists which were in the act of being raised, having found a lurking–place in some dark corner under the seats of the spectators. From this he was probably dislodged by the tumult of the dispersing multitude, and had been compelled, therefore, to make an appearance in public when he least desired it, not unlike that of the celebrated Puliccinello, at the conclusion of his own drama, when he enters in mortal strife with the foul fiend himself, a scene which scarcely excites more terror among the juvenile audience, than did the unexpected apparition of Sylvan among the spectators of the duel. Bows were bent, and javelins pointed by the braver part of the soldiery, against an animal of an appearance so ambiguous, and whom his uncommon size and grizzly look caused most who beheld him to suppose either the devil himself, or the apparition of some fiendish deity of ancient days, whom the heathens worshipped. Sylvan had so far improved such opportunities as had been afforded him, as to become sufficiently aware that the attitudes assumed by so many military men, inferred immediate danger to his person, from which he hastened to shelter

himself by flying to the protection of Hereward, with whom he had been in some degree familiarized. He seized him, accordingly, by the cloak, and, by the absurd and alarmed look of his fantastic features, and a certain wild and gibbering chatter, endeavoured to express his fear and to ask protection. Hereward understood the terrified
creature, and turning to the Emperor's throne, said aloud,—"Poor frightened being, turn thy petition, and gestures, and tones, to a quarter which, having to–day pardoned so many offences which were wilfully and maliciously schemed, will not be, I am sure, obdurate to such as thou, in thy half–reasoning capacity, may have been capable of committing."

The creature, as is the nature of its tribe, caught from Hereward himself the mode of applying with most effect his gestures and pitiable supplication, while the Emperor, notwithstanding the serious scene which had just past, could not help laughing at the touch of comedy flung into it by this last incident.

"My trusty Hereward,"—he said aside, ("I will not again call him Edward if I can help it)—thou art the refuge of the distressed, whether it be man or beast, and nothing that sues through thy intercession, while thou remainest in our service, shall find its supplication in vain. Do thou, good Hereward," for the name was
now pretty well established in his Imperial memory, "and such of thy companions as know the habits of the creature, lead him back to his old quarters in the Blacquernal; and that done, my friend, observe
that we request thy company, and that of thy faithful mate Bertha, to partake supper at our court, with our wife and daughter, and such of our servants and allies as we shall request to share the same honour. Be assured, that while thou remainest with us, there is no point of dignity which shall not be willingly paid to thee.—And do thou approach, Achilles Tatius, as much favoured by thine Emperor as before this day dawned. What charges are against thee have been only whispered in a friendly ear, which remembers them not, unless (which Heaven forefend!) their remembrance is renewed by fresh offences."

Achilles Tatius bowed till the plume of his helmet mingled with the mane of his fiery horse, but held it wisest to forbear any answer in words, leaving his crime and his pardon to stand upon those general terms in which the Emperor had expressed them.

Once more the multitude of all ranks returned on their way to the city, nor did any second interruption arrest their march. Sylvan, accompanied by one or two Varangians, who led him in a sort of captivity, took his way to the vaults of the Blacquernal, which were in fact his proper habitation.

Upon the road to the city, Harpax, the notorious corporal of the Immortal Guards, held a discourse with one or two of his own soldiers, and of the citizens who had been members of the late conspiracy.

"So," said Stephanos, the prize–fighter, "a fine affair we have made of it, to suffer ourselves to be all anticipated and betrayed by a thick– sculled Varangian; every chance turning against us as they would against Corydon, the shoemaker, if he were to defy me to the circus. Ursel, whose death made so much work, turns out not to be dead after all; and what is worse, he lives not to our advantage. This fellow Hereward, who was yesterday no better than myself—What do I say?— better!—he was a great deal worse—an insignificant nobody in every respect!—is now crammed with honours, praises, and gifts, till he wellnigh returns what they have given him, and the Caesar and the Acolyte, our associates, have lost the Emperor's love and confidence, and if they are suffered to survive, it must be like the tame domestic poultry, whom we pamper with food, one day, that upon the next their necks may be twisted for spit or spot."

"Stephanos," replied the centurion, "thy form of body fits thee well for the Palaestra, but thy mind is not so acutely formed as to detect that which is real from that which is only probable, in the political world, of which thou art now judging. Considering the risk incurred by lending a man's ear to a conspiracy, thou oughtest to reckon it a saving in every particular, where he escapes with his life and character safe. This has been the case with Achilles Tatius, and with the Caesar. They have remained also in their high places of trust and power, and maybe confident that the Emperor will hardly dare to remove them at a future period, since the possession of the full

knowledge of their guilt has not emboldened him to do so. Their power, thus left with them, is in fact ours; nor is there a circumstance to be supposed, which can induce them to betray their confederates
to the government. It is much more likely that they will remember them with the probability of renewing, at a finer time, the alliance which binds them together. Cheer up thy noble resolution, therefore, my Prince of the Circus, and think that thou shalt still retain that predominant influence which the favourites of the amphitheatre are sure to possess over the citizens of Constantinople."

"I cannot tell," answered Stephanos; "but it gnaws at my heart like the worm that dieth not, to see this beggarly foreigner betray the noblest blood in the land, not to mention the best athlete in the Palaestra, and move off not only without punishment for his treachery, but with praise, honour, and preferment."

"True," said Harpax; "but observe, my friend, that he does move off to purpose. He leaves the land, quits the corps in which he might claim preferment and a few vain honours, being valued at what such trifles amount to. Hereward, in the course of one or two days, shall be little better than a disbanded soldier, subsisting by the poor bread which he can obtain as a follower of this beggarly Count, or which he is rather bound to dispute with the infidel, by encountering with his battle–axe the Turkish sabres. What will it avail him amidst the disasters, the slaughter, and the famine of Palestine, that he once upon a time was admitted to supper with the Emperor? We know Alexius Comnenus—he is willing to discharge, at the highest cost, such obligations as are incurred to men like this Hereward; and, believe me, I think that I see the wily despot shrug his shoulders in
derision, when one morning he is saluted with the news of a battle in Palestine lost by the crusaders in which his old acquaintance has fallen a dead man. I will not insult thee, by telling thee how easy it might be to acquire the favour of a gentlewoman in waiting upon a lady of quality; nor do I think it would be difficult, should that be the object of the prize–fighter, to acquire the property of a large baboon like Sylvan, which no doubt would set up as a juggler any Frank
who had meanness of spirit to propose to gain his bread in such a capacity, from the alms of the starving chivalry of Europe. But he who can stoop to envy the lot of such a person, ought not to be one

whose chief personal distinctions are sufficient to place him first in rank over all the favourites of the amphitheatre."

There was something in this sophistical kind of reasoning, which was but half satisfactory to the obtuse intellect of the prize–fighter, to whom it was addressed, although the only answer which he attempted was couched in this observation:—

"Ay, but, noble centurion, you forget that, besides empty honours, this Varangian Hereward, or Edward, whichever is his name, is promised a mighty donative of gold."

"Marry, you touch me there," said the centurion; "and when you tell me that the promise is fulfilled, I will willingly agree that the Anglo– Saxon hath gained something to be envied for; but while it remains
in the shape of a naked promise, you shall pardon me, my worthy Stephanos, if I hold it of no more account than the mere pledges which are distributed among ourselves as well as to the Varangians, promising upon future occasions mints of money, which we are likely to receive at the same time with the last year's snow. Keep up your heart, therefore, noble Stephanos, and believe not that your affairs are worse for the miscarriage of this day; and let not thy gallant courage sink, but remembering those principles upon which it was called into action, believe that thy objects are not the less secure because fate has removed their acquisition to a more distant day." The veteran and unbending conspirator, Harpax, thus strengthened for some future renewal of their enterprise the failing spirits of Stephanos.

After this, such leaders as were included in the invitation given by the Emperor, repaired to the evening meal, and, from the general content and complaisance expressed by Alexius and his guests of every description, it could little have been supposed that the day just passed over was one which had inferred a purpose so dangerous and treacherous.

The absence of the Countess Brenhilda, during this eventful day, created no small surprise to the Emperor and those in his immediate confidence, who knew her enterprising spirit, and the interest she must have felt in the issue of the combat. Bertha had made an early communication to the Count, that his lady, agitated with the many anxieties of the few preceding days, was unable to leave her apartment. The valiant knight, therefore, lost no time in acquainting his faithful Countess of his safety; and afterwards joining those who partook of the banquet at the palace, he bore himself as if the least recollection did not remain on his mind of the perfidious conduct of the Emperor at the conclusion of the last entertainment. He knew, in truth, that the knights of Prince Tancred not only maintained a strict watch round the house where Brenhilda remained, but also that they preserved a severe ward in the neighbourhood of the Blacquernal, as well for the safety of their heroic leader, as for that of Count Robert, the respected companion of their military pilgrimage.

It was the general principle of the European chivalry, that distrust was rarely permitted to survive open quarrels, and that whatever was forgiven, was dismissed from their recollection, as unlikely to recur; but on the present occasion there was a more than usual assemblage of troops, which the occurrences of the day had drawn together, so that the crusaders were called upon to be particularly watchful.

It may be believed that the evening passed over without any attempt to renew the ceremonial in the council chamber of the Lions, which had been upon a former occasion terminated in such misunderstanding. Indeed it would have been lucky if the explanation between the mighty Emperor of Greece and the chivalrous Knight of Paris had taken place earlier; for reflection on what had passed, had convinced the Emperor that the Franks were not a people to be imposed upon by pieces of clockwork, and similar trifles, and that what they did not understand, was sure, instead of procuring their awe or admiration, to excite their anger and defiance. Nor had it altogether escaped Count Robert, that the manners of the Eastern people were upon a different scale from those to which he had been accustomed; that they neither were so deeply affected by the spirit of chivalry, nor, in his own language, was the worship of the Lady of the Broken Lances so congenial a subject of adoration. This notwithstanding, Count Robert observed, that Alexius Comnenus was a wise and politic prince; his wisdom perhaps too much allied to cunning, but yet aiding him to maintain with great address that empire over the minds of his subjects, which was necessary for their good, and for maintaining his own authority. He therefore resolved to receive with equanimity whatever should be offered by the Emperor, either in civility or in the way of jest, and not again to disturb an understanding which might be of advantage to Christendom, by a quarrel founded upon misconception of terms

or misapprehension of manners. To this prudent resolution the Count of Paris adhered during the whole evening; with some difficulty, however, since it was somewhat inconsistent with his own fiery and inquisitive temper, which was equally desirous to know the precise amount of whatever was addressed to him, and to take umbrage at it, should it appear in the least degree offensive, whether so intended or not.

CHAPTER THE THIRTY-FOURTH

It was not until after the conquest of Jerusalem that Count Robert of Paris returned to Constantinople, and with his wife, and such proportion of his followers as the sword and pestilence had left after that bloody warfare, resumed his course to his native kingdom. Upon reaching Italy, the first care of the noble Count and Countess was to celebrate in princely style the marriage of Hereward and his faithful Bertha, who had added to their other claims upon their master and mistress, those acquired by Hereward's faithful services in Palestine, and no less by Bertha's affectionate ministry to her lady in Constantinople.

As to the fate of Alexius Comnenus, it may be read at large in the history of his daughter Anna, who has represented him as the hero of many a victory, achieved, says the purple–born, in the third chapter and fifteenth book of her history, sometimes by his arms and sometimes by his prudence.

"His boldness alone has gained some battles, at other times his success has been won by stratagem. He has erected the most illustrious of his trophies by confronting danger, by combating like a simple soldier, and throwing himself bareheaded into the thickest of the foe. But there are others," continues the accomplished lady, "which he gained an opportunity of erecting by assuming the appearance of terror, and even of retreat. In a word, he knew alike how to triumph either in flight or in pursuit, and remained upright even before those enemies who appeared to have struck him down; resembling the military implement termed the calthrop, which remains always upright in whatever direction it is thrown on the ground."

It would be unjust to deprive the Princess of the defence she herself makes against the obvious charge of partiality.

"I must still once more repel the reproach which some bring against me, as if my history was composed merely according to the dictates of the natural love for parents which is engraved in the hearts of children. In truth, it is not the effect of that affection which I bear to mine, but it is the evidence of matter of fact, which obliges me to speak as I have done. Is it not possible that one can have at the same time an affection for the memory of a father and for truth? For myself, I have never directed my attempt to write history, otherwise than for the ascertainment of the matter of fact. With this purpose, I have taken for my subject the history of a worthy man. Is it just, that, by the single accident of his being the author of my birth, his quality of my father ought to form a prejudice against me, which would ruin my credit with my readers? I have given, upon other occasions, proofs sufficiently strong of the ardour which I had for the defence
of my father's interests, which those that know me can never doubt but, on the present, I have been limited by the inviolable fidelity
with which I respect the truth, which I should have felt conscience to have veiled, under pretence of serving the renown of my father."—*Alexiad*, chap. iii. book xv.

This much we have deemed it our duty to quote, in justice to the fair historian; we will extract also her description of the Emperor's death, and are not unwilling to allow, that the character assigned to the Princess by our own Gibbon, has in it a great deal of fairness and of truth.

Notwithstanding her repeated protests of sacrificing rather to the exact and absolute truth than to the memory of her deceased parent, Gibbon remarks truly, that "instead of the simplicity of style and narrative which wins a belief, an elaborate affectation of rhetoric and science betrays in every page the vanity of a female author. The genuine character of Alexius is lost in a vague constellation of virtues; and the perpetual strain of panegyric and apology awakens our jealousy to question the veracity of the historian, and the merit of the hero. We cannot, however, refuse her judicious and important remark, that the disorders of the times were the misfortune and the glory of Alexius; and that every calamity which can afflict a
declining empire was accumulated on his reign by the justice of
Heaven and the vices of his predecessors."—GIBBON'S *Roman*

Empire, vol. ix. p. 83, foot– note.

The Princess accordingly feels the utmost assurance, that a number of signs which appeared in heaven and on earth, were interpreted by the soothsayers of the day as foreboding the death of the Emperor. By these means, Anna Comnena assigned to her father those indications of consequence, which ancient historians represent as necessary intimations of the sympathy of nature, with the removal of great characters from the world; but she fails not to inform the Christian reader that her father's belief attached to none of these prognostics, and that even on the following remarkable occasion he maintained his incredulity:—A splendid statue, supposed generally to be a relic of paganism, holding in its hand a golden sceptre, and standing upon a base of porphyry, was overturned by a tempest, and was generally believed to be an intimation of the death of the Emperor. This, however, he generously repelled. Phidias, he said, and other great sculptors of antiquity, had the talent of imitating the human frame with surprising accuracy; but to suppose that the power of foretelling future events was reposed in these master–pieces of art, would be to ascribe to their makers the faculties reserved by the Deity for himself, when he says, "It is I who kill and make alive." During his latter days, the Emperor was greatly afflicted with the gout, the nature of which has exercised the wit of many persons of science as well as of Anna Comnena. The poor patient was so much exhausted, that when the Empress was talking of most eloquent persons who should assist in the composition of his history, he said, with a natural contempt of such vanities, "The passages of my unhappy life call rather for tears and lamentation than for the praises you speak of."

A species of asthma having come to the assistance of the gout, the remedies of the physicians became as vain as the intercession of the monks and clergy, as well as the alms which were indiscriminately lavished. Two or three deep successive swoons gave ominous warning of the approaching blow; and at length was terminated the reign and life of Alexius Comnenus, a prince who, with all the faults which may be imputed to him, still possesses a real right, from the purity of his general intentions, to be accounted one of the best sovereigns of the Lower Empire.

For some time, the historian forgot her pride of literary rank, and, like an ordinary person, burst into tears and shrieks, tore her hair, and defaced her countenance, while the Empress Irene cast from her her princely habits, cut off her hair, changed her purple buskins for
black mourning shoes, and her daughter Mary, who had herself been a widow, took a black robe from one of her own wardrobes, and presented it to her mother. "Even in the moment when she put it on," says Anna Comnena, "the Emperor gave up the ghost, and in that moment the sun of my life set."

We shall not pursue her lamentations farther. She upbraids herself that, after the death of her father, that light of the world, she had also survived Irene, the delight alike of the east and of the west, and survived her husband also. "I am indignant," she said, "that my soul, suffering under such torrents of misfortune, should still deign to animate my body. Have I not," said she, "been more hard and unfeeling than the rocks themselves; and is it not just that one, who could survive such a father and mother, and such a husband, should be subjected to the influence of so much calamity? But let me finish this history, rather than any longer fatigue my readers with my unavailing and tragical lamentation."

Having thus concluded her history, she adds the following two lines:
—

"The learned Comnena lays her pen aside,
What time her subject and her father died." [Footnote: [Greek:
Laexen hopou biotoio Alexios d Komnaenos
Entha kalae thygataer laexen Alexiados.]]

These quotations will probably give the readers as much as they wish to know of the real character of this Imperial historian. Fewer words will suffice to dispose of the other parties who have been selected from her pages, as persons in the foregoing drama.

There is very little doubt that the Count Robert of Paris, whose audacity in seating himself upon the throne of the Emperor gives a peculiar interest to his character, was in fact a person of the highest rank; being no other, as has been conjectured by the learned Du Cange, than an ancestor of the house of Bourbon, which has so long given Kings to France. He was a successor, it has been conceived, of the Counts of Paris, by whom the city was valiantly defended against the Normans, and an ancestor of Hugh Capet. There are several hypotheses upon this subject, deriving the well–known Hugh Capet, first, from the family of Saxony; secondly, from St. Arnoul, afterwards Bishop of Altex; third, from Nibilong; fourth, from the Duke of Bavaria; and fifth, from a natural son of the Emperor Charlemagne. Variously placed, but in each of these contested pedigrees, appears this Robert surnamed the *Strong*, who was Count of that district, of which Paris was the capital, most peculiarly styled the County, or Isle of France. Anna Comnena, who has recorded the bold usurpation of the Emperor's seat by this haughty chieftain, has also acquainted us with his receiving a severe, if not a mortal wound, at the battle of Dorylseum, owing to his neglecting the warlike instructions with which her father had favoured him on the subject of the Turkish wars. The antiquary who is disposed to investigate this subject, may consult the late Lord Ashburnham's elaborate

Genealogy of the Royal House of France; also a note of Du Cange's on the Princess's history, p. 362, arguing for the identity of her "Robert of Paris, a haughty barbarian," with the "Robert called the Strong," mentioned as an ancestor of Hugh Capet. Gibbon, vol. xi. p.

52, may also be consulted. The French antiquary and the English historian seem alike disposed to find the church, called in the tale that of the Lady of the Broken Lances, in that dedicated to St. Drusas, or Drosin of Soissons, who was supposed to have peculiar influence on the issue of combats, and to be in the habit of determining them in favour of such champions as spent the night preceding at his shrine.

In consideration of the sex of one of the parties concerned, the author has selected our Lady of the Broken Lances as a more appropriate patroness than St. Drusas himself, for the Amazons, who were not uncommon in that age. Gaita, for example, the wife of Robert Guiscard, a redoubted hero, and the parent of a most heroic race of sons, was herself an Amazon, fought in the foremost ranks of the Normans, and is repeatedly commemorated by our Imperial historian, Anna Comnena.

The reader can easily conceive to himself that Robert of Paris distinguished himself among his brethren–at–arms and fellow– crusaders. His fame resounded from the walls of Antioch; but at the battle of Dorylaeum, he was so desperately wounded, as to be disabled from taking a part in the grandest scene of the expedition. His heroic Countess, however, enjoyed the great satisfaction of mounting the walls of Jerusalem, and in so far discharging her own vows and those of her husband. This was the more fortunate, as the sentence of the physicians pronounced that the wounds of the Count had been inflicted by a poisoned weapon, and that complete recovery was only to be hoped for by having recourse to his native air. After some time spent in the vain hope of averting by patience this unpleasant alternative, Count Robert subjected himself to necessity, or what was represented as such, and, with his wife and the faithful Hereward, and all others of his followers who had been like himself disabled from combat, took the way to Europe by sea.

A light galley, procured at a high rate, conducted them safely to Venice, and from that then glorious city, the moderate portion of spoil which had fallen to the Count's share among the conquerors of Palestine, served to convey them to his own dominions, which, more fortunate than those of most of his fellow–pilgrims, had been left uninjured by their neighbours during the time of their proprietor's absence on the Crusade. The report that the Count had lost his
health, and the power of continuing his homage to the Lady of the Broken Lances, brought upon him the hostilities of one or two ambitious or envious neighbours, whose covetousness was, however, sufficiently repressed by the brave resistance of the Countess and the resolute Hereward. Less than a twelvemonth was required to restore the Count of Paris to his full health, and to render him, as formerly, the assured protector of his own vassals, and the subject in whom the possessors of the French throne reposed the utmost confidence. This latter capacity enabled Count Robert to discharge his debt towards Hereward in a manner as ample as he could have hoped or expected. Being now respected alike for his wisdom and his sagacity, as much as he always was for his intrepidity and his character as a successful crusader, he was repeatedly employed by the Court of France in settling the troublesome and intricate affairs in which the Norman possessions of the English crown involved the rival nations. William

Rufus was not insensible to his merit, nor blind to the importance of gaining his good will; and finding out his anxiety that Hereward should be restored to the land of his fathers, he took, or made an opportunity, by the forfeiture of some rebellious noble, of conferring upon our Varangian a large district adjacent to the New Forest, being part of the scenes which his father chiefly frequented, and where it is said the descendants of the valiant squire and his Bertha have subsisted for many a long year, surviving turns of time and chance, which are in general fatal to the continuance of more distinguished families.

Lightning Source UK Ltd.
Milton Keynes UK
UKHW010626131221
395525UK00001B/126